Goodbye Piccadilly

Deep and fast-moving clo
rose.

Nothing could be seen with the naked eye so it was left to radar and the weather satellites to record the phenomena in their special and various ways.

The tidal streams were baulked and then held by the moon's increasing pull, springing to their highest peaks. The waters to the north of Scotland were stopped from voiding naturally into the Atlantic – were drawn back into the North Sea where The Lady Kuklos ruled.

Her breath raged and the seas banked beneath her, held in thrall by her retarding winds. Very slowly she made them run to the south, down the eastern coast of the British Isles towards the bottleneck of the Dover Straits where the high tides piled up against her forward winds, rolling higher and heavier – forced to wait for the surge she sent against them. Already high from the moon's rising influence, they peaked and swilled and waited.

When the two walls of water conjoined, they must assault the land through the estuaries. *There was nowhere else to go.*

Also by Tom Barling
in Magnum Books

THE OLYMPIC SLEEPER

Goodbye Piccadilly

TOM BARLING

MAGNUM BOOKS
Methuen Paperbacks Ltd

A Magnum Book

GOODBYE PICCADILLY
ISBN 0 417 05680 X

First published in Great Britain 1980
by Eyre Methuen Ltd
Magnum edition published 1981

Magnum Books are published
by Methuen Paperbacks Ltd
11 New Fetter Lane, London EC4P 4EE

Made and printed in Great Britain
by Hazell, Watson & Viney Ltd
Aylesbury, Bucks

Acknowledgements

Many people have been instrumental in helping to research parts of this book and I am indebted to the following:

Maureen, Wendy and Patrick, David and John.

And the man whose encyclopedic knowledge of weather, tides and all things nautical deserves very special mention, Dave Sutton, to whom this book is dedicated.

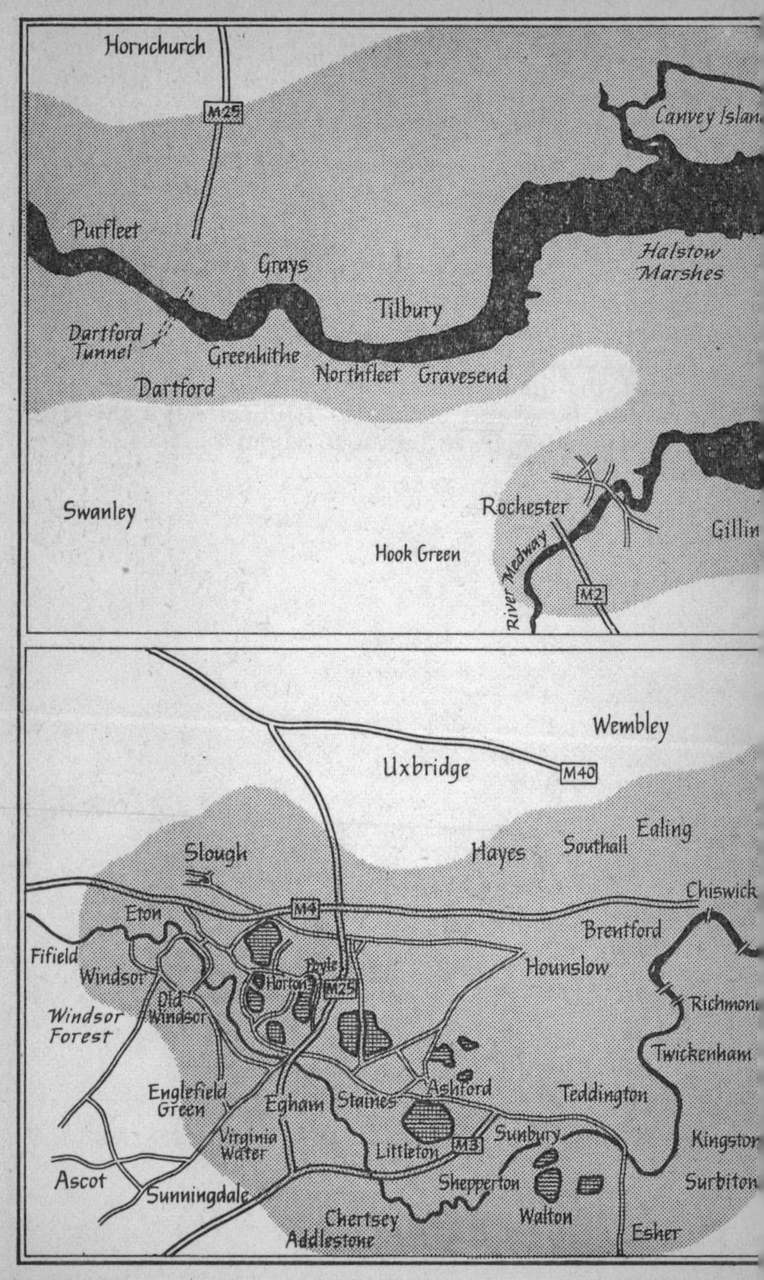

Hornchurch
M25
Canvey Islan
Purfleet
Grays
Halstow
Marshes
Tilbury
Dartford
Tunnel
Greenhithe
Northfleet
Gravesend
Dartford
Swanley
Rochester
Gillin
Hook Green
River Medway
M2
Wembley
Uxbridge
M40
Ealing
Slough
Hayes
Southall
Chiswick
M4
Eton
Brentford
Fifield
Poyle
Hounslow
Windsor
Horton
M25
Old
Windsor
Windsor
Forest
Twickenham
Englefield
Green
Egham
Staines
Ashford
Teddington
Virginia
Water
Littleton
M3
Sunbury
Ascot
Shepperton
Surbiton
Sunningdale
Walton
Chertsey
Addlestone
Esher

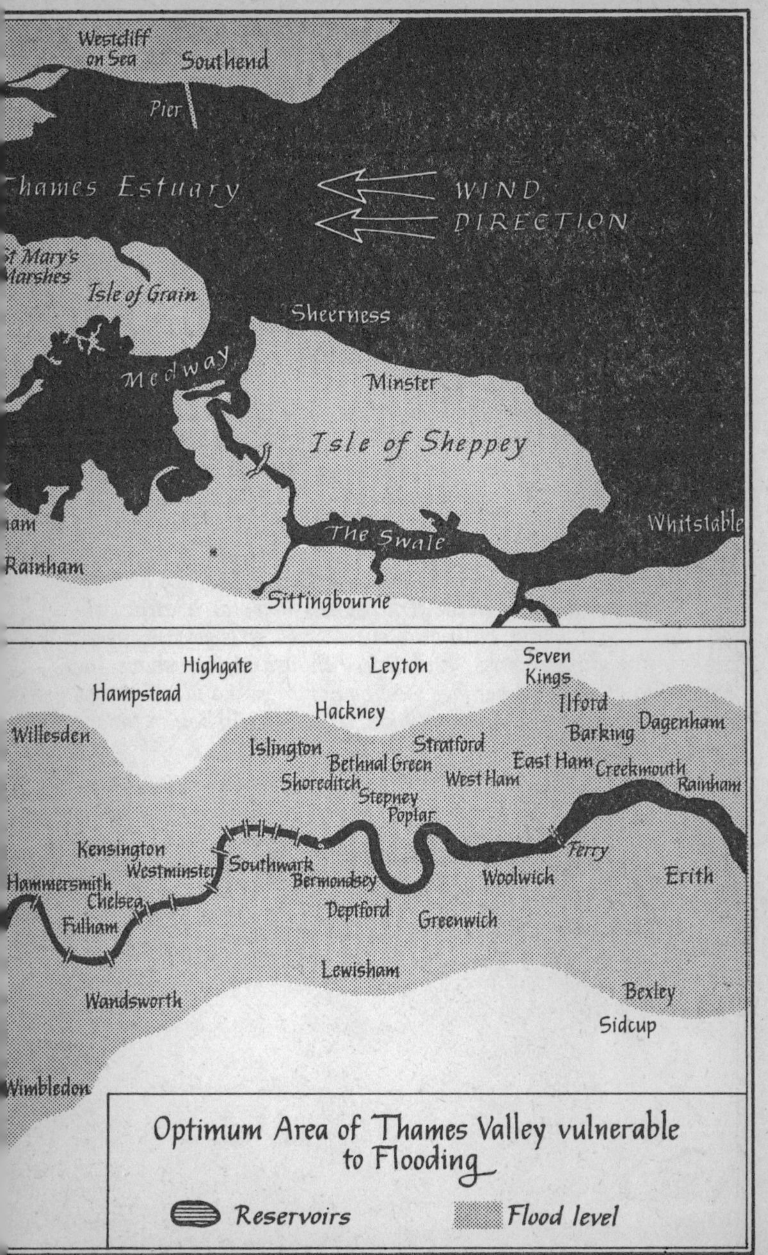
Westcliff on Sea
Southend
Pier
Thames Estuary
WIND DIRECTION
St Mary's Marshes
Isle of Grain
Sheerness
Medway
Minster
Isle of Sheppey
Whitstable
The Swale
Rainham
Sittingbourne
Highgate
Leyton
Seven Kings
Hampstead
Hackney
Ilford
Willesden
Dagenham
Barking
Islington
Stratford
Bethnal Green
East Ham
Creekmouth
Shoreditch
West Ham
Rainham
Stepney
Poplar
Kensington
Ferry
Westminster
Southwark
Hammersmith
Bermondsey
Woolwich
Erith
Chelsea
Deptford
Greenwich
Fulham
Lewisham
Wandsworth
Bexley
Sidcup
Wimbledon
Optimum Area of Thames Valley vulnerable to Flooding
Reservoirs
Flood level

Prologue

The Lady Kuklos

She was born quietly and invisibly at the roof of the world.

She had been an anonymous part of the dense, cold air of the polar region which rolls continually to the south, forming fronts against the warmer, more stable air advancing from the Azores. Great, slow balls of warm air rose to buffet her and as she threw out shy coils to tease and then to envelop them, they massed higher, climbing all the time, eluding her overtures of union.

With a slow shudder, she separated herself from the cold sameness around her and began to circle in dance with the warm barrier of air she faced. Turning slowly at first, she tried to bring her temperature up to that of her silent partner. As she threw out more coils, the pressure at her centre dropped and she began to advance through the stratosphere in a stately anticlockwise spin, gathering bulk and speed. She was a mile deep, twenty-five miles across, and thirty-thousand feet above the Arctic Ocean. She set her face west by north-west and ran across the pack ice at a speed of twenty knots, seemingly bound for the West Indies.

And nobody knew she was there.

1

Monday 1 October

21·28 hours

It was raining glass rods.

Hacking straight down from a lowering sky and snapping back as a million dancing dollies before flooding the gutters and washing into the drains where it roared and chuckled along the old Victorian sewers that ran with the river to the east and to the outflows below Eastcheap.

The streets were awash and vapour clouds formed haloes around the street lights and hung in cowering banks in the wet night air. Traffic signs and signals made bright splashes of primary colour above the crawling traffic and the Thames was an oily surge lost in pale mists. A sharp and quartering westerly lashed the empty pavements and cut between the supports of the elevated motorway above the A40 and the deserted stalls of Brentford market. It was too cold for sleet and snow could not form in the wind. It was a bad night for sleeping rough.

Charlie Glass adjusted the newspapers inside his sodden overcoat and shivered and cursed and held a precious bottle up to his face. He wanted the drink and the forgetfulness each burning mouthful would bring. He also dreaded the thought that it might all be swallowed before oblivion came. Most times it worked and he slept inside a warm cocoon where the dreams of failure could not make him scream himself awake. But there were other times when the booze turned to stone in his gut and filled his mouth with scum and fear and foul things flapped and crawled inside his skin. Charlie licked his mouth and thought of the bad times, all the bad times, and held the bottle tighter.

Bastard luck had brought him to this, bastard bad luck.

They'll pay, he told himself. Just who *they* were was never clear to Charlie. He was never able to give *them* a collective face he could hate. They were the police, social workers, the Sally Army, other alcoholics, people with homes and bank accounts, those with bottles who would not share, those without bottles who begged; anybody in fact who had more or less than Charlie Glass.

Charlie shifted inside his makeshift shelter of milk crates and plastic sheeting and smelled his own unwashed stink. His legs were cramped and his feet were frozen inside his broken boots. Shivers of self-disgust racked him and he swore monotonously, the litany of a loser.

Bastard army, bastard luck. *Bastards.*

But he had the bottle. Charlie twisted off the foil cap and took a long draught of his supermarket whisky, forcing it past his larynx with a great effort – don't taste it, don't savour it, just feel the effect, that was the great thing. Don't let it come up off the empty stomach and be coughed to waste. Hold it down.

Charlie kept it down and gaped as the raw fumes rose in his throat. *Better,* he thought.

Charlie had been Sergeant Glass in Korea where he had fought the Chinese and been mentioned in dispatches twice. A three-star general had pinned on his medals and shaken his hand for the cameras. He had been everybody's friend in the bars and his photograph had made the front page of the *Daily Mirror*. He was sent home to help in a recruiting drive. At Aldershot, in the Sergeants' Mess, he had smashed the throat of an NCO who had sneered at his Glorious Gloucesters and then drowned in his own blood.

The court martial had been open and shut. A long lecture about the regiment and honour and then the sentence. Ten years in the glasshouse and a dishonourable discharge with no pension rights. No cushy civvy job on retirement, no help from the ex-servicemen's associations. Just ten grinding years with no remission and the big elbow on to the street.

Sergeant Glass marched into the military prison but it was Charlie who shuffled out. Charlie with the arthritis, the bad feet and a thirst as long as his legs.

Charlie gulped more whisky and managed not to

puke. It was working.

He dug an Old Holborn tin out of his pocket and began remaking stubs into a long smoke. There was less tobacco in the butts now that most people smoked filter tips and Charlie cursed them for it.

He did not notice the car right away. He had lit up and was breathing stale Virginia smoke before the extra light from the headlights registered on his fuddled mind. Charlie froze. Nobody stopped here without good reason, that was why he had chosen the place. It had to be the *Filth*. The bloody Filth, the law in one of their Pandas, creeping up on him when he had the bottle with the price tag still on the cap and him with no receipt and no story made up. He had to take a look to make sure, even though it was the last thing he wanted to do.

Charlie eased the edge of the plastic sheet aside and squinted out into the darkness. The heads had gone out and the car was barely outlined by the sodium lights from the eastbound lane of the A40; it showed no side-lights either. It was a big saloon, a Bentley that could have been maroon or brown, – the yellow tungsten light made everything muddy and indistinct. The windows were tinted and Charlie could see no movement inside. He bared his gums in a humourless smile. Lovers, he thought, parked for some nooky in the dark. He could give them time to settle down to it, then go over and put the bite on them for a few bob. Most randy bastards paid Charlie when he caught them with their bugles in the breeze. Charlie pinched out the end of his smoke and put it back in the tin. He capped the whisky and slid it into his side pocket and buttoned the flap over it. He was about to slide from his shelter when the driver opened his door and stepped out on to the hard shoulder. Charlie stayed very still.

A big man walked around the front of the car and looked all round him with jerky moves of his head. He waited for a long minute, then opened the rear offside door and leaned in. Charlie heard him hissing as he lugged something from the back seat, something that flopped and snagged itself between the seat and the frame. The man untangled it and lifted a bundle up into his arms, adjusted his grip and stood still, listening to traffic through the hush and crackle of the rain. Then, with sudden haste, he walked into the shadows and Charlie lost sight of him.

When he came back he was empty-handed.

Charlie watched him climb into the car, start the ignition and bring on his lights. With hardly a sound, the Bentley made a turn and was gone in the direction of the roundabout where it was swallowed up in the gloom. An articulated lorry and trailer barrelled past and Charlie had the elevated section to himself. And the bundle.

Charlie edged from his shelter and hobbled in the direction the man had walked. He came to the concrete flanks of the ramp of the M4 and felt his way along it until his boot snagged in cloth. He leaned over and felt the stitched edge of good wool. A blanket, a good quality blanket that Charlie could sleep in tonight and sell tomorrow.

There were knots of rope around the bundle and Charlie worked at them with stiff fingers, wondering what was inside. Probably some bloody dog the driver was dumping. A hit and run. Maybe he had knocked it down and was saving himself the trouble of facing a neighbour, or it was his own pooch and he didn't want to pay a vet for disposing of the carcass. Charlie had seen stranger things down on the canals and in carparks.

The rope was good too, good washing line with a waxed surface. Stuff worth a good few coppers and it all added up, but the knots were taking too long in the dark. Charlie needed a light. Back here, Charlie figured, he could risk it.

He fished out his Woolworth's torch and laid it on the ground where the beam would not show out on the road. The work went faster. He found the main knot and unravelled it, pulling the rope away. The bundle sagged apart and Charlie whipped the blanket aside.

The body had no muzzle and no tail.

It was bound up in a foetal position with the arms lashed around the raised ankles. It wore a bottle green sweater and a single grey sock with a green tag hanging from it. The legs and buttocks were naked and a crust of dark blood had formed around the inside and back of the thighs. Bruises showed blue against the white skin. The face was framed by yellow hair and one eye was wide open in a fixed stare and the pupil was very blue. The other eye was red and suffused and very different. The mouth hung slack and small milk teeth showed against the blackened tongue. A trail of dark claret ran from beneath the cap with its yellow piping and yellow fleur-de-lis badge.

Charlie Glass reared up, took a step back, and vomited.

Then he started to run.

He was into the busy roundabout before he came out of the shock and he did not see the braking artic before it scooped him up and threw him across the bonnet of a swerving saloon. By then he was beyond caring.

22·02 hours

Soho was a blur of brilliant neon with little foot traffic and the pubs had most of the business. The bookstores were closed with lit windows and the lobbies of the club cinemas were empty under their bright marquees. The Old Compton Street arcade was loud with striped anoraks and hard rock as electronic targets exploded and racing cars swung through continuous chicanes on the screens. The pintables pinged up scores in hundreds and thousands and a couple of foreign sailors stood in the entrance and watched the rain strike down around two black whores in a doorway across the street. None of them looked at the parked blue Cortina with misty windows and dirty plates.

John Coward had the car heater blowing over his soaked shoes as he wiped condensation from the windscreen and Frank Cave coughed around one of his small cigars. A long hour had crept by and the informer was late. Coward knew the snout was scared of the information he carried and the thought made Coward all the more patient. He bit off a yawn and wiped off his side window.

'Is that him?' asked Cave.

'Where?'

'There he is,' said Cave in a gout of bitter smoke as a man came up past the corner Wimpy and crossed over to make a show of reading magazine titles as he used the window to see up and down the street. The shoulders of his raincoat were as slick as a seal pelt and rain dribbled from the brim of his hat.

'I see him.' Coward flashed the heads, engaged first gear and turned up into Frith Street to a dark patch of road beside the hospital where he pulled into the kerb.

'He saw us, John,' said Cave.

'He'll still be cautious. He'll come up Greek and around into the square at the top. Come down at us from the north side.' Coward hoped he would be quick about it. It was close to ten and neither man had been home since the previous night. Even Cave's Maggie would be fretting and Coward refused to think about where his wife might be. Coward's eyes were grainy with liver spots and he could taste his coated tongue. Another eleven minutes crawled by.

The man came out from the motorcycles and the shadowed paving of Soho Square and walked quickly down the centre of Frith Street between the parked cars. He came abreast of the Cortina and ducked into the back seat, thumping the door closed. Spray from his hat hit the back of Coward's neck as he settled himself and his breath clouded with the cigar smoke.

'You took your time.'

'Had to, Mr Cave. Had to. If them faces knew I was talking . . .'

'Nervous are we, Goldy?'

Goldy snorted and sucked at his teeth, his bony face averted.

'Gutless, Mr Coward. I don't mind the small stuff, you know, the usual, but this – this is out of my league.'

'All right, Goldy. How much are you asking?'

'It ain't that. It ain't the money. Not all of it. I mean, you know me.'

'How much?'

'Fifty won't go nowhere. This has got to be paid for. We're talking about my neck. I'll have to keep my head down for a good long stretch. A couple of hundred maybe. It ought to be a monkey.'

'Five hundred? Nothing's worth that,' said Cave.

'This bloody is. Barclays or Nat West would slip me a grand for this, and you know it.'

'The clearing banks only pay out that sort of money once there's been an arrest and a conviction. They only work on results. Proof and proven facts. We work on a lot less and pay in cash money. You know that full well, Goldy. Tell us what you've got and we'll tell you what it's worth,' said Cave, his manner hard and uncompromising, leaving Coward to play Mr Nice.

'I dunno about that,' mumbled Goldy. 'Why don't I just forget it? I told you it scared me.'

'Suit yourself. You can't peddle this anywhere else.'

'Then I won't peddle it at all, will I?'

'Then do the other thing,' snapped Cave. 'I should be home with my nearest and dearest, not sitting here with a loser like you.'

'All right, Frank,' said Coward smoothly, shifting the rear mirror on its axis to show Goldy's face. 'Let's have it, Goldy. I've always been straight with you, there's no need for all this moody.'

'I know that, Mr Coward. This ain't no piddling thing. It's too rich for my old blood. I wish I didn't know, honest. They're gonna do the . . .' Goldy trailed away and hunched inside his raincoat, his unshaven chin rasping against the raised collar.

'They're going to do what?' prompted Coward.

'You'll see me right, Mr Coward?'

Coward said yes.

'The Bank of England,' said Goldy, flinching.

'The bloody *what*?' laughed Cave.

'The Bank of bleeding England,' said Goldy, 'I knew he'd cackle, Mr Coward. But I'm telling you.'

Cave bit at his cigar and Coward fought to keep his face straight, as he said:

'Name me some names, Goldy.'

'I can give you three,' said Goldy, and did so. The names were big enough to be involved in almost anything. The policemen exchanged glances. There was no chance that Goldy could have got close enough to overhear anything involving those men. They were strictly part of the upper establishment, the penthouse set.

'Where did you pick this up?' asked Cave.

'At this club in Brixton. I was working the kitchen and these two faces was talking on the other side of the partition by the manager's office. They didn't know I was there because of the washing machines. They're electric, you just load the dishes in and switch on. Make hell of a racket. Anyway, these two was talking about a driving job for a face with a clean heavy goods licence. The driver had to be one of the lads, like, trustworthy, for all the usual reasons, but no form. Five grand was mentioned.'

'Sounds like some driving job.'

'That's what made my ears flap. That and one of them mentioning the Gnome in the Garden.'

'Kellerman?' asked Cave.

'Yeah, the Gnome. Kellerman of Covent Garden. That proves how big this caper has to be. Kellerman only fronts for them three names I gave you. Ain't that right?'

'Go on.' Coward hoped his voice was neutral.

'They said it was a currency job because this artic had to go overland to Zurich. There was too much of it to go by couriers. The safest way was by lorry from Harwich to Ostend, and then to Switzerland. They said it couldn't go from none of the other ports 'cause they wouldn't be working. Bloody funny that.' Goldy thumbed a mucous dewdrop from the end of his nose. 'I mean, what does that signify?'

'It's your story,' said Cave.

'Yeah, ain't it? Well, one of them said he knew someone who was tailormade for it. He said he didn't want to use the phone, he said he'd go over to this bloke's house and talk face to face. They said okay and went off. Well, I went out through the alley at the back and saw these two come out into the street. I couldn't follow them both, so I chose the one who'd said he might know a driver and watched him collect his car. I got the number and wrote it on a fag packet. Here it is.'

Cave took the fold of grubby card and opened it out. 'Is

that all?'

'Just about. He had this Jag and I was on foot. I ain't got 3·5 litres under my hood, have I?'

'So where does the Bank of England come into it?' sneered Cave.

Goldy brought his raised collar up around his hatbrim in a long, eloquent shrug. 'Got to be. Where else has all that paper money lying around in bundles? Enough to need an artic to cart it away? It don't take a big brain to sort that one out.'

A flurry of rain lashed the car and a mini roared past to squeal into the square.

'Well, what d'you reckon to it? I got to be off,' said Goldy.

'What do you think, John?' Cave asked Coward.

'Could be.' Coward caught Goldy's reflected eye. 'Have you told us all of it?'

'Pretty much, I reckon. I've stuck to the club job, but neither of them faces has been back. And I can't exactly ask about them, can I?'

'No. You stay there though, you could come up with something more.' Coward sounded doubtful.

'Only if it's worth my while.'

'It might be. Give him a score, Frank.'

'A lousy twenty,' yelped Goldy, his shoulders dropping as his neck rose. 'That's like nothing.'

'It's all it's worth at present,' said Coward.

'Look, they might never come back. What then? Just me up to my armpits in bloody suds. That's choice, that's lovely.'

'Just do it.' Coward reset the mirror and turned on the ignition. 'There'll be twenty more each time you come to us with kosher information. No fairy tales.'

'I never done that. Never, and you know it.'

Cave held out four folded notes. 'So don't start now, that's all he's saying.'

The fivers disappeared inside the folds of the raincoat and Goldy climbed out without another word. Cave wound down his window.

'This club, what's its name?'

'The bugger-something.' Goldy dug around in his

pockets. 'Here. It's on this matchbox.' He dropped the match folder into Coward's palm. 'They give them away. I'll get back to you.' He turned and stepped away without using his heels in the direction of Shaftesbury Avenue, and was lost in the wash of rain and glaring lights.

'The bugger-what?' asked Cave.

'The Bugalloo Cabaret Club,' read Coward.

'Funny way to find out Goldy can't read.' Cave threw his stub into the night. 'I've had it, John. I don't know whether to laugh or cry. Every time I blink I see red, I'm so beat.'

'Then don't blink.'

'Thanks a lot. Has old Goldy got something or not, d'you think?'

'Who knows?' Coward swung out and drove around the square into Oxford Street, knowing full well it was closed to all traffic save buses and taxis. 'Goldy's given us good information in the past. But this, this is both too little and yet too big to throw away. I think I'll write it up as a report and drop it on Maitland's desk. He likes the cerebal exercise.'

'*Commander* Maitland, please,' Cave said wearily, staring out at the brash frontages of the big stores as they slid past. 'You are a mere Detective Inspector and I am a Detective Sergeant, an altogether lower form of life. In all things we must show due respect to our elders and betters.'

'Shut up, Frank.' Coward turned into the back doubles and made towards Regent's Park, grateful for the ordinary street lighting.

'It could be De La Rue's works, where they print the currency,' suggested Cave. 'But the security is supposed to be impregnable. Or one of the Mint warehouses.'

'Impregnable? Every time there's a better mousetrap, along comes a better mouse. If men can build it, another man can crack it,' yawned Coward, cornering sharply.

'The law according to Coward,' said Cave. 'Coward's Law.'

'Right now, all I'm thinking about is bed. Big soft mattress. Fluffy white pillows. A hot belly against cool sheets.'

'A hot belly against what?' mocked Cave, leering sideways.

'You crude animal. Shut up and let me drive. Where shall I drop you?'

'Camden Town. I'll walk up the road.'

'Fine. Christ, just to get home.'

'Will you have a meal waiting?' asked Cave.

'No chance.'

Cave asked abruptly, 'At the risk of a poke in the mouth, are things all right at home, John? Between you and Nancy?'

'Do you think this rain will ever stop, Frank?'

'Look, I know I've got no right to pry, but we have been together for going on three years. That's almost like being married.'

'How long *has* it been raining? Must be all of a fortnight.'

'You don't have to tell me. It's just that Maggie thought that things were just a bit tense when we were last over.'

'It's probably closer to three weeks.'

'I'm just trying to help, John.'

'Yes, three weeks of solid rain.'

'All right, I won't ask.' Cave folded his arms.

'What did you say, Frank?'

'Nothing.'

'That's good, Frank. That's very good. I approve.'

'I know you like to keep things to yourself, but sometimes it helps to talk,' said Cave as Coward turned out of the park and set the Cortina down along Parkway. 'You can be too private.'

'Talking certainly helps you, Frank. Except you don't have any problems, do you?'

'Only because I'm lucky. It's nobody's fault if . . .'

Coward cleared his throat with a brief cough of laughter. 'I'd love to hear Maggie's views on that. I'll bet she has a good deal to complain about. You must be hell to live with. I'll bet you squeeze the toothpaste in the middle and leave a ring around the bath. I'll ask Maggie the next time I see her.'

'We're talking about you, not me,' Cave protested.

'I'm talking about you.' Coward slowed outside a cinema showing a double Disney bill and pulled into the kerb with the engine running.

'Don't change the subject. Mr self-contained, that's you. I just wanted you to know you have a friend you can talk to if you wanted.'

'Camden Town, Frank.'

'You won't listen . . . what?'

'Camden Town. You're here.'

'Why didn't you say so?'

'Good-night, Frank.'

'All right, all right.' Cave climbed out on to the pavement and leaned through the open window to say, 'The offer's there, John.'

Coward forced a smile. 'Say hello to Maggie for me.'

Cave watched him turn across the intersection and swish off towards St John's Wood.

'Insular bastard,' he said to the night sky.

* * *

The roundabout was awash with revolving blue lights from the Pandas and hazard triangles reduced the traffic to a single-line crawl. A saloon with a splintered windscreen had its front wheels up on the central reservation, and the police had moved the articulated lorry to the westside of the North Circular where they breathalysed the German driver and had him answering questions in literal English. The woman from the saloon was being hysterical about her Pekingese running off after the accident. A woman constable held the woman's wrists and was wondering whether to slap her sensible.

Charlie Glass lay on the grass where he had been thrown and where two ambulance men were straightening his limbs and deciding how to move him. A traffic sergeant was going through his pockets for identification with ginger fingers and dropping what he found into a plastic bag. There was blood on the broken whisky bottle he found in the overcoat pocket. He showed it to the ambulance driver who wrinkled his nose and snorted through it.

'It's a buttock wound, missed the big artery by millimetres. They won't thank us at St George's for delivering this one. His hair's alive. I'm not spraying him for chinches. They'd be all over the ambulance and we'd be off the road for fumigation.'

'You can have him,' said the traffic sergeant, hastily moving away. 'According to the artic driver he ran out of nowhere under his wheels. From his breath he's swimming in shoe polish and meths. A real Whisky Joe.'

Charlie was wrapped in a blanket and lifted on to a wheeled stretcher. Breath bubbled in his throat and his scraped face rolled from side to side. Saliva ran from his gaping mouth. The three men slid him into the ambulance and the attendant climbed in beside him, wishing it was his turn to drive. 'Make it a fast run,' he told the driver. 'Apart from the broken ribs and the possible internal bleeding, his blood pressure's way, way down. We don't want him dead in transit.'

'Seven minutes, or I'm a Chinaman.'

'All right, Bruce Lee. Chop-chop.'

'I've gone.' The driver closed the rear doors, climbed behind the wheel and started the siren. The traffic sergeant waved him up the ramp to the flyover into the city centre and watched the ambulance race away. Then he went back to the hysterical woman and the problem of her missing peke. He was scratching his wrist when he arrived in time to see the woman constable give the woman an open-handed slap. The woman sagged and wept quietly.

'Technically, that's an assault on the public,' said the sergeant.

'What are you scratching for?' asked the woman constable, patting the woman's shoulder.

'The tramp was alive, ugh.'

'Have you found Mrs Willoughby-Smith's dog yet?'

'No. She's in no fit state to drive. Best take her back to the station for some hot tea and sympathy.' The sergeant's smile was sour under the spotting rain.

In the ambulance Charlie started to moan and gabble. *'He was dead, dead. Couldn't have been more than seven or eight. His face was all . . . he had no trousers and his little dick*

. . . aaaaaahhh . . .'

The ambulance man held Charlie's filthy hand as the light poles and traffic whipped past the tinted windows.

'Easy does it, old lad, easy . . .'

'Aaaaaaaahhhh . . .' Bile spattered on the blanket and Charlie's yellow eyes widened around the washed-out pupils. His grip bruised the other man's knuckles. *'Aaaaaaaahhhhh . . .'*

'Easy, easy . . .'

22·04 hours

The parking slot came up too fast.

The new Cinturati tyres squealed as Giles Prebble brought his Bentley to a halt bare millimetres from the wall, throwing himself forward against his seatbelt. He cursed, released himself and climbed from the car with pounding temples, blaming everybody but himself for his own inattention.

The headache that had started on the motorway was worse, a pernicious clamp that made thinking difficult, shooting his peripheral vision through with hurting bands of colour, each band a different wavelength of pain. The whine of a landing Trident set his teeth on edge and brought a wave of nausea.

When the trauma had passed, Prebble leaned himself against a concrete upright, fumbled a capsule from his silver pillbox and swallowed it dry.

The effect was almost immediate.

There was the familiar punch to the heart, the taste of metal foil on his tongue, the rush of light giddiness as the stomach cramps left him; the sliding backflip as his inner ear re-established up and down. There was the careful sipping of air until each of the hurting lights blinked out to leave him clear-eyed and able to listen to the landing jets and the rain without flinching. He watched his hands for tremors before moving.

When he reached the pedestrian exist of the multi-storey carpark he was himself again, and he viewed the rainswept terminal buildings with mounting distaste. He should have brought an umbrella to save his clothes from a drenching. He paused in the harsh spill of the overhead lamp.

His topcoat was Barathea and the fur collar was not spun nylon. His suit was Savile Row, his shirt sea-island cotton and his shoes were handlasted in Switzerland. Sandy hair receded from his fleshy face and grew thickly as sideburns below his small lobeless ears. His brows were blond understatements over eyes the colour of dried kelp, giving him a perpetual air of faint surprise. His nose was broad with thin nostrils and the cleft in his chin was deep enough to hide a finger joint in. His hands were large-knuckled and long-fingered and he wore a gold-mounted bloodstone on the huge little finger of his right hand. He shaved twice a day and his chest hair was an abrasive blond pelt. He smelled of pressed expensive blooms and his bulk made him seem shorter than his six and a half feet.

He was thick in the waist and heavy in the wrists and his shirt cuffs or watchband could have circled a slim girl's neck. Prebble practised roles and behaviour patterns like the social chameleon he was, and could switch personas at will. He had surprisingly small feet and had trained himself to walk ponderously for effect, small careful steps, as though testing surf for sharp pebbles.

His eighteen stone was heavily muscled beneath a sleek layer of good living, and although he walked with the mannered gait of a fat man, he was capable of the silent and sure speed of a wing three-quarter. None of his business partners knew he regularly worked out with weights or that he could swim two miles and run over soft ground for two more without becoming breathless, should the occasion warrant. That intelligence was something Prebble liked to keep to himself as he did many other things, including his reliance on the explosive and highly illegal capsules a Swiss chemist made up for him at high risk and for higher profits.

Prebble made a slow dash for Terminal Three and stopped just inside the automatic doors to shake droplets of water from his coat.

The airline desks were besieged by short-tempered

passengers and all the available benches were occupied. Many people sat on their luggage or on newspapers spread on the floor. The air was hot and stale and the indicator boards were crowded with delayed flights.

Prebble ploughed through the crowds using his bulk to clear a path for himself, and made for the Executive Lounge where he knew he could sit in comfort over a brandy in a decent glass without the press and staleness of the tourist-class passengers.

He was wrong.

He passed a group of clergymen on the way in and thirty or forty people were calling to each other over drinks and cameras flashed at the far end of the room by the long draped windows. A damned press conference or somesuch. There were several brown faces with dog collars and serious expressions and the topic of conversation seemed to be apartheid.

Prebble poured himself a liberal measure of Remy Martin and found himself a comfortable seat in a recess by a large smoking stand where newspapers were spread on a side table. He consulted his half-hunter. There were twenty minutes to kill before the direct Los Angeles Jumbo landed. When he had checked the stop press of both evening papers, he lit a cigar and buried his face in the *Financial Times* to avoid looking at the black faces all around him. The article on the European Monetary Fund was all predictable stuff and barely held his attention. He had been reading for only a few moments when his elbow was rudely jogged.

'Sorry, it's the crush,' came an apology in a harsh London accent.

Prebble grunted without raising his eyes.

'Mr Prebble, isn't it?'

Prebble glared up at the thin, dark and untidy man in a brushed denim suit with a medallion on a chain where a Christian tie ought to hang. The long face was vaguely familiar.

'You are mistaken,' said Prebble, rustling the pink pages.

The thin man moved in so that Prebble was unable to open his newspaper to shield himself. 'Really? I covered the by-election in seventy-four when you stood as an English Independent. Let's see, yes, your platform was Free Enterprise and England for the English, wasn't it? You barely saved your deposit, and the left-wing herberts wanted to ride you out of town on a rail. Lovely copy for a wet Tuesday that was. I was on the Manchester end of the *Daily Express* in those days. I interviewed you a couple of times. *When* I could get past your campaign heavies.'

'I repeat, you are mistaken, Mr . . .?'

'Sadler. Shall I spell it for you?'

Prebble's face began to mottle.

'I should like to read my newspaper, Sadler. So, if you'll excuse me?' Prebble's tone and expression were not polite.

'You're Prebble all right. Can't be two like you. Unique.'

Prebble did not reply.

'What are you doing nowadays? Now that politics has kissed you good-bye?'

'Minding my own business, an ability you seem to lack.'

'That's my living, old son, since we're trading clichés.'

Prebble's hands tightened on the newsprint.

'No comment.'

Sadler saw and grinned.

'Why not? You haven't had much press coverage lately. You used to court it like a whore on piece-rates, as I remember. You seem to have dropped out of sight – have you lost your taste for public life? There was a time when you gave the Honourable Enoch a good run for his money with your racist remarks.'

Prebble folded the paper carefully and laid it in his lap. He pointed his cigar at Sadler. 'Take your impertinence elsewhere, Sadler. Go and join the varicoloured throng of clerics behind you. They might welcome the opportunity to save you from drowning in your own mediocrity and the various products of United Distillers.'

Sadler brayed laughter that turned heads.

'And you're a great personal friend of my editor, right?

Or is it the publisher you've got in your pocket? One word from you and snap, Sadler joins the ranks of the unemployed. You were going to say that, weren't you?'

'It's tempting, but no. Go and drink the holy wine or whatever they're serving at this circus of brotherly love. There's no story in me. Say good evening and good-bye,' Prebble said through his teeth.

'I'll go when you've said something nasty about coons or gollies,' taunted Sadler, liquid slopping from his glass. 'Give me something reactionary, something I can puff up into a half-page with a suitable picture and caption. Something I can build a retrospect on.'

Prebble forced a sigh as though he were dealing with a wilful child, privately telling himself to keep it light and not to allow himself to be drawn into uttering anything too provocative. This was neither the time nor the place. 'I understand,' he said, his eyes lidded, 'that newsprint and matchsticks account for half the trees felled in the world. A sobering thought for anybody other than a person like you. I should reconsider this silly idea, if only in the interests of conservation. None of the cretins who stumble through the comic strips in your rag would be interested in a single word I say. Give them page three nudity and gossip, that's the diet they flourish on. When the enlightened Victorians decided to educate the masses, they thought the proletariat would read poetry and take up punting. Instead, the workers learned to fill in pools coupons and calculate the odds on the favourite at Newmarket. A glaring miscalculation, wouldn't you say?'

'May I quote you on that, Mr Prebble?' asked Sadler, leaning closer and smiling wider to show sharp discoloured canines.

'Better to be misquoted than have you invent some libellous nonsense, I suppose.'

'How about your views on the Prime Minister?'

'Do we have one?' asked Prebble.

'And the Foreign Secretary?'

'I understand that travel broadens the mind. In his case, it seems to have affected a lower part of his anatomy.'

'You would have been terrific on television, Prebble.'

'Don't confuse wit with wisdom. Remember, I was denied the silver screen during my election campaign. So much for free speech and access to the media in our sorry excuse of a democracy.'

'Now that is a quote.'

'Oh, I've pleased the little scribbler. With luck, the union members who set the type will spell my name wrongly and choose a picture of somebody a trifle more photogenic. Now, if you'll excuse me, I have to meet someone.'

As Prebble rose to his feet a motorized Nikon whined and an electronic flash seared his eyes.

'Just one for the files,' said Sadler. 'Shall I send a print or two for your scrapbook?'

'Save it for your own, Sadler,' snapped Prebble, sidling from his corner, his face flushed and angry.

'Oh, you know about that, do you?' said Sadler, his eyes suddenly quick and watchful.

Prebble merely shook his head and moved away towards the Arrivals Hall, walking his fat man's walk. Sadler's smile became strained and disappeared. He was no longer drunk as he tapped the rim of his glass against his lower lip, thinking deeply.

'We all through here, Sadler?' asked the photographer, an old pro with bad feet and five children. 'What say we drink up and get this stuff back to the office?'

'Have you got a long lens with you?'

'A one-fifty and a thousand-mill zoom, why?'

'Fast film?'

'Eight hundred ASA.'

'Load it and fix your long zoom. That reactionary old fart is up to something. I can feel it in my water.'

'Who, that Prebble? I thought he was a lost cause. I only snapped him because you signalled.'

'That's as maybe. Blokes like Prebble never give up once they've got a taste for power. He's as hungry as ever. But why would he turn up in the middle of a Church Unity delegation to South Africa, if not to be provocative? I checked with the girl on the desk. He's not flying anywhere. Let's get after him.'

They found Prebble at the Arrivals gate directly opposite the Customs channels. He had propped himself near the barrier and was smoking calmly. There were only two flights clearing, a delayed flight from Montreal and the Los Angeles flight which was on time. Sadler commandeered a luggage trolley and wheeled it against the roller front of a closed kiosk. He helped the photographer to stand on it so that he had a clear view over the heads of the crowd. The thousand-mill was too long and the photographer changed over to the one-fifty. He muttered about focal lengths and depths of field as he took readings with a Lunar Six. The trolley bar was cutting into his feet, too.

Sadler ignored him except for an abrupt: 'Just get it in bloody focus.' Then they waited.

The usual assortment of passengers began to emerge through the sliding frosted-glass doors, wheeling baggage and dragging children. Businessmen with their single cases and no duty frees in plastic bags, tourists with their cameras and matching luggage.

'He's moving,' said the photographer. 'He's seen someone he knows. Definitely.' His camera began to whine through film. Sadler craned to see. Prebble was walking parallel with the barrier, not looking at anybody in particular. Sadler scanned the faces and picked on one that seemed likely since Prebble kept pace with the man.

He was well over six feet, wide in the shoulder and narrow in the hip. He had a short crop of sunbleached hair and a Californian tan. His forehead was broad and freckled and his eyes were the blue of Boston stockings. His cheekbones were high and sharply defined and his nose was a short pug above a thin mouth and a button chin. He wore a casual oyster jacket over a chequered shirt, white duck trousers and white shoes with golfing tongues, and he carried his bags as though they weighed lightly. He and Prebble reached the open concourse together and nodded hello without shaking hands.

'Get them together,' ordered Sadler.

'I've got them, I've got them,' hissed the photographer, breathing out steadily to keep his heartbeat from spoiling his steady aim. He got a last shot of the backs of their heads before they were through the doors and out on the concourse. 'Do we follow them?' he asked, lowering his camera.

'Not unless they go into London. Prebble lives out in the wilds of Surrey somewhere. That's in the opposite direction to our deadline and my bed,' said Sadler, helping the photographer down. 'Let them go.'

'Get this film back to processing then?'

'Yes. Look, Ted, keep this last batch to one side, will you? Have them drop the contact prints on my desk when they're ready. I don't want them going into the general library files just yet.'

'Working angles again, eh? You and your private crusades. You know the *Herald* won't print none of this, so you keep it by you just in case. You want my opinion . . .'

'I don't. Just hold the Brownie like you're paid to.'

'Temper, temper.' The photographer began packing his gear into his bags. 'I'll mark this roll for your personal expense docket.'

'You do that,' Sadler said absently, his mind on other things.

Outside, the rain had eased to a persistent drizzle teased by maverick gusts of wind. Prebble led the way to his car and asked about the other man's flight.

'Bumpy as hell and the landing was punk. I thought we were going to bounce right up again. I guess the pilot is a frustrated astronaut. I'm glad to be down.'

'Jetlag and plastic food does not commend itself to me, Mr Calloway. Thirteen hours in one of those steel coffins leaves me completely wrung out,' said Prebble as they went up the stairs to level three of the carpark. 'I need to rest up for two clear days.' He had not offered to carry either of the American's cases, nor had it occurred to him to ask. Their voices were covered by the clattering echoes from the bare concrete stairwell. They pushed through the swing doors and Prebble unlocked the Bentley's boot for Calloway's luggage. He then opened the passenger door.

'Do climb in, Mr Calloway.'

'Henry,' said Calloway. 'Call me Henry.'

'Very well.' Prebble settled himself behind the wheel. 'Though I must say that I am not used to being addressed as Giles. Most people call me Prebble. Odd, isn't it?'

'That your preference?'

Prebble considered the question as the Bentley purred down the exit slope before replying: 'You know, it probably is.'

'Suit yourself. You know we were being photographed?'

'Were we? How interesting. Tell me, were there two men? One of them in an awful blue sacking suit, and the other a nondescript in a jacket and rumpled slacks?'

'One of them had a denim suit, black hair, thin. The other guy had the Nikon. What's going on, Prebble? I taste trouble.'

'Members of the yellow press. Don't fret yourself, they're absolutely nothing to worry about. One of them has chosen me as a sort of a hobby. I had him investigated some time back. I'm usually thorough.' Prebble stopped at the barrier and paid the Sikh in the tollbooth, carefully avoiding hand contact and brusquely refusing his change. He drove out in a surge of power, sideslipping into the one-way system that ran around to the tunnel and the motorway.

'You people give gratuities to parking attendants?' asked Calloway.

'Hardly. I should have given him the right coins if I had had change. I will not allow those animals to touch me, nor will I handle anything they have touched. Especially money. A great germ carrier, money. I accept only new notes at the bank, and I insist on mint coins in unwrapped slugs.'

'Jesus alive, that's a wow of a fetish if I ever heard one.'

'To each his own, Calloway, and I mean that literally.'

'They told me you were wild when they briefed me, but this is something else. How do you get along in restaurants? Half the hotel kitchens of the world are staffed by coloureds.'

'One makes sacrifices. I avoid eating out whenever possible. On the rare occasions when I do, I patronize either Greek or Italian restaurants. Those concerns are usually family run, and are staffed by aunts, cousins, uncles and nephews. Not a black in sight. You see? There's a logical answer to any problem.'

Calloway eased his shoulder muscles, pressed back against the leather backrest and lit a Camel with a plain Zippo. 'Those media boys at the airport are a problem. Put your mind to that.'

'No problem. In fact their interest may well prove to be helpful.'

'You want to explain that?'

'Not at present, but I will.'

'See you do, Prebble. I'm supposed to keep a low profile. That was part of the deal.' Calloway snatched smoke and blew a little at the windscreen.

'You want the money and none of the risk, eh? Let me remind you you're being paid very well for the information you carry. It had better live up to my expectations. You claim you can predict weather accurately. Proving that to my satisfaction is the only thing that need concern you. I hope that's clear.' Prebble almost purred, hissing his esses.

'I can do it. I've checked my figures through the computers at Stanford. It all firms up, you'll see that when you check them through your own systems. I'll even give you the date and the hour.'

'Better and better. I like a man who is confident.'

'I'm that, Prebble. You won't like how soon the big wave's due.'

'Won't I?' Prebble sounded patronizing.

'How does three days from now sound?' asked Calloway, watching for a reaction. Prebble's top lip tightened and beaded with moisture.

'You're sure?'

'As I'll ever be.'

'Well,' said Prebble. 'Well, well.'

They had been driving west and now Prebble turned on to the Staines road, running along the periphery of Heathrow Airport. The sodium lights bled into the low, drifting clouds and the low scrubland was a featureless expanse beyond the bright ribbon of road.

'This isn't much of a detour,' said Prebble, ignoring the

sweat around his mouth. 'I wanted you to see how close two of our targets are to the airport and the Thames. It's more apparent from the ground than on any map. Usually it's the other way around.'

The Bentley ran beneath dripping oaks and the odd stark elm. On the right, a dark bank began to loom up, high and impressive above the outer wire fencing.

Calloway blew more smoke. 'Which one is that?'

'King George Sixth Reservoir, and on this side of the road, the Staines Reservoirs.'

Calloway peered through the batting windscreen wipers, pointing off. 'What are those animals up there?'

'Sheep. The authority runs them to keep the grass cropped.'

Calloway's thin lips peeled back from his big white teeth and his laugh was cold and humourless. 'Then those warning signs lie. You can't run guard dogs with sheep. Jesus alive. Two fences and a flock of sheep between us and all that beautiful water. You'd think they wanted us to blow them. When we take those walls out, the Dambusters will lose their record.'

'And the capital city they fought for,' Prebble said with some satisfaction. 'Compared with what we're about to do, the Luftwaffe's efforts pale to gnat spits.'

'Good-bye, London,' said Calloway.

'Literally,' agreed Prebble, accelerating.

* * *

She had grown since her birth.

She had doubled her depth to two miles and spread her skirt seventy miles wide. She was now in the Western Atlantic and lower by several thousand feet. She was also becoming visible as she picked up salt crystals in her coils. These in turn attracted moisture that vaporized and streamed out to form tresses of cloud around her head. Her brow was fringed with cirrus and she draped her shoulders with a flowing cape of cumulus.

She breathed now. Her violent progress threw squalling winds ahead of her. Great gusts that heralded her coming. Soon she would be low enough to breathe on the sea. To throw up waves, to chop their towering crests into spume. She left a wide trail of rain and sleet behind her.

She began to rotate eccentrically as the world turned beneath her, distorting her path, turning her point by grudging point towards the Bahamas. But still she ran on, and still she grew, swooping down towards the ocean, darker and darker; more and more substantial.

And still she was paid no mind.

2

Tuesday 2 October

06·30 hours

At precisely 6·30 a.m. Coward's Sony alarm-radio cut into the middle of the early morning weather report, blaring at full volume:

'. . . an overnight low of nine degrees centigrade. The rain is expected to continue throughout the day and into the evening when there will be scattered showers throughout the south-west. Temperatures will rise to a high of eleven degrees, dropping rapidly during the late afternoon. Fog patches are likely . . .'

Coward sought the volume control and fumbled the sound to a mutter without opening his eyes. The predawn chill struck at his naked arm; he drew it back inside the covers and automatically sought the warmth of his wife's hip. It was not there. His hand encountered a cold, shallow dip for the fifth time in as many days and brought him fully awake with a sudden sick fist in his stomach. He lay on his side and listened to the quiet of the bedroom and of all the other empty rooms of the apartment Nancy had left behind. She had stripped the place of everything that was hers.

'. . . flooding is reported in the north of Scotland. In the area of the infamous Pentland Firth, an SOS has been received from a Liberian coaster . . .'

Coward threw back the duvet and shrugged into a towelling robe as his feet worked themselves into his old slippers with the broken backs. He stretched through a long yawn then padded out along the passage and into the living-room.

There was a depressed oblong in the nap of the living-room carpet where her piano had stood and the big panoramic windows were without curtains. Nancy had taken the scissors to them. She had taken her clothes and her sheet music, her earthenware and cutlery, kitchen pans and spices, her antiques and *objets d'art*, the small collotypes of composers and the huge portrait of an illustrious forebear who had died from a French ball on the Heights of Abraham moments before General Wolfe himself had succumbed. What extremes of hatred, Coward wondered, had made Nancy take a hacksaw to the central heating pipes and a hammer to the light fittings?

In the kitchen Coward spooned instant coffee into a mug and plugged in the cheap kettle he had bought the previous day, making a mental note to pick up some plates, cups and a frying pan. Perhaps if he phoned the freezer people they would deliver a bulk order of food when they fitted a new plug and lead to the machine itself. All it contained at present was a pool of water, a selection of plastic bags and a scraper.

Coward abandoned the idea of toast when he found the sliced loaf had developed a green culture mould. He poured hot water over the coffee and took the kettle into the bathroom to shave. Nancy's good-bye note was still taped to the mirror over the sink pedestal. A masterpiece of brevity, it read:

Goodbye, Shitlegs, Nancy.

It worked out at a word a year, thought Coward, working lather into the dark stubble on his upper lip, and why shitlegs? Her language had always been pithy and downright earthy when they made love, but *shitlegs*! That was too much.

The telephone began to warble as Coward scraped his face. He ignored it. The receiver was no longer connected to the wall anyway. He sluiced his face, combed through his black and wiry hair and went into the bedroom in a vain search for a laundered shirt. He settled for a grey rollneck sweater, navy trousers and a houndstooth jacket with patched leather elbows. He spread newspaper on the kitchen table and smeared Kiwi over his black shoes, spitting on them and buffing them to a high shine as the persistent telephone jangled at him.

Coward vaguely remembered a launderette just beyond the Lords roundabout, and he thought about using it before work, rejecting the idea when he remembered it was Cave's turn to pick him up in his old Ford. There was always tomorrow, he supposed.

Coward sipped his second cup of coffee as he looked out at the park through the curtainless living-room windows. The sky was stitched through with dull threads of cloud scudding towards the north-east. Gulls swooped through the sodden plane trees and squabbled on the banks of the Regent's Canal. Beyond, in the open zoo pens, a herd of Waterers Deer stepped about on thin, nervous legs, their tails to the wind. It promised to be the kind of a day central heating salesmen dream of.

The phone stopped ringing just as somebody began to hammer on the front door. It was just after seven. Coward dumped his cup and cracked the door against his foot. Cave's nose and one eye showed between the gap. He was breathless.

'Oh, you're up,' he puffed, 'your phone must have been jumping off its hook. Maitland's been calling for hours. Your doorbell needs a new battery and your lift's out of order.'

'I'll be right out. Just get my coat.' Coward started to close Cave out but he bored inside, grinning painfully.

'I need your pisser, if you'll excuse the expression. I've been in traffic for half an hour and I've got a twenty-minute bladder. The road's up, single line all the way.' He was down the passage and into the bathroom before Coward could reply. Coward left the door ajar and swiftly closed the bedroom and the living-room from sight. The cistern flushed and Cave emerged, zipping up.

'All right, Frank, what's the rush all about?'

'Von Maitland's doing his upper-class nut. He breathes fire. Any coffee going, John?'

'Sorry, no. Why?'

'I'm gasping.'

'Maitland's temper, I meant.'

'Oh, since when did Maitland tell me anything? He only called me because he couldn't raise you. There's your phone now, shall I get it?'

'Leave it. Let's go.'

Cave was busy noting the bareness of the passage and

the hallway where pictures had hung and furniture had stood. 'You had a burglary?'

'Redecorating. The stuff's in store.'

'What it must be to have money. Maitland was his bristly unlovable worst. He wants you fastest, his own words.'

'Then deliver me. He told you nothing else, no clue?' Coward ushered Cave from the apartment and towards the stairs. They went down three floors, crossed the lobby and emerged in drizzle. Cave drove through almost empty streets.

'We're to meet him on the spot, not at the office. He says he'll brief you there. Probably on his second coronary already.' Cave used his teeth and his free hand to strip cellophane from a fresh cigar.

'Not before eight, Frank. We agreed, remember?' Coward took the cigar and threw it into the glove compartment. 'Now where is "there"?'

'The old café near the M4, just beyond Chiswick. By the junction with the North Circular. I reckon fifteen minutes with the wind behind us.'

'Not without a siren,' said Coward, wishing he had brought a carrier of washing with him.

08·15 hours

Calloway had woken late with no jetlag and the appetite of an emperor.

A housemaid with peasant's calves and Irish freckles had brought him a tray of English breakfast and iced Florida orange, the London and New York *Times*, and a pot of perfectly brewed Java blend. He savaged the crisp bacon and devilled kidneys over the OPEC oil crisis headlines, a page two editorial on the latest British political scandal, and a rejigged potboiler about Nixon's future in the world arena. Complete with an archive half-tone of him smiling across at old Chairman Mao himself. *Is Dicky that Tricky*? was the rhetorical headline.

Calloway drank his third cup of coffee and skimmed through an article on the real possibility of an imminent new ice age. He abhorred popular science reporting as a rule, but this offering was risible nonsense. To his certain knowledge the reverse was more probably true. If anything, the polar caps were shrinking as the world sea-levels rose. The reasons were as complex as they were interesting, which is why he had majored in marine studies, and the study of global tidal movements in particular, to the exclusion of everything else – including any form of personal attachment. Like his meals and his rest, Calloway fed his sexual appetites at the nearest oasis and paid what it was worth. No emotional involvement, no ties, and no regrets; just the brief professional contact and away with the dawn.

Calloway saw himself as a cerebral sea-captain who caught the tide with no backward glance towards the land. Yes, just that, he thought, and it suited him just fine. And, he reminded himself, if Prebble lived up to his reputation, a woman would be forthcoming when Calloway needed one. Correct in every detail, from eye and hair colour, to age and bust measurement.

Calloway scratched himself and got out of bed for a soak and a shave. He ran the water as hot as he could stand it, was liberal with bath oil and scrubbed last night's Boeing from his muscles with a stiff brush. He rinsed a rime of lather from his matted blonde chest and lay back with his first Camel of the day.

He loved water. It was better than a woman. It could be warm and cleansing, cool and bracing, could dance with reflected light from a dying sun, be all the hues of the rainbow and as dull and as threatening as ancient lead. It could bear you up or suck you down. It could not be compacted and would always find its own level. It could punch holes in concrete and scour a town into the sea in bare moments. It could grind granite into the finest talcum and be harnessed to power all the cities of the world. It was seas and oceans and rivers and lakes and waterfalls and rain. It was home for the stately whale and the deadly cholera virus. It was both boon and curse and the earth was a dead ball of rock without it. It was also the ultimate weapon. Control the sea and control . . . everything.

Calloway stopped himself from leaving the bath to

check the computations in his briefcase. They were correct to the nearest hundredth decimal place repeating. The computers at Stanford had checked them twice. There was no error and Prebble Marine had bought the data dearly without a quibble. For once, the British were ahead of the game.

Back in the bedroom he found a note on the freshly made bed. It invited Calloway to join his host on a tour of his experimental station.

Calloway threw on clothes and went down the Tudor stairs to Prebble's library by way of the banqueting hall with its minstrel gallery. Men on a portable scaffold were regilding the Poynter coat of arms and painting a fresh, fierce expression on the rampant cockatrice that formed the crest of the helm. Prebble, it seemed, was hot for preserving tradition.

Distant thunder echoed in the vaulting.

Calloway knocked and Prebble said, 'Come.'

A woman leaned across the desk as Prebble signed something with a cramped flourish. Calloway was brought up short, surprised by his own surprise. Why eluded him momentarily. Was the sight of Prebble with a woman such a bizarre tableau? And why did he feel wrongfooted?

She was one of those willowy English roses whose faces had dominated the soap-ads of Calloway's puberty; the face more striking than starlet pretty, the hair more ash than blonde, the eyes more amethyst than Hollywood forget-me-not, and her controlled smile parted from teeth that had grown in her mouth all by themselves without a dental cap in sight. She carried herself and her simple suit with born assurance, and her gaze was direct and interested; certain Bel Air ladies of Calloway's acquaintance could have taken lessons from her.

Her long hand lay in his paw as she said:

'I am Mrs Prebble. How do you do, Mr Calloway. I'm sorry I wasn't here to greet you last evening. It was just a little too late for me, d'you see.'

To Calloway, his own 'A pleasure,' sounded as gauche as a juniper off an Ohio plough.

'Madeleine rises with the lark and sets with the sun.' Prebble could have been expressing pride in a favourite hound or a thoroughbred mare.

Calloway was sorry when she took her hand back. She kissed the air near Prebble's ear, said dinner was at seven and was gone. Prebble shuffled papers and sat down to write his name several times.

'Do you shoot, Calloway?'

'Clays.'

'Any game?'

'Not since High School. I used to plink gophers with a ·22 Ruger my daddy gave me for graduation.'

'Well, the birds are finished of course, but we're thinning out the pigeon tomorrow, and a few rabbits. They seem to be infesting the south pasture. Might be some sport, care to join in?'

'Very much.'

'Good. You can use my Ridley-Scott. Shall we go? I'm having a test run I want you to see, and it's scheduled to start in half an hour. It might make a few things clearer to you.'

'Fine.'

'Do you have your figures with you?'

'In my room.'

'Fetch them and meet me at the car.' Prebble showed satisfaction. 'Half the county will be here tomorrow, Calloway. A fact that pleases me beyond measure, even if they only come to drink my cellar. Being a social pariah in this country is no joke, I can tell you.' Prebble chewed at something he would not swallow, something as dark as crow meat.

Calloway thought about that on the way back to his room. It stopped him thinking about Madeleine Prebble.

08·22 hours

The westbound lane through Chiswick was solid.

Cave drove on the wrong side of the road with his heads on full, sounding his horn. A lollipop lady yelled at them and the traffic sergeant who pulled them in at the roundabout nodded over their warrant cards with more sweat than rain running down his face. He pointed off at a police motorcyclist. 'Follow the lad on the Noddy-bike, he'll get you through. And the sooner the better. Of all the places to dump a body. Bloody criminal, this time of the morning.' He seemed unaware of any irony.

The A40 was sealed off by hazard triangles and a double strand of orange and white tape and the detoured traffic tailed back in all directions. Maitland's Daimler and a forensic utility truck stood side by side on the disused stretch of tarmac to the rear of the defunct café. A uniformed constable in an orange surcoat waved the Ford through his portable barrier as the motorcyclist U-turned away. Maitland's driver told Cave to stay in the car and had Coward follow him to the Daimler where Maitland lounged in the back seat. Coward climbed in beside him and said, 'Good morning.'

Maitland drank sweet tea from an engraved pewter beaker, one leg crossed under a bulky report folder, his right hand clicking a gold ballpoint. Last night's brandy had pinked his eyes and his jowls sagged from lack of sleep. His white hair was long at the nape and ragged about the ears in direct contrast to the carefully docked black moustache that followed the contours of his nostrils and overhung his upper lip. He had dined with the Home Secretary and was paying for it this grey October morning. He pointed the clicking ballpoint at Coward.

'You took your time.'

'Cave got me as soon as he could. My phone's on the blink.'

'If you weren't such a damned fine thieftaker, I'd assign you to a school crossing in one of the outer suburbs.'

'Somebody mentioned a body, Sir,' said Coward, not biting.

'Too much loose talk. One of those Traffic Wallies, I suppose?' Maitland spoke as though he resented the lifting of wartime restrictions and gave Coward the impression he missed the sandbags and crosses of sticky paper on the windows of Whitehall. 'Looks like a sex crime. Young lad, can't be more than eight or nine years old. Bit of a butcher's shop.'

'Regrettable, but more in the line of the CID, surely.'

'Not if I say otherwise, Coward. And I do. There are similiarities to December last. And other things . . .' Maitland blew on his tea and swallowed it down. 'This'n could be the work of the same lunatic. If you remember that other body last Christmas time, hidden under bracken in a wood just outside Newbury. Badly mutilated. Massive internal injuries caused by the introduction of a long, sharp probe into the anus. When you stroll over and take a look at this poor little devil, you'll pretty soon see what I mean.'

'I still don't see why we should . . .'

'I want you to keep a watching brief. Play uncle to the local CID boys. You know the sort of thing, reporting directly to me.'

'You're telling me less than usual.' Coward did nothing to curb the edge in his voice. He remembered the sex crime of the previous year very well, but it should still have been a CID matter. Unless the child was the son of a political figure, or if the Home Office, for reasons best known to itself, was applying pressure. Maitland expected assumptions from his people without the luxury of a direct brief from himself. Coward described it as silent patience with blank cards. It was the way Maitland played his game.

'Less and less,' agreed Maitland.

'Will I ever know why?'

'Leave the "why" of it to me, Coward. If you need to know more, then I shall inform you. I thought you had learned to curb your constant questions.' Maitland scratched an eyebrow over one swollen lid. 'I am handing you a murder investigation. Does there have to be any other reason for my action except to say that you are one of my more able officers?' The smile was as faint as a scratch on concrete.

'I see,' said Coward, not seeing at all.

'Good, good.' Maitland's smile lost itself in the edges of his moustache. 'One has to pay for sitting at table with the mighty, you know. And that includes the resulting hangover.' The electric window hummed open and he tossed tea grouts onto the tarmac where they steamed briefly. 'How did you get on with your snout last night?'

Coward repeated Goldy's information almost verbatim as Maitland said nothing with less showing on his face. Coward finished and there was a long rain-lashed silence until Maitland broke in with:

'Does he suffer from a vivid imagination, this informant of yours?'

'He has none at all.'

'Take your word on this occasion. Well, keep me posted. By the way, you'll likely be travelling for a while. The reason will become apparent when you've spoken to the CID chaps.'

Dismissed, Coward climbed out and collected Cave. They crossed the carpark between heaped bags of rubbish and building debris. A group of men were working under the flyover in an area sealed off by more tape and flashing lights. Cave and Coward trudged towards them.

'What are we into, John?' asked Cave.

'A juvenile murder investigation. And don't swear at me under your breath, Frank. I can't see why either. Reading between the lines though, I'd say that the Home Sec has taken an interest for some reason.'

'I see,' said Cave.

'I've already said that. It did me no good either.'

'Said what?'

'Nothing. Who's that in the sheepskin coat and the sporty hat?'

'Which one?' Cave said, midmumble. 'Oh, him with the Doc. That's Dutton. Inspector the last I heard. Bit of a hardnose. Why don't you let me clear the way a bit. There's bound to be some sniping.'

'No thanks, Frank. Mr Nice and your Mr Nasty will do,' said Coward, lengthening his stride.

A flashgun was popping and a long lead was being connected to a powerful vacuum cleaner. Canvas sheets had been spread around the body and the blanket it lay upon. Resentment was apparent as the two Special Branch men introduced themselves. Cave said he knew everybody as Coward shook hands with Dutton and the doctor who was chewing on a cold pipe.

'I've been waiting to hand over to you . . . Sir,' said Dutton.

'Not just yet. If at all. How far have you got?'

'Our status,' said Dutton, 'is as follows: following set procedures, I have instituted . . .'

Cave's voice slashed at him. 'Inspector Coward doesn't want to hear all that old toffee. Let's not play Hendon Reviews. He wants the cream off the top. Not the manual quoted at him.'

'My sergeant's right.' Coward's tone was mild.

'And if you think we're from CIB2, forget it,' said Cave. 'If some villain thinks you twisted his balls too hard, that's not our affair.'

'Not so loud,' Dutton jangled a pocketful of change and flushed. 'All right, already. A passing motorist phoned this lot in at 5·14 this a.m. Thought it was a hit and run and made himself scarce before the traffic lads got here. I was rousted out of bed and got here at 6·50 on the nose. There were two uniformed lads here already. It . . .' Dutton jerked his chin at the body, 'was lying much as you see it now. The ropes binding the blanket had already been untied and there was a cheap torch beside it. Someone had thrown up there, under that cardboard box. I made sure it wasn't one of our lads – maybe they've got stronger stomachs nowadays. I remember my first body. I threw my ring to the other side of the river.'

'And me,' said Coward.

'I'm analysing it,' said the doctor, 'It's mostly bile and alcohol. It's recent, that much I can say.'

'And you think what, Dutton?' asked Coward.

'The body was dumped by a car, I'd say, and then found and opened up by somebody with more curiosity than sense. That would have been sometime last night. The torch we found was lit, and there's a tramp's jungle off under the flyover about fifty feet away. Somebody was using it to sleep rough. We're doing a rundown on the local bums who use this stretch to camp out. There's a flourishing local community of the buggers. We'll have to pull them all in. The Panda Wallies won't like picking some of those flyblows up, I can tell you.'

'And you've asked for the incident lists from the local station covering last night, Inspector?' asked Cave politely.

Dutton nodded yes. 'One of the uniformed lads told me there was an incident at the roundabout. A vagrant ran under a lorry. I'm chasing it up. Could help, could be nothing.'

'First impressions, Doc?' said Coward.

'In cowboy language, a filthy sick mind did this to the poor benighted little sod. He's been bounced off half the hard surfaces in Christendom. He's been abused, battered and buggered. I don't feel inclined to give you a personality profile of this loony, all wrapped up in the current soft-option jargon. What he is capable of is more to the point I'd say. And you'd best catch him sharp as you like.'

'Dr Buford isn't one of your usual bleeding hearts,' said Dutton.

Cave was doing some heavy, forced swallowing as he and Coward crouched next to the doctor over the boy. Dr Buford produced an expanding metal wand and pointed it at the swollen neck.

'To preempt the usual questions about cause of death and all that,' he said. 'Take your choice. Crushed oesophagus, trachea and larynx, swollen tongue. Up here, impacted skull on the lip of the eye socket, suffusion and displacement of the eyeball itself. The scalp is split in several places.' The wand ran down the chest. 'Broken ribs, and down here, the sphincter has been slashed through and there seems to be a foreign object in the anal tract itself. And last but not least, the penis has been severed.' The pointer touched the dead lips. 'And been forced into the boy's mouth. It was placed there after the boy's death, otherwise there would have been a deal more bleeding than seems to have taken place. Any one of these injuries could have killed him. None of them would have been . . . quick.' Buford pulled himself upright, using Coward's arm. 'I've seen some nasties in my time. But this . . .'

Coward was glad he had not eaten breakfast. 'Time of

death, Doc?'

'You'll love this,' said Dutton, rattling money.

'It would be a very rough guess.'

Dutton cleared his throat with a laugh. 'Rough is right.'

'Perhaps a week. Maybe longer.'

Coward knew his face reflected his surprise.

'Terrific,' said Dutton. Cave was clicking his tongue against the back of his upper teeth.

'Then where's the smell?' asked Cave. 'It would stink to the skies.'

'The clue's in the eyes. See that filminess?' said Buford.

'Yes.'

'It's been kept in a deep freezer. On ice.'

Nobody said anything as wind lifted the corner of the orange blanket and stirred the boy's hair. Traffic sound boomed from the elevated section and a commercial flight shuttled above the low cloud. Cave took great care lighting a small cigar and Dutton took his hands from his pockets and looked at the fingers of one hand.

'I'll be able to tell you a good deal more once I've got the body back to the mortuary, Inspector Coward. There might be some dermis under the fingernails. He would have fought, I think,' said Buford, closing his wand with a snap.

'I hope he marked the bastard good,' said Cave.

Coward looked at Dutton. 'Any reason why the doc shouldn't get moving?'

'No. We've got all the pictures and marked out the site. All we need to do is sweep the area and do some dusting for prints. I've got some Wallies and Cadets coming in, they're promised for nine o'clock.'

'Fine, that's your baby, Dutton. Sergeant Cave and I will go on to the station house. I want to check through the missing persons. Somebody must have missed the boy.'

'I've got that moving, Sir,' said Dutton. 'Should all be waiting on my desk. I'll see you back there.'

'Do that.' Coward laid a hand on the doctor's shoulder. 'You'll have to do me some cosmetic work. We can't send out ID prints with his face like that.'

Buford bit his pipe stem. 'I'll try.'

09·15 hours

The man lay on the gold bed in the chocolate room and watched the naked woman pout out at the grey, wet morning. She held the big white telephone close to her ear, listening to it ringing. Light from the window threw shadowed rain on to her body so that she seemed to run with water like the glass panes, and made it difficult to see if she was crying. She took hard, dry little bites of smoke from a menthol More and her charm bracelet rattled as she jerked the cigarette in and out of her mouth. The man knew each and every charm for she had a story made up about all of them, all bawdy, and all involving her blasted husband.

There was an Adam and Eve inside a hinged and hollow apple, a white enamel mouse eating gold cheese inside a cage, and a lot of arrows that pierced hearts, underlined her initials and transfixed a lovers' knot. There were keys and locks, butterflies and scarabs, an omega sign and a manikin with an articulating penis. Nancy liked that sort of thing.

She had a long slender back and her bottom was a hard double pear above longer and more slender legs. Her hair was scraped back from her face and caught at the nape by a black velvet bow. Her profile was all fine bone with a mouth that stopped short of being too wide and too full. Ash fell from her cigarette and made a grey mark on the orange oriental carpet. Nancy ignored it. She ignored anything that did not suit.

'If you get off the phone, darling, we can order breakfast,' said the man, drumming his fingers on his flat belly.

'Shut up, darling.' Nancy's voice was a low husk, almost masculine, except when she was aroused or amused. Then it took on a less abrasive tone. That, thought the man, happened less and less lately, and more was the pity. He reached his drink from the Chinese bedside table, sipped at it and made a face. It was just last night's melted ice and flat tonic with a tired lemon twist floating in it. As flat and as tasteless as Nancy was becoming. Her quicksilver moods swung between wilful displays of temper and maudlin sulks. She slept badly and coughed through the mornings until her throat spray eased her breathing. He needed coffee and some breakfast.

'Nancy, room service.'

'Shut up, lover.' Nancy's bellow made the rich hotel room sour rather than cosy.

'Charming.' He lost the dead drink, read the time by his ten-programme digital and threw his legs to the floor. It wasn't even ten yet and the day was already spoiled. 'He isn't going to answer, you know. He'll be off writing traffic tickets or whatever the hell he does before breakfast. Boring, Nancy love.'

Thunder growled as Nancy swung from the hip.

'Go and stick your talent under the shower, sweetie. Leave the thinking to the adults. I don't keep you around for your sparkling wit. Your talent's in your lap, go and powder it.'

The man stood and looked down at himself.

'I could always tuck it into my Y-fronts and take it walkies.'

'When I say so,' said Nancy, slapping the receiver against her breast. 'And not a moment before.' A soft flash of distant lightning made her dark eyes bright and hot.

'Your wealth is extremely attractive. Such a pity you aren't.'

'Oh, baby wants to quarrel,' Nancy told the phone.

'Not particularly. Let's have breakfast and fight on full stomachs for once. I'll shower and you order.'

'Starve, you're getting flabby.'

The man forced a smile. 'I'm in better trim than that fuzzy pig you walked down the aisle with. Feed me, I'm much more fun to fight with.'

'Leave John out of this. Don't even think about mentioning him.'

'Mention who? After breakfast I'll tell you how much I love the fuzz.'

The heavy telephone was suddenly in the air and struck the man on the cheek before he could raise an arm. He swore and clutched at his face as the telephone reached the end of the extension cord and fell on to the gold bed.

'Bitch!'

'I warned you. Leave John out of . . . *anything*.'

The man saw the smear of blood on his palm, and barely whispered as he held it out for Nancy to see.

'This is going to be very expensive and painful, Nancy dear.'

'Get out. I'm finished with you. Out.'

'If he's important, why cuckold him at every opportunity?' sneered the man.

'Shut up, pimp.'

'Sure, I'm bought and paid for, but you couldn't stay with him, could you? Couldn't pull off his twig and berries and have him sit in your lap, could you?' The low, wheedling voice kept on at the same monotonous level as the naked, muscular man skirted the bed, closing in on the furious and frightened woman. Nancy could only see his blooded hand and hear his awful, droning half-truths.

'What I do, I do. My affair, mine,' Nancy said shakily.

'And mine. This time the tame stud won't jump through the hoop. Just tell me how you married the poor bastard and tried to emasculate him in a welter of puerile domesticity. And ended up being smothered yourself. You tell me.'

'I want you out.' Nancy saw the line of new blood on his cheek and jaw, a thick bead of it gathering on his chin. She wanted to claw it or kiss it away.

'Not until we finish the truth game, Nancy dear. Tell me how he wouldn't stand behind your chair and light your foul little cigarettes when you entertained your coven of rich bitches to high tea. You have to have somebody like me for that, don't you? He wouldn't play, would he?'

'You distort everything, you shit.' Nancy was crying as she cast around for something to throw. She flicked her cigarette and it struck the man's shoulder in a shower of sparks. His naked heel ground the stub into the carpet and he ignored the pain. He drew a rectangle in the air close to her face.

'A portrait of Mr Nancy Fitzgibbon-Coward. A masterpiece of failure. The frame's worth more than the picture.'

Nancy threw herself forward with raking nails.

The man caught her neatly, trapped both elbows in a firm grip and forced her forearms up against the joint. Her mouth dropped open as the pain stole her breath. She brought up a knee. He took the blow on the outside of his thigh, changed his grip and threw her in a thrashing heap across the gold counterpane. The man flipped her on to her face and straddled her. She bunched her muscles and arched her back but he held her, using his superior weight to hold her down.

He whispered into her hair.

'You have to be punished for that, don't you?' His thumbs found the muscles in her neck and ground down, making Nancy gasp.

'Yes . . .'

'Yes,' the man said, thinking, *Christ, I earn my money. She's just another lunatic woman willing to pay for the quickest route to hell. Sometimes they pulled back, sometimes they didn't. This one would go all the way with the flags flying. She wanted to die.*

He stole a glance at his wristwatch as he sought another pressure point. When he had finished he would make her serve him breakfast with her eyes bound. His stomach growled in anticipation.

10·31 hours

Dutton's office was a doorless cubicle with a metal desk, a swivel chair, a pinboard and a telephone off a central bull pen where constables and detectives worked in open plan under rows of fluorescent tubes. The double-glazed windows were filmed with dirt and the grey-painted walls were scuffed by chairbacks and dappled by handmarks. An institution clock ticked off the seconds, a big tear-off calendar gave today's date and there were dead flies trapped in the light fittings. The ducted heating barely kept the chill from the room and the bare tiled floor struck up cold through Coward's shoes. He had riffled through all the teleprints and killed the missing juveniles file twice. It was Cave who came in with the right picture with matching dates and a profile flimsy stapled to it. He skimmed it across Dutton's desk and Coward caught it before it found a home on the floor.

'Surrey CID just printed this through to us direct. Quicker than going through Central,' said Cave. Good old Frank knew every short cut and invented more. In his book, the shortest distance between two points was through the side door and chatting up the right WPC clerk. Cave grinned around his second cigar. 'Peter Michael Petrie. Eight years old. Both parents living and together, which makes a refreshing change. Reported missing nine days ago. Went to a cub meeting at the local hall and never came home. Lives – *lived* – at an address in a village called Easter Without. Heard of it?'

'No. Have you, clever clogs?'

'Found it on the map. It's in Surrey. If we leave now, we can be down there for a lunchtime pint and a ploughman's. There's a decent pub with accommodation.'

Coward regarded the fuzzy ten-eight of the smiling boy in his uniform, his cap askew on uncombed hair, one sock adrift and his knees scuffed. 'And you phoned ahead to the local station, of course.'

'You're the "Sir" in this team. Privilege of seniority. I told the switchboard to put the call through in five minutes. We'll need a WPC on standby down there, if we have to inform the parents.'

'The Petries might be churchgoers, Frank. Check with the local vicar. He'll certainly know the boy by sight, cub groups are usually run in close accord with the church. Anything to make it easier. They'll have to be brought up here to the mortuary for the identification, of course.'

'Sure, but we could stand back – let the local police handle it.'

'I don't think so,' said Coward.

'You wouldn't . . . *Sir*.' Cave held up a hand, warding

off censure. 'All right, I'll get on with it. We going down there?'

'Yes, and don't get the idea I'm being noble or sentimental. I want to see both parents up close as soon as possible. Murder's usually a family affair.'

'Usually, but this . . . the pattern's out of that league.'

'On the surface, Frank, on the surface. They still have to be eliminated as suspects. Apart from that, this investigation is spread over three counties at present. We have to consolidate. The Petrie boy came from Surrey and his body was found in Hammersmith. This vagrant of Dutton's is probably in one of the London emergency hospitals.'

Cave snapped fingers.

'He is, St George's. Name of Charlie Glass. Do we need him up front?'

'A possible eyewitness? Bet your pension we do.'

'That's not on. The old fellow's still under according to the medics in charge down there. Won't be available for interview for at least twenty-four hours. Don't frown at me, they're their words, not mine. Dutton went purple too. You'd think we were going to rubber-hose the old berk the way those doctors talked.'

Coward shrugged. 'We'll have to live with that. Tomorrow's soon enough anyway. We've got enough legwork in Surrey to keep us occupied. Maitland can handle our end of the red tape, but poor old Dutton will have to sing and dance over his paperwork if he's to continue on the case.'

Cave's 'shame' was patently insincere. 'I'll tell him. He's below, booking in his forensic evidence. Diesel dust and puke. What a life.'

Coward reached for the telephone. 'Meantime, I'll talk to our office and then Commander Maitland.'

'MBE, OBE, Sporran and bar.'

'Out,' said Coward, dialling New Scotland Yard. Cave grinned and went. Coward gave the switchboard his extension number and the answering machine cut in. He said his personal code and the voice print ident gave him the green light and played him his message tape.

Goldy's voice said, 'Guv, they come back. Give us a

meet at point four. Usual time.' There was a click as he cleared down and a drunken Nancy said, 'Don't try to find me, Shitlegs. We are through. Finished. Ended and over.' Her voice was slurred and vicious.

Coward swallowed a hot tennis ball and said stupidly: 'What?'

'Kiss Maitland's arse for me.' A man's voice fuzzed in the background and Nancy snapped something indistinct before the telephone clattered in its cradle. The tape beeped and rewound itself.

Coward was both flushed and cold. He gripped the receiver as ways of hurting her back tumbled in his mind in a mad, negative spiral. There were visions of torn and bleeding flesh and a pleading voice he wanted to batter into silence. He was staring at the ten-eight bromide. The sight of the smiling and dead cub scout calmed him for no reason he could fathom. He ran a gentle thumb over the face and told the tape to erase itself; listened to it do so, broke the connection and redialled Maitland's number.

When Cave came back, Coward was sitting with his chin in his palm looking at nothing at all.

11·05 hours

Nancy turned the shower control from hot to cold and stood under the cold needles for as long as she could stand them. Spun back to hot for a moment, lathered herself and rinsed off in tepid. She dabbed herself dry and oiled herself from shoulder to toe, inspecting her skin minutely as she did so. Her labia and groin were tender to the touch but the man had not caused bruises or broken the skin anywhere.

Her throat bothered her, more of a dull nag than a true throbbing. She used the medicated spray on her tongue and was eased in moments. She worked cold cream into her face around the eyes and the scores at the corners of her mouth where age and self-abuse showed first. Not that it mattered any more, not if the consultant and his sophisticated machines were right. *Damn the doctors, damn the injustice.* Her lips clamped together briefly as she suppressed the sudden black fire of depression; pushed the self-pity from her. Right or wrong, justly or otherwise, it was the nowness of things that truly mattered. Not the might-have-beens of an uncaring future that would not include her.

Perhaps the philosophers were right, perhaps it was true that when self died the world died too. That would be amusing. More amusing still, if, by a deliberate act of will, she stilled her heart prematurely and killed the universe along with herself.

Nancy threw back her head and laughed her vibrant man's laugh.

God, what a final and ultimate irony.

She caught her own eyes in the ormolu mirror and locked into them. The face laughed but they did not. They knew more than the face knew, far more, and had a hell of a lot more at stake. They knew why she had killed John in her mind, had deliberately assassinated their marriage and destroyed their home. She, Nancy, had done that. Not the foul crab in her body. Dear dead John would not see her when the grain of her skin had turned to porous stone and her body was rotten tissue on an ugly framework of bones. Nobody would. She must find a way of avoiding that ultimate indignity. She would make the leap into infinity long before her will was sapped and her essence was trapped inside a wasted shell. That travesty of Nancy would be seen by nobody.

Nobody.

She leaned in towards her beautiful reflection, close enough for her breath to bloom the mirror with moisture. She pursed her lips in a pretty, silent kiss. 'I promise, Nancy,' she told herself. 'As God is my judge, I promise.'

Then she smiled and the eyes were softer and less remote. Somewhat mocking, she realized, and was pleased. Self-mockery had the taste of life in it, self-pity did not. Nancy released her hair from the waterproof cap and untied the black bow. She combed her hair down her back with a hundred long strokes from either side of her face and was careful with the centre parting. In her ears she pinned matching sapphires and coated her long lashes with dark liner. Then, using her most vivid gloss, she painted her lips and her nipples. She slipped her feet into delicate gold slippers and, wearing nothing else, returned to the bedroom where the man waited for her.

The heavy curtains were drawn and the lights were dimmed. The gold bed was a raft of delicate light in the blackness. Without a word or a sideways glance, she lay down upon it with her legs together and her arms spread. She kept her eyes trained on the ceiling.

The man came to her side and, gently raising her head, placed a small pillow beneath it. He spread her hair in a black fan with careful strokes of a soft brush and, leaning over, brushed his lips against her stomach.

'Now,' he said quietly, 'you are ready and the calmness will come if you will it. Good . . . good.'

She felt the cold anaesthetic pad against the crook of her left arm followed by the numbness. She did not see or feel the hypodermic draw a little blood before it discharged the hallucinant drug into her veins. The world behind her lids made a long clockwise spiral and she was through an explosion of colour where a voiceless choir made the dark side of reality retreat from her in a slow, single and sliding note of comforting melody.

11·06 hours

Charlie swam up through the amber liquid that tasted of hundred proof into a blinding headache.

His mouth was all fur and feathers and his eyes grated in their sockets. Sound came to him in lapping waves from an interior location. There were bright female voices and the organized clatter of busyness. A curtain swished on rails and a bedhead was adjusted with cheerful solicitude. He smelled disinfectant and boiled vegetables. A spoon clattered in a plate. Charlie opened the edge of one reluctant eye and found focus. A bloody hospital ward.

He was on his back on a comfortable mattress and had been bedbathed in astringent surgical spirit. He was wearing soft, much-washed pyjamas and bandaged wadding kept his head from making proper contact with the pillow. He wiggled his toes and was shocked by the nakedness of his feet under the covers. *They* had turned him into a vulnerable thing, as clean and as naked as an old pink baby. A bloody geriatric. That was the new word for old incontinents with no wealth and no standing in the welfare state.

Charlie's sense of outrage was diminished by the pressure inside his head. It was as if his tightening skull was about to evict his brain, forcing the grey cells out through his ears like ectoplasm. Charlie was too angry to be frightened. A pint of stout would help. Hadn't he heard somewhere that they prescribed Guinness in State hospitals nowadays? He wondered where they kept the crates of bottles. They also kept alcohol in stock. Mixed with flavouring it would swill down a treat. The first thing was to get up and reconnoitre. Have a forage like in the old days. For Charlie it was as natural as breathing, it was how he survived. He lay still and quietly planned – *they* must not know he was aware.

He must have slept.

He came to with a start. There was a pneumatic collar around his right arm and air squeaked through a rubber tube as his blood pressure was taken. His ribs felt caved in and he was thirsty enough to consider water as a reasonable thing to swallow.

The nurse was young and chunky with a scrubbed face and short copper hair beneath her white cap. He was no longer in the general ward. It was a small room with a single chair beside the bed. Charlie's heart began to thump. A young copper sat in the chair with his helmet on his lap.

Charlie remembered the small corpse in the weak torchlight.

They had his card marked. That was it. The bastards had him marked down as prime suspect number one. Not this kiddy, Charlie thought fiercely, keeping his features slack, his eyes hooded. Not Charlie Glass.

* * *

She was black and violet and pewter and she hid the light. Her great central eye looked up into deep space where she saw both the sun rise and the moon fall from grace. Her eye was quiet but her head was more violent. A great wall of cloud that ploughed forward, throwing winds before her, hacking down at the Atlantic and blasting the middle air with howling gusts. She was a great palling thunderhead whose power was based on appetite. She drew power from the main cold front behind her. The more power she generated, the more she needed to consume.

She was dressed now. In a great flowing cape of cloud and disturbed air that trailed back behind her for many miles. She threw up storms and left a thunderous veil of cumulo-nimbus in her wake. Ships ran from her when they could and aircraft skirted her or stayed grounded until she had passed.

The top of her head was four miles above the ocean. She furrowed the sea with her broad chin, banking it up into great mountain ranges. Then, lifting her head, she allowed those shifting monuments to crash back into the depressed valleys.

Men plotted her as she swung more and more from her original course, ever swinging towards Europe.

3

Tuesday 2 October

11.59 hours

The M4 was left far behind before Cave lost his temper.

The light was poor and he drove on dipped heads along congested B roads past dripping hedgerows where stands of balding autumnal trees raked the cloud ceiling with their bare uppermost branches. He was tired of the rain, tired of the job, tired of the sudden upheavals that took him so far away from home; tired of giving darling Maggie half-reasons for his absences. He was also damned tired of driving with the silent and introspective Coward for company. He was about as much fun as the swishing wiper blades. Less. For the last hour he had gnawed at his thumb without a word.

Cave put himself back into the Cowards' bathroom and studied the room minutely. The peach bathrobe that Maggie drooled over no longer lived on its hook behind the door. The glass shelves were empty of the usual clutter of scents and lotions, and there were no female deodorants or menstruation tablets in the medicine cabinet. No tweezers, moisturizer, lacquer or bath salts. And the pictures missing from the hall – the framed prints from an antique Japanese Pillow Book, the row of tiny original Bewick woodcuts. Nancy would never have let them out of her sight. It was obvious to Cave that she had upped and left her husband.

Coward did not see Cave punch the wheel as he mouthed a savage expletive. He was reconstructing his last conversation with Maitland who had listened to Coward's update before saying:

'I did say I thought you would be travelling, did I not?'

Coward thought, *Not from reading tea-leaves you didn't*, and said, 'You did indeed.'

'Good fishing country. A lot of fine private water. Had you the time, which sadly you do not, you could have taken your rods.'

I'm after more than dace or bloody gudgeon. 'Pity.'

'Yes, pity indeed. You'll see that the usual supply of questionnaires are to hand, won't you? In case it becomes necessary to institute a mass interview of all the males above fourteen years of age? Best you go and see the leading figures in the area first, JPs and suchlike, have them set an example for the rest of the populace.' Paper rustled over the line as Maitland turned pages. 'I understand the local squire is some chap called Prebble, Giles Prebble. He should be one of the first on your list. See that he is, will you?'

'Yes.' Coward was brushed by a distant memory. 'Isn't there a dossier on him in the political section?'

'That's the fellow. Had a go at a couple of by-elections. Has right-wing sympathies of a sort. Bit of an England-for-the-English merchant. Still, I'm sure he'll be more than anxious to help over a matter like this. On his door-step, so to speak. Duty and all that.'

'Was he cleared over that votes shuffle, or is he still on the pending file as a doubtful? I might need to see the file, refresh my memory.'

'Oh, I don't think that's necessary, Coward. Not under these circumstances. Not the thing at all. Not that sort of an op, is it?'

'Isn't it?'

'No, Coward, it is not.' Maitland's voice was less airy. 'According to the local electors' register, there're about two hundred souls of voting age in and around Easter Without. It seems to have evaded being part of the commuter belt. A nice trick. Ah, and the village church seems to have some character, architecturally speaking. Early perpendicular tower of flint rubble. In 1642, the Poynter family erected a fine example of a painted stone memorial in the west nave. Look out for it, I should.'

Coward's head, feet and hands felt weightless. *Why the bloody Michelin Guide? He'll be asking for brass rubbings next.* 'Really.'

'Do I detect a note of sarcasm, Coward?'

'Sarcasm, Commander Sir?'

'Yes, sarcasm, and I do. The current vicar's name is

Poynter. It might be that he's part of the same family. Can't be a coincidence, I'm sure. Worth noting, I'd say.'

'Shall I check that out on your behalf?'

'Only if it comes up in the course of casual conversation. Not the sort of thing that requires a direct question, I should have thought. Still, suit yourself.'

What is he whittering on about? Coward pressed his hand against his swimming temple. 'I'll consider my approach with care, Sir.'

'You'll need to. That's the point. The local church hall is the only suitable public building for you to use as your Murder HQ. I should think it would be both prudent and wise to cultivate the vicar's good-will.'

'Thanks for the advice.'

'Not at all. Call me once you have your telephone lines installed.'

'I'd like the Prebble file.'

'Goodbye, Coward.' Maitland cleared down and that was that. Or is it? wondered Coward. All that Olde Englyshe travelogue had to have some significance, didn't it? Coward was slammed sideways in his seat as Cave overtook a juggernaut on the inside with his horn blaring, shaving past with his offside tyres churning up the grass verge.

'Looking for a ticket, Frank?'

'He's awake, everybody,' said Cave, drifting into a long curve and bumping over a humpbacked bridge. 'Whoopee. I'll bet that woke up your breakfast.'

Coward waited for his stomach to settle.

'What breakfast? You promised me a pint, remember?'

'I'll swap for some clues.'

'About what?' asked Coward, half-guessing.

'This trek into darkest Surrey. It's my business when you go all broody on me. And don't say it isn't if I think it affects the job.'

'Just drive, Frank. You know as much as I do.'

'Just drive, just drive,' mimicked Cave. 'Move over, you daft trout!' he yelled at a woman turning an old Volkswagen at an intersection. 'Women should stay home, barefoot and pregnant. Not messing about on the roads in clapped-out Kraut cars.' He accelerated beneath bowering trees and out into a flat stretch between raw, furrowed farmland. The sky was a ridged grey vault where rooks wheeled with ragged outstretched wings. An old green and white iron sign said: 'Easter Without ¼ mile'. They had left metrication far behind.

'Heads or tails?' said Coward, flicking a coin.

'What for?'

'The boozer or the vicar first.'

'What a cat's got. I've got to eat, and you're changing the subject. Why is Von Maitland playing Geppetto with our strings? He's got us bumping around in the dark for no reason I can see. If this is a cover for something else you might just tell me.'

'You know Maitland.'

'Like I know the crack in my bum. I know it's there but I've never seen it. Just sitting on it is an act of faith. Christ, John, you're as elusive as Carlos.' Cave swung on to a pub forecourt, ripped on the handbrake and allowed the engine to idle. 'Well?'

Coward sighed and closed one eye.

'You've guessed as much as I have. When I know more, you'll be the first to know. Until then stay *shtumm*. Now, that may be tough for a garrulous clown like you, but that's how it is.' He stared one-eyed. 'Do I get my pint, or not?'

Cave blew out his cheeks, shook his head, started to say something then changed his mind. He killed the ignition and opened his door.

'The best in the house, Inspector,' he said, 'With a splash of egg-nog and a green cherry.'

'Thank you, Sergeant,' Coward said formally.

13·00 hours

The publican gave Cave directions to the vicarage and he found it with little difficulty. The manse was a Victorian disaster at the end of a drive lined with old redwoods and mature rhododendrons. Tall, gaunt and ivy-covered, it loomed above a depressed lawn and a sunken garden. A small grey woman answered the bell pull and led them into the vicar's study where old volumes ran from floor to ceiling and apple logs burned in the fireplace.

The Reverend Poynter was a short and balding butterball with prominent eyes and teeth, a muddy complexion and a strong baritone voice that drew echoes from the high ceiling cornices. His glances were as brisk as his handshake and once initial eye-contact had been made, his eyes roved at will. He stood before the fire with his belly out, his hands clasped in the middle of his back as he smiled the Special Branch men into old darkwood chairs with tapestry backs and brass-nailed edges. He offered tea made by his housekeeper and accepted one of Cave's small cigars whilst Coward told him of the Petrie boy's death and asked for a character assessment of the parents.

Poynter showed distress and smoke trickled between his ugly teeth.

'Tragic,' he said. 'But what you've told me is confirmation of what I've feared all along. Peter was not the sort of boy to roam, far from it. We all hoped that he would turn up after a trip to the bright lights all the same, even though it would be totally out of character. I suppose he was assaulted . . . sexually, I mean.'

'Yes.'

'There are times,' said Poynter, 'I do not like the world at large. And prayers or condolence seem so pitifully inadequate.'

Wind snarled in the chimney and the flames sputtered around a knot.

Poynter rolled the cigar between his fingers. 'I can help with the mother, I think. I know Mrs Petrie very well. But her husband is something else. He works on the Prebble Estate as a gamekeeper of sorts. The shooting around here is very good. From what I hear, Petrie has been drinking heavily of late and is inclined to use his fists rather too freely. I'm not suggesting he ill-treated the boy, far from it, he idolized him. But his wife is another matter . . . and his attitude to the scouting movement is . . . well, what can I say?'

'Anything that might be relevant,' said Coward.

Poynter smoothed a ruck in the carpet with a toecap. 'All the gossip comes to me, you know, it goes with the living. I suppose the police must hear much the same sort of thing.'

'Pretty much.'

'Yes . . . my Christian charity is spread extremely thin too often these days. When it gets too much, I go out into the orchard and punt a few windfalls about. It seems to help.'

'I swear down the loo and flush it away,' said Cave with a straight face. 'Inspector Coward jogs in Regent's Park.'

'So long as it works, eh?'

'It works,' lied Cave, flicking ash into the fire.

Poynter picked a shred of tobacco from his lower lip. 'I suppose you have to know, Petrie has made some unfortunate remarks about our scout master, Mr Ferris. Quite unfounded of course. You'll probably hear about them during the course of your enquiries, and I suppose it's best if you hear it from me first, without the distortions and gilding. The Parochial Council did consider legal action at one point, but I was able to change their minds, thank God. Something like that can get out of hand in a small community like this.'

The small grey woman brought tea things on a tray and went away. Poynter poured from a silver pot, adding milk and sugar. Nobody wanted the biscuits.

'You were saying?' Coward jogged.

Poynter cooled his tea with a puckered mouth.

'I should like to excuse Petrie's behaviour over this matter, but the truth is, he started his campaign against Mr Ferris long before Peter disappeared. Several anonymous letters were written and received. His wife brought one of them to me, one she had found in the house. She was very distressed. A truly Christian woman. None of us will have an easy time with the man when we go to the house.'

'My handwriting,' said Cave.

Poynter stopped blowing into his cup. 'Pardon?'

'Leave him to us, Sir.'

'Why didn't you report these letters, and Petrie, to the police?' asked Coward. 'That would have been best.'

'I didn't see it that way. I believed we could handle it

within the village. I spoke to him and the letters stopped. All seemed well until Peter . . .' Poynter sighed into silence.

Coward let it drop. It could wait.

Poynter said suddenly: 'I understand you'll want the use of the church hall.'

'Do you?' Coward showed mild surprise.

'Yes, your superior in London – Maitland, is it? Seems a very civilized chap. Most interested in the tower and the family ties with the village. Very distant, I told him, but binding all the same. The Poynters go back to the Conquest.'

'He telephoned you,' said Coward. Cave muttered and his spoon clattered in his saucer.

'Just so. I told him the hall would be made available. The scouts and the Mothers' Union can meet here in the conservatory. They can tie their knots and call bingo to their hearts' content. Your people will have to cover the expense of heating and lighting of course.'

'Fine,' said Coward.

'No problem,' said Cave. 'When does Petrie finish work? We like to see both parents together. The boy was very badly beaten about and the identification won't be pleasant.' He swallowed the oversweet tea without making a face.

Poynter helped himself to another cup. 'We've a few minutes yet, I sent my housekeeper off on her bicycle with a note for Mr Prebble. He'll send Petrie home. I preferred not to use the telephone – we still have a manual exchange and operators have big ears. We'll go in your car if you don't mind. Mine isn't at all well, something to do with the transmission they tell me.'

They talked about general nothings for ten minutes or so and then left.

11·05 hours

The entrance to the experimental station was down a concrete ramp cut into a hump in a pristine lawn less than a quarter of a mile from Prebble's manor house. He and Calloway could have walked there in more clement weather conditions. Mossy cairns camouflaged the many air-ducts and the faint hum of generated power rode on the wind.

In reception they were issued with lapel ID cards, coveralls and felt overshoes. Calloway's cigarettes and lighter were taken into care to enforce the smoking ban.

Beyond a double set of self-sealing rubber doors the air pressure rose and electronic drones monitored their progress into a control room where banks of screens received live colour images overlaid by constantly changing indexes of figures. An angled observation window commanded a high view of an acre contour model dotted with buildings, scored by road systems and cut through with water courses, both natural and artificial. Men on elevated gantries called off check lists into the sound system and linked digital clocks pulsed off a countdown in minutes and seconds punctuated by bleep tones.

Prebble ignored the screens, moved directly to a programme console and set it to 'receive', his hand out towards Calloway, his face tense. The American opened his case and handed him the printout of his weather prediction. Neither man spoke until Prebble had typed the figures into the computer, made a control tape and linked that to the various visual displays.

'Let's at least be comfortable, Calloway. No sense in you standing on one foot like some miscreant waiting for a whipping.' Prebble waved Calloway into a swivel bucket beside him and locked in a master control, pressing a 'commit' button. A series of reds blinked around the gantries with a warning warble. 'Still confident?'

Calloway nodded as he trimmed a ragged nail with his teeth, not trusting his voice.

'Four minutes, gentlemen,' Prebble said into an opened mike, looking aside at Calloway. 'Impressive, don't you think? The only larger model than this was built in Hong Kong. This, though, is far more sophisticated.'

'Four minutes, control,' the speakers echoed several times in various accents.

'We have laid in assimilated power and sewage lines, all the sub-stations and pumping stations for both water and the electricity supply. And we've built stress and tolerance factors into the road systems, and a series of coloured dyes will mark the spread of pollution.' Prebble explained.

'Surge building,' said the speakers.

Calloway identified the area immediately below him as Windsor and Slough with London Airport and Staines beyond. Several large reservoirs formed a bright ring to the west of the main river and the rivers Colne and Wraysbury. He followed the Thames through Chertsey, Molesey and Hampton to the sudden southern swing through Twickenham and Richmond, the curve between Brentford and Kew, the humping swings through the London Boroughs and the City, the dogleg at Greenwich and the widening flow to the east past Southend and Sheerness to the Channel beyond Maplin Sands.

The whole of the Thames Valley in miniature lay below him. Prebble was right, it was impressive and must have cost several small fortunes. Calloway's estimation of Prebble rose several points; the Englishman's boast of being thorough was more than borne out by the incredible detail of the model and the sophisticated hardware he used to monitor the effects of the miniature flood he was about to create.

'Three minutes,' said the speakers in concert.

'Watch screens one through three,' said Prebble. 'They cover the Dogger Bank, Felixstowe and Clacton. You'll see the sea-surge follow that coastal line, swing past Blackwater and the Crouch and gather at the estuary mouth before forming a blanket between Canvey and Sheerness.'

'Factor One surge achieved, control. Building.'

'Understood.'

'What time scale are you operating?' asked Calloway, patting his flanks for cigarettes that were not there.

'Seventy five per cent acceleration. Every fifteen minutes on the model is an hour of real time. Also, to plot the water levels when they rise above the norm, red dyes will be released to mark the areas and height of the flooding. When they mix with the blue, brown and yellow dyes from the sewers and the water mains, we'll be able to measure the probable extent of pollution.'

Calloway made a simple mental calculation. It would take six hours to simulate a twenty-four-hour period. If he and Prebble stayed until the end they would be late for dinner at seven. Again he wondered why he was considering Madeleine Prebble. It was senseless. Especially in view of how important this test was to his calculations. If he were wrong he knew his life would not be worth the proverbial plugged nickel.

'Two minutes and thirty seconds. Factor Two surge building.'

'Stand by to mark,' said Prebble.

'Standing by, control.'

'Mark.'

'Marked, control. Building to Factor Three and release.'

'We'll be monitoring a thirty-six-hour period. That gives us a convenient break for dinner and time enough to get back here for the final results at ten this evening. It doesn't do to upset one's wife, eh?'

'No,' said Calloway, suddenly absorbed in the test. It was as if Prebble had read his mind.

'We have ninety seconds to release of surge. Counting down from sixty seconds.'

'Control counting,' said Prebble, cueing the video recorders. He mumbled a song under his breath, one that Calloway found vaguely familiar. An old veterans' song from World War One.

'. . . Goodbye, Piccadilly, Farewell, Leicester Square . . .'

'Sixty, fifty nine, fifty eight . . .'

Calloway felt his scalp crawl. Prebble was stroking the inside of his thighs as though it were an act of private sexual foreplay, and his forehead glistened. He smiled at Calloway and there were small bubbles at the corners of his mouth. He licked them away and said:

'Still certain of your figures?'

Calloway looked away at the screens. 'Yes,' he said, wishing his voice was steadier, wishing he had the money and was light years away from Prebble and his oddly wanton smile; the dead flecked eyes that bored at his own.

'We'll soon know . . . we'll soon know,' hissed Prebble, licking more saliva bubbles.

A lazy hump of water had formed on screen one and was advancing to the south as a wide and shallow arrow. The simulated destruction of London had begun.

14·45 hours

The Petries lived in one of a row of ugly grey cottages down a pretty lane bounded by hawthorn and poplars. A muddy Land Rover was parked at the door and a grocery bicycle leaned against the fence. A tortoiseshell tom lounged in an empty windowbox on the sill and a net curtain stirred two doors down. Poynter waved towards the movement and it stopped abruptly.

'The local busybody, Mrs Elphin,' he said, using the Petries' knocker twice.

A wiry man in work clothes opened the door with a jerk. The stubble on his chin was smeared with clay and his loose mouth twitched with a life of its own. 'In here,' he said, and they all crowded into a small front room warmed to blood heat by central heating. A large and plump woman sitting in an uncut moquette chair was introduced as 'the wife'. Her eyes were huge and ringed in purple, her pupils enlarged by Librium. She made a mewing in her throat when she saw the vicar and her hands made fluttering movements in the air. Poynter caught them both and crouched beside her, speaking softly.

'You've found him,' said Petrie, leaning in the doorway. 'You've found Peter.' It was not a question.

'Yes,' said Coward. 'I regret to have to tell you . . .'

Petrie pointed a blunt finger over a fist. 'Don't give me that "sorry" stuff. Where is he?'

'His body was found in Chiswick.'

'And you're bringing him home.'

'You have to identify him first. Not that there can be much doubt, I'm afraid.'

Mrs Petrie freed her hands and dug them into her hair,

wailing and looking for something in Poynter's face. She did not find it. Poynter got her hands back between his before she tore tufts from her scalp. The comfortable rolls of flesh on her face seemed to be shaking themselves from her skull.

'You arrested the bastard yet?' asked Petrie.

'Nobody has been arrested, Mr Petrie.' Coward moved to block the man from his wife's sight.

'He done it. Ain't no question.' Petrie's finger drilled at Coward's shoulder. 'You get him or I fucking will.'

'This is hardly the time to utter wild threats,' said Coward, holding the man's wild stare.

'I mean it. That's my kid we're talking about.' The muscles in Petrie's shoulders rolled and bunched. 'And you can shut her mooing up, vicar. It's bleeding hearts like you that make her wetter. That's all I've had since this started. Whine, bloody whine. I'll have justice out of you bastards, see if I don't.'

'That's enough of that,' said Cave.

'Up yours. He sees a bitch, you wag your tail. I'm talking to him.' Petrie's finger stabbed at Coward.

'Even so. I'd sit down if I were you,' said Cave.

'You ain't me. In my house I say what goes. Get Ferris and I'll listen. I can dump the both of you if I fancy.'

Cave's 'Really?' was quietly ominous.

'I just said so.'

'This isn't helping.' Coward could have cheerfully punched a hole through the lathe and plaster wall beyond Petrie's head. He brushed the pointing finger aside instead. There was something unhealthy squirming down in the depths of Petrie's bright eyes, as much a warning as a fog maroon. Coward had seen many similar faces in solitary where they nibbled the buttons from padded walls or muscled the steel door from a cell with nothing more than manic strength and a chair leg. For a man in Petrie's state of mind anything was a weapon.

He chose a nobbly blue ashtray that weighed a good two pounds.

He came out of the doorway in a leaping swing, scooped up the glass ashtray and bored past Coward, his arm arcing down at his wife's head. Cave's foot took a leg out from under him and spoiled his aim. Petrie's forearm caught Poynter at the base of his neck and drove him to the floor where he rolled in a ball and showed a darn in his black sock.

The ashtray skied off into splinters.

Petrie railed at his wife as he fought for balance, his words jumbling together into a solid cudgel of abuse. Her eyes were dumb lavender blooms pinned to her wet, upturned face.

Coward shouldered air and spittle from Petrie's mouth a moment before Cave caught him around the waist and heaved him bodily away. Petrie kicked off a gumboot and it jammed itself in the fireplace gas logs. He and Cave spiralled off into the hall where they scraped a portrait of General Kitchener from the wall and overturned a vase of dried flowers.

Cave's fingers did something near Petrie's mastoid bone and the man was a sudden limp weight with his fringe over his face.

'I'll take his legs,' offered Coward.

'He doesn't mean it,' wailed the woman.

'He's mine,' said Cave, his breathing normal, his eyes a smidge whiter. 'I'll take him for some fresh air and a talking to.' He opened the kitchen door and dragged Petrie through and out into the back garden where the light was failing fast. Coward closed him out and went back to the front room where Mrs Petrie sobbed into Poynter's chest.

'He doesn't mean it,' the woman wailed over and over. 'He doesn't mean it . . .'

'I did try to tell you,' Poynter said over her ample shoulder. 'There, there, my dear . . .'

Coward sucked a scraped knuckle and thought of straitjackets.

'She can't stay here.'

'I suppose I could arrange something, Inspector.'

'I want more than that. I want a positive yes.'

'All right, yes. I'll take her back to the manse. One of the local women will look after her.'

'Wait.'

Coward went outside where Cave had Petrie up against the side of a garden shed full of junk. Petrie's face was flattened against the rough, warped planks. Coward took the car keys from Cave's pocket and said, 'Well?'

'This should have been left to the local CID. And the doctor. Bloody Maitland. He keeps blacking out and his pulse is jumping like a ferret in a sock. Confined observation is what he needs.'

'Give me a couple of minutes then bring him back inside.'

Coward took the keys to Poynter, told him to drop the woman at the vicarage and bring the car back. They got her into her hat and coat, found her bag and shoes and got her out and into the car. Poynter drove off in almost total darkness and a light drizzle.

Cave had Petrie seated in the living-room when Coward went back inside. Petrie reminded Coward of a fur seal waiting for a two-ounce ball from a culler's gun.

'He didn't do it,' said Cave, doing something ugly with his mouth.

'No.'

'Nor did Mrs Petrie. These two might hate each other, but they both cared for the boy. Go on up and take a look at his bedroom. I'll bet it's as neat as a museum. This is no domestic killing, more likely some tanker driver or commercial traveller had the boy away for a nasty private party.'

'I'm not arguing, Frank.'

'You're not doing any strong nodding either. Even if we ought to be involved, which we shouldn't, this shouldn't be our area of operation. Anything matey here, or his wife, could have to say will be a matter of record with the local CID boys. This whole mess smells of a copy-cat murder – too much like that one in Newbury last Christmas.'

Coward sighed into an overstuffed chair to watch Petrie sob into his hands. Cave was stating the obvious in his usual direct manner.

They sat and waited for the vicar to return.

15·30 hours

By three-thirty that afternoon a transformation had taken place on the model.

The flanks of Chapman Sand and Holehaven Creek had turned pink, and red streaks cut into Tilbury Reach from the Lower Hope. Grays Thurrock and Swanscombe Marshes were crimson blankets spreading west into Dartford and the Avely Marsh beyond Purfleet. A rolling figure-of-eight marked the erratic undertow of the lower levels of Erith Reach.

The River Darent was a pale pink finger pointing towards Dartford.

The reclaimed industrial areas of Barking and Dagenham were taking on colour as the surge sped along Halfway Reach, the colder, denser seawater rolling under the lighter river water, bearing it up and spilling it outward from its path into the residential areas either side of the Thames. Fierce cross-currents formed where the two levels met and spread as the crest advanced on Silvertown and the Royal Docks. The power station at Creekmouth was up to its footings in red water and the Roding was backing towards East Ham and the M11.

Prickly sweat had formed on Calloway's back as the automatic systems recorded the surge and fed data into the computer. Canvey Island and most of Foulness had disappeared under a spreading brown stain of polluted water.

'Four minutes to Phase Two.'

'And hopefully, the optimum moment,' said Prebble, engaging another bank of switches that showed green lights. Illuminated signs blinked on beneath the switches and Calloway read their legends aloud.

'Datchet, Queen Mother, Wraysbury, King George VI, Staines 1, Staines 2 . . .' – all the names of the reservoirs to the south and west of London Airport.

'Stand by,' said Prebble, his throat dry.

Calloway swallowed saliva and watched the screens form images of the reservoirs, all of them red with dye.

'Counting down at sixty seconds,' said Prebble, turning the switch lights to amber.

'Stand by to mark. Detonation in sixty seconds.'

'Marking.' Prebble turned the lights red and uncovered the detonator button, his thumb poised above it. The seconds ticked off and sweat rolled down Calloway's nose. There was a sudden gonging and the figures on the visual display froze as they were overlaid by a flashing word: ABORT.

Prebble was on his feet, closing down systems, working the console with controlled haste, his features contorted. Within moments, the console was in neutral and the water was retreating from the model as the powerful pumps drew it all back into the underground storage tanks. The men on the gantries had their faces turned towards the control booth.

Prebble said, 'Stand by,' into the main speaker and perched himself on the edge of his swivel as he regarded Calloway with cold detachment.

Calloway did not wait for any outburst.

'Your timing was shot, Prebble. You have to blow the reservoirs before the big blow comes. The river has to be at flood level before the surge reaches the coast. You have to commit yourself at least twenty-four hours in advance if you want to proceed at all.'

'So much for your expensive expertise,' Prebble sneered.

'I never said there wasn't any risk. All I'll guarantee is that the anticyclone will hit some time during the early hours of Friday next. You have to decide what to do about that. If you decide to chicken, I'll pick up my marbles and go home.'

'No,' said Prebble. 'I'll ignore your graphic cheek this time. Don't ever talk to me like that again.' His tone made his meaning clear. His hands gripped the upholstered arms of his chair and his fingertips had dug through to the metal. 'What we will do is revise our timings until we get it right.'

Calloway wanted to say, 'And miss dinner?' but he held his tongue. There was something about Prebble that frightened him badly. Something he could only describe as unhealthy. He needed time and quiet to work out what it was. 'Okay,' he said. 'Whatever you say.'

'Start calculating,' Prebble said in a near normal voice, turning back to his controls. They worked in silence as if nothing had happened.

15·59 hours

There were three Pandas, two GPO vans, a mobile Incident Centre trailer and several unmarked saloons outside the village hall when Cave drove up. A wireman hung in a cradle from a nearby telephone pole and his mate listened through earphones in an opened manhole. Uniformed men carried files and equipment into the hall and the notice board was being dismantled and replaced by a larger official one. Cables ran through the door and made a tangle underfoot.

Dutton had a map laid out in the boot of his Hillman and was reading it in the beam of a big silver flashlight. He straightened up as Cave swung in beside him and nodded as Coward climbed out. Cave took Petrie into the hall where he handed him into the care of a uniformed sergeant and a WPC who made mothering noises.

'Look,' said Dutton. 'Hardly four o'clock and it's dark.' His topcoat was pearled with moisture and the brim of his hat shone wetly. 'I've been seconded to this investigation. If it was your doing, thanks.' His expression was blank and the torch drew bright circles on the ground.

Coward decided to leave him wondering. He shrugged a shoulder at the hall.

'That was the boy's father my sergeant took inside. When the police doctor arrives I want him to run the tape over him. He looks as if he's about to fall apart. His wife, Mrs Petrie, will have to make the ID. He's likely to run up the wall and keep going.'

'I'll see to it. The doctor's due within the hour. What about the press and telly boys? We'll have to tell them something.'

'Not until we've a positive ID, you know the form. Tomorrow's soon enough for them to get their headlines. Have you got the local electoral rolls for our enquiry lists?'

'Yes. We can start processing just as soon as the centre

stops being a circus.'

'I'd like them ready for a morning start. I also want the address of a man called Ferris. Run him through CRO over your car radio.'

'Right away.'

'Incidentally, the vicar has the Petrie woman at the vicarage. Send somebody with a bedside manner. Oh, he also tells me the phones work from a manual exchange. I don't like that.'

Dutton agreed but shook his head.

'Our lines will go directly into the national grid, so that's no security problem. We could indent for a scrambler.'

'Whatever seems fit. Your decision.'

Dutton's pocket went quiet as he digested the implication. He switched off the torch and became a shadow in the dusk. 'You'll sign the indent? It would carry more weight.'

'Yes, Dutton. But you handle the press. See what you can dig up on Ferris. I want to leave here in an hour, and I want a chat with him before I go.'

Dutton closed himself into his Hillman.

Cave had emerged in time to hear the tail-end of the conversation.

'Not like you to act on hearsay,' he said.

'This isn't the usual investigation, is it?' Coward said. 'If it's just Petrie's shout down spite road, I want it eliminated up front. Now, you can stay here tonight, or come back to town with me. It'll mean a dawn start tomorrow if you do.'

'So it's a dawn start. Worth it to see Maggie's face. We can bring both cars back tomorrow in that case.'

The GPO engineer was descending the pole and phones began to ring on test from the hall.

'Who brought Dutton in?' asked Cave.

'Need you ask? I'll give you just one guess who the police doctor will be, too.'

'Lovable Doc Buford and his amazing little black bag.'

'For some reason we're to be a right, tight little team with no strangers. A big lid on a small pot.' Coward shivered in the chill and knew his instincts were right. For once, Cave had nothing to say.

Dutton opened his car door and the interior light threw hard shadows around his grin.

'Leon James Ferris. Aged forty two. Male Caucasian. Thinning hair and mole on left cheek. Has an alias and's been a bad lad,' he said. 'He's been clean since the late sixties. Seems he liked young men and disliked girls. He was given treatment at Broadmoor, had his sentence suspended. Chummy's a sexual deviate with violent tendencies.'

'Ouch,' murmured Cave, his attention on Coward who said:

'Have them print that through with pictures when our wires are working. The sooner he and I have that chat the better.' Too many things nagged at him without proper focus. The information too readily fitted their requirements. Why he thought so could wait for later analysis along with all the other gathering intangibles that surfed around in the back of his head.

Dutton scribbled the address and pointed the cottage out on his 1:25000 scale map. It wasn't far.

'Will you bring him in, Inspector? We ought to get every word on tape. Hit him fast and hard. Don't give him time to claim the headaches or that his mother hated his pet rabbit.'

Coward made no comment, gave no sign he had heard, staring off where the invisible moon hung above the low rainclouds.

'I'll drive, Frank,' he said, as though he were alone with his shaving mirror.

Dutton watched them motor away without pursuing the matter of taped evidence. Fifteen years in plains had taught him the wisdom of strategic silences. They committed you neither way. He had neither agreed nor demurred, but his thoughts were his own affair, weren't they? Whoever or whatever Coward might be, he did not control CID procedures. Dutton's report, like his views, were his own very private affair. He locked his car and walked into the hall grinning a small hard grin that left his eyes bland and blank. When Coward returned he would walk into the smoothest-run Incident Centre ever.

Bar none.

*   *   *

She had settled her course now.

She ran in towards Europe at a rate of four hundred miles a day.

And she was accelerating.

She was one hundred miles long and six miles high and she roared in an ecstasy of anguish. The sea rode high beneath her.

4

Tuesday 2 October

16·16 hours

The rain was a rolling veil in the Ford's headlights, a clinging elusive thing, all the more oppressive for its lack of substance. It drifted between the hedgerows and slanted in dance in the roundels of occasional lights, climbed in dribbles up the windscreen as the rubber blades banged back and forth through it, spotting and clearing, spotting and clearing; wipes of immediate detail with the obscure distance lost in the grey sprawl beyond the headlights' beam.

Coward bumped along a track gouged by tractor tyres where the clay slick had formed into yellow puddles dimpled by rain. At a junction between barred gates a tarmac lane dipped to a neat drive of rolled gravel guarded by a lych-gate overhung with rambler vines and bordered by beds of pruned roses and ice plants. A concrete heron gazed into a fishpool beside a pile of raked leaves. Coward coasted to a halt, certain that any car noise had been covered by the downpour.

Salem Cottage was thatched, had carved dragon posts and matte white infill between the timber uprights. One of the lower windows was lit and a coaching lamp cast a wedge of light on to the front door. Water ran from the eaves in vertical lines to break over the roof of a mustard Land Rover with fog lights and a towing bar. Cave took note of the number and checked that there were no keys in the ignition as Coward used the brass owl knocker. A voice called something indistinct from inside and a curtain moved. Then nothing. Coward knocked again. More nothing.

'The back,' said Cave, and hurried off towards the side of the building.

At the corner he came to an abrupt halt and took a hesitant step back, stopped, glanced sideways at

Coward and spread his hands wide with the palms forward and the fingers apart.

'Police,' he said, 'Mr Ferris?'

A dark barrel slick with rain and factory polish hovered at navel height, the double bore describing a slow, nervous circle. The man holding it a smudge of face in carpet slippers, one knuckle and the bridge of his nose picked out by a chink of light.

'Don't move. Who's with you? How many?'

The voice reminded Cave of his schooldays when the milk monitor's balls were dropping and he quavered and boomed in turn with acne rioting on his cheeks. The man's fear dampened the inside of his collar and prickled his spine, and he damned himself for not drawing a revolver from ordnance, forgetting the forms and the song and dance. The spill of light from the opened side door ran up his legs to the second button of his topcoat. He wished all of him showed, seeing himself as the other man must have seen him, half a man with all the important features a sinister blank. To move into the light meant going forward into the shotgun. He stayed where he was and made a delicate pointing gesture with his left index finger.

'That is Inspector Coward,' he said carefully, listening for cracks in his voice that were not there, 'and I am Detective Sergeant Cave. If you are Mr Ferris, we want to talk to you. But not with that thing in the way.'

'Talk? Talk about what? You're with them.'

Cave wondered what birdshot would do to his diaphragm.

'We're the police, Mr Ferris.'

'No.' The denial was as flat as a sheet of Croxley Bond.

Coward had moved back to the Ford and was leaning across the driving seat. He clicked on the car lights in stages. Sides, dipped heads, and then full beam. The man leapt into brilliant focus, he and Cave in a cone of brightness like exhibits in amber.

The mole on Ferris's cheek quivered above the whorls of unshaven hair and his shuddering belly seemed to be operated by a wind pump. His moving face gave his eyes a peculiar stillness. Cave knew it was crunch time.

'Tell you what,' he said. 'Let's go inside and put the kettle on. Tea or coffee, it's all the same to us.'

'I've talked to the police. They won't listen.'

'We'll listen.'

Coward held his warrant card where it could be seen.

He said, 'Let's talk inside. After you, Mr Ferris.'

'Just to talk?' Ferris spoke as though the concept was beyond him.

'Just to talk.'

'I haven't been well. It's all this . . .' Ferris sniffed something gluey back into his throat.

'Shouldn't be standing out here then. Not in weather like this.'

Cave saw the 12-bore waver, droop and swing down to score a groove in the wet gravel. The hammers were uncocked.

'No.' Ferris turned on his heel and shuffled through the side door, head down on his chest. He could have been sent off to wear the cap of disgrace in a corner, only the dragging gun made him an adult. Cave closed in beside him to forestall any change of mood, any attempt to bring the gun to bear. He need not have bothered. Ferris slid it into an umbrella stand and flopped on to a leather chesterfield, his hands dug deep between his thighs.

The room had charm. There was a lot of open studding and old brickwork matched in with modern fabrics and good pieces of period furniture. The carpets were hand-woven by peasants and sold by Bond Street smoothies. Bullrushes stood in a Greek amphora and a stuffed squirrel dealt cards to a badger in a smoking jacket inside a Victorian case. A gilded wooden eagle spread its wings over a small collection of cups on the mantel above the open fireplace. Ferris had let himself go, but his home was immaculate.

Coward closed the side door and broke the shotgun, spilling two unused Ely-Kinloch cartridges into his palm. One firing pin was missing and the other was bent at right-angles. Both barrels were clogged with dust and fine money-spider webbing. He showed Cave without comment and unnoticed by Ferris who pored over his lap as though the contemplation of his trapped wrists required effort from his whole torso.

'See to him, Frank.' Coward pointed through the ceiling.

'Whatever.'

Coward made for the open staircase and climbed to the upper storey where four doors led off from an L-shaped landing. There were two bedrooms, a study and a bathroom that was tiled in vicious pink and flecked gold. The small bedroom was a white box with chipped paper walls and a single bare divan, a bare polished wooden floor, a row of Penguins on an open shelf, an empty bedside table and a lamp and had nothing to say to anybody. The other one was a symphony in black.

Black sheets, pillows and a duvet covered with an ermine counterpane. The ceiling and walls were covered in jet fabric and the carpet was a black deep pile shag. The fitted wardrobe had black hessian facings, ebony Formica uprights and strings. The only white thing in the room was a small flower embroidered on the breast of a pair of silk pyjamas. The drawers held ordinary socks and underwear and regular streetclothes hung from the racks.

Coward went back to the bathroom and the medicine chest.

Ferris suffered from haemorrhoids, used cotton buds for his ears, preferred soluble aspirin, shaved with disposable Schicks, rubbed his scalp with dandruff lotion, kept an aerosol for summer feet, another for easing his back muscles, a tincture for sore gums and a vibrator in a soft chamois bag.

All his scouting trophies and literature were in the study, a cheerful room with open beams and deep oak mullions at the windows.

The book collection had items going back to the earliest days of the movement, some of them with portraits of, and forewords by, Baden-Powell. A fat red foolscap binder contained Ferris's own history of scouting written in careful flowing script. His rosewood desk contained all the usual personal junk neatly arranged in the drawers.

Among the pictures on the walls were several group photographs with bell tents in the background, and a waist-shot of the younger Ferris sporting his badges and flashes and a pointed hat with a cleft crown.

There were no pornographic books or magazines, no fetish items, no transvestite clothing. Nothing that was strange or incriminating that might give a clue to the man's perverse sexual appetites. Less in fact than the average suburban home or bachelor flat or station house common room, which could mean anything or nothing. Ferris was either clean or careful. Coward allowed himself a final shudder over the hideous bathroom tiles before closing them away and going below.

Ferris sat much as he had left him. Cave was perched on the arm of an overstuffed chair, guarding both exits without seeming to. He made a face at Coward's negative headshake.

'Mr Ferris wants protection.'

'From whom?' Coward sank into a Heal's recliner.

'It sounds like the whole damned village.'

'They won't leave me alone,' whispered Ferris, pinching his clogged nostrils, sounding martyred and nasal.

'Oh, yes.'

Ferris raised his head. 'You don't give a toss, none of them do. I should have known better than to expect otherwise. You two are just as bad. All those whispers and the calls. The filthy notes. I feel dirty. Fouled.' His palms squeaked as he washed them together between his clamped thighs. 'You could make them stop, but you won't. You'll take their side.'

'Will we? How did you get those marks on your face?' said Cave.

Ferris squinted as though trying to hide the faint scores in the deep lines at the corner of his eyes. Sweat glittered in the middle button of his chins.

'I . . . fell. Yes, I fell.'

'On to the side of your face.'

'That's it.'

'And got that egg on the back of your head at the same time.'

Ferris almost touched his pate.

'I suppose so.'

'He supposes so.' Cave sounded unconvinced and slightly sarcastic.

'Well, yes. I did. Yes.'

Cave snorted. 'Liar.'

'You can't say that. You can't.'

'You pathetic little pouf. Why are we wasting our time on him, John? Let's just take him into custody and sweat him. He must have done it.'

'Done what?' Ferris seemed to see both men and the room for the first time, shaken out of his self-pity. 'Done what?'

'We've found the boy, Ferris.'

Ferris mouthed 'the boy' without sound. Then, clearing his throat: 'Peter?'

'You perverted little bastard. This is your second murder, isn't it? I'll have you before the psychiatrists wrap you in cotton wool and write long explanatory files about your bruised libido,' snarled Cave.

'Second?' Ferris wondered, seeking warmth with his skipping eyes. 'Second? Second what? What's this got to do with Peter?'

'He was your second. The first was Newbury ten months ago.'

'What are you saying? Please . . . what?'

'You had him, then killed him.'

'No.'

'No gets you nothing, Ferris. You did it, and we'll prove it. First there'll be me working you over. You'll spend your nights in with the drunks and the other offal. You'll stink of their puke and scratch with their lice. There's always a dirty cell for the likes of you. Then, after the trial, you'll go to prison. The other prisoners will have you all to themselves. You know what the regular lags are like with fuckpig child molesters like you, don't you? You've had some of that before. You won't know if your arse is punched, drilled or countersunk.'

Ferris broke wind at both ends. A long double raspberry of pure terror. The resulting stink was as pungent as disturbed mulch.

Cave's expression of disgust made Ferris look away to lock eyes with Coward, his eyeballs as white and as wet as freshly peeled eggs. Ferris freed his hands and held them out like a supplicant for sanctuary at the steps of Notre Dame.

'Please, don't let him do anything to me. You're an inspector. He has to do what you tell him, doesn't he? Please, oh Jesus, please? I can't take any more violence. I want to be dead. Truly dead. But I can't . . . do it to myself. It's a mortal crime, you understand that. I know you do. Your face says so. Please, damn you, please?' A great bubble of wind became a choke and then a sob. The chubby fingers twined and tensed into a double fist of despair.

'I admire your taste, Mr Ferris,' said Coward.

'What?'

'You've decorated this place beautifully.'

'I have?'

'Admirably. Did you choose all the fabrics yourself?'

'Yes . . . I, yes.'

'Very nice. Don't you think so, Frank?'

'Fucking poufsville. Let me have his balls off.'

'Not just yet. Mr Ferris is no fool. He knows it's best to help us with our enquiries, to tell the truth. Look at him. He's not one of your average villains with an IQ in the low eighties. He's a historian, did you know that?'

'Him? He couldn't suck cock without a diagram.'

'A very nice prose style, Mr Ferris. I took the liberty of reading some of your work. It helped me to understand you. I hope you don't mind?'

Ferris shook his head, his mouth working around what Coward had said. Cave stood and smashed a sudden fist into his chairback, twisting his face into a fierce parody of uncontrolled anger, forcing blood into his cheeks.

'Fuck this for a box of soldiers. Let me sink a couple into that fat gut. Put a knuckle sandwich into that lying shit's mouth. We can say it was self-inflicted. He looks a sorry enough bastard to me, and the shrinks'll love it.'

'Coffee, Frank.'

'You what?'

'Make some coffee and bring a cup for Mr Ferris.'

'Me make a drink for that perverted turd?'

'That's an order, Sergeant. Do it, unless you want to hand me your resignation now. Mr Ferris isn't foolish. I told you. He's going to help us.'

'Anything,' said Ferris, flinching away from Cave.

'Fuck.' Cave went off to bang around in the kitchen.

Coward reached out and squeezed Ferris's wrist to regain his attention. He winked solemnly.

'Best not to annoy Frank. A good officer, but a terrible temper. There are times . . .' Coward clucked, his smile cold.

'You won't let him . . . touch me?'

'Up to you, isn't it?'

Ferris was unable to answer.

'He doesn't like pederasts. Hates anybody who interferes with children. If he really believed you had anything to do with that boy's death, well, I couldn't hold him back. And do you know? I don't think I'd want to.'

'But I'm not.'

'Not what?'

'Not a pederast.' Ferris toyed with a hank of quiff on his temple. 'I'm a homosexual. A consenting adult, although God knows, I don't get that many offers. And it doesn't mean I interfere with children. If you know anything, Inspector, you know that to be true. Do you think I'd be allowed around young people, be allowed to run a scout pack if there was any chance of my being . . . like *that*?'

'You convince my sergeant. Your record isn't that savoury.'

'My record.' Bitterness gave life to Ferris's voice. 'That was a long time ago in Leeds. In those days the police, especially the provincial police, had less imagination than the average potato. I was being blackmailed by a much younger man. He was AC/DC. A young thug. After a while I could no longer pay what he asked. I went to the police. They took a statement and interviewed him. No arrest and no caution. He waylaid me and I was beaten unconscious by him and one of his friends. When

I came to I was arrested for soliciting a minor for immoral purposes. The rest you know. What you don't know, is how it is in prison for somebody like me. I have no physical courage. I also suffer from sympathetic reflexes. That means, if I try a punch with my left hand, my right hand reacts too. I have enough coordination to walk so long as I remain calm and take my time. Otherwise I trip myself up. You asked about bruises. I'm covered with them.'

Coward said nothing.

Ferris carried on, almost dreamily, as if he had rehearsed this speech in his mind many times. 'In prison, I was put in a cell with two other men. A cell designed for a single occupant. Those two animals found out I was . . . what I am, and I became their private property. They told me what to say and what to do at all times. When they had used me for their own relief, they loaned me out to others. They humiliated me with every waking breath. I even ate my own ordure for their pleasure. That's what finally saved me from them. I was admitted to the prison hospital, and when I was discharged as fit, I went into voluntary solitary for the rest of my term.'

Coward grunted sympathetically.

'Not a new story, is it?'

'I've heard similiar.'

'Perhaps, if you sent me back, I would find the courage to finish it. It might be worth it if there is absolution in afterlife.'

'Is that a request, Ferris?'

Ferris's smile was a sickening caricature of the real thing.

'I'm finished anyway.'

Without heat, Coward said: 'You are a sorry bastard. Maybe Frank is right about you. You've had your little whine, now let's have some straight talk out of you. Why do you want protection?'

'Request withdrawn, Inspector. Do you subscribe to the will of fate?'

'Do you?'

'Perhaps. To sleep the long sleep has its attractions.'

Both of Ferris's index fingers curled in against his palms. 'If only I had the courage to make that one shot.'

Coward leaned out of his chair and slapped the unshaven face. Shock registered in the slack mouth and the staring eyes.

'You hit me. You said . . .'

'I said talk straight. Otherwise *he* comes back.'

'I thought you *cared*.'

'I said I'd listen. I've listened. I don't waste caring on a slab of suet like you. There is a small, very dead boy who deserves more sympathy than you ever did or could. There are his parents. Two decent people, half out of their minds with grief and loss. Tearing themselves and each other apart because their only son is gone – wiped out by a sick mind that isn't so terribly different from your own. That boy was probably all that held their union together. Apart, they're as dead and as mutilated as their boy. Your petty-minded self-indulgence doesn't rate in that scale of grief, so save it, Ferris. Forget yourself for once and try crying for them.'

Coward bit off his words; clamped down on his temper, wondering if his show of indignation was based on anything more noble or worthy than his own desperate feeling of loss. His own tragedy, asking himself if he was capable of true compassion when it was not echoing his own sad view of things.

You're tired, John, excused a small, chill voice inside himself. *Stamp on this character, feel better for it. Go on, indulge yourself.*

The telephone saved him.

Mostly because of the riveting effect it had on Ferris. As soon as it rang, Ferris reared back against the chesterfield, slicked with sudden perspiration, his hands over his ears.

Coward lifted the receiver and listened. There were no pips before a voice said:

'We're coming for you, cornhole. You hear me, sodomite?'

The following mechanical purr underlined the quiet menace of the county-accented words. Cider and cheese and whipped double-cream. Dorset, Wiltshire? Devon or Somerset? wondered Coward, dialling the exchange to trace the call. He checked himself, finger on the last zero. This wasn't the Yard. It wasn't even London. This was the arsepiece of noplace. The real boondocks. Coward thought better of wasting his time and rang off, slamming the warbler into its cradle.

Cave was putting earthenware mugs of coffee onto an occasional table with a marquetry top and brass feet, his eyebrows up.

'Nuisance call,' Coward explained. 'The worst kind.'

'Must have been. Look at Chummy.'

Ferris was openly weeping as he slumped on the couch, his skin the colour of old hemp.

'I couldn't take that, day after day.'

'Poor sod. What the hell's wrong with this village, John? Christ, all we need now is a case of animal buggery, a family up for incest, and we've got the whole classical scenario of low English country life. Throw in a village idiot, the local witch, brandy smuggling and some shipwrecking, and we can sell it to BBC2 as a serial.'

Coward sipped at the scalding instant brew.

'I don't know, but I'll find out. Sure as eggs.'

The phone rang again.

'Frank, get down to the Incident Centre. I want a constable up here with recording equipment. Like now.'

'You've got it.' Cave went, throwing gravel from the tyres.

From that moment on, the telephone rang every two minutes. All the voices were different, only the content remained the same.

18·18 hours

Coward found that Dutton had worked miracles.

A generator gave independent lighting and power, aluminium and glass partitions gave the Incident Centre three single offices, an interview room and a general bull pen with stacking chairs, teletypes and telephones, an index-sorter and enough deskspace and wall panels for everyone. A duty roster had been posted and a xerox was chuffing out forms. An automatic drinks dispenser gave a choice of drinks, all of them tasting of something more than the usual ersatz and plastic. There were individual desklamps and the heating did not dry the back of the throat.

Coward refused one of Dutton's untipped Player's and sipped at a beaker of tea given some edge by Dutton's hipflask of good malt. Cave had taken a second constable over to Salem Cottage and was due back shortly. Doctor Buford was working on Petrie in the interview room.

Coward gave Dutton a rundown on his interview with Ferris. When he got to the nuisance calls, Dutton leaned on both elbows and coughed ash into his lap, all attention.

Coward tugged at an earlobe. 'And there's more to those calls than first appears. It's damned well organized for one thing. Ferris is terrified. He's all marked up too, been worked over pretty thoroughly. More actual bodily harm than grievous. Just enough to make his bottle go.'

'There was dermis under the Petrie boy's nails.'

'I thought of that, and we'll check it too. No choice. I just somehow don't think that's it, though.'

'That's one hell of a guess,' said Dutton.

'Maybe not. It's all too pat. Too simplistic. I get the feeling we're being channelled.'

'You'll have to explain that.'

Coward dug at his ear. 'To you and me both. This isn't Dan and Doris country by a long chalk. Poynter the vicar has said as much. And Petrie's convinced that Ferris has something to do with his boy's disappearance and death. Now ask yourself, where would he get an idea like that?'

'Why don't I ask you?' Dutton brushed at a thigh.

'Nasty calls and beatings don't just happen like spontaneous combustion. There has to be a source, a certain somebody who kicks it off, gets it started. Not some nebish. Not some sick introvert, the kind who sends anonymous filth through the post. It has to be somebody with a bit of clout, with some standing in the community. Farm workers don't just up and take their sickles and flails to a man with no good reason. You know villagers, they're more likely to care for the halt and lame than to ostracize or bully them. This whole thing doesn't fit any known pattern.'

'You make it sound like Bavaria in the thirties,' said Dutton, and both men lapsed into an odd embracing silence that went on too long. Dutton stroked his other knee. 'Shit, I wish I hadn't said that.'

'And if one knows, they all know.'

'Those that didn't would guess what's going on.'

'Have you ever tried keeping a secret in a small community?'

Dutton shook himself. 'I'm a London boy myself. But I was evacuated during the war for a bit. A small place called Mousehole. You couldn't sniff before somebody blew your nose for you. You only had to think hungry and somebody was round with a couple of bacon rashers and the bread to spread your margarine on. You didn't have to say, they knew.'

'That's the nice side. What we've got here is the obverse of the coin. Some nasty bastard has got it in for Ferris, and, whatever any of us thinks of Ferris personally, it's our job to see that he gets protection. He might well be our prime suspect, but I'm damned if I'll have our investigation coloured by the mud and shit that's flying around. Or personal prejudice. I hope that's made plain to all our people.'

Dutton snatched smoke back into his throat and it trickled from his nose in two thin plumes.

'Coward,' he said. 'I'm older than Grannie, and I suck eggs like a veteran. That last remark sounded like a cheap motion of censure to me. No wait, hear me out. There's just you and me, and you don't have your sergeant here to do your double act with. So let's clear the air. I'm known as a hardnosed bastard, and that's how I want it. I want villains to cross the street when they see me coming. I catch thieves, I don't catch cold. I don't plant evidence, and if I did, I wouldn't get caught doing it. I build my cases on hard facts, not manufactured fairy tales, just honest-to-God detection and a little insight into people's minds. A10 put me through the mill twice when Robert Mark was cleaning house. Twice, old son.

And I walked out clean. There isn't a Wally on the force that hasn't had some wanky villain with a smart shyster brief bubbling up all kinds of silt to the DPP. Well, let them. It's part of being on the force. You swallow it and get on with the job. And that, *Mister* Coward, is what I plan to do. If Ferris murdered that kid I'll have him for it. *If* he did it. If he didn't, I don't want to waste the time of day on him. I want the sick bastard who did. Not his fucking poodle. And you can make that plain to your people.'

Coward crunched his empty beaker and hit the wastebin dead centre.

'That's the third speech that's been made to me today, Dutton. Every mother's son seems to want to tell me what makes him tick. I must have that sort of a face. I just hope you feel better for it. And, just out of interest, how many times has a superior told you much the same thing? Probably using saltier language.'

'Maybe all of them, it's standard bull.'

'Then do me an enormous favour, will you? Don't state the obvious again. We're both here because we were told to be. Right?'

Dutton was having trouble with his face. The muscles would not arrange themselves into a single, set expression. He finally employed four hundred facial muscles to grin.

'It was a bit strong, wasn't it?' he said.

'Just a bit.' Coward climbed to his feet. 'That was good malt. Let's have the doctor in, shall we? Go through the details of the autopsy and get the Coroner's enquiry under way.'

'Coward?' Dutton had killed his cigarette and locked his thumbs. 'I'll pass the word.'

Coward shrugged. 'One of us has to.' He held the door prior to opening it. 'Where's that tramp laid up?'

'St George's. I've had him moved into a private room where we can keep an eye on him. We'll get a statement when he wakes up. If he wakes up. His name's Glass, and the local station knows him from way back. He's been on more drunk and disorderly's than a bishop's got mitres. The lorry threw him a good twenty feet. But you know these winos, lying to the law is second nature. He wouldn't know the truth if it came in a three-star bottle.'

Coward let that go. 'Have ballistics run a test on the shotgun Ferris had. He doesn't have a licence for it, can't have with his prison record, and yet there were two new cartridges up the spout. I'd like to know where he got them.'

'Good question.'

'I also want a lift of those taped nuisance calls. For voice analysis. Those voices are as distinctive as finger prints. We'll match them against anybody we talk to on the telephone. So that means every call that comes through here gets recorded.'

'I'll have to bring the equipment in. Won't be here until tomorrow morning.'

'You'll have it tonight. I'll see to that.'

'You blokes in Special have it all your own way. Scramblers . . . analysers. Like having a key to a discount warehouse.'

Dr Buford came in, biting on his cold pipe.

'I'm sending Petrie home. I've given him something to keep him quiet. Who's this fellow Ferris? All I got was Ferris this, Ferris that.'

Dutton fumbled another Player into his mouth.

'Was that wise, Doc? What d'you think, Coward?'

'We had nothing to hold him on. We'll just take the precaution of keeping an eye on him.'

'Some hope.' Dutton scratched a match alight. 'Unless you've got another dozen men up your sleeve.'

'Sorry. Cover for me, Dutton. If my department calls I'm out and about. Back tomorrow morning.' Coward held the door ajar.

'Charlie Glass?' grinned Dutton.

'Amongst other things.'

'What about this Ferris?' asked Buford.

'Another good question. You tell him, Coward.'

'I've got a better one for you.' Coward stepped out and leaned back around the jamb. 'How long was that boy kept on ice?'

'Within an hour of dying. Let's say a week. Why?'

'There isn't a deep freeze at Salem Cottage.'

Dutton watched the door close with a slipped grin.

*   *   *

Meteorologists had given her a temporary name. Doris. A simple name to write on their plots, to give out on weather reports, a simple name for the media. A film star's name. Only one of them knew Doris was an ancient Greek Goddess whose special dominion was the sea. And that she had an uncertain temper.

The word spread and she was given a more permanent and private name. The Lady Kuklos. The Greek origin of the word 'cyclone'. It was an apt name since literally translated it means 'The coils of the snake'. They marked her position with a capital K in a red circle.

5

Tuesday 2 October

20·05 hours

Cave drove Coward into London through heavy traffic.

Below the runs of sodium the motorway was a dark trench where angry red rearlights jockeyed through a mist of tyrespray and clouding backwash, and approaching vehicles were whipping white ghosts across the invisible centre reservation. Both streams cruised at top speed, ignoring the restrictions on the illuminated overhead panels; a flood of steel lemmings whose collective instinct was to rush homeward to the capital with no thought of caution. Heavy rain and dense fog always seemed to have the same soporific effect: as though each driver travelled in his own blind womb where what was unseen offered no danger, where lack of vision was worth a thousand crossed fingers and a million St Christophers.

They were twenty minutes late when Cave parked on a double yellow line in Wardour Street next to a uniformed foot patrol. He flashed his warrant card as Coward went looking for Goldy along Chinese Gerrard Street where the brash frontages turned the milling oriental faces to wax. This was the mecca for ethnic dishes and buddhas, for chopsticks, porcelain and parasols, dried fish, noodles and hammered duck carcasses. There were bundles of horse and handrolled grass smokes, goldfish kites and paper dragons, a little illegal gambling and the services of girls in rooms north of Shaftesbury Avenue. Posters of the Queen and Bruce Lee shared equal space in the shop windows and none of the supermarkets had ever heard of Kellogg's or General Mills.

He turned into a narrow side door between an old restaurant and a new curio shop. The passage was sharp with joss fumes and glass bead curtains acted as an early warning system. A shadowy blue figure appeared at the top of a flight of stairs, thumbs hooked outside the patch pockets of his Cantonese jacket. There was a glossy slick on his shaven head and twin gold crowns glittered in his mouth. He was slender and fast and was called Tiger Joe Yellow by his students. His true name was Ting Pu Fook and he spoke seldom because of a cleft palate and an indifferent command of English. He sneered his polite sneer at Coward and drifted off into the shadows of his cubby hole to sip ginseng tea, puff Pall Malls and paw his collection of girly magazines.

Coward went up two more spotless flights and rapped on a steel fire door where incense smoke gathered in whispers in the pigmented spill from orange wall lights. An almond eye stared out through a peephole before the door opened inward on carefully oiled hinges. Tainted smoke rolled out on to the landing, sweet with the tang of dried white poppies. A rich dead smell that set the teeth on edge as though a filling had ground on silver paper. It was a long dark room and a snooker bin light concentrated focus on a green baize table where dice rolled snakes and deuces and paper money shuffled softly as softer voices made hard side bets.

Coward lost himself in the peripheral darkness and watched three straight sevens thrown before moving into a curtained alcove and the automatic door beyond. The girl in the cubicle there did not look up from her piles of currency and the abacus she used to make her conversions. She like everyone else in that establishment had her role to play and had learned not to show curiosity.

The benches in the shooting gallery were empty of smokers. Only the truly wealthy could afford raw opium in their pipes since heroin profit had almost wiped it from the market. Goldy sat on a pallet on the floor, his back to the wall and his hand full of gun. The big and ungainly Army Colt seemed to be attracted to Coward's midriff by magnetism.

Coward chose a fretted bench and sat on it, swung his legs onto the mattress and laid his head on a hard silk cushion. A tassle tickled the side of his face and neither man spoke for a long count of ten.

Goldy finally said:

'I almost gave you up. That chink didn't want to let me in at first, until I gave him that password you told me. Then he hustled me up here and locked me in. I been sitting here smelling that heathen stink all day. I'd trade a pint for a breath of clean air.'

'I hope you needed to do this, Goldy. These favours don't come cheaply, and they have to be paid for.'

'On my life it was, guv. Do you think I'd come beetling up here if it hadn't all gone ugly? My gut's like a bleeding grinding works.'

'Oh, yes?'

'Oh, *yeah*. I'm still trying to sort it out in my head. This is all new to me.'

'So why are you all tooled up like Billy the Kid?' asked Coward, watching the blood pulse inside his closed lids.

'Why do you think? When did you ever see me with a shooter? I don't even carry a shiv, you know that. When did you see me armed?'

Coward waved a lazy thumb. 'When I walked through that door.'

'First and last time, I tell you.' Goldy began to wheedle. 'Look, guv, I took this off a bloke. Don't that tell you something? I took it *off* someone.'

'Why?'

'Why? Bloody why? Because he had it pointing right up my nose, that's why. I still dunno how I did it, but I did. Look, he was waiting for me. Last night. Outside that Bugalloo Club in Brixton. You told me to stay working there, so I done just like you said. I was in the side alley by the kitchens. I was dumping this bag of kitchen garbage, and he comes out of the dark and says was I me. I says yes. He says good and heaves out this cannon and shoves it at me. It was all too quick to think. I heaved the sack at his head and gave him a boot in the cobblers. He went down, cracked his head, and I was off and running.'

Coward raised himself up without haste.

'With the gun.'

'Yeah. He sort of handed it to me as I went past. I tell you, if I'd swilled that alley down like they'd asked me earlier, he would have got me. As it was, he lost his feet in a lot of old gravy slopped all over the cobbles. He went over backwards with his hand and the gun straight up in the air. I grabbed it and shlepped off.'

Coward held out his hand and Goldy gave him the Colt. Goldy looked like a gnome who had lost his pond and his fishing pole, a live dewdrop on the end of his elongated nose.

'I told you I was on to something bloody prodigious.'

'That you did. Watch you don't swallow those long words. What did he look like?' Coward worked the ammunition clip into his palm. It was a full load and the spring was lively under his thumb. The action was clean when he cocked it and squeezed off a click.

'Like an Irish Cherokee. Straight, Mr Coward. He had these high cheekbones and squitty eyes just like Sitting Bull. But his mouth was sort of curly and his teeth were slabby, like a Mick's. About your height, maybe an inch or two shorter. Stocky with big hands. Short checked jacket, red and black, zip pockets. Denims with frayed cuffs. Them laceup combat boots in brown with yellow stitching.'

'You noticed a lot for a man throwing rubbish, kicking cobblers and running off with guns.'

Goldy looked discouraged.

'I've had all day to remember. How long do I stay cooped up here?'

'How long do you want to stay alive?'

'As long as Methuselah. At least you're taking this serious,' said Goldy. 'I've been thinking it through. I swear I never tipped my hand. I'm too old to have asked any daft questions. I didn't even blink when the Kellerman walked in there last night. Him and the manager giving each other the old pals act. How did they get on to me? My head's going round with it.'

'Maybe you talk in your sleep.'

'Ha-bleeding-ha.' There was no humour in Goldy. He shrank within himself as if making himself a smaller target, rank with fear.

'You're sure it was Kellerman you saw?'

'He was as close as you are. You know his laugh,

sounds like a train in a tunnel. Couldn't be off being him.'

'I know his laugh,' said Coward.

'Have you traced that car registration I gave you?'

Coward mentally kicked himself for the oversight.

'Maybe one of those faces saw you, Goldy. When you followed them out to their cars. You boobed somehow. Here,' he passed Goldy some folded notes. 'Buy yourself a toothbrush and whatever.'

'Nobody sees me when I'm tailing. I've lost your blokes before now.'

'Only the ones you were supposed to see. Just stay out of sight and do whatever Joe Yellow tells you to do. And Goldy, keep your smart remarks to yourself, no "chinky" gags. Joe has a temper and enough cutlery to convert you into sliced bacon.'

'So long as he gets me out of this junkies' dosser. The stink's giving me a blinder.'

Coward pressed a hidden bell behind an embroidered drape.

'Has this manager at the Bugalloo got a name?'

'Hammond. Like the organ. How about a bottle, guv?'

'Ask Joe, he's your lifeline. And do some more thinking. That contract on your head means you've stamped on some villain's patch. The clue's with you, under your hat. Somebody thinks you're worth a couple of grand. This shooter is loaded with dum-dums. One shot would have turned you into a crowd.'

'Jesus, can I keep it?' Goldy nodded at the Colt.

Coward shook his head. The door swung open and he stepped through, pausing to look back. Joe Yellow sneered over his shoulder.

'I thought not,' sighed Goldy, clutching his raised knees.

'See you, Goldy.'

'Yeah, don't be a stranger, eh?'

Joe Yellow led the way below and stopped at his cubbyhole. He gobbled and sneer-smiled something Coward translated with difficulty.

'Yes, Joe, he's important. And yes, you keep him under wraps. Anything happens to him and I'll have your cue off at the navel. By tomorrow morning I want him squirrelled away permanently. Your place on the docks is ideal. Don't look so surprised. I've known about it for months. And you've got my word it'll stay our little secret so long as you stay useful and amenable. That means you do it right. I'll let you know if he needs a trip abroad. Have a route mapped out just in case. Something a trifle more sophisticated than those packing cases you use for illegal immigrants. I'll get back to you in a couple of days.' Coward patted Joe's cheek and went down and out into the rain to weave through tourists and puddles and knots of football supporters full of Wembley fervour. Coward was glad he would not be around when the pubs turned out and they had drunk themselves savage.

Soho had once been a village. Now it was a square mile of honky-tonk and tourists.

At the corner of Gerrard and Wardour he checked on his rear as he bought both late editions from a street newsvendor. The parked cars seemed to be empty and nobody looked out of place which meant nothing. Coward's spine was jumping with an old feeling he had come to trust.

He took his change and made for the Ford. Cave might have seen something he had not. Coward opened the passenger door and skimmed the *Standard* at Cave, swinging his leg over the sill.

Wind raised his hair and ripped the *Evening News* from his hand, slapping it around Cave's head. The door yawed and cut into his shin. The newsvendor folded over and sledged across the paving as his boards sailed off into the air and through a window across the street. A passing car was gusted on to the far pavement and sideswiped a railed area. Smashed glass began to frost the street and any sound was lost in a whipping pressure wave.

Coward tasted hot pennies and sulphur and his ears screamed with a silence he tried to swallow away. He heard the sea roar in snatches as a wash of red batted off the buildings, winking on shattered panes, playing on the crumpled bodies, painting motion where there was stillness.

Cave was outside and leaning both hands on the discoloured bonnet, saying things that could have been profound or stupid. It was academic. Nobody was listening.

One of Coward's legs dragged as he went away from the Ford, around the corner and into the shambles of Gerrard Street. Glass crunched unheard under his feet. Most of the facias at the eastern end had lost their colour and brashness and billowing smoke made a lazy, bitter fog. People ran or staggered or stood like dummies. Jets of flame tore from a gap that had been Joe Yellow's emporium. Coward made for it and found himself looking up into a burning interior where wallpaper and plumbing and floor joists danced in the shimmering heat. A fretted cot hung from a hole where the third floor had been, and a vellum lamp dangled in the hot updraught. The bead curtains and the staircase had fallen in and Coward stood on a charred girly magazine without seeing it.

Then a scarecrow was beside him, tugging weakly at his arm, gold caps in his working mouth. Apart from a clean, grazed knee showing through torn trousers, he could have been any colour under the grime. Joe Yellow was as black as a Gambian and crazy with rage and pain. Coward heard snatches of what he was saying in a jumble of Hong Kong argot and gobbled English. Reaction to the blast had stolen his strength and coordination. Coward shook him off and did not see where he went. He just was not there any more. It did not seem to matter.

A fire engine was nosing in around the buckled hoardings of Newport Place, and a Panda swung in from Soho Market. There was nothing to say, nothing to be done. Coward stumbled back to Cave and the Ford, half falling into his seat.

Cave obeyed a traffic policeman who ordered them to move away and threaded his way through the side streets into Haymarket and Piccadilly, moving north as fast as he could. They parked in St John's Wood at precisely 8·52.

It felt much later to both of them.

20·45 hours

Madeleine Prebble met her husband and Calloway in the hall when they entered hurriedly, brushing rain from their clothing. Part of her noticed the marked contrast between them. How taut and athletic the American was beside the sleekly upholstered Giles. Both men seemed pleased with themselves and their work at the experimental station. What went on there was beyond her, although she did know it seemed to make a great deal of money. She was gratified of course, but only in the abstract. Prebble's business was way outside her sphere of influence or interest. It was simply what kept Prebble from being underfoot during the daylight hours, and sometimes, albeit rarely, some evenings and weekends. She viewed such activities with tolerant detachment just so long as she was never expected to hold dinner parties with odd numbers – or left to entertain house guests when he was absent on a business trip.

Of course, some of Giles's business guests were social dullards, and she was more than grateful he had abandoned his political ambitions. She had hated wearing hats and rosettes and judging contests for bonny babies and jam-making. And smiling grimly through recounts that invariably ended in defeat. The welfare of the estate workers was another matter entirely. Which was why she had to speak to Giles immediately and in private.

'Foul weather,' Prebble grumbled heartily, shedding his coat.

'Wretched,' agreed Madeleine. 'Giles, if Mr Calloway would excuse us . . .'

Prebble felt a twist deep inside him. Madeleine's pallor, the way she forced her back straight, held her pretty head, all of it told him more than she realized. It took surprisingly little to pretend ignorance, to be bluff.

'Drinks, Madeleine. A watery sun over a drowned yardarm. You know the form. Bourbon, Calloway, or are you a Scotch drinker?'

'Either, so long as it's built high.' Calloway too had

seen the wrongness in the woman's face. The . . . anguish? He could not be certain, but he sensed he was in the way.

'I have to talk to you, Giles. In private.'

'Oh.' Prebble looked about as though the floor had become unstable beneath his feet. 'Then, yes of course.'

'Why don't I help myself? I can cope, I'm sure.'

'Good of you, Calloway.'

'Yes, thank you.'

Calloway took himself off to the withdrawing-room and the huge drinks cabinet, the woman's face superimposed over the drowned Thames Valley model. Hell, he would celebrate alone. He had been right about the timing, all his work had been vindicated. He poured Jack Daniels over ice in a crystal tumbler and listened to the study door open and close, cutting off the whispered voices. Damn the woman, she was getting to him in some inexplicable way. He carried his drink to a footman's chair and slumped to stare into the blazing elm logs. He had been *right* and Prebble had to make the big decision or back away. Calloway had no way of knowing which way the big man would jump, and realized he cared little either way. So long as he got away with a whole skin, the whole thing could go hang.

'Well, Madeleine?' said Prebble, putting the desk between himself and his wife. He might have to sit down and he did not want to sag into one of the visitors' chairs. He needed the high leather back of his own swivel. 'What's wrong in the kitchen?'

'Nothing so domestic. Mr Poynter's housekeeper cycled out here with a note addressed to you. Since you weren't here, and since she said it was urgent, I opened and read it. It was a request to send Petrie home. Although it didn't say so, I think they must have found the boy, Peter.'

'That's good news, surely?'

'No, Giles, it isn't. When I told Petrie to go home he went as white as a sheet. He knew, you see. It had to be bad news.' Madeleine took a long breath. 'I think he must be either dead or badly injured. There are other things too. I later telephoned the Petrie cottage and there was no reply. Also, the police seem to have moved into the church hall. Poynter called me later, less than an hour ago in fact, and asked me to inform the Mothers' Circle members to meet at the manse until further notice. He was very reticent about it, he just said the police were using the hall. I asked about the Petrie boy and he was downright evasive. He was almost rude.'

'Well, we are living in his family home,' said Prebble.

'Now, Giles, that isn't an issue with me, and you know it. He's never been anything but courtesy itself with me. You and he don't seem to hit it off, that's all. He has nothing but praise for the preservation works we've been carrying out up here. You know he'd rather be off saving souls in Africa than playing squire. Perhaps your remarks about aborigines and kaffirs deserving a dusky god has a lot to do with his guarded attitude towards you.'

'Delicately put, Madeleine. He'd hate me if he weren't such a Christian gentleman.' Prebble trowelled sarcasm into his voice, his mind racing on other matters.

'We won't go into that.' Madeleine toyed with one of her fluted sleeves. 'I was intrigued about the church hall, so I telephoned Mr Ferris to ask if the scout troop too was barred from using the hall.'

Prebble said nothing with a supreme effort. He opened his humidor and selected a cigar for something to do with his hands.

'The telephone rang for a long time. I know Ferris has been unwell lately, and I thought he might be lying down. I was about to ring off when somebody else answered and asked me my name. I gave it of course, and asked to speak to Ferris. It seems the poor chap is unwell and couldn't come to the telephone. The man I spoke to – it could have been a doctor – suggested he take a message. Giles, I do think you ought to drop in and see how he is, he's one of your employees after all.'

'I will if I can make the time. We are under pressure at the station you know. And please don't lecture me on people versus profits. This government contract is the most important we've landed. I do employ in excess of a hundred people in my plants, and the welfare of the majority must come first.' Prebble cut at the air, using the cigar like a baton. 'I'll see him after the weekend. And that's a promise. I think I must be more concerned about the Petrie boy than the state of that hypochondriac's upper respiratory tract.'

Madeleine searched for the correct words. She had to avoid another mindless squabble that ended in the use of dry semantics, a test of wills in the arid middle ground of their relationship. Separate beds and separate lives that came together when they played host and hostess to a world of strangers who professed friendship was a charade she played with less and less conviction. There had to be more to life than passing port to the left and withdrawing to leave the men to their cigars. She tried not to think of the difference children might have made. Probably none, she decided, except that she would have run a nursery as she ran the house, faultlessly and without complaint. Just another exercise in good housekeeping. There were no right words.

'They are our people, Giles,' she said simply.

'*Noblesse oblige,* eh Madeleine? You're right, of course. I'll enquire about the Petries and see Ferris on Monday morning. Will that satisfy you?'

'Must I say thank you?'

'As you say, it's my duty. If you'll hold dinner for fifteen minutes I'll make some enquiries right away.'

Madeleine let the issue drop. As usual, Giles was going through the motions, making all the right noises, as though people were ciphers in an equation he could solve by moving them in columns, separating them with the clever use of the decimal point. She drifted away through the banqueting hall, blind to the fresh gilding and paintwork on the cockatrice, not registering the odour of drying varnish. She went into the modern kitchen and lost herself in a conversation in Spanish with her Andalusian cook.

Prebble stood stock still until Madeleine's footfalls had died away and he could only hear the old house shifting as rain hushed on the windows. He looked at the cigar as though he had never seen it before, returned it to the humidor and unlocked one of his desk drawers where a red telephone lay. He unlocked the dial and made a local call. It buzzed twice before being answered.

'Magpie and Stump.'

'Prebble,' said Prebble. 'You've heard about the church hall?'

'I heard. The cops must have found the kid's body.'

'I still think it's a local matter. You agree?'

'Yes.'

'The sooner the better.'

'Tonight?'

'If it can be arranged. Are you confident it can?'

The laugh came too close to the mouthpiece, distorting unpleasantly.

'Easily. And about time. That pouf bastard . . .'

Prebble kept his voice low and controlled.

'That, as always, is my decision. You never make a move until I order it. If you understand, say so.'

Pause. 'I . . . understand.'

'Discipline, Sergeant. Power can only be directed downward. Tell me you understand.'

'And loyalty must work in both directions. But yes, I agree.'

'Tonight it is then. Make no further contact. You will hear from me. Understand?'

'Yes.'

'Take one squad.'

'Yes.'

'Good.' Prebble rang off, dialled Ferris's number and heard the policeman answer. He cleared down without speaking, relocked the telephone and the drawer, rapped his fingers on the desktop and, rising abruptly, went to the windows and opened the drapes. There was little to see through the streaking rain and condensation. Prebble saw the view in his mind's eye. The stand of oaks on the rise before the long shallow dip into the wide and shallow valley where the village lay. The hills beyond crowned with forest and alive with deer. His valley and his people. He was trembling all over with more than fear, more than anticipation. He was in control of his own destiny and the future of the Home Counties if he had the courage to move on Calloway's intelligence. He decided he could afford to sleep on it.

Prebble stayed at the window until his hands were still and he no longer snatched at his breath. Then he went to make polite conversation with Calloway; suddenly hungry and in need of a very dry martini.

* * *

The Lady Kuklos held her course. Accelerating.

But as she moved faster, she began to lose power. Her eye was cooling and closing. She called to her little sisters and gathered them to her, those small, spinning eyes of warmer air in colder, outer coils, and absorbed them. Rebuilding her strength. It was a continual process. She ate those little sisters and made them part of her greater self. Ever rushing forward.

6

Tuesday 2 October

20·52 hours

Cave trailed into Coward's apartment, still dazed by the Gerrard Street blast. He wanted to go home, to snuggle up to his naked wife and fondle away the depression, to pump through a transcendental climax to release and ease and dark, dreamless sleep; to let eight straight hours give him back his sense of perspective. But that was impossible. A surfeit of adrenalin demanded more than a domestic physical encounter with Maggie. Much, much more. He had to know the 'why' of the thing and nothing less. Now it was multiple murder.

He turned on the bedroom radio to catch the end of the nine o'clock news, turning up the volume so that it could be heard in the kitchen. The report on the explosion was short and confused. There was no casualty count and nobody had claimed responsibility. The IRA or the Triads were mooted as possible suspects. A more detailed account was promised for later that evening and a station jingle led into a singing commercial. Cave left it on and found Coward at the kitchen sink. He looked like a stranger at his own graveside.

Coward's eyes were withdrawn as he backtracked, gleaming less than the glass in his hair and in the folds of his coat. The smear of soot on his cheek was as overstated as a theatrical scar.

Over and over he visualized Goldy converting to gobbets of flesh and Type O vapour, the money he held dusting into green dandruff. Dying before his brain registered the flash of power that had wasted him. The girl and her abacus, the dice and the gambling Chinese. Joe Yellow and his third-degree burns. The gutted, burning building. The prostrate football supporters.

All gone save in his memory, which would fade all too soon, gone into infinity like the dying dot on a powerless television set.

He was filling the kettle from the tap for tea. That all-comforting, all-embracing English panacea for the ills of the universe, whatever their magnitude.

Baby dead, marriage dead, made redundant? Have a cup of tea.

Except there was no tea in that deserted kitchen that had once been the hub of his home. He smashed his fist down on to the draining board and used the pain to boost his consuming angry frustration. He resisted Cave's attempt to turn him around, relented and was shaken by the shoulders as his name was shouted at him.

'I'm all right.' He did not pull away. He made himself smile cynically, feeding that other emotional facet of his nature that was glad the dying had been done by others whilst he was safe and alive and capable of an honest erection, could smell spring blooms and covet a jiggling breast, could swear and defecate and breathe the ozone from a surging sea. All that and more, and he wanted more. He wanted all there was.

'I'm all right.'

'Well I'm not,' Cave was saying forcefully. 'I need reassurance, old mate. Buckets of it. That was no Chinese cracker going off pop back there. The Tongs don't go in for bombs. They like the personal approach, long knives and blood on their sleeves. That bomb was for us, or Goldy, or just you. Half of Chinatown goes up in smoke and we're pissing around with some local murder that don't amount to a burp in a bottle. Get us back where we belong, John. Back after the likes of Kellerman and Carlos. Back with the adults. Or my stripes come off and I'll sell insurance or open a pub.'

'You want to take them off? Take them off!' snarled Coward. 'I've had your carping up over my head. You want the truth? You can have it. Resign and do me a favour.'

Cave's fist came out of nowhere. Coward rocked with the blow and blood burst from his lower lip. He said quietly:

'Thank you.'

Cave's hands moved in the air, fluttering with regret,

wanting to take it all back. He could not believe it had happened. He turned away, groaned, and slumped against the worksurface, patting his pockets for a cigar.

'What can I say?' he asked.

'Nothing.'

'Damn it, John. This is stupid.'

Coward said nothing without moving. Only the pulse in his neck showed he was alive.

'Look, take a poke at me.'

Coward did not react.

'Anything. Something. Just do it, will you?'

Two joke bottles extolled the virtues of a liquormart from the bedroom, cockney voices struggling with bad copy. A baritone bawled through a downmarket plug for retail furniture that was offered at amazing discounts and was probably made from chipboard and sacking.

'I ought to hit you again,' flared Cave, crushing a cigar between thumb and forefinger, knowing he was compounding his stupidity.

Coward's attention focused beyond Cave, on a note taped to a kitchen cabinet, to a pile of laundered clothes that were soiled that morning; to a bubbling casserole in the Moffat.

'This your doing, Frank?'

'So I poked you, I don't know how else to apologize.'

'No, Frank. This.'

'What, damn it?'

'This.' Coward retrieved the fold of Basildon Bond and held it close to Cave's nose.

'Oh, that.' Cave smelled the seasoned meat and knew it had nothing to do with Nancy. Not her style at all.

'Yes, that.'

'Well, I called Maggie to say I was coming home, and she sort of asked about you and . . . she had this afternoon free. And this key Nancy gave her a long time ago, and . . .' Cave shrugged. What did it matter now. He was beyond apologizing for a simple act of kindness. Hell, it was trivial in the light of what had just happened.

'And you just happened to say you thought Nancy wasn't here.'

'Well, you know Maggie.'

'I'm beginning to. You deserve each other.'
Coward read:

Dear John,
This was my idea.
I've changed the duvet and sheets. I'll bring the other bedding back when it's dried and aired. I poked around with a screwdriver and your phone seems to work now. I've hung your shirts in the wardrobe, and I put a few groceries in the fridge. Tea in caddy. Don't shout at Frank. Shout at me. Love and stuff,

Maggie XXX

P.S. Have Frank eat with you. I've gone to movies.

Coward crumpled the note, made as though to toss it away, changed his mind and handed it to Cave who skimmed through it. He frowned at the last line.

'Terrific. She mothers you and abandons me.'

Coward dabbed at his mouth with a tear of kitchen towel.

'Your fault for minding my business for me.'

'Well fuck you and the camel you rode in on, Coward.'

Coward put all his steam into a punch at Cave's upper arm.

'Shit and derision.' Cave exploded, clutching himself.

'It doesn't end there, Frank.'

'Well, go on then,' Cave offered his chin.

'Oh, no. Since you've had the baldfaced audacity to adopt me, you can lay the table and serve up. And do the washing-up afterwards.'

'I'd rather take the poke.'

'When I say so. I'm going to clean up.' Coward went to the bathroom and closed the door. Cave's face reflected the pain in his arm. It would be stiff for hours. Serves me right for mixing with the welterweight champion of C Division, he told himself, shaking his head. Coward could have murdered him. He whistled as he searched cupboards and drawers for the essentials, careful to keep the kitchen door open to command a view of the front door. Coward was going nowhere without him. Coward had been building up to something over the last two days; Goldy's death might just have pushed him over the edge. He was as close to losing his temper as Cave had ever seen him. There were stories about Coward before he married, and some of them had to be true. How hard and unorthodox he and his methods were then, and how successful. The details were lost in carefully worded reports by superiors who wanted the villains off the streets and buried any 'irregularities' in a welter of semantics.

As Cave had heard himself say only twenty-four hours before, being partners for three years was as binding as marriage. Perhaps more so. All right, so he had had his shout and made his threat of resignation. He knew he would back Coward to the limit.

He was spooning food on to warmed plates when Coward padded from the bathroom wrapped in a multi-coloured beach towel, old slippers on his bony feet. They ate in silence filled with private surmise and conjecture that would become a bull session if Coward was in the mood.

22·00 hours

Constable Midgeley checked his watch for the umpteenth time and yawned impatiently. He was thirsty and out of Woodbines. It shouldn't have taken Constable Tucker this long to nip down to the Magpie and Stump for two quarts of brown and cigarettes. They had tossed a coin in the traditional and democratic way and Tucker had lost. But that was no reason to dawdle. He had the longer legs anyway, the great beanpole, and it was no treat watching this chap Ferris snoring and twitching in sleep on the chesterfield – what with him jumping at every sound and breaking wind like a carthorse full of oats. Roll on the morning shift and out in the fresh air, even if it was lashing down out there. Even the telephone calls had stopped, they at least had given some spice to the proceedings. Midgeley bet himself that Tucker had stopped for a crafty one in the public bar. On a night like this it would most likely be empty and he'd consider the risk worthwhile. Well, bugger him.

Ferris rolled on to his side on the couch, his ample

buttocks looming from beneath the loose-knit coverlet. Charming, thought Midgeley, why didn't he get those titty great blondes to guard like Mike Hammer or Nick Carter? Still, he did feel some compassion for the fat man. He was falling apart with nerves. He was the colour of old sacks and his eyes had retreated into their sockets. Whoever was making those calls had a lot to answer for.

There was a scratch on the gravel and a rap on the side door.

About time too. Midgeley worked the bolt and the chain as softly as he could. Let the poor chap sleep. He swung the door inward and saw Ferris move out of the corner of his eye.

'Come in,' he hissed, his eyes averted. Tucker did not come inside. Midgeley turned to stare out into the darkness. What was Tucker playing at anyway? He opened his mouth to say something sharp. The side of his head went numb and no longer belonged to him. He was puzzled until a great balloon of pain ate his reason. His legs turned to string and his vision doubled. He clutched at the door with rubber fingers that would not grip the gloss surface. He went down on one knee, begging his eyes to tell him the truth. There was a whoosh of air that smashed into his forehead and compacted his spine. He slipped forward very slowly, twisting from the hip to collapse on his side. The last things he saw were a pair of Ferrises who refused to join together like they should, both mouths open wide. Four great eyes watched him slide through the coconut matting.

He did not hear Ferris scream as men in brown field uniforms moved in to take him away.

23·45 hours

The rain still rained.

Cave watched coloured bulbs chase themselves around a club marquee as the garish pink name blinked on and off, playing peek-a-boo with sleeping Brixton. Bugalloo, blink. Bugalloo, blink.

Coward was inside and his car was tucked away in the lee of a railway viaduct.

Cave had pretended to go home when Coward had gone into his yawning act. He had driven away, doubled back to cruise around the block and coast silently to a halt across from the entrance. Coward had eventually come out and pointed his Cortina towards Brixton. Cave did not tail him once he was sure of his destination – he took a parallel route and caught every stoplight in South London. After that, finding Coward's car and the club had been downhill all the way. Easy.

All the mountains in the world were inside the Bugalloo.

Cave checked the load in the Smith & Wesson ·38 he had lifted from Coward's shirt drawer, tucked it in his waistband, locked his car and slanted across the street, passing the club lobby like a pedestrian ducking the rain.

There were the usual grainy blow-ups of busty, siliconed girls in strings and feathers, their unlikely names blazing from dayglo banners. A negro in pink frills and mohair chewed a match into a telephone, his patent boots hooked over the back of a second chair. A heavy man with thick white hair and an olive tan leaned on a counter counting his fingers. His forehead unpuckered with relief when he found his second thumb. Maybe ten was his lucky number.

The side entrance was down a narrow, cobbled alley lined with steel bins. A fire door was propped open to let kitchen heat escape into the night. A pair of winos scooped racks of cutlery through suds and a chef poked at pats of ground meat on a hot plate. None of them noticed Cave pass through the kitchen and step out into the passage beyond. Cave had the impression that they would not have cared if they had, as though thinking was something other people did and was none of their business.

The passage was long, barely lit and serviced the stage, dressing-rooms, office and customers' restrooms. Cave had it all to himself. He stood in the semi-darkness and listened, building a sound picture of the club interior beyond the padded swing doors with obscured, circular windows.

A bass line thudded from coffin speakers and an

amplified guitar twanged through bumps and grinds with complete panache and no finesse. High heels rapped on a stage as a woman took them off to whistles, slow handclaps and her own squeaky version of 'Mad About the Boy'. Straying darts of brilliance from a revolving glitter-ball made a whirling kaleidoscope on the passage wall, some of it spilling on to Cave. He cracked the doors and looked in on the paying guests.

There were about a dozen dotted around the tables, evenly divided between blacks and whites. Three women dressed as hostesses sat in a bored line with boosted bosoms and dull eyes. A Spaniard in white tended bar and a girl in fishnet served drinks from a tray.

Coward was not to be seen, but he had to be on the premises somewhere. Cave backed off to search the passage.

A length of tired velvet winged the stage area and he saw up into the nose of the wiggling blonde who was down to her twirlers and earrings and the metallic paper stars gummed to her flanks. Her flesh shivered under the body paint like liquid cement in a mixer, about as palatable as week-old porridge.

The dressing-room had a screen, some cracked mirrors, a rack of shiny gowns, a row of head-dresses and varicoloured wigs, and smelled of spirit gum and old face powder. All the gold cane chairs were empty.

There was nobody in the Ladies, and the door marked *Office. Private* was locked and would not yield to a credit card.

Cave went into the men's room.

A man with red hair and a black moustache fooled with the flies of his dress suit, shyly, like a used car salesman promoting a vehicle he need not lie about. A conman with genuine gold watches guaranteed for life. His expression was all wrong and showed too much of too little, as if Cave was Christmas and the Second Coming rolled into one compact bundle.

As Cave stepped around the self-closing door he sensed movement to his side and rear. He was struck across the shoulders and his numbed arm went dead.

Sucker, he told himself. *Go into a roll*.

He was caught by the ears from behind and his head was jerked painfully upward and back. His wet shoes skated on the tiled floor. An expert kick in the tendons at the back of his knees collapsed him forward and down in a sprawl. He hit the floor with his face and it smelled of ammonia and Dettol, blinding him with involuntary tears. There was no purchase for a kick and no strength in either arm. He had to lie there and take it, damning himself for a fool.

His gun was taken and he heard it cock a moment before it kissed the side of his neck.

What a bloody silly way to go, he thought. *In a lavatory with a borrowed gun.*

He was hooked up by the collar as though he weighed nothing and slammed into a kneeling position. *This is it,* he told himself.

He blinked his vision clear and found himself in the smeary wall mirrors. He hardly knew himself. His hard, square face wore a comical look, one side of it slicked with dirty water. A clown washed of make-up. Cave could not accept his end from an anonymous source. He had to know who had his finger on the trigger. And if the bastard laughed; bared so much as an eyetooth, Cave would kill him somehow, even if his body was dead.

The reflected man was not laughing, and when Cave saw who it was his stomach rolled badly, casserole aftertaste in his mouth.

'If you can't fight, wear a big hat, Frank,' Coward said into his ear.

'Damn me for a second-hand maidenhead!'

Coward levelled the Army Colt at the man in the dress suit, who was sidling towards the door. 'Back against the cubicle, you.'

The man froze and looked sad.

Cave accepted the Smith & Wesson and a hand to his feet. Mumbling furiously, he crossed behind Coward, leaned over the washbasins and sluiced his face, dabbing it dry with a paper towel. His hands jumped with returning circulation.

'Who's Ginger?' he asked, still damning himself.

The automatic cisterns flushed, filling the relative

quiet with spitting water. The group thumped through the walls and the red-headed man watched the gun, his moustache twitching.

'He's Hammond, the manager. You gave him a nasty surprise. He thought you were one of his minders off the door.'

Cave leaned against the towel dispenser. 'He doesn't look much.'

'He isn't, until you know who his friends are.'

'So impress me,' said Cave.

'A certain gnome from Covent Garden.'

'Oh dear, that means he's in trouble. Right up to his flash bow tie.'

'It makes him dead,' said Coward.

'Won't Kellerman take exception to that?'

'I wouldn't be surprised. But that's the idea, Frank. It'll show him just how vulnerable he is.'

'You poor sod,' Cave told Hammond. 'You see how important it is to pick your friends with care? And now you have to pay for it.'

Hammond's bright blue eyes ricocheted between the two men as he teased his cheek from the inside, making and rejecting possible moves, possible ploys. He seemed to be coming up with nothing but zeroes. His tongue bounced from cheek to cheek and one hand kneaded his crotch.

'I don't know any Kellerman,' he said.

Coward just looked at him.

Cave tutted. 'Now that's a fib.' He hit Hammond low down and bowed him over himself, escaping breath sounding like a tearing sheet. Cave held him by the collar and went through his pockets for keys. They hung from a brass ring and Cave shook them in front of Hammond's contorted face, asking which one opened the office.

'The Chubb. Christ, I think something's broken,' Hammond groaned.

'Only my heart, sunshine.' Cave straightened him up. 'Show us, like a good lad. And Hammond, use the right sequence of turns. We don't want any alarm bells ringing, do we? This is a private party. If we find ourselves with company, you'll go to hell chewing on your own dick.'

'Shit, all right. I can't . . . breathe.'

'Shame.' Cave hustled him out into the passage and watched him open the door as Coward watched the doors into the clubroom. A comedian was being blue close to the mike, fuzzing his consonants. Laughter came in coarse waves. Inside the office there was little to be heard through the soundproofed walls. Cave threw Hammond into a corner in a heap as Coward went through the desk, dropping anything of interest into a black refuse sack. The rest made an untidy pile on the floor.

'The safe, Frank,' he said, leaning back in Hammond's chair.

'You heard him, Hammond,' said Cave.

Hammond raised streaming eyes. 'More than my life's worth. I can't, straight.'

Cave leaned over him, pulling him up by the hair. 'Wrong. That's exactly what your life's worth. Open it.'

'They'd . . . Christ, they'd crucify me, and twice on Sunday.'

'That's Kellerman all over.' said Coward.

'I didn't say that. I didn't mention him. Do me a favour, do me over, but lay off the safe. They'd bury me in concrete.'

'And we won't?'

'I'll risk it.'

'Fine.' Cave caught Hammond's right wrist, hooked it back against the joint and broke his little finger. Hammond bit through his tongue, turned sap green and lost consciousness. Cave lit a cigar and waited for him to come round. Coward went through a filing cabinet as though nothing had happened. Ten minutes later Hammond worked the combination, sobbing quietly to himself.

There were two sets of accounts and the same number of VAT returns. A large manila stuffed with maps and folded drawings on architect's flimsy, a steel cash box full of notes, mostly twenty pound denominations, a rough daybook, two desk diaries and a black leather telephone book. Coward scooped it all into the sack and sealed it with Sellotape.

Hammond seemed to be trying to remember a childhood prayer.

'Look, at least leave me the money,' he said. 'I can try to make a run with that. Get abroad somewhere. South America. If I stay here I'm done. Straight.'

Coward took him by the shirt front and jerked him close.

'Listen, you shit. A bloke named Goldy wasn't given that choice. He's spread all over Gerrard Street with a lot of other innocent people. Your big friends did that. I hope they do the same to you. You aren't going anywhere. Just you tell Kellerman what I said when he comes to cut your ankles off at the throat, Hammond. You tell him.'

Hammond went into a spasm of kicking and swearing, punching out with his one good arm. Cave chopped him across the throat, crossing a short left to his jaw. Coward looked down at Hammond as if he wanted to spit on him. Cave waited for instructions.

'Take him next door. Cuff him to the cistern pipe in the first cubicle and prop the door open. He'll make a nice diversion.'

'What for? We can go out through the kitchen.'

'Not when I'm through with it.' Coward went out and waved Cave out into the passage. 'Wait for me outside the Gents. We're going out through the front.' Hefting the sack, Coward pushed into the kitchen. The winos had gone and the chef was rolling a cigarette over a sinkful of rinsing vegetables. Coward showed him the gun and the roll-up dropped into the greens.

'There's the door,' said Coward.

'Yeah,' said the chef as if he had never seen it before.

'Use it.'

The chef nodded, lifted his coat from a hook and walked quickly into the alley. There was a brief running of feet then silence.

Coward fired a cluster of two into a bubbling deep fryer and hot oil ran out on to the floor in two boiling spouts. He struck a kitchen match, lit the corner of a glass-cloth and threw it into the spreading oil. It went up with a whoosh of bright flame and black smoke, eating the range and the long butcher's table. Flames ran up the wall and the gagging smell of burning electrics filled the room. Coward backed out, met Cave, and they walked into the club.

The comedian was still blueing it up and the laughter was as unsubtle as his material. The three hostesses had joined one of the tables and the girl in fishnet poured sparkling wine, the cheap label hidden by a cloth.

In the lobby the negro chewed his match over an evening paper and white-hair had lost interest in his hands. He had found something much more interesting in his ear, foraging diligently. His questing finger went still when he saw the two Special Branch men emerge from the dark interior, his eyes snapping at the black bag.

Coward frowned at him.

'Your manager has got himself locked in the lavatory,' he said. 'I thought you ought to know.'

'You being fucking funny?' asked white-hair.

'Am I being funny, Frank?'

'Not you.'

'He says I'm not being funny,' said Coward. He brought the Army Colt into view and slid out the magazine. 'Here, this belongs to a friend of Mr Kellerman's. See he gets it back.' He wiped off the butt and grip and dropped it on the counter.

The negro spat out the match and stood up, rolling his eyes.

'What's your fucking game?' asked white-hair, grabbing at Coward with both meaty hands. Coward's free fist made two short crosses and white-hair found himself holding his windless stomach and a mashed lip. A lock of hair fell over one dazed eye.

Cave grinned at the negro.

'Oh, yes, and your kitchen's on fire. Probably an electrical fault. The emergency number's nine, nine, nine.'

The negro's lips disappeared inside his mouth and popped out again as he said, 'Sheeit.'

'Whatever you say, Masumbula. Remember, nine,

nine, nine.'

The negro grinned for no reason at all when his sensitive nostrils picked up the first whiff of smoke. Whitehair cursed and held himself.

'Good-night,' Coward said pleasantly, holding the glass door for Cave. They strolled on to the pavement and watched the alley grow bright and smoky. They could have been promenading on vacation. The rain had ceased to drizzle and the gusting breeze barely stirred the puddles.

'Time we weren't here,' said Coward, making for his car.

'I'll follow you.' Cave crossed to his Ford, thinking, *Let Kellerman pick the bones out of that.*

The fire had caught hold in the upper storeys and people were streaming from the lobby in aimless confusion, milling around on the pavement under the blinking sign and the chasing bulbs. The negro came out supporting Hammond, his grin still in place, amused by a joke nobody else could see. Hammond's bowed head was a crimson rosette against his chest and his legs were rubbery. The marquee went dark when somebody threw the switch. Cave drove away with the negro's smile in his mind, wondering about it until he caught up with Coward and realized they were headed towards Hampstead.

That meant Maitland and the carpet.

Groaning, he wished Coward drove more slowly.

01·30 hours

Beyond the privet and the iron railings the Georgian façade was spotlit and there were Rolls and Bentleys in the drive. After a draughty wait of several minutes, Coward and Cave were led to a circular library by a tall, silver man and told to wait. White Corinthian columns divided the books and supported a ceiling where cherubs gambolled with trailing swashes of Latin and decorative escutcheons. The curtains and carpets were dull moss and the furniture had been crafted around the time of Waterloo. The curved doors were Honduras

mahogany with complicated brass locks and handles.
Cave scratched his nose to cover a yawn.

'What time is it?'

Coward peeled a cuff from his digital.

'Tomorrow morning.'

More time droned by without diversion or comment. One of the Rolls swished away, and then another. Maitland came in and made a production number of seating himself. He crossed a leg, picked invisible lint from a crease, recrossed his legs and hooked an elbow over the chairback. He cocked an ear as if listening for the fizz of seltzer as his raised foot nodded on a trapped nerve. He spoke as though he ought to have been alone with his books and the pinking central heating pipes.

'There is a good reason for your being here, Coward?'

'I think so.'

'And you, Cave?'

Cave stifled another yawn. 'The inspector tells it better than I can.'

'Let's hope so.'

Coward said: 'We can make this a formal request to be reassigned, or a discussion on the merits of alternatives.'

'We could also play charades or wrestle Indian style. Request denied. Now explain why you aren't in Easter Without.'

'Gerrard Street.'

'That is a location and not an explanation.'

'And Goldy Stern.'

'In the event that a Stern is not an ornothological rarity, and is in fact a person known to yourself, Coward, you will now wish to explain how this man and this London Street are related, won't you? And, before I know it, I shall be listening to the reasons for your wish to be reassigned. I don't want to hear anything of the sort. I want you to leave for Surrey straight away. Now. This instant.'

'There was an explosion in Gerrard Street this evening.'

'I know, Coward, I know. A matter for the Bomb Squad, the Anti-Terrorist Squad, the SAS probably, and the media. It has nothing to do with you. Good night, both of you.'

'Bullshit, Maitland,' said Cave. Very softly. Very succinctly.

An eyebrow detatched itself from over one of Maitland's eyes, rising slowly into the wrinkled, blushing forehead.

'Take care, Sergeant.'

'Of what? My career? My pension? You can eat my badge right now.'

'Buttered and sautéed, Cave,' said Maitland.

Coward wished he smoked. To spill ash and blow smoke into Maitland's face. He dug his fists into his pockets and the linings protested.

'He'll do it, Frank. And parboil your butt before it hits the pavement at the back of the Social Security queue. Commander Maitland won't countenance insubordination. He doesn't listen to verbals either. He likes carefully typed reports using red and black ribbons. The prose should be simple yet distinctive. Giving enough leeway for clever addenda in the margins, written by his gold Parker in violet ink.'

'Two with one blow, Coward?'

'If you like, Commander. I can't stop you. I don't know that I want to. Me and Frank could try mini-cabbing.'

'Not without a licence. And I predict you'd both find one hard to come by. Go back to Easter Without like good fellows. Much the best.'

Coward was pacing in a tight samba square, his shoulders hunched, eyes down.

'Goldy was my snout,' he said. 'He died in that bang. He should have died the day before, from a ·45 dum-dum. Somebody owes for that.'

'Usually, Coward, yes. But in this instance, not,' said Maitland. 'Anyway, you can't be certain he was there, in Gerrard Street. He'll probably turn up with a hangover.'

'He was there and so was I.'

Maitland was smoothing his moustache with thumb and forefinger as though it were a pet that snuggled up to his top lip.

'I see.'

'Good.'

'It changes nothing, Coward. And you, Cave. Climb into your respective cars and go back to Surrey. I'll forget you were here.'

'A club in Brixton caught fire tonight, Commander. One of Kellerman's.'

'And you're making a connection, are you?'

'I am.'

Maitland tugged at one end of his moustache, winced and let it alone.

'Don't. You'll be claiming you were there as well. Damn it, both of you. Go away and do what you're told.'

'So I wasn't here, I wasn't in London at all, is that it?'

'It is.'

'Not Gerrard Street or Brixton?'

'Neither, Coward. Both expunged from the memory.'

Coward bared his gums and his upper teeth.

'Sounds fair, eh, Frank?'

'Maybe that's why he's a Commander,' mumbled Cave, wondering where all these convolutions were going. Coward had a sleeve full of unplayed cards and seemed to be changing reams of unwritten laws.

Maitland stood up. Coward freed a fist from his pocket, straightened an index finger and pointed it at him.

'Just remember you said that, Commander.'

'You remember it, Coward.'

'Good-night, Commander.'

The silver man closed the door on their backs, and Coward and Cave stood on the porch watching the eaves drip. A watery smudge of grey could have been the moon through the scudding cloud, coming and going like a dull torch. The privet was a jumble of wet arrows and the railings were a row of soaked assegais thick with paint. All the expensive cars had rolled away home and the spots were turned off.

'I did enjoy that,' said Cave. 'Bullshitting him like that. Worth a month's pay.'

'Let's hope that's all it costs you, Frank.'

'Yeah? What the hell was that Mexican bean-dance of a conversation all about? You lost me after the first if and but.'

'Mean?' Coward rearranged his collar. 'It means we go back to bloody Easter Without like proper little coppers. It means that that's where the action is. It means he ain't saying nothing to no one.'

'Which means?'

'We do our job with our backs together and our eyes open wide. The cunning old bastard is playing a double game where the top and bottom are the same thing, Frank. And us? We're in the pigging middle.'

'The middle of what?'

'Everything, Frank. Every little thing. If thy head be corrupt, cut off thy head.'

Cave showed incomprehension until a lightbulb clicked on inside his head. 'If he tells us what he knows, we'll maybe let somebody above him know what it is, and . . . the plug gets pulled on all of us?'

'Something like that, Francis.'

'Then he knows full well what we did in Brixton? He knows about Gerrard Street. And he'll cover for us.'

Coward put his hand over Cave's mouth.

'Shut up, Frank. Walls have ears.'

They walked down the drive and out into the road. Up on the first-floor landing, Maitland took his finger from the door mike switch and smiled wanly in the darkness. He knew he would sleep for the first time in days without the aid of a soporific. It was a relief.

* * *

The Lady Kuklos showed clearly on the satellite pictures as a great bearded eye. Her winds prevailed at seventy miles an hour.

She swept into the North Sea and seemed to hesitate.

7

Wednesday 3 October

09·00 hours

The atmosphere inside Salem Cottage was as grey as the morning.

Dr Buford had gone to the County Hospital in the ambulance with Constable Midgeley. He just bit on his pipe and shook his head when asked to give odds on Midgeley's chances of recovery, his silence more oppressive than anything he might have said.

Dutton looked down at the chalk outline where Midgeley had sprawled, up at Constable Tucker with his blackened eyes and partial amnesia, across at Sergeant Cave and his small cigar, and finally at Inspector Coward and his nothing expression.

Dutton lit another Player and thought of great dollops of ordure dropping on him from a great height. He felt like the mythical djinn, who, formed of fire and trapped in an enchanted bottle, promised death to the man who released him from silent captivity. Then, mellowing as the millennia passed, he swore to give the empire of Asia in exchange for his freedom. Djinn-like, Dutton knew he would strike the first person to speak to him, then, as the silence became heavier and more prolonged, prayed somebody would say something. Anything.

He had burned through five Players in fifteen minutes and his throat was as sore as his head. Blame for the cock-up had to find a home somewhere, and he could see himself as the prime target, firmly holding the business end of the shitty stick; just a matter of time before Coward pointed that long, accusing finger. Dutton was a circus of contradictory emotions. If Coward let him off the hook, Coward was a useless wet. If he didn't, he was a hardnosed mother-humper hot for his granny's cat.

Dutton threw his cigarette out through the open door, wondering if Midgeley would make it. He had bled from the ears and the front of his scalp was spongy to the touch. Two hard blows had done that, and could have come from any direction, inside or outside the cottage. But how had Ferris got both Midgeley *and* Tucker? Tucker had come to his senses in a ditch not a hundred yards from the Magpie and Stump. The fat man *could* just have caught Midgeley off guard. But Tucker was six feet plus and built like a brick outhouse. Ferris was five-six and overweight. It was about as likely as raising day-old chicks in a fridge. And the place had been ransacked. Not the work of an hysterical, houseproud and homosexual pudding with a persecution complex.

Dutton found himself dragging at a fresh cigarette. Shit. He pinched it out, and as he found a home for the long stub behind his right ear, caught Coward looking at him with kindred awareness in his slate eyes. Double shit, it was going to be all right.

'Are you thinking what I think you're thinking, Dutton?'

'I reckon. This mess is about as kosher as a bowl of trotters. If Ferris had got Midgeley, why did he bother with Tucker if all he wanted to do was get away? The Land Rover was right outside the door. He had the keys and a full tank. He could have taken off in any direction he chose. But he didn't. We're supposed to think Ferris ran after Tucker, knocked him cold, then went off on foot without a topcoat, any money, or his credit cards.' Dutton turned to Tucker. 'What do you remember?'

Tucker touched the makeshift bandage over his temple. Both eyes were shading from green to purple.

'Somebody got me from behind. Held me. Then I went down and out. I . . . the next thing, I was throwing up and it was light. It's all hazy.'

Dutton looked sour.

'I'll bet. What were you before you joined the force?'

'Chicken farmer, sir.'

'Practise your plucking. You may need it.'

'Yessir.'

'Beats mini-cabbing,' Cave said enigmatically.

'Sit down before you fall down, son.' Dutton waved Tucker into a chair. 'Have you been upstairs yet,

Coward?'

Coward had found the telephone under a pile of cushions and torn magazines. The tape machine was still connected and the tape in place. He rejected the cartridge and dropped it into his pocket before replying.

'Yes. There are a couple of things I want to show you.'

Up in the study the books had been scooped to the floor and the chair overturned. Ink splashed the white walls and stained the sagging curtains. A portable typewriter stood on the untouched desk, paper in the roller, several lines of elite face hammered on to it.

Dutton read:

> To the police.
>
> I did it.
>
> I wanted to show the boy tenderness but he would not stay quiet or help me when I wanted him. He had to die after that because of the people knowing what I had done. Nobody understands how it is with someone like me. Special and different and outside. It is my cross. I was born with it and I cannot carry it any further. I have to die like the boy died and I will do it my way. My way. My decision. The law of your social machine has no right in this. Take your revenge. Spit on my body if you find it. Abuse it. It will not matter. I will not be inside it. I am truly outside now. With God who is my saviour and my one true friend.
>
> Together we have the last eternal laugh. I leave you insiders this hell on earth and go to God consenting.
>
> May Our Will be done.
>
> Leon James Ferris.

Dutton bit back a crude remark, saying instead, 'I've read some right and tight ones in my time, but this is one for the Black Museum. A classic straight out of Peter Pan and Wendy. A perfect suicide note and confession all wrapped up in pink ribbon. Any aspiring forensic shrink could make his name with a thesis based on this. Neat, clean and to the point.'

'And?' said Coward.

'Just ask me why I don't buy it at face value? Go on, ask me?'

'I'm asking.'

Dutton spaced his words. I . . . don't . . . bloody . . . know. I just don't.'

Coward pointed off at the tumbled books.

'Down there is a red foolscap binder. Tucked just inside and peeping from the top are some newspaper clippings.'

Dutton bowed over. 'So?'

'I'll bet you they're reports of another child murder. In Newbury last Christmas. Don't handle them. I want them checked for prints. Here, use these tweezers.'

Dutton snagged the yellowed scraps of folded newsprint and opened them out on the desk. They were mostly cut from the *Newbury Recorder*, with one from the *Sunday People* and another from the *Daily Express*.

'A horrendous crime,' read Dutton. 'Brutal slaying. Yeah, this is the one. Another convenient clue.'

'Too convenient, Dutton. I read through that binder yesterday. It's a history of scouting written by Ferris in longhand. Those clippings weren't there.'

Dutton watched Coward tug at an earlobe and asked: 'You're sure?'

'As I'll ever be.'

Dutton made a long nod of confirmation, took the cigarette from behind his ear and bobbed it on his lower lip. 'I smell conspiracy with a big fat C,' he said, and rasped a match alight, drawing smoke deep into his lungs. 'But to what purpose? After what you said last evening, I have to ask, how much more do you know about this than me? Your department don't get involved in peanut murders.'

'It's your penny, keep talking.'

'Expect nothing and that's what you get,' Dutton mourned. 'All right, keep it dark. Just don't reckon on me acting dumb until I'm grey enough to collect my pension. There's only one way to find out what's inside a tin that's lost its label, and that's to open the bastard. We may be digging with different spades, Coward, but it's the same sodding hole in the ground.'

'Who's arguing?'

'So we agree it is a conspiracy on several levels?'

'What else?'

Dutton lifted his hat, raked his hair and jammed it back tighter, the brim low over his face.

'So let's go and find out how many,' he said, leaking smoke.

They turned to find Cave leaning in the doorway.

'Your relief constables have reported for duty. I stuck Tucker out in my car so he couldn't talk to them. It seemed best.'

'It was.' Dutton made as though to pass but Cave stayed where he was.

'Correct me if I'm wrong, Inspectors both, but wasn't our directive to approach the top people of this corner of the sceptred isle and have them fill their questionnaires first? With a lot of good-will and handshaking thrown in? An exercise in public relations. To set an example to the rest of the unwashed proletariat?'

'Do you want to answer him?' Coward asked Dutton.

'Out of the mouths of babes and sergeants.' Tumblers clicked into place as Dutton added the thrown hints into streams of logical progression, amazed by how much could be said without using direct language. 'What's the name of the local squire?' he asked.

'I think it's Parboiled or Prebble or something,' said Cave.

'You *think*.' Dutton grinned like a poison victim. 'You don't think, you know. All right.' He spread his fingers from his palm. 'So I state the obvious. I think I know what you fellows are up to. How your minds work. All tangents and no straight lines.'

'That's good. Isn't that good, Frank?'

'Bloody terrific, Inspector, Sir.'

'You characters.' Dutton edged Cave out of the way and headed for the stairs. 'It's like working with Tom and Jerry.' At the stairhead he paused, looking back. 'Silly question number two,' he said. 'Do we phone ahead in the name of protocol?'

'Hell, no,' said Coward. 'We'll take them as we find them.'

Dutton clumped downward.

'That's what I thought.'

10·20 hours

Prebble stood on the sloping lawn with his hounds around him and took in the morning. Woodsmoke rose from the tithe cottages beyond Salem Wood and the grass beneath his feet gave off the raw badger-scent of waterlogged earth, counterpointing his own body heat and the warmed rubber of his Gannex shooting coat. The hounds smelled of straw and beechmast, casting about after puffballs of their own breath, trembling and sleek and anxious to follow the guns. Their anticipation of sport was sometimes better than the hunt itself.

The sun was a dead white ball in the pewter overcast, showing without heat. A shrouding ocean of ground-mist washed over the valley and steamed in the beeches bordering the farmland to the west. Cattle floated legless in the hollows and foraging rooks hunted the unseen furrows, cawing from beneath the blanket.

Prebble scanned the valley rim, fret after rising fret of pale watercolour tones, pastels of olive and russet and lilac washing together somehow without merging, ever changing and ever the same, displaying more moods in a single hour than any man could hope to express in a lifetime of frenetic emotion. The valley had been part of the kingdom of South Saxony before William of Normandy granted it to Françoise Poyntier for his gallantry at Stamford Bridge, and was Prebble's for as long as he could hold it. A part of Prebble, and yet apart from him. It would abide after Prebble had gone, simply by being.

Prebble knew he would only be remembered by other men for what he had done and been. The valley would neither know nor care. One day perhaps, it too would be gone, its trees felled, its shelving sides levelled to support concrete towers and metalled roads and be peopled by those with nowhere to look and nothing to breathe save the fumes from their own waste. Prebble shuddered. Not if he had his way. He turned and looked back at the house.

An awning covered the flagged terrace and portable tables were set with linen, silver and heated trays of breakfast foods. Iced Methuselahs of champagne stood in buckets and mulling irons heated over a glowing brazier beside barrels of fined ale. There were loungers, a stand of double umbrellas and shooting sticks, a rack for guests' guns and a steel safety cabinet stocked with cartridges of various bores.

The 'old money' county set would not have seen a shooting party on this scale for years, perhaps decades, thought Prebble, partly proud, partly dismissive.

Madeleine had a genius for this sort of thing, and she had done exactly what Prebble had requested, perhaps more. When Prebble had casually wondered how many of the silver place settings would have gone missing by the end of the day, Madeleine had supplied a simple answer; to have each setting engraved with a guest's name and present them as gifts. The unimpressed would leave theirs for the kleptomaniacs to steal, and the genuine friends would be gratified; a simple matter of loss transformed into a gracious act.

The scheme appealed to Prebble's game sense of humour, such as it was. As muscles atrophy from lack of exercise, and humour dies without a keen lateral sense of the ridiculous, so pomposity can only float on a raft of overweening self-regard where no deflating torpedoes of wit are either aimed or fired.

Prebble guarded his flanks with sarcasm and the big stick of financial power. His strength came from the certain recognition of the other man's weakness. It suited his purpose to be seen as a flabby man who waddled rather than strode, to seem breathless and lacking in physical strength, to avoid ball games or any contact sport with a weak smile and talk of weaker ankles. In the boardrooms of the city he clove corporate skulls like a kingmaker of old and several of his guests had been brought down by his manoeuvres, totally unaware of his involvement in their company affairs until, through impartial intermediaries, he had offered them a solution to their problems, leaving him in control of some part of their holdings. Prebble was a saviour who ruined before offering financial unction.

If any ten of the men under the awning knew what he had done to them, twenty barrels of birdshot would have spread Prebble over an acre of his own turf. He told the dogs to stay and went to join his guests, showing no more expression than a shaved knee.

Madeleine entertained a group of Lloyd's underwriters, enchanting several million dollars with an anecdote about one of the crustier restorers, gilding better than he did. She wore simple brown tweeds with a split skirt and soft calf boots in tan. One of Prebble's old fishing hats crowned her ash hair, as high-fashion as any triple-figure creation from Knightsbridge. A brilliant yellow neckscarf glared at the mist. Calloway lounged beside her, hanging on every word. Prebble noted all this and more, moving from group to group without settling.

A small man in hornrims came out of somewhere and attached himself to Prebble. His hair was greased back from a small, smooth forehead and his small, hard mouth was a prim slash, the lips clamped together over a permanent bad taste. His suit had been tailored to create the illusion of optimum height and his shoes had elevated soles. He was five feet of nothing straining for a ten-foot shadow. He bobbed his head at Prebble and said:

'I understand we're shooting as a pair.' His voice came from somewhere beneath his feet.

'Delighted,' lied Prebble, scooping champagne from a tray and downing half. 'I thought it would give us a chance to talk.'

'So long as it isn't one of your usual diatribes, Prebble. For once you'll be listening. You'll be listening to me. You've seen the morning papers?'

'Briefly.'

'It's in the qualities and the tabloids. They'll be swarming down here by mid-afternoon, and I don't plan to be here. It couldn't have come at a worse time.'

'What couldn't?' asked Prebble, feigning ignorance. The small man was incredibly astute on occasion.

'What d'you mean, what?' Salmon spots burned on Kellerman's cheeks.

Prebble drained his glass and lost it without seeming to. He smiled at an old duck of a dowager who was going back for her third portion of kedgeree. She owned a thousand acres of weeds and lived in a rundown cottage with a dozen cats. She was titled and crazy and worth millions. When she had gone, Prebble said, 'My dear Kellerman, you make it sound like my fault. A local murder is a distressing affair, but you must take my word, the matter will be cleared up in the next twenty-four hours. Let's just leave our chat until we're out on the shoot. We'll be starting in a matter of minutes. The mist is burning off nicely.'

'Damn the mist,' snapped Kellerman, refusing a drink from a tray, his bony face ugly. 'I'm talking about more than your local murder. I lost a club last night.'

'Oh, hard luck on the insurance company,' said Prebble, nodding at a colonel and his lady. 'Glad you could both come. *Later*, Kellerman.'

'I'm not standing around while you play host, Prebble.'

'Oh, but you are.' Prebble turned away as his sleeve was tweaked and looked down into washed-out old eyes below a blue rinse. 'Yes, my lady?'

'Restaurants have doggy bags, you know. I read that in a magazine. It seems terribly unfair on the cats. My cats for instance.'

Prebble signalled Madeleine and said:

'I had that in mind myself, Lady Presthurst. My wife must have read the same magazine. We'd be delighted if you'd accept a catbag from our kitchen. We had one made up especially for the dear felines.'

'How kind, Mr Pobble.'

'It's Prebble, my lady,' Prebble corrected as Madeleine came up. 'The catbags for her ladyship, please, Madeleine.'

'Of course.' Madeleine's smile was as brilliant as her scarf. 'If you'll come with me, Lady Presthurst?'

'Chicken must be off the bone, you know. The splinters get into their little throats,' said the old woman, making for the kitchen.

'We'll remember that,' Prebble called after her, giving

his wife an eyes-up look.

Madeleine said, 'Thank heaven she broached the subject. She's been shovelling kedgeree into her handbag since she arrived. I'm glad we didn't serve soup. Cover for me, will you? I'll see she is driven home. All that champagne on an empty stomach will have her swinging from the chandeliers. Shan't be a moment.' She did not look at Kellerman who watched her float away as if she wore tassels and glitter-dust under red spotlights. The tip of his tongue wet his cramped lips.

'How did you rate a looker like her, Prebble?'

Prebble bowed to speak into Kellerman's right ear. 'Make yourself agreeable, you jumped up snotty little bantam. Or else. As of today, I don't need you and your seedy little organization. As a matter of fact, I'm in two minds about having you thrown off the estate. Take a hint, there's a good chap.' When he straightened his face was pleasant and one eyebrow was cocked.

Kellerman blanched.

'Not that simple, Prebble. If anything, you need me more than ever. Gerrard Street has to be paid for, and the price is suddenly doubled.'

'And just how do you propose to present your bill? Something like, for producing one bomb with timer mounted on a second-hand car, one hundred and twelve pounds fifty pence, including VAT?'

'One way or the other, you'll pay.'

'Zero to that. A gentleman pays his gambling debts but never his tailor. You, Kellerman, are less than a tailor.'

'And you're a gentleman? You can try buying all this highflown company if you've a mind to, but . . .' Kellerman made a sweeping gesture, ' . . . just how many of these gentlefolk d'you think will *return* your hospitality, eh? Ten to one even the daft old cow with the cats wouldn't split a tin of Kit-E-Kat with you under her roof, let alone the rest of them. You can't buy into this crowd if they don't want you. You're hung meat like I am. At least I know where I belong.'

'I wonder, Kellerman, I wonder.' Prebble's hot eyes belied his smooth tone. 'Small in mind, smaller in stature.' He broke off when a woman in orange waterproofs and scuffed golfing shoes confronted him, her hand thrust forward. She was Betty Peveril-Saunders, half-sister to the Lord Lieutenant of the County. She bred dogs and shot to Olympic standard. She and Prebble shook hands like men, crushing each other's knuckles.

'Morning, Prebble. When do we take out the guns? The morning's dragging on a bit and I've brought one of my younger pups to put under fire. You know what their attention span is when they're young. Best to get them blooded on a rough shoot. You don't mind?'

'Not at all. Is your husband here?'

'Poor old lad's got a tummy bug. Left him in bed on a diet of toast and brandy. Kill or cure. Where's Madeleine?'

'Talking cats with Lady Presthurst.'

Mrs Peveril-Saunders looked pained. 'Moggies,' she said down at Kellerman. 'Good targets for a ·22. You aren't planning to walk the shoot in a town suit, are you?'

Kellerman said no. He had a change of clothing in the car.

Whistles sounded from the rough ground below the beeches. The beaters were ready. Mrs Peveril-Saunders wagged a finger in Kellerman's face. 'Hop to it then, or you'll be left behind,' she told him. 'Who's the blond young man with the city types, looks like an American?'

'He is. His name's Calloway,' said Prebble.

'Holds his gun like a walking stick. He looks like he needs mothering.'

'That's why I teamed him with you, Betty. If you don't mind?'

'Mind? No. I can handle two pups with a hand tied. Leave him to me.' Mrs Peveril-Saunders strode away.

Kellerman threw back his head and laughed. A harsh bray that turned heads.

'And you want eccentrics like that cluttering up your living-room, Prebble? If she'd been born in the East End, she'd run a corner shop and breed greyhounds to run at Harringay Stadium. If that's class, I'm Eric the Red.'

'Go and change, Kellerman.'

'Not rising, eh?' sneered Kellerman.

Prebble merely looked at him without comment.

'I'll be five minutes. Got a gun for me?'

'Oh, yes,' promised Prebble. 'That I have.'

Guns were streaming down the lawn in twos and threes as the dogs quartered the ground and let go with the odd bark. The mist had thinned to a haze, fat banks of it hugging the hedgerows. The sky had warmed to pearl and the sun cast orange light from a lemon orb.

Prebble selected a short lady's gun for Kellerman, broke it and loaded two twelve-gauge cartridges, pushing them home with metallic plumps. He closed the gun and set the safety. It wouldn't do for Kellerman to have an accident right here and now. Prebble was loading his own pump-action Browning when Madeleine reappeared, cradling her Winchester and nursing a frown.

'Well really, Giles,' she said. 'You haven't sent Henry Calloway off with Betty Peveril-Saunders. She'll throw him under the nearest gorse thicket just as soon as they're out of sight of the house. You know what a maneater she is.'

'Don't fuss. I thought you'd like to make up a threesome.'

'Like to? More like a necessity. And I shall have to sprint, she covers ground like a marine. Oh, as I was pouring Lady P into a car, three men drove up and asked to see you. I explained the situation, but they were very insistent. Understandable, I suppose.'

'What circumstances.'

'The poor Petrie boy. They're policemen.'

'When did you tell them to come back?'

'I didn't, they wouldn't. You'll just have to see them, Giles. Betty's half-way over the paddock stile. Follow on when you can.' Madeleine patted Prebble's lapel and took her gun away down the lawn.

Prebble felt pressure in his upper chest and he stroked an eyebrow as he controlled his breathing. A tall and lean man led two others out under the awning. His hard slate eyes found Prebble and held him as he covered the flags between them. The second man was square and muscular and a shade shorter. The third wore a pork pie hat over a flat copper's face and swung his arms inside a sheepskin coat.

'Sorry to trouble you, Sir,' said the one with slate eyes, no apology in his voice. He introduced himself and the other two men. Prebble said he wondered what he could do for them as if he didn't know, and Coward showed him the questionnaires he wanted filled out by the whole household. 'Today,' he said, and he wasn't asking.

Prebble said, 'Of course,' offered them glasses of ale and noted his bluff manner did nothing for any of them.

Cave said he didn't mind and helped himself from the barrel, easing suds into a pewter tankard. Dutton looked pointedly at the champagne as Coward sat and said:

'Petrie, the father, works for you.' A bald statement.

'As a gamekeeper. Morose sort of a chap, but good at his job. There's been some drinking, but so would we all if our positions were reversed. Have you any idea who killed the boy? His disappearance has unsettled the village no end. Rumours, you know.'

Coward let that go.

'Just to set an example,' he said. 'I'd like you to account for your movements during the afternoon and evening of Monday last.'

'That was October first,' added Cave, foam on his lip.

'Easily. Here at my experimental station during the day. At London Airport in the evening. I went there to meet an American colleague. I drove myself and we were back in time for a late supper. I remember conversing with a reporter in the lounge. Can't say I liked the fellow.'

'You know his name?'

Prebble counted three as if remembering.

'Sadler, I believe. One of those inky scribes who confuse loudmouthed impertinence with in-depth reportage. You fellows in blue know the sort.' Again, his tone and manner struck iron pyrites as if these men had never heard of gold. Prebble held on to his temper, pinching his eyebrow.

'We'll check,' said Dutton, reading the vintage from a Brut label.

'Do,' said Prebble. 'Would you care for a glass?'

'Another time. Is Salem Cottage on your property?'

'On the very edge. It overlooks the Lord Lieutenant's bottom land. I lease it to a former employee of mine. I say former although he still draws a salary. He's on three months' leave in lieu of working out his notice. It seemed best.'

'Did it? Has he got a name?'

'Ferris. Why, does he figure in your investigation?' The Browning jogged on Prebble's forearm.

Coward looked at it. 'Put that down, will you, Sir? It's pointing at my foot.' Adding, 'Should he?'

'The safety's on, but you're right, it is dangerous. Should he what?'

'Should Ferris figure in our investigation?'

'Who said he should?' Prebble's back was turned as he racked the gun.

'You said there was talk.'

Prebble turned back. 'I said there were rumours, Inspector. I did not link that observation with any remarks I made about Ferris. Because his work suffered due to his illness does not mean I link him with these unfortunate rumours. That was your doing.'

'But there have been rumours.'

'Yes, I said so. Come now, I have a degree in law, don't play the prosecutor with me. Say what you have to say in plain language.'

'I thought I did. Am.' drawled Coward.

'Perhaps we're both mistaken.' Prebble tried to smile and Coward returned it with interest, switching it off just as suddenly.

'What's wrong with Ferris, medically?'

'Nervous complaint of some sort. Progressive. He finally lacked the ability to concentrate. Our work at the experimental station needs complete precision, there's no room for error. Ferris made several, and the cost of finding them and setting them right was prohibitive. I can't tell you what we do, suffice it to say we are currently engaged on a government project. If any of you is senior enough to have the security clearance, you can check.' Prebble seemed to think that none of them had. His smile showed eyeteeth.

'So you had to let Ferris go.'

'Yes. I cushioned the blow as best I could.'

'Generously, I'd say. This nervous complaint of his, was it treated locally?'

'I believe so. Ferris does hold your interest, doesn't he?'

Dutton shoved his chin at Prebble.

'Did you know he had a prison record when you employed him?'

'Who, Ferris?'

'Yes, Ferris. Did you?'

'No, why should I? He was highly qualified and his references were excellent. Marine engineers of his calibre are few and far between. Three years ago, when I hired him, there were less. And his private life was and is his own affair.'

'Why do you say that? And with so much . . . emphasis?' Coward was staring.

'Malicious gossip bores me,' said Prebble, tightening his mouth.

'But you run a high-security operation. You just said so.'

'Not when I employed him. That is a very recent development. You're obviously going to insist, so I'll tell you. There was some sort of trouble with the Parochial Council, something about his unhealthy liking for children. Ferris ran the local scout group, and naturally, any suggestion of improper behaviour on his part would cause concern of a very high order. A proper enquiry would have cleared the air. Poynter the vicar would have none of it. His values are as turned around as his dog collar in my opinion, and I've said as much.'

'A trial of morals, Sir?' said Cave, swallowing ale.

'A simple enquiry, Sergeant.'

'You and Poynter quarrelled about it.'

'Absolutely not. Children quarrel, gentlemen have a difference of opinion.'

'Nice distinction.' Dutton scribbled nonsense into a notebook.

'*Nice,*' stressed Prebble, 'is a woman's word. My views are diametrically opposed to Poynter's. He should return to his mission in Africa and sit in the dust with his hottentots. They loved his views on equality, though I dare say they barely understood them. History is against Christian teaching on that point in the dark continent. They have lived with despots, both black and white, for a thousand generations. Poynter would have us all as barefoot as they, just as equal, and just as poverty-stricken. Fortunately, our climate and social system makes that simplistic notion of universal brotherhood both impractical and unacceptable.'

Coward sensed a chink in Prebble's shell and went for it.

'How does Poynter get along with Ferris?' he asked.

'They could be bed partners for all I know.' It was out before Prebble gave himself time to think. He knuckled his brow. 'No, I take that back. I don't know how intimate they were or are. They had to work together over the scout group. Ask Poynter.'

Cartridges popped several acres away, racketing in the valley walls. Prebble looked off and said, 'They're in the south meadow. I really must join them. Now, is there anything else that cannot wait until another time?'

'Dutton?' said Coward.

'We'd like the questionnaires today.'

'I've already promised that. They'll be completed by this evening.'

Coward slapped his knees and levered himself upright.

'I'll have them collected.'

'No. *I'll* have them delivered. I have a houseful of guests, and policemen in the shrubbery tend to create unwarranted tensions.'

Coward thanked Prebble for his cooperation, forestalling Dutton's next line of questions. Prebble nodded and took up his Browning.

'Will you, or have you, arrested Ferris, Inspector?' he asked.

Coward showed surprise.

'What for?'

'Murder, what else? That would be the charge, if there were a charge, would it not?'

'That's a case of three and twelve making six,' said Coward.

'Really? All the same, if he's on your list of suspects, he'll need legal advice and, should it come to it, a defence lawyer. I'll expect to be informed. He's an employee of mine after all.'

'And you're an employer who cares for his people.'

'One has a duty, you know.' Prebble looped a cartridge belt over his shoulder. 'What would you rather have if you were Ferris? Prayers from a vicar, or the best brief money can buy?'

Coward said nothing as the guns sent crows up from Salem Wood to beat around in cawing circles. He scratched his nose with a thumbnail. When the racket had died a little he said:

'If there is a suspect list, Mr Prebble, Ferris would most certainly be on it. But then, so would you.'

'And the cook. And the office cat, eh?'

'Something like that.'

'Something a lot like that. Let me see you to the door. I have a tardy guest who needs hurrying along, so it's no trouble.' Prebble edged around Coward and led the way through the house. He did not offer to shake hands as they trooped past him out on to the drive. The huge door closed without a whisper and left them with the parked cars and the chatter of a startled jay.

'I've got that old feeling,' said Cave, lighting up a Manikin.

Dutton snorted and adjusted his hat.

'And I've got answers looking for questions,' he said. 'That fat slug constricted my windpipe with all that old toffee.'

Coward had glimpsed a smudge of a face at one of the windows.

'Not so close to the house,' he said, walking across the gravel to his Cortina and opening the door. He sat behind the wheel and tapped the rim. Cave took the back seat and Dutton the front, both slamming doors.

'Take a look at the purple Rolls, Frank.'

'I see it. It usually lives in Covent Garden. Kellerman.'

'I saw him inside when we were talking to Prebble. He

ducked back out of sight when he saw us. That's Prebble's tardy guest. I thought he was going to ruin his underwear.'

'Who's Kellerman?' said Dutton, swivelling in his seat.

'He's up at one of the windows watching us. Don't look.' Coward let out the handbrake and turned down the drive towards the road.

'Why didn't you jump the little shit then?' asked Cave.

'There are some poplars along here. We can't be seen from the house. Frank and I are getting out, Dutton. I want you to drive back to the village hall. Here.' Coward passed him a cigarette packet. 'Run that car registration number for me. Also, station a man at the turnoff out of sight. I want every car number that goes in or out from Prebble's place. I'll meet you at Salem Cottage in an hour.'

'Who the fuck's Kellerman, first.'

'Run him through CRO. There isn't much, but it might give you a clue.'

'Fucking Tom and Jerry again.'

Coward drew in under the poplars and slid out. Dutton hauled himself behind the wheel, closed the door and wound down the window.

'Have you seen what a Browning 12 gauge can do to a man, you two? If that thing's for rabbits, Prebble collects noses and tails. There wouldn't be much else left.'

'Tell that to Kellerman.' Coward joined Cave in an overgrown ha-ha under the trees. Dutton swore, clashed gears and drove away.

Cave found a fox track through rusty nettles and turned to help Coward up the slope. They followed a ragged blackthorn hedge into a thicket of holly and stunted silver birch where they paused to get their bearings.

The manor was etched against the sky and the dark woodland to the south. The great slope of the lawn ran down towards them and terminated in boggy land guarded by a new wire fence hung with red signs that read: *Electrified Fence*. Scrub and conifers blocked the view of the road to the north-east, and an ornamental lake showed from the bottom land to the north.

'There they go,' said Cave, pointing off.

The unmistakable figure of Prebble moved along the brow of the lawn, a smaller man trotting beside him.

'Ba-bang,' Cave sighted along his finger. 'A cluster of two, and down goes you.'

'Wishful thinking, Frank. We'll have to follow the fence on this side until it runs back up towards the house. There's a fallow field, a hedge, and the one beyond looks ploughed. I think the south meadow Prebble mentioned is beyond that, over the rise.'

'That's a fair old hike.'

'It leads straight to Salem Cottage.'

'Except there's a bloody great wood in between.'

They were both sweating when they reached the far side of the ploughed field, their shoes fat muddy clogs. They perched on a stile and cleaned them with twigs, taking a breather. The air was still and damp from the threads of mist. Guns sounded from the south and west. Cave had something on his mind. He said abruptly:

'There was another familiar number plate near the Rolls.'

Coward wiped a toecap with a fleshy leaf. 'Well?'

'An Alfa Romeo. Red with a black vinyl hardtop.'

'Oh, yes.'

'London plates and a leopard skin wheelcover.'

Coward dusted off his hands and dropped the leaf into a furrow.

'That's right, Frank.'

'You saw it.'

Coward swung over the stile and dropped on to grass on the other side, looking off towards a tangled copse of naked trees. 'It's Nancy's. She once told me she had a friend who lived this way. Madeleine Tawnton. That'd be Prebble's wife. They were at school together. Small world.'

'Well, that puts us right in it.' Cave jumped the stile and circled to face Coward. 'What can we do with your wife on the premises?'

'What do you think we were going to do?'

'Nail flaming Kellerman.'

'For what? Knocking off rabbits? I wanted to see what

sort of a shot he was. Maybe just show up and spoil his aim. That's all, Frank.'

'I wouldn't buy that with a Hong Kong shilling.'

'Try, it's true. Come on, and put your fists in your pockets.'

'You aren't more interested in discovering who might be escorting her, by any chance?'

Coward threw Frank to the ground and dropped across him. Leaves blew from the evergreen hedge and shot sang off into the furrows. The double roar clattered off into the high ground, returning as echoes. Cave stopped trying to defend himself and pulled his gun. Pellets had struck his face and hand. Coward rose on all fours and sprinted for the trees. As he crashed into the outer growth of the copse somebody wailed from G into high C, holding the note until a cough brought it to an end.

Coward was tumbled by a root and he ripped down through spurs of holly into a sheer-sided hollow where tangles of briar and leaf-mulch trapped one arm. He flipped himself onto his back and got his arm back, casting about for something to help haul himself to his feet. He grabbed at a branch, heaved, and it came away in his hand with a tired, rotten snap. He fell back awkwardly.

The coughs had become hawking and spitting between groaning intakes of breath. A stomach emptying the hard way.

Coward rolled over and over across the clinging, boggy ground, spreadeagling himself on the huge, twisted root of a leaning oak that angled up and out of the hollow. Using boles and clefts as handholds he made the rim and levered himself on to hard ground where he stood still to listen.

The slatted light caught at his clouding breath in snatches, turning it solid in the maverick beams. The vomiting had stopped and he heard footfalls scrape through the carpet of leaves, making off to the west. He followed in a soft, jogging run.

The trees thinned and grew together again, finally opening out into an open depression around a solitary, mature plane tree. A shotgun lay in the golden leaves next to a smear of breakfast, and tracks led off away towards the main shooting party. Coward halted sharply. He stayed where he was and watched the slender woman in black stumble out into the open ground beyond the fringe of trees, fall, rise, and make her erratic way over the crest of the meadow and out of sight. He found it hard to breathe, to think, to do any damned thing but stand there. He stared down at the ground trying to pull himself together.

He had two shadows.

One grew from his legs and the other joined the first at the hip, turning slowly on the carpet of leaves, somehow connected to the dark cast from the plane tree. He raised his face into the sunlight, lidding his eyes against the glare shafting down through the upper branches of the naked plane and found what had made the woman run.

Cave found him there and said what they both knew: 'That was your Nancy, John. And this is her gun.'

'And that?' said Coward.

Cave followed his eyeline up into the lower branches where a limp, plump weight turned on the end of a hemp rope, the inturned and naked feet pointing ten rigid toes at the ground as many feet below. The round, suffused head leaned over against the right shoulder, hanging from a neck both stretched and bent at an impossible angle. The popped red eyes stared at everything and nothing with detached intensity as the body turned from east to west, paused, then swung the other way, moving through the cold, dappled light in a sad, final waltz without music. The far gunfire sounded like party fire-crackers lit by uncaring neighbours.

'Poor, bloody Ferris,' said Cave. 'He went and did it.'

There seemed little else to say.

* * *

The Lady Kuklos spread her cape between the Orkneys and Stavanger on the Norwegian coast, grinding in an angry circle.

Her charged breath blew all about her. The sea swilled into banks beneath her. Faltering. Hesitant. She was losing strength again. Decaying where many of her ancestors had blown themselves into nothing. Her winds spiralled from her, blowing to every quarter. Her centre cooled and her failing winds seemed to be unravelling her.

She thought she was dying.

8

Wednesday 3 October

10·58 hours

Coward made a slow circuit of the tree and said:

'Like hell he did. He was lynched.'

Cave's 'What!' was lost as Coward ploughed on in a thick, shaking voice. 'At least six of the bastards. They came from the west, over there, in a direct line from Salem Cottage. See how they churned up the leaves when they dragged him to the tree? Can you see that poor, fat bastard shinning out on that limb, tying off the rope that far out from the trunk? Shoving his head into the noose and jumping? Of course you can't.'

'What about this?' Cave leaned down over the shotgun.

'Leave it.'

'She turned both barrels on us.'

'She fired to attract attention. To bring help. She wasn't even looking at us when she fired. She was looking up at *that*.' Coward spat in disgust and cuffed a dribble from his mouth. 'Time we weren't here.' He began walking rapidly to the west.

Cave almost hesitated before following.

They left the trees and followed a shale trench shored up by elm posts and crossed a rustic bridge above a swollen stream where drowned bullrushes bowed with the current. They skirted an overhang of rhododendron and crossed a stretch of scrub to a bare hillock studded with elm stumps where Coward paused. Members of the shooting party were hurrying across the south meadow, too far away to be recognizable as individuals. The sky was darkening rapidly. Leaden cumulus banked in from the north-west, driven by a high-altitude wind, too high to stir the bare deciduous branches or the thick stands of conifer. It began to look like rain.

The first fat drops rapped down when Cave and

Coward were deep in Salem Wood, rattling in the canopy like wooden sabres, plunking down into the brown cushion of pine needles. The guns had fallen silent.

The Cortina was already parked outside the cottage when they broke cover and dashed the last few yards in the open. Dutton sat on the chesterfield burning a Player and sipping black instant coffee. The two constables played pontoon at a corner table. Dutton offered his cigarettes without commenting on the pellet marks on Cave's face. Coward took one and stabbed his mouth with it as he sat heavily.

'You don't smoke,' said Cave, slackjawed.

'I do now.' Coward drew fire from Dutton's Swan Vesta, eating the first gulp of smoke whole, holding it in his lungs until he said: 'Give the lads a break.'

Dutton told the constables to return in half an hour and they left, driving off in a Panda. He pulled several Polaroids from an inside pocket and fanned them out on the couch. 'There are all your car numbers,' he said. 'I went back and took all of them. There must have been sixty of them. Then I ran them through Swansea. Half the cream of Debrett's and Burke's Peerage are up there supping Prebble's champers. And, if you hadn't noticed, a relative of yours, Coward.'

Coward blew smoke and stayed quiet.

'He knows,' said Cave. 'She also found Ferris. Hanging in a tree.'

'The fuck you say!'

Dutton rolled his cigarette between his fingers, bit smoke from it and said: 'How is it that you fellows know she found Ferris, and you aren't up there sorting it out? Or is that another obvious question, meaning I'm too linear in my thinking to see the clever curves you two can see.'

Neither man said anything as they stared at him.

Dutton looked at each of them, then between them, then away.

'I should play it safe and report you two for misconduct and a dozen other infringements of regulations and procedures. I should also give up smoking and remember my wife's birthday. Me, Daniel Dutton who hates the sound of Special Branch.'

'Daniel?' said Cave. 'Sweet.'

Coward held his Player like a pencil and stayed silent.

A hard flurry of rain smashed against the window and wind rattled the doors.

'All right,' Dutton held up a hand. 'I've taken my deep breaths, now tell me the score using simple words. And make it convincing. Young Midgeley has compound fractures of the skull and Tucker has concussion. I need reassurance.'

Coward went through the events as they happened, adding his views on how Ferris died.

'And now comes the favour,' said Dutton.

'Oh?'

'Don't "Oh" me, Coward. Let me lay it out for you, let's see if this is close enough for you. I answer the call from the manor when they get around to reporting the body. I then go there as nearest senior officer to the scene. I seal off the site, set the forensic boys to work, and take verbal statements. Then, because I am already assigned to a case, the Petrie murder investigation, I hand it on to the local Surrey police. Making certain that they don't get sight of the suicide note, and making *quite* certain they know his record and his medical background. I do this without informing any of the residents or staff up at the manor, or any of the local inhabitants of Easter Without. Which means I can gather in all the questionnaires as if Ferris's death was a separate matter, write an official "Pending Investigation" on the file, and carry on as if nothing had happened. You two meantime, are free to break heads and hearts whenever the fancy takes you. And me, I'll be the poor career copper who carries the can if it all goes nasty, which it probably will.' Dutton leaned back against the couch and blew a fat O of smoke.

'How can you be sure Prebble will call us? He might go direct to the local police,' said Cave.

Dutton leaned at him. 'Not if he's implicated in the conspiracy or the murder. He'll want it all in one tight bundle. Right?'

'True,' admitted Cave.

'Maybe,' corrected Coward. 'A definite maybe, but a maybe all the same. Can you keep the locals out for twenty-four hours, Dutton? Before you let anything go?'

'If that's what it takes, yes.'

'We're asking a hell of a lot,' said Coward.

'You bet your last sixpence. You can't go up there and take a statement from your own wife. Against regulations. Paragraph B, subsection whatever. No, Uncle Dan has to pull your conkers from the barbeque.'

'I owe you, Dutton.'

'Damned right. And that goes for you too, Cave.'

'You've got it.'

'Now explain why you're being so . . . amenable.'

Dutton's thumbnail ran a white line down his fleshy nose.

'The sight of that kid's body for starters.'

'And?'

'I checked on Kellerman's file, made a couple of calls to mates at Vine Street. Spoke to a fellow on the Fraud Squad. Had a chat with one of the Narcotics lads at Customs & Excise. Then, using a certain back door, I got a dip into a file on some fellow called Prebble. That answer your question?'

'That's a locked file. I can't even get to it,' snapped Coward.

Dutton looked sleepy.

'Yeah, it's got stopped somewhere between the Home Office and New Scotland Yard. I even got the name of the sweetheart who pulled it. At least the name of the face who indented for it last and put a "Closed" stamp on it.'

'I think you just committed suicide, Dutton.'

'I might have if I'd gone through channels. There's this fellow in Records who makes copies of files when us straight 'uns from CID are given the block. He made a Xerox before the file went upstairs. He only discovered it had been withdrawn from circulation when he decided to do an update on it. So, nobody's neck's near the chopper.'

'Who pulled it?' asked Cave.

Dutton grinned.

'Commander Cecil Makepeace Maitland, OBE and bar and star and all that noble graffiti on a lavatory wall.'

Coward went purple and coughed smoke between his knees.

'I thought he'd do that,' Dutton chuckled as Cave banged Coward's spine. Coward shrugged away and threw the long butt into the fireplace where it lay smouldering.

'Now, this other car number you wanted run,' said Dutton. 'The one on the fag packet. That's registered to a face called Eliades. Cypriot extraction, been in this country since '52. He's got more form than Red Rum. Sub-post offices were his meat until he went down for a Securicor robbery. He was almost tied to a killing in Aldgate two years back. An eye witness went missing and the case was dismissed on the second day of the hearing, insufficient evidence. The witness stayed missing, and that was that.' Dutton looked at his notes.

'The victim was a woman, a Mrs Pell, she ran a dress manufacturer's, a sweat shop, mostly staffed by immigrant women who sewed away for twenty-five pence an hour. When the safe was opened it was full of foreign currency. Her bank safety deposit box was an Aladdin's Cave of jewellery, most of it turned out to have been stolen on the Continent. Mrs Pell ran a money laundry and fenced stolen stones. It seems she was treading on Kellerman's toes. She gave a better rate and wouldn't tie in with him. Mind you, all this is just street talk, nothing you could call hard evidence. Eliades would have talked if we'd got a conviction for the shooting, but that wasn't to be. He went free, Mrs Pell's husband cleaned out the safe and the deposit boxes and buzzed off to South America. Somebody failed to mark the cash or the jewellery as evidence, so it wasn't held.'

Cave scratched his chin and yawned.

'Seems like a balls-up all round. Maybe deliberate.'

'Yeah,' agreed Dutton. 'CIB2 stabbed around at it and came up empty. And they were thorough too. All they dished out was a reprimand or two.'

'That makes Eliades a contract shooter, right?' said Cave.

'In my book it does,' Dutton too yawned.

Coward rose and stretched.

'You know it, I know it, we all know it. Just try proving it.' He reclaimed the Player from the hearth and ground it against the firebox. 'Have we got one case or two that overlap, or somehow tie together? We've got a dead boy and a suicide who admits to the murder. We've got Prebble tied to Kellerman socially. We've got a dead snout killed by a bomb in Gerrard Street just hours after somebody tried to shoot him.' (Dutton stopped yawning when he heard that.) 'Talk of a big currency robbery that involves both Kellerman and this Eliades character, a conspiracy to hound Ferris which results in a lynching by persons unknown, and Prebble, the racist who tried to rig a poll during the previous election. A man who is working on a secret government contract, a man who also employed Ferris. There aren't enough rolls of pink ribbon in the world to tie that lot into a neat package.'

'Don't leave out the blocked file. Or Maitland,' said Dutton.

'I'm not, Dutton. Far from it. I just hope the three of us can trust each other, that's all.' Coward slapped his fist against an open palm. 'Charlie Glass, that's the name, isn't it?'

'Yeah, what about him?'

'How tight have you got him locked up?'

'The usual, a copper by his bed day and night.'

'Not enough. I want it tighter.'

Dutton looked puzzled. 'Why?'

'Because, my old flower, you're going to let it be known we have an eye-witness. A definite, one hundred per cent, gold-plated kosher witness who can positively identify the man who dumped Peter Petrie's body.'

'Let who know, for instance?'

'Prebble. You're going up to the manor. Make it sound like you swallow the suicide bit and that the description of the man who dumped the body sounds remarkably like Ferris. Except, and this is important, make it loose enough to describe Prebble himself.'

Dutton thought for a long moment, dogged his butt,

took a mouthful of cold coffee, made a face and nodded.

'It's funny,' he said, thinking aloud. 'But for height and hair colour, they could be twins in a bad light.'

'Right,' agreed Cave. 'We still don't have a motive though, do we? Why would Prebble want Ferris posthumously nailed to a child murder?'

'I could think of several. All racist,' said Dutton.

Coward was suddenly impatient to go.

'Has Glass been shown an identikit or been questioned?'

'How? That lorry caved his chest in. He's a sick old man. You know how these old winos live. Cabbage leaves and red biddy. You and I wouldn't last a week on that diet.'

'Leave him to me, I'll coax him through the picture book. All I need is a snap of Prebble.'

'Oh, easy.' Dutton was sarcastic. 'Just point your Polaroid and ask him to say cheese.'

Coward's smile transformed his face. He slapped Dutton's thigh.

'Easier than that, Prebble gave me the answer himself. The reporter, Sadler. He must have files of pictures. From the way Prebble described Sadler, they've had run-ins before.'

'He didn't sound fond, did he?'

'You need me?' asked Cave.

'No, Frank. Stay and dig around, but stay away from Prebble and the manor. Dutton'll book you in at the Magpie and Stump, won't you, Dan – that's where you're staying?'

'Yeah.'

'I'll call you,' said Coward. 'There's the Panda back. You don't need me for a lift.'

They cleaned the ashtrays, washed the cups and locked up behind them. The rain was being driven by gale force winds and it was as dark as evening when they went outside. Coward drove off in his Cortina and Dutton and Cave took the Panda back to the Incident Centre.

16·30 hours

Coward found a space for the Cortina in Henrietta Street, walked through into Monmouth Street, passed the Thorn Building and Peppermint Park and went into the side door of a shop next to a modern office block. He climbed to a third-floor office, rapped on a half-glazed door and waited. Carpet slippers shuffled, a bolt was shot and the door opened inward with a melon face in the gap. The eyes were two sooty holes in the pan make-up and grey streaked from the centre parting of the rinsed hair. The wrinkled mouth was thick with pink gloss and the teeth were moulded porcelain.

'Hello, Peggy,' said Coward. 'How's my girl?'

'It's you, Mr Coward, dear. Let's get the chain off.' The old woman freed the door and ushered Coward inside, chattering. 'He's not been well, dear. The cold gets into his chest, but will he listen? He will not. I keep him rubbed in with Wintergreen and Vick, and give him lots of hot lemon. He just grunts and leaves his vest off. You'd think he wanted to die, the old fool. I talk my drawers crooked, it doesn't make a jot of difference. He's addled.'

Coward grinned with genuine fondness. Peggy had been a whore in Soho for thirty years before retiring to play house with old Gluckman, her most regular client.

'He's too wicked to die, Peg. He's slightly older than God and more wicked than Lucifer's Uncle Jack.'

Peg's outer office was worn and outdated and scrupulously clean. Knitting lay on an easy chair beside a bleached oak desk and two brown filing cabinets. An old grey cat lay on the worn linoleum beside a two-bar electric fire with imitation coal below the lit bars. The walls were covered completely by Peg's collection of framed photographs of old Western movie stars. Hoot Gibson, Johnny Mack Brown, Lash LaRue, Tex Ritter and Gene Autry made a top line above a sepia William S. Hart, a still of Gary Cooper in *High Noon*, a hand-tinted Roy Rogers on a rearing Trigger, a young John Wayne in a *Republic* white hat, and a full-length Tom Mix leading Tony by the bridle through movie cactus. Jack Elam,

George Kennedy, Jack Palance and many others made a border of baddies.

Peggy knocked at an inner door and, pushing Coward through, closed it at his back.

Gluckman, wrapped in a loose dressing-gown over heavy pyjamas, crouched in a bentwood rocker surrounded by machines that kept him in touch with the world money market. A tickertape chattered and CeeFax monitors blipped up FT Indexes, Dow Jones Averages, current trading from Le Bourse and the closing prices from Tokyo. An illuminated wallchart showed the present float of the European Money Snake, the Irish Punt nudging low despite an alleged rise against sterling.

Gluckman was as old and as shrivelled as mummified oatmeal. Only his eyes showed life. Two polished chips of anthracite in bony hollows either side of a desiccated nose. He said:

'I spy strangers,' as though from the floor of the London Exchange. Then with surprising strength, he bawled: 'Peggy. Pour the malt.' More quietly he added, 'I hear you're up in the world, a Special Branch Inspector yet. You shouldn't be welcome, you stay away so much, but you are. Sit, sit.'

Coward made himself comfortable in a chair and wondered what kept Gluckman alive. 'You look as well as ever,' he said.

'Shoo,' said Gluckman. 'A regular cowboy like one of Peg's movie bums. Maybe with muscles and a stetson . . . it's not so likely. You're a liar, Coward, but I like to hear lies. It beats listening for my heart to stop beating. Maybe we should trade a little of my business savvy for some of your vitality, eh?'

'No trade, Mr Gluckman.'

'So formal?' Gluckman tapped his hairless skull. 'That means he wants to tap what's up here. Where's that crone with the whisky?'

'She lets you drink?' asked Coward, brows up.

'She should stop me?' Gluckman slapped a caved-in cheek. 'Nothing else warms.'

Peggy banged in and served them both with amber

drinks. Leaning close to Coward she whispered: 'His is cold tea and ginger ale. He can't taste, so I won't waste.' She told Gluckman to sip his slowly and left.

The old man bared his gums at the closed door.

'She thinks I don't know what she pours me. Ersatz. Garbage. I have a bottle of my own.' Gluckman took a bottle of Glenfiddich from inside his robe. 'Next time you come, you bring me another.'

'I already did.' Coward passed over a bottle from his overcoat pocket. It was snatched and hidden before Gluckman said his thanks. It was a game they played every time.

Gluckman settled himself with a chink of glass.

'You heard the bang last night? It lifted me out of my bed. The whole sky went red. It was the IRA maybe?'

'I was out of town. Perhaps.' Coward suddenly realized how close Gerrard Street was to where he now sat.

'Best place. London is a sewer. Anyway . . . what is it this time? Gold into India, or D Marks out of Cambodia? What?'

'Hypothetical question. If I were Kellerman and I had a load of sterling, a pantechnicon full, and I took it from here to Switzerland, who would I be trading with?'

'You think I'm Interpol with such a question?'

'I think you're better. Am I wrong?'

'Dead I'm better. They'd give you a long list of probabilities. Me? I'll give you a simple answer. Nobody.'

'You mean you don't know?'

'Listen, I know. I say nobody, I mean nobody.'

Coward just looked at Gluckman.

Gluckman made an impatient sound through loose lips.

'Listen, who would buy such quantities of sterling outside the British Isles? And for how many shillings to the pound? Nobody. Such amounts would be a drug on the market. Only governments could afford to buy. And they wouldn't. Kellerman knows that, the clutz. He would have to ship it back here and do a deal with the Treasury. And they would declare war.' Gluckman paused, fingered a liver freckle below one eye and nodded. 'Maybe under the right circumstances it's . . . possible.'

'It is?'

'Who knows? For an answer, you get a definite maybe. How many millions are you talking about exactly?'

'Several hundred at a guess. Perhaps all there is.'

'Dumb move. Even Kellerman couldn't think of doing such a thing. You think he's considering something like this really? In hypothesis, of course.'

'I think so, yes.' Coward sipped his malt.

'It makes no sense. Given that the UK was a banana republic in the middle of a civil war, it might. Shifting the currency out of the country to deny it to victorious rebels has been used before in South America. But even then it won't work unless all the other major assets of the country go too. I'll explain: supposing all this country produced was bananas, right? The rebels are about to take over. You, the government, sell the entire crop to a foreign concern, all wrapped up in an ironclad contract the rebels couldn't break, right? The rebels come to power and they're bankrupt. No assets, no bananas. The entire crop belongs to the foreign contractor.'

'Until the next crop the following year.'

'So it would appear, until the rebels read the fine print and find that the crop for the next ten years had been sold at a fixed price.' Gluckman poured his tea and ginger into a small corner sink without moving from his rocker and poured himself a stiff measure from the hidden bottle, knocking it back in one. He shuddered from head to foot. 'You see?'

'If that's the case, what are the UK bananas?'

'Treasury gold. North Sea gas and oil. Offshore mineral rights. All overseas holdings. Tea plantations, sugar crops, oil installations, coffee crops, even bananas. A whole screed of things like that. UK companies have many foreign holdings that cover anything from shipping to mining. Bananas of a high order, things that can be bought and sold without setting foot in the old country.'

'It's too big an op for the ordinary asset stripper, Gluck.'

'He addresses me in diminutives, yet,' Gluckman complained. 'Listen, Mister policeman, it's possible. You think it isn't?'

'I think I don't know.'

'It's possible . . . *if*.'

'If what?'

'If you neutralize the armed forces, the RAF and the Royal Navy, and you destroy the credibility of the Central Government. Then it's easy.'

'That's nonsense,' Coward said, hoping he was right.

'Listen to him,' Gluckman gripped his robe and leaned out of his rocker. 'You think Russia didn't do that in Eastern Germany, in Poland, in Czechoslovakia? You think they didn't try in Egypt before Nasser blew wise and tossed the engineers and the advisers out? You think they aren't doing that now in the Yemen, in Ethiopia, in Mozambique? You think they won't do that in South Africa if somebody doesn't wake up soon? I won't even *talk* about South America. You British are so complacent. You think,' Gluckman pointed east, 'twenty-two miles of Channel is your frontier, your shield against aggression? You're forty years out of date.'

Gluckman choked and wiped his mouth with trembling knuckles. His skin was transparent and the heavy veins there were blue-black. He lay back in his rocker, saying weakly, 'I shouldn't get excited. Particularly with a fool from a nation of fools.'

'Behave, Gluck, or I'll call Peg.'

'For what, to watch me die? I can do that all by myself.' Gluckman took slow shallow breaths and his voice was stronger. He sneered at everything in the room, his jagged gums as pink as fangs. 'You want something on Kellerman that isn't hypothetical?' he asked slyly.

Coward just nodded. Thinking, *is he crazy or right*?

'Kellerman's so smart he outwits himself with his manoeuvres. He's making moves in the market. Shifting share blocks, liquidating holdings. He uses brokers, but I know it's him. For six months he's been quietly shifting his business from the City, he's broking out of the Continent now, and to others who don't know him like I do, it looks like simple diversification. To me, it makes a pattern. A crazy pattern that maybe makes no sense. But others are following him, move for move.'

'Who particularly?' asked Coward.

'Take your pick from a dozen. Not a nebish among them,' Gluckman watched Coward from the edge of his eyes, making him work for the information.

Coward stabbed in the dark.

'Giles Prebble, Peveril-Saunders?'

'That's two of them. What does that do for you?'

'Nothing and everything.' Coward admitted. 'Will you give me a list of the others?'

Gluckman slid a cream sheet of typed names from a drawer in the CeeFax console and held it across his lap. He was enjoying himself.

'You should have come to me sooner, John. I've been sitting on this since the middle of September. Old men like company.'

Coward smiled gently.

'Don't chide me, Gluck. I come when I can. Tell me about the crazy pattern. Maybe we can make it sensible together.'

'No offence, you don't have the nous. Take my word, all these fellows are keeping in this country are their current accounts. Even their properties, houses, lands, are owned by foreign paper companies. Make what you can of that.'

'More to the point, Gluck, what do you make of it?'

'They've sold their bananas to themselves. Holding them out of the country so the rebels inherit a bankrupt regime.'

'Who are the rebels, then?'

'Ask. I told you it was crazy. There's something else, and you can make what you want of it. A coaster came out of Lisbon and was on its way to Northern Ireland. The manifest was heavy machinery. It rounded the Lizard and sank. There was one distress call before it disappeared. No survivors. The insurance investigated and paid up. It wasn't such a big claim. One of the underwriters was hurt badly, he talked to me about it. I checked it out just for interest. The cargo was owned by a company registered in the Cayman Islands. This Prebble owns a major share, don't ask me how I found out. I just did. That cargo had been on three other ships before it was loaded on the coaster that sank, and had originated in America. I thought an insurance fraud maybe. I checked some more and that cargo, machinery it wasn't. Arms it was.'

Coward started to speak. Gluckman cut him off.

'No, Mister policeman, it wasn't meant for the IRA. I figure it was landed in the West Country. That coaster went down on a calm sea, no wind, nothing. I couldn't help my friend the underwriter, but you? You can do something with those few bones.'

Coward thought in silence for a moment and said: 'I'm spinning on a carousel, Gluck.'

There was no answer. Gluckman's head had flopped back and his mouth had sagged open. He snored through a throatful of bubbles. Coward teased the list of names from between the old man's fingers, wrapped the dressing-gown across the thin chest and tiptoed into the outer office. Peg smiled over her knitting.

'He's asleep?'

'Dropped right off in the middle of a sentence.'

'He does that more and more. Did you bring him a bottle?'

Coward said yes he had.

'I'll fill it with tea and put it back where he hides them. I pour him pretend drinks, he pours them away and drinks from his bottle. He thinks it's whisky and he's happy. You want some of the real stuff, Mr Coward, dear?'

'No thanks, Peg. I'd like to use your phone.'

'Feel free.'

Coward dialled the *Morning Herald* and chased Sadler through several extensions without luck. The switchboard transferred him to a copy-editor he knew slightly and who suggested Coward try *Mothers* drinking club in Frith Street. Coward thanked him and cleared down. The grey cat was making a figure of eight around his feet. Peggy toed him away.

'As randy as Gluck used to be,' she said wistfully. 'Come soon, he doesn't see many people now.'

Coward promised he would, kissed her leathery cheek and left. He got to the Cortina before a traffic warden, drove to Duck Lane, parked, and walked around into Frith Street. At *Mothers* he mumbled a name into the doorphone and the lock was released electrically. He walked down carpeted stairs to the bar-room.

Mother himself was pouring drinks at the bar, mincing about in a kaftan and insulting his clients at the top of his voice. Nobody was offended. The place was decorated in seedy Spanish baroque and filled with commercial film-makers, advertising men and Post Office engineers. An old scene-painter and a Xerox operator hugged the bar and an account executive bored a tall secretary with his life story. It sounded as though his wife understood him all too well.

Mother blew Coward a kiss, called him a butch bitch and served him with an honest measure of whisky. He pressed change into Coward's palm and pointed Sadler out, his eyelashes fluttering. Sadler, a thin, sallow man in a denim suit, leaned over a plump Welsh girl with a giggle and a long gin and vermouth. Neither looked sober.

Coward decided against subtlety. He jogged the girl's drink into her lap, apologized, bought another, and whilst she cleaned up in the Ladies he said to Sadler: 'I want to talk to you about Giles Prebble.' He showed his warrant card. 'Cut loose from the lady, this is important.'

Sadler swallowed his drink, killed his smoke and made for the exit, saying, 'Well, come on then. She'll find another friend.'

On the windy pavement Sadler stopped.

'If this is the old frighteners, forget it. Tell Prebble bent coppers give me wind, not the wind up. So, kindly piss off, old darling.'

Coward's tone was mild. 'You'd best have good reason for saying that.'

Sadler's long face twisted into a sour grin.

'My reasons go into print, whatever your name is. Read all about it in the morning edition. I sell words in the same way you sell your badge and truncheon. To the highest bidder.'

'I'll buy a copy of your rag. Nothing like the view of the impartial press. That is of course, if the printers aren't on strike, or your legal department doesn't put the dampers on your copy. Always the same, when you hacks are on the skids you all make noises of outrage. Corruption in high places. Do us both a favour, Sadler, you more than me, don't call me bent. Once more and I'll show you some real police brutality.'

Sadler digested that in silence. He dug a cigarette from somewhere and wasted four matches trying to light it. The smoke he breathed was snatched away and blown down the street. He shivered from cold and said:

'I wish I was sober. I'm so bloody used to being threatened, I wouldn't know an honest man if I fell over one. So what chance has a copper got?' He raised his eyes and made them focus. 'All right, I'm listening. What can it cost me?'

'I hear you were out at Heathrow the other evening.'

'So?'

'So you saw Prebble, spoke to him.'

Sadler looked wary. 'You could only have got that from him.'

'That's right. You're his alibi.'

Sadler squinted, holding one eye closed.

'I'm hearing things. You want to give me that again?'

'You heard right the first time. A gallon of Java Blend might help.'

'You buy, I'll listen.' Sadler began walking, taking careful steps. He and Coward wove through side streets to the Wardour Street Sandwich Bar where Coward bought large blacks as Sadler flopped into a booth. A ponce who worked three girls from St Anne's Court drank up and left, hiding his face inside his collar. He did not know Coward from Adam but he had a nose for the law.

'You have quite an effect on the natives.' Sadler drank noisily, swilling aftertaste from his palate.

'You're not so drunk.'

'Instinct. I can keep track even when I'm legless. This stuff tastes like hippo mud. What about this alibi?'

'Do you confirm it?'

'For what it's worth. What's it to you anyway? Wait on, little clicks in my brain tie things together. Some kid got himself killed by a sex maniac, a kid from Easter Without. That's Prebble's village. It came over the wires early this morning. I sent one of the lads down. Maybe I should have gone myself. Am I connecting, whatever your name is?'

Coward said nothing.

'Going too fast for you, eh? Cards on the table. Is he tied to that?'

'I don't know.'

'That means you're not saying. Fair enough. For now, anyway. I still don't know you aren't on his payroll though, do I?' Sadler gulped the last of his scalding coffee and stared over the cup-rim. 'Fuck the brutality, you know I could be right. You *could* be bought and paid for. I've got a wired rib from trusting the wrong copper.'

Coward pushed his untouched coffee across the table.

'Drink that and listen, Sadler. My name's Coward. Special Branch. I can make your life a misery if I want to, and you know why. All that left-wing crap you were involved in at one time would be enough for a long detention. I want your cooperation, and I'll do whatever is necessary to get it. You'd be the one to suffer if I slapped you inside for . . . oh, let's call it prevention of terrorism.'

Sadler looked pained as the alcohol drained from his eyes.

'The same old stuff,' he sighed. 'The bully-boy bull-shit. So I ghosted a few squibs for armpit underground magazines when I couldn't get typeset in a daily. It happens all the time. You think anybody in the Street likes to give copy to mags like the *Pink Dwarf* or the *Gay Politico*. Sometimes it's the only way.' He shrugged. 'That or leak it to the foreign press.'

'And who was it leaked the security details of the Paris Commission to the Bader-Meinhoff?'

'Guilty, and I don't have to explain it. It tightened things up.'

'And the OPEC meeting.'

'Wait one millisecond. Did you say, Coward?'

'Drink the coffee.'

'You're Coward?' Sadler said unsteadily. 'I spent a year chasing you for a story. That big car fraud they worked between London, Birmingham and Rotterdam? You wrapped that up with no loose ends, except for a couple I dug up. You cost me a fat scoop. I was weeks ahead of *World in Action* on that one. Why didn't you say so before? Jesus, I'm a fan.'

'The coffee, Sadler.'

Sadler was making mental adjustments.

'I don't need it. I'm as sober as Lord Longford at a Festival of Light christening. If you're after Prebble, his tail is in a sling. I've been after that pompous racist sea-cook for five long years. I can't get a thing printed. Well, nothing you wouldn't wrap fish and chips in. What do you need? You've got it. Anything.'

'Some good, current photographs.'

'Easy. They'll only strengthen his alibi though.' Sadler told Coward about Heathrow and the American Prebble had met there.

Coward said those pictures would do fine.

'Do?' Sadler looked offended. 'Listen, I've got all there is on Prebble. Right back to his school days. I know his collar size and which side of the bed he likes to sleep on. Heck . . .' he broke off. 'But you? There's something unkosher about how you're doing this. Contacting me. Talking like this in *this* place. You're shoving your elbow into a fat barrel of nasty, Coward. Perhaps my enthusiasm is misplaced. Maybe you are just a laundry detail after all.'

'You want to think that, go ahead.'

'Throw me something. I still remember what it was like to have ideals. I like to think there's more to journalism than football results and full-colour cleavages.'

Coward unfolded Gluck's list of names to show the top three. Sadler almost grabbed at it. He leaned back against black vinyl and took several breaths.

'So,' he said. 'So, so, so.' Nodding.

'Well?'

'That explains a lot,' said Sadler.

'Does it?' said Coward, thinking, *What?*

Sadler could have been relating the details of an elusive dream.

'I can guess at the rest of the names. I'll just bet there aren't any coppers' names on there. There ought to be, of course. But you'd want them out of it and Prebble in. It's natural. You don't have the clout to get that high. You'd have to be a Commander at least. So it's an imperfect world.'

Coward's neck burned. *Hints and bloody riddles. Implications.*

He said nothing as Sadler looked at him. A negro pushed down the aisle and plumped into a seat. He was joined by a brunette with bright make-up and chocolate fingernails. The other tables were filling up and the takeaway queue wound to the door.

'The old boys' team. Column 88 to the core. Upper-class tearaways with their own private armies. So right-wing they'd hang Maggie Thatcher as a Red.' Sadler watched Coward with amusement. 'I do believe I'm telling you something you didn't know. I *don't* think.'

'This,' said Coward, looking around, 'is no longer the place to continue this discussion.'

The negro was slanging Coward in the mistaken belief he could not be understood. The girl giggled into her toasted salami and pickle. To her, Coward was a square straight. Fair game for the black barbs. The byplay was not lost on Sadler. He jerked his head.

'There's one of the reasons the old boys act the way they do.'

'I wonder why?' said Coward.

'No you don't,' said Sadler, rising to his feet. 'None of us do, really. We all have prejudice of one kind or another. It doesn't have to be racial. Some of us argue that the immigrant influx has come too suddenly. Taken us by surprise. That we need time to assimilate. To adjust. You're prejudiced against villains. But you have to think like them to understand them and to catch them. You use them one against the other, throwing bones to the smaller ones to get them to inform on the bigger ones. Big fleas and little fleas. Our dark friend here is as prejudiced as any of us, only he thinks he has good cause. He rationalizes his attitudes like all of us.'

The negro caught the last of what Sadler was saying, realized he was the subject and stopped chewing. Sadler gave him a sunny smile.

'Shall we?' he said to Coward, making for the door.

Coward glanced back through the steamy glass. The negro's thumbs had met through his sandwich, his face gorged with blood. The brunette no longer giggled. She worried her lower lip with small, sharp teeth.

Sadler waited for a hole in the traffic, crossed rapidly and went into a doorway between a film company and a viewing theatre. Coward caught up with him in a first-floor bar. It was tatty, warm and had dark corners with booths.

'My usual, Fred.' Sadler went to a booth and left Coward to pay for and carry the drinks across. Sadler took the bottle of Perrier water and filled his glass with it. Coward sipped a watered whisky.

'Do I get to see the rest of that list?'

'More than that if you like. You can give me all you have on the bastards. Do some digging on my behalf,' said Coward.

'Are you going to insult me with money?'

'Up to you.'

'For once I'll say no. That way I'm not bought and paid for. I work with you, not for you. Do we exchange information?' said Sadler, liking the sound of what he had said.

'Later. If there's no other way.'

'Meaning *if* you can't settle this matter through the due processes of law? Don't answer, it's obvious. I'm going to like this.'

'Don't bank on it.'

'Which means,' said Sadler after a pause, 'you can't offer me any protection because you have none for yourself.'

Coward let that alone.

'Or you'll dump me if you have to. Which?'

'Probably both.'

'Well, that's honest.'

'Surprised?'

'An understatement, Coward. One word of warning, and I'm not giving you names, those old boys have long arms and deep pockets. When they buy it stays bought. Or it becomes valueless. I know of a copper who wouldn't stay bought. He was purged so totally, none of the rags would listen, let alone print what he might have said. Bears thinking on.'

'And that includes your own rag.'

'Do I look happy about it?'

'Stop hinting, Sadler. Give me one solid bone or forget it.'

'You won't like it.'

'Sadler,' Coward warned. His hand squeaked around the glass.

'All *right!* You want a name, I'll give you a name.'

'Well?'

'One of yours. Maitland.' Sadler pressed his shoulders against the back of the booth, almost punched there by Coward's expression. There was a long screaming pause.

'Make that stick,' said Coward.

Sadler found the courage to say, 'I can't. It was the last thing that purged copper told me before he tanked himself full of vodka and drove his Princess into a motorway bridge. He said, and I paraphrase, "They've even got old Maitland on the stick. They'll save him for the end". Something like that.' Sadler's fear turned into a kind of rage. 'I don't know how they got to Maitland. Prebble's a weirdo and he can smell it in others. Maybe Maitland was bent for small boys or basset hounds. Suicidal cops don't make the most rational witnesses.'

Coward made fists and laced them together.

'You're damning yourself with street talk, Sadler. Cheap, unfounded junk. Labelling Cabinet Ministers or punk rock stars as homosexuals is a fashionable gutter press tactic. Allegations without substance.'

Sadler's hands fluttered up and down his drink.

'You came to me, remember? Not the other way around. Sodomy, buggery, what does it matter? That's consenting adult stuff. I don't want Prebble on that. I want him on the political level, where it counts.'

'There is no political level. Prebble's been old hat for years. He couldn't sport a Liberal button or sell a pot of red paint to Transport House. He's an untouchable right across the three-party system.'

'That's how much you know,' said Sadler.

'Facts, chum. Facts.'

'You won't find him at the rallies or the hustings. He'll never speak from a platform or display party posters in his window. But he's there all right. Behind the scenes where money and influence can buy the ear of a rising candidate. Look there, Coward. Look at that list of names and tell me I'm not right.'

Coward found himself linking Gluck's bananas with the rows of sleek cars outside Poynter Manor, adding blanks to question marks. He dragged himself back to what Sadler was saying.

'. . . so I've maligned one of the big boys in blue. So what? We're talking about democracy, Coward. Or is that an overused, clichéd concept that means as little as love or human rights? You think that funny coming from me? All right, it's funny. I drink too much and I screw anything with the right equipment. I scratch around in the silt to make a living. Make headlines from starlets' indiscretions. Do the dirty on pampered celluloid characters. It wouldn't get bought and published if there wasn't a market. The public gets the kind of press and police it deserves.' Sadler had not raised his voice once. It was all delivered in a hard whisper that rocked with passion.

'A bum with aspirations for the greater good, eh?' said Coward.

'Comical, isn't it?'

'Yes, it's comical.'

Sadler called to the bar.

'Fred, two large whiskies.' He eyed Coward. 'Unless you won't drink with me.'

'Me?' Coward smiled wryly. 'You ain't the only one with a red nose.'

'Then why do I want to apologize all the time?'

'To whom? You or me?'

'Fucked if I know, Coward.'

'You decided you could afford a conscience. Your

decision.'

'Yeah.'

'Give me a number where I can reach you day or night.'

Sadler scribbled on an envelope. 'My mother's place in Fulham. She still keeps my room the way it was before I left home to join the army. I go back there when I need to think. She's eighty-four and she still tucks me up and brings me hot milk in bed. Forty-three years old and I still find times when I need it. Laugh, and I'll throw one.'

'Who me?' said Coward. 'Cheers.'

'Yeah,' said Sadler. Unsure.

17·02 hours

Kellerman sat in the back of the hushing Rolls-Royce deep in thought.

It had not been a good day for him so far, he would have to do something positive to improve it. His small, ugly face had the bone-scraped look of a man emerging from deep shock. Prebble had shat on his own doorstep with the arrogance of the fool he was. Kellerman could hardly bring himself to rerun Prebble's encounter with Coward, his treating a thieftaker of Coward's stature like local constabulary filth was unpardonably dangerous. Crassly stupid.

Kellerman's scrotum contracted and he wriggled a knot from his underwear. With hindsight, he knew he should have seen Prebble's mania for what it was, and not have been blinded by profit. Prebble had the ghetto mind and the tunnel-vision of a commited social climber. Had he been an ordinary thief with pretensions, he would have shoplifted at Harrods and stolen his bread from Fortnum and Mason's Food Hall, but he wasn't, he wanted power.

Kellerman had warned Prebble about Coward as they walked to join the shoot. Prebble had listened impatiently and drawled:

'Your courage is more minuscule than your body, Kellerman. This Coward is only a man, and a policeman at that. If he troubles you, kill him.'

There had been no time to protest. The hysterical woman had run screaming from the copse and talked of finding a dead, hanging man. Kellerman knew from Prebble's face it had to be Ferris. More shit on the doorstep instead of a nice clean disappearance in a convenient gravel pit.

Then the police had arrived in the shape of Inspector Dutton, who had talked of suicide as he watched for reactions. Prebble obliging him. Madeleine looking stricken. He, Kellerman, saying as little as possible. The woman who found the body having a vomiting fit and needing a doctor. Dutton taking statements and going away. Prebble toasting the closing door with a raised glass.

The whole thing had smelled of choreography.

He's only a policeman. Kill him, echoed in Kellerman's mind.

He might even have spoken the words aloud. It did not matter, he was alone in the back of his soundproofed car and nobody had overheard him. Why not?, he decided.

Kellerman reached for the carphone and waited for the operator to respond. Coward would have to go. And Prebble. The eyewitness Dutton spoke of? Perhaps. It was time to cut loose, forget the profit and take the loss. There was no longer any other choice. Kellerman gave his code and asked for a number in Maida Vale. It was answered after the third buzz.

'Yes?' said a coarse, bored voice.

'Give me the Cypriot,' said Kellerman.

'Wait.' The receiver clacked on to a hard surface and steps went away along a bar. The pause was filled with juke box noise, the murmur of drinkers. Softer steps approached and Eliades said, 'I'm listening.'

'Covent Garden,' said Kellerman.

The 'Yes' was cautious. Tense.

'You owe me a free ride. The jockey you sent for the last race fell. One of my stables was burned, and there's no insurance. I've taken a loss. You understand.'

'Yes,' said Eliades, breathing close to the mouthpiece.

'You'd better. This time I want you in the saddle. Personally. No novices like last time. Any falls, and I'll have you barred from the course for life.'

Eliades breathed more heavily, not responding.

'Well?' Kellerman said briskly.

Eliades sounded sullen. 'I understand. Yes.'

'Good. There are two races at two different courses. They have to be ridden on the same day. Tomorrow.'

'No,' Eliades snapped. Furious. 'I have to go over the courses first, to study the terrain. I don't know the territory. I need to train for a week.'

Kellerman brayed without humour.

'You don't understand. There is no time for training. Your contract is void unless my conditions are fulfilled. No other trainer will touch you if you don't make the rides tomorrow. You have no choice.'

'I'll be in Covent Garden in an hour,' said Eliades. 'We'll discuss it then.'

'No discussion. You will collect your riding instructions. That's all.'

'I think we must talk. I insist.'

'Listen, another contract jockey is only a phone call away. Bear that in mind.'

'One hour,' said Eliades.

'Very well. *We'll* be waiting.' Kellerman rang off with a slam.

As he rode along the Cromwell Road he made two insurance calls. It paid to be careful with a contract shooter like Eliades, and Kellerman was in no position to leave anything to chance. He would have Eliades followed on the jobs. If he failed, he would die. That made everything neat.

Kellerman decided to eat Italian and phoned his reservation ahead to Gennaro's. Pasta would settle his stomach.

21·08 hours

Madeleine led the ladies into the withdrawing-room, leaving the men to their port and cigars.

Dinner had been six courses and four wines. Poilly Fuisse with the caviare and cold consommé, old Burgundy with the beef and wild duck, claret with veal in green waistcoats, and a sweet young Italian with the shredded orange in meringue scallops. The cheeseboard had been as international as the guests' business interests. Madeleine saw the ladies served with coffee and liqueurs before slipping away to Nancy's bedroom.

Nancy lay propped on pillows, her bedside tray untouched. There was chalk under the fine grain of her skin and her hair looked brittle. She snatched smoke from a menthol More, blowing it out before it reached her lungs. Her smile was as artificial as the flowers on her robe.

'God, but I feel ugly,' she said. 'If you're going to make noises like the school matron, don't. I can feel sorry for myself without help.'

Madeleine leaned a hand against the fourposter.

'You've eaten nothing,' she said.

'Everything tastes of straw. Isn't it foul?'

'Would you like something lighter? Some eggs?'

'Straw eggs, how disgusting. I suppose you've guessed. That fool of a doctor would have said something.'

Madeleine swallowed her denial, she had never been able to lie to Nancy. 'Yes. How long have you been ill? You could have told me.'

'And have you clucking it all over the county?' Nancy mimicked a county drawl. 'Dahling, haven't you heard about poor, dear Nancy? No? Dahling, it's tragic. Cancer, you know. Isn't it riveting and awful?'

'That's unfair, and you know it.'

'What do you know about what's unfair? God.' Nancy brushed the air as though cobwebs clogged her breathing. 'Oh, sit down. I'm not made of glass.' She slapped the counterpane. 'Sit, damn you.' When Madeleine had done so, she said: 'Do I look awful?'

Madeleine shook her head. 'No.'

Nancy laughed. 'It's all turning to straw. Tastes, my hair . . . there's no life in it at all. Straw. At least it won't last much longer. Two months they've given me.'

'Is there no treatment? Radium?'

'Of course there's treatment. But no guarantees. I decided not to become an invalid, that's all. When the time comes, I shall explode in a shower of pixie-dust and float away on the wind to pollinate flowers. Arum lilies I suppose, they are the traditional blooms for funerals, aren't they?' Nancy lifted Madeleine's chin and looked deep into her eyes. 'No crying, my girl. I'll not have it. I only accepted your invitation in order to see you one last time. If that fool of a man hadn't let me find him hanging in that tree, I shouldn't have had an attack. We should have parted without you knowing. Swear you'll say nothing.'

'Nancy . . .'

'Swear. I'll not have the little time left spoiled by pitying looks.'

'I swear.'

'Good, we can stay friends. You never met my husband, did you?'

'No.'

'I've left him. He doesn't know either. Nor shall he. When he gets around to hating me enough he'll find somebody else. He'd make an awful widower.'

'It's all so calculating.'

'Pray you have the courage to do the same if, God forbid, it happens to you, Maddy. Don't turn the world into mourners. Now I'm tired. I'd like to rest. I shall be leaving very early. I shan't see you before, so, good-bye, Maddy.'

They shook hands like men, a firm clasp of hands. Nancy pulled Madeleine towards her and brushed both cheeks with her lips. When she pushed away her smile was bright and real.

'Live a long time, Maddy. I intend to. If I last sixty days, each day will be a lifetime. You see, I have the gift of knowing how long I have left, and I don't intend to waste a moment of it.'

Madeleine had no words. She shook her head dumbly.

'Go away now. Remember me as I was.' Nancy rolled over and pressed her face into the pillow. 'Leave the lights on. No more darkness.' She waited for the door to close behind Madeleine before she let the tears come, knowing her brave front had fooled her friend without bringing comfort to herself. There was no comfort. Just the certainty that she must finish things herself before the pain and the addictive hallucinants stole the last of her will.

Madeleine had made for her dressing-room and sat before her mirror, brushing her hair, unwilling to return below before she had control of herself. She was haunted by Nancy and her sixty days, unable to mourn the passing of such a vibrant personality without seeing the emptiness of her own existence. She saw her husband older and heavier and less inclined to the physical. Separate lives and separate beds under a roof that did nothing but keep out the rain and house history, killing the ghosts of what might have been.

She wanted to make love suddenly. To share warmth and whispers with a body ridged with muscle and pelted with hair. Her breasts pricked against her dress and her thighs tensed inside the silk. She thought about the policeman with slate eyes who had filled the doorway that morning, his features somehow grafted on to Calloway's frame.

Madeleine ran cold water and threw it into her face, badly spotting her dress. She would have to change before returning to her guests. When she went below, she was in control again.

19·14 hours

Coward had his identity checked five times before he got to interview Charlie Glass.

The old man, strapped to his bed and reeking of hospital soap, sulked aloud. He had been washed weak, they had cut his hair and his strength, he wasn't allowed a breath of fresh air or allowed to drink anything but orange stuff diluted in the ale Adam washed his leaf in. Tea was for sickly virgins and flatfooted rozzers with the down on their cheeks. A man needed a man's drink. And food that stuck to the ribs, not pap that tasted of baby milk.

Identify anybody? Not without a drink and some baccy. Look at photographs? Not without two drinks, his trousers and his freedom. He knew his bloody rights.

Charlie threw a fit and his bedpan, yelling for Guinness and justice.

Coward left him with two police marksmen for company and left for home. Sadler's Vanden Plas fell in behind him.

Coward dawdled along the Edgware Road, turned into Chapel Street and suckered Sadler into the cross-town traffic heading across Baker Street. By the time Sadler had made an illegal U and turned north again, Coward was into Regent's Park, swinging south past the Zoological Gardens.

As he turned into the forecourt of his apartment building, a plain panel truck took up station across the road.

If Coward saw it he gave no sign. He was carrying a black plastic bag when he went inside.

Eliades turned sideways across the wheel to the man with red hair.

'Well?' he said.

'That's him,' said Hammond through swollen lips. 'Definitely.'

The negro in the back laughed softly, turning a switchblade to catch the light. 'You be right, white ass.'

'Shut up, Moses.' Eliades slid the offside door open. 'Out, Hammond. See you in South America. If you make it.'

Hammond tumbled on to the windswept pavement, turning his beaten face up at Eliades. 'Wish me luck, Ellie?'

'Luck.'

The negro's laugh followed Hammond as he took himself off, cuddling his broken hand and favouring his torn left leg.

'You think Kellerman let him make it?' Moses asked the Cypriot.

'Would you? Come on, we've got work to do.'

Eliades unzipped a leather cricket bag and began assembling a high-velocity rifle.

'No,' said Moses, working a woollen ski helmet over his hair and pulling on white cotton gloves. 'That man's dead meat for certain.' He loaded a silenced Sterling-Pachette and did not laugh.

20·15 hours

Coward forked the last wedge of scrambled egg and toast into his mouth and washed it down with scalding tea, crosslegged on his living-room floor.

He had separated the contents of the black plastic sack into piles, laid Dutton's Polaroids in line with Sadler's bromides of Prebble and Calloway with Gluck's list of names and the Swansea print-out of registered car owners. The aerial drawings of the Thames from Hammond's safe fitted together into a long paper snake.

One thing was certain. Goldy had been right.

Coward reached for the phone, dialled, and with the connection ringing in his ear, stripped the cellophane from ten Piccadilly, fumbled one into his mouth and lit it with all the panache of a child in a school playground. When the silver man had put Maitland on the line he said brusquely:

'I'm not scrambled. We must meet and talk. But not there.'

'Where are you?' Sharp and breathy.

'At home.'

'Alone?' Sharper.

'Yes.'

Maitland allowed background hiss for a long count of ten.

Coward let him. There was a lot for the Commander to think about. Rain and wind flexed the double-glazed window panels and an octopus of pale smoke formed around his head. He flicked ash into his empty cup.

'You seem to have disregarded my orders once again.'

Coward gave the silence back with interest.

'Can you say why, without being indiscreet?'

'I wouldn't try.'

Maitland's 'Typical' was dry. 'And this truly cannot wait.'

Coward counted to five. 'Not if you want me *not* to be discreet.'

'That sounds . . . ominous.'

'Doesn't it though.' Coward's phonehand ached with tension.

Maitland strung a lot of m's together, said, 'Wait for me,' and cleared down.

Coward listened for bug clicks under the dialling tone, heard none, replaced the receiver and sat very still for several minutes, missing comfort, missing furnishings, missing Nancy.

He went along into the hall for his revolver and brought it back into the living-room, wondering where to conceal it near at hand. He checked the load and decided to leave it in plain sight, laying it on the carpet where he planned to squat. The cigarette had died of neglect in his fingers and he drowned the stub in the teacup. He killed the overhead light and sat in the spill of a standard lamp.

And waited.

* * *

Death seemed very close.

She called her sisters to her, her very act of dying making her more attractive to them. Two answered the call. Rushing towards her, anxious to fill the power vacuum she was creating. They fell against her and she took their young strength into her greedy coils and grew magnificent again. Spiralling at their centre as they moved around and into her.

Her faltering winds grew in strength and she screamed with mounting fury.

9

Wednesday 3 October

20·36 hours

Eliades had circled the block three times in the panel truck and walked around it slowly twice more. There was only one entrance at the front, the side walls were sheer and blank, and the balconies overhung the front, shielding the windows from a shot from the narrow street. There seemed no way of making the contract from outside. The memory of Mrs Pell made him shy of a risky contact shot.

Mrs Pell, with two shots in her ample chest, shrieking and defecating, scrabbling for the gun with her heart clinically dead. Only a third shot to the head had thrown her down and away from him, spraying Eliades and the racks of wedding gowns with exploded bone and brain tissue. He could still smell her. Now he preferred the long-range hit. Less involvement, more room to manoeuvre, to improvise, to use the back-up man more sensibly.

Moses had found the ideal spot. He was learning.

Eliades brought the infra-red night-scope up to his eye and scanned the face of the apartment. *Beautiful*.

He lay on a flat roof between muttering extractor ducts, soaked by rain, sweating under his hood. Inside the building below him, their days and nights reversed for public convenience, exotic nocturnal animals slept in artificial sunlight. Before him, the deer terraces sloped away to the Regent Canal, rose from the far bank to the outer ring road and the floodlit frontage of Coward's block. Apartment 3A, third-floor front. No traffic swished in the rain and the pavements were empty. Eliades thanked the Blessed Virgin for that small plus in a situation filled with negatives, counting off rosary beads in his head, whispering the prayers like a mantra, calming himself. Calm enough to think, *Shit on Keller-*

man. Knowing the midget shit was washing him from the slate along with Prebble and this armpit copper, Coward.

Eliades saw again the ticking nerve in Kellerman's cheek, the twining fingers over the sweating palms. The nervous turning of the water glass on his desk. The little bastard was cleaning house, cutting away the dead wood before he was sucked down with it. Eliades knew fear, knew it intimately. Nervous partners and frightened targets added up to much the same thing, trouble for him. And Kellerman was trouble. Eliades did not need to be a genius to see that successful or not, Kellerman had had his card marked as a future danger. Goodbye, Eliades.

Making the hits tomorrow would be too soon and too late. By precipitation, by making the contracts good tonight Eliades earned himself a good twelve-hour start on the heavies with a paper for his backside. He grinned. While they looked for him in Regent's Park and Surrey, he would be looking for Kellerman in Covent Garden.

Beautiful.

Eliades worked the cup of the sight into his eye socket and lined it up with the lit third-floor window. He could have been on the balcony itself, it was so close and clear. He braced his forearms and leaned the long barrel in a cleft in the brickwork.

Show yourself, beauty. Surrey is a long drive.

* * *

Moses had both windows wound down, his nightglasses trained on the dim smudge that was Eliades on the Mammal House roof. He panned across to the third-floor window on the opposite side of the street, then back again.

Shee-it! If Ellie couldn't hit that mother-fucker copper in the headbone, he couldn't shoot shit in a can.

Moses tucked the glasses in the dash and broke open a fresh stick of gum. He would have preferred to have kept the motor running, but Eliades had said no, it would have been noticed. Cool and quiet makes for happy hits.

Moses admired Eliades without liking him. *Sure, there was no honky shit going down, Eliades could have been colour blind, he was so impartial. Maybe he didn't like anybody too much*. Moses had never seen him fooling with a chick. He didn't ball with guys either. *Well, bless him for that, more chicks for Moses. Moses the magnificent. Man, with the money from this caper . . .*

Moses snapped back to the street. The far lights had changed and traffic approached. He felt for the ignition and kept his hand there.

Ready.

'Are you lost?' somebody asked through the offside window.

Moses gagged as he swallowed his gum. He should not have daydreamed. He should have seen the patrolling copper long before he reached the truck. *Now what*?

'This is a restricted parking zone,' said the constable. 'Permit holders only. Residents.' He was young and bearded, leaning through the window at Moses, taking in his negroid features, sniffing for alcohol or funny cigarettes, checking the tax disc on the windscreen, prejudice in his manner.

Play it his way, Moses thought wildly. The Sterling could be anything under the blanket on the passenger seat. Nothing else was out of place. *Play the mother-fucker for a Charlie Horse*. Moses rolled his eyes and went into his coon act, grinning and showing a lot of tongue.

'Yes *sir*, I'm the lostest nigger in whitesville, officer,' he crooned idiotically. 'Supposed to pick up this fish tank for Oxfam. For the charity shop. Go to Albany Street, they say. And I go, except it ain't where they say it is. And me, I'm driving around and around until my eyes is crossed permanent. And I'm doing *them* a favour, you know?'

'A fish tank?'

'Yessir.'

'For the Oxfam shop?'

'That's what they said. Seventy-two, Albany Street. I've been round this park twenty times. I figure shit, I'll tell 'em I can't find no seventy-two.'

'It's behind you, down Parkway. Over on the northside of the park. Didn't they give you a name? A telephone number?'

'Nossir. Just the truck and the number and . . . *go.* And that's it.'

This copper ain't buying it. Ain't buying nothing. Moses kept his hand on the switchblade in his pocket, the other on the ignition key. *Lean over, cut him in the throat, and drive away. No, that leaves Eliades without wheels.*

The constable was looking amused.

Don't relax. Wait.

'Go on, drive away. I haven't seen you.'

'Yessir. I'm gone.' *Did he say that? He did, go.* Moses cut the engine in, snicked into first and swung out. A Bentley just shaved past, turning into the apartment forecourt. Moses braked, corrected and made a turn on two wheels, leaving rubber on the wet tarmac. Yelling: 'Good-night, officer.' Thinking, *Shee-it!*

20·41 hours

There was a head at the window.

The target had suddenly risen to stand in profile, looking down at his feet, pulling at his lip, every hair pin-sharp.

Beautiful.

Eliades went to work. He spread his elbows, lined up the crosshairs, took the stock into his shoulder, emptied his lungs with a long, controlled outbreath, found the trigger with the second pad of his right index finger. One slow blink to lubricate the eyes, squint, focus and steady up . . . hold it . . . start the pressure . . .

A horn sounded. A sharp blip of protest. Tyres squealed from the road. A motor roared in first, changed into second, power-slipping.

Eliades straightened his finger, jerking it forward against the trigger guard, lowered the rifle on to the brick sill, took a breath.

The panel truck was wobbling away towards Camden Town. Somebody stood on the pavement where it had been parked. A policeman. A Bentley had pulled on to the forecourt, brakelights blazing.

Stay calm. It's all part of the game, Eliades told himself.

Just another good reason for proper preparation. Going off half-cocked was for amateurs, cowboys. Eliades lay still and waited. The constable started walking south. By that time, the window was empty again.

Eliades ignored his stiff legs and the cold in his back.

He had all the time in the world. As long as it took.

*   *   *

Maitland came out of his reverie in time to take avoiding action.

He saw the panel truck U-turn behind him as he turned his Bentley on to the forecourt, realizing quite suddenly how close he had come to a collision. Sounding his horn had been a futile gesture, pure nerves. He yawned behind his driving glove and watched the constable across the street with swollen, grainy eyes, hoping not to be involved in what could only be a minor traffic violation. The constable had drawn his notebook, looking off after the diminishing panel truck. After a long count of three he tucked it away and walked off, leaning into the wind.

Thank heavens.

Maitland locked his car and took the elevator to the third floor. The door to Coward's apartment was closed to but unlocked. Maitland pushed inside the bare hall and called Coward's name.

'In here.'

Coward sat on the living-room floor surrounded by piles of paper. An electric Cona hob was plugged into a wall socket and bubbled hysterically. Apart from a single standard lamp there was not a stick of furniture in the room. Coward could just have moved in, or be in the process of moving out. He did not look as though he lived there. Maitland smelled tobacco smoke and wrongness.

He said good evening.

'Pull up a carpet tile and sit down. Coffee?' Coward

sounded and looked wooden.

'No, I'll stand.' Maitland checked his watch.

'You may as well make yourself comfortable, Commander. This is going to take some time.' Coward looked at his revolver without touching it. 'Was that you screaming about down there?'

'What? Oh . . . no, some clown in a van cut across me as I turned in. A near miss. The Sunday drivers seem to come out on weekdays now.'

Maitland's voice could have been absorbed by the walls for all the impression it made on Coward.

'We've all got troubles, Commander.'

Maitland rode his irritation and rapped: 'Meaning what?'

'Just that.'

'Games, Coward? Do we couch our questions in rhyming couplets?'

'Not any more. D'you know what all this is?' Coward's palm circled the air above the papers.

'Not until you tell me. And I think that had better be soon, don't you?'

Coward raised his head, looking directly at Maitland for the first time, his eyes bright and fierce in dark hollows. Darker triangles of shadow formed under his cheekbones, his mouth a taut line between the lower points.

'Those are phoney VAT returns for the Bugalloo Club. Two daybooks, one for the taxman and the other for private consumption. That goes off to the Customs and Excise anonymously. It's too small-beer for us. This, on the other hand,' Coward pointed at a second sheaf of papers. 'This is a list of men you should recognize.'

Maitland stifled a yawn. 'Really?'

'Arthur Peveril-Saunders, the Lord Lieutenant of Surrey. He's a friend of yours, isn't he?'

'Yes.'

'And Thornton Barclay the financier?'

'Yes.'

'Soames Peachey, James Crawford-Hunt, Tom Elthorne?'

'Again, yes.'

'And Giles Prebble?'

'No.' Maitland almost sneered.

'But you know him. You know him as well as you know the others.'

'Not quite the same thing, is it?'

'Straight talking, Commander. Stuff the semantics. There's no time for any of that old toffee.'

'Very well, the first five men you mentioned are indeed friends, the degree of friendship could be qualified as "social". Just that and nothing more. The last-named does not move in quite the same social circles.'

'Not until today, perhaps. I think they've been in each other's pockets for a lot longer. Maybe you just didn't know about it. Maybe the circle closed and pinched you out.' Coward toyed with an unlit cigarette, willing something to show in the other man's face, watching Maitland closely. 'They were all shooting and back-slapping on Prebble's estate this morning, when a man named Ferris was found hanged in a tree, one of Prebble's trees. This Ferris ran the scout pack Peter Petrie belonged to, and, until recently, was employed at Prebble's experimental marine station.' The Piccadilly had turned to shreds in Coward's fingers. 'You don't look surprised, Commander. You don't look anything.'

Maitland shrugged and took his time sitting down. He leaned back against the wall, his long legs straight out ahead of him, the ankles delicately crossed. He lifted his lapel to smell the carnation pinned there. Finally he said: 'How would you suggest I looked? Being cross-examined by a subordinate is a new experience and does nothing for me. Therefore, nothing shows. You do seem to have linked Prebble, somewhat tenuously for my taste, with some of my "friends". In almost the same breath, you mention a murder and a suicide. Am I supposed to draw conclusions from any of that?'

'But you have, Commander. I didn't mention suicide.'

'So, that proves my point. The one conclusion I drew was erroneous. Not all that surprising I'd say.'

Coward brought a knee up under an elbow and supported his chin in a cupped palm. 'Try this for a link. All these men are members of a financial consortium, which, until recently, was a power in the City. Now their groups of companies operate from outside British waters. Prebble is a director of all those companies. So is our old friend Kellerman. It's all here in black and white.'

Maitland smiled into the bloom on his lapel.

'I happen to know that.'

'Like you knew they were all cosied up on the social scene, hmm?'

Maitland's mouth turned down behind the carnation.

'Your name wouldn't be on the headed notepaper, would it, Commander? Not the first time a high-ranking copper has guinea-pigged for favours.'

Maitland stiffened, rolling his shoulders inside his coat.

'It would not.'

'Let's fly one,' Coward persisted. 'Let's just say it could have.'

'Let's not. That makes me guilty by association.'

Breath popped from Coward's mouth. Almost a laugh. He stifled it before it became anything. 'Why not? The old boy network still flourishes in this country. Comprehensive schools didn't even dent it. Yeah, I'm inclined to bet they approached you, you could be useful to "chaps" like that. I'm also betting you turned them down flat.'

Maitland's left eyebrow rose a millimetre.

'Benefit of the doubt, Coward?'

Coward shook his head. 'Nope. I have to believe that because the alternative makes one of us dead.'

'I suspect mostly me,' said Maitland. 'You have the Smith & Wesson.'

'Don't pre-empt me, Commander. You only turned them down when you found out what was really behind this high-flown financial flim-flam. Or at least, when you'd made a pretty shrewd guess at what they must be up to. But when you turned them down you put yourself in something of a bind, didn't you? You realized you couldn't turn them in without involving yourself.'

Maitland's 'Oh?' was neutral.

'Sure, why else did you pull Prebble's file from circulation? What have they got on you?'

Maitland moved his head from side to side, his eyes dull, saying nothing.

'I'm pulling molars, God,' Coward told the ceiling. He looked back at the silent, tensed Maitland. 'You've had me and Frank Cave on this murder hunt, hoping we'll turn up independent evidence that lets you and your conscience off the hook. You could have been straight with me. Did you think I'd flush you from office? Yank your chair out from under you?'

'Wouldn't you? Always supposing I have dirty linen.'

Coward looked sad. 'You have. I wasn't sure until now.'

'You're guessing, my boy. What have I been involved in? Apart from being offered a seat on the board of a reputable company?'

'On a board with Prebble and Kellerman, Commander. Reputable that ain't.'

'Pure supposition,' Maitland said, folding his arms. 'Show me some hard facts before I doze off.'

'Okay. Fact: the consortium is playing funny-money on the international market. Fact: Kellerman is planning a massive illegal currency export. Fact: the consortium landed an arms shipment in this country. Fact: Ferris used to work for Prebble Marine. He's supposed to have sexually assaulted and killed Peter Petrie then hanged himself. Fact: Prebble Marine is working on a secret government project. Shall I go on?'

'Do.' Maitland smoothed his lapel, smoothed his shirt collar, smoothed his hair and his expression.

Coward stabbed a finger at him.

'This map of the Thames came from the Bugalloo safe. It shows the water spread in case of flood, projected water depths throughout the city, installations that would be affected. Power stations, British Rail, the Underground system, telecommunications, water supplies.'

'This information can be picked up from any local council office.'

'Sure it can. What's interesting is this second area marked in red. You see,' Coward traced the lines with his finger. 'The spread is far wider and much deeper than the inner area. Look at this – ten feet in Piccadilly, twelve in Leicester Square. It shows the whole Thames Valley under water. Jesus.' Coward rocked on his haunches.

Maitland patted a sideburn, hiding behind a sleepy expression.

'Is that it?' he asked.

Coward came back from somewhere.

'No. Also marked in red are these locations: the Bank of England, the Post Office tower and the highest point of Hampstead Heath. There are several other points marked on the map that I can only guess at.'

'Guess aloud,' said Maitland.

'Emergency military installations?'

'Is that a question?'

'Only if you can answer it, Commander.'

Maitland said nothing.

Coward showed no surprise. He fumbled a cigarette from the pack and lit it clumsily, one-handed. The other hand lay close to the revolver. He coughed smoke and said: 'Well?'

'It's your story, Coward. All I can add to it, for what it's worth, is that none of it really ties together. Could you go to the DPP with this as the basis of a prosecution? I doubt it.' Maitland chafed his ankles and his hip. 'My circulation isn't what it was.' He rose to his feet, stood on one leg and worked the other backwards and forwards, turning the shoe from side to side. 'Better,' he said, and walked stiffly towards the windows, his back to Coward. 'On the whole, I'm rather disappointed. I was hoping for more than this . . .' His arm trailed through the air after his dying voice.

'There's more, Commander. A whole lot more. Your crocodile tears are premature. Look. This map is stamped: "Prebble Marine",' said Coward with hard emphasis. 'Another link between Kellerman and Prebble.'

'Really,' Maitland's breath clouded the window.

'Yeah, really. It's also dated: 5th-6th October. Today is the third. Whatever is about to happen, will happen, or will start to happen in two days' time.'

Maitland larded his voice with affected exhaustion.

'And what is going to happen, Coward? Work the oracle for me.'

'I telephoned the Meteorological Office and asked them.'

'And what did they say?'

'According to them, those are next optimum dates for a high tide from the North Sea. Something to do with low air pressure in the North Sea and the sun and moon working in conjunction. If that is backed by a prevailing northerly gale-force wind, bingo, massive flooding in the Thames Valley.'

'Hardly oracular, Coward.' Maitland's breath formed a halo on the glass around his head. With his face edge-lit by the single lamp he could have been a medieval saint in modern dress. 'The newspapers have been double-spreading that doom and woe for months. Just how do you tie a possible flood to this . . . hypothetical caper of Prebble's? You make him and his alleged group sound more daunting than the hordes of Attila the Hun.'

'Stuff your scorn, Maitland,' Coward said with disgust. 'They've obviously got you wetting yourself. Christ, I hate to see it.'

'That's another hypothesis you'll have to prove, Coward. Your womanly intuition is hardly enough to convince even you, let alone me. And those in high places, the ones you would really have to convince, would laugh at you. If they weren't yawning with boredom.' Maitland's voice had an underlying quiver. 'If you were in your right mind, I'd introduce you to the fellow in charge of the emergency services for London, including the military wing, of course. A chap named Rawlings. Major-General. He'd lay these phantoms of yours to rest for you, I'm sure.'

'Fine,' said Coward. 'We'll go and see him together. Tonight. Now. I gave you your chance to clean house by the side door. I figured I owed you that much. Now we'll do it by the book, and to hell with your career and pension.'

'Oh? Writing me off, Coward? Not as easy as it sounds. Let me tell you . . .' Maitland turned to find the ·38 levelled at him. He nodded as though it confirmed something to his own satisfaction. He added: 'No point saying anything, I suppose. You'll just act in your own bull-headed way and take no from nobody.'

Coward frowned and said, 'You're writing yourself off. Why? Your attitude would be laughable if the situation wasn't so blasted serious. It's bloody obvious these characters mean to use the flooding of London to their own advantage. If what you'd read in the newspapers had stuck you'd know that the new Thames barrier is by no means complete. You'd also know from just looking out of the window that it's been raining solidly for three weeks. Also, there's a bloody great northerly blowing in right now. There have been storms along the east coast for days, and parts of the upper Thames have flooded already.'

Maitland wiped a hole in the bloom his breath had formed on the window and stared out into the night.

'And Prebble has caused all this, eh? Is he now the breath of God? Can he blow up storms at will?'

Coward made a fist alongside his shivering gunhand, shouting: 'How can I get through to you? I've given you enough information to act. We've moved on far less for lesser reasons. We'll go to Rawlings. Let him make up his own mind.'

'Perhaps he'll let you count sandbags for him,' sneered Maitland.

'Bloody sandbags don't mean diddly-squat to a twenty-foot wave. D'you know what 30 per cent of Joe Public answered when asked what they'd do in the event the Thames overflowed? Where they'd go to escape from the water? Eh? Down the bloody Underground, that's where.'

Maitland made no reply.

'Just think of the loss of life. Idiots fighting to drown themselves, kicking each other to be first down the escalators.'

Maitland moved a hand to his lapel and dug inside it.

Coward cocked the revolver and stepped up and aside, blocking the door with Maitland between himself and the window.

'Hold it,' he said. 'Forget you even thought of it.'

Maitland faced him fully, his hand inside his coat. 'Wrong again, Coward.' He drew out a stiff white envelope. 'This is my resignation. I'll go with you to see Rawlings . . . as my last official act. I merely wanted to see if you had the balls to go through with it. There's nothing more . . .'

There was a double *pock*.

Something slashed through Coward's hair and plunked into the wall. Disturbed air whacked near his face. A second carnation pinned itself to Maitland's lapel and pumped blood up at the ceiling tiles. His shirt turned red through a ragged hole in his tie and his jaw went oddly slack. He took a faltering step, dropped the envelope and held both hands out to Coward who went forward to meet him, catching him as he sagged, lowering him to the floor. Kneeling beside him.

There was a starred hole in the double-glazing. A figure of eight with an open centre.

Two shots. Meant for me, thought Coward automatically. *Where from, though*? He raised Maitland's head, turning him carefully on to his side to prevent blood flooding his lungs. *Waste of time. He's too heavy already. Everything's gone out of his face. Retreating.*

'Rest,' he said aloud.

The angle from the street is too sharp. He has to be back in the park. Farther back. In the zoo. Right.

'Rest, Commander.'

Maitland's eyes widened, glazed and froze. Whatever he was seeing was outside the room. Beyond the high clouds. His mouth yawned open, brimming with blood. As Coward watched, one last gout flowed down the side of his jaw and a thick pink bubble formed between his lips.

He was gone.

Be there. Please just be where you should be. I'm coming.

Coward made for the front door on his elbows and knees.

Just be there.

21·17 hours

Eliades forgot about the cold and stiffness in his limbs when he saw the grey-haired man walk to the naked window and talk out at the night, blurring his features with his breath.

Two targets now. There could be no witnesses. Coward must be sitting on the floor. Why didn't the bastard use furniture like other people? His head would have shown and he could have been popped long before this other bloke arrived to complicate things. All right, swallow it. Do what has to be done.

Eliades practised panning shots along Maitland's line of sight, following an invisible clay until his movements were rhythmic and instinctive.

Squeeze, pan, sight. Squeeze and back. Beautiful.

But where the hell was Moses and the truck? The Pesevenghi!

Eliades' legs were soaked and frozen and his back was stiffening up. He breathed on his hands to keep the fingers supple, fighting the cold with thoughts of the pleasure to come.

Madonna in tights. My feet are cemented in a glacier. Calmly, man. Calmly. Think of the cocaine capsule breaking under your nose. The first snort of dust exploding back in your head. Under your palate where the roots are. The shafts of strength shooting into your loins. Up into your member. Swelling and extending it. Until you are attatched to it, not it to you. Then the women under you. Boring in until they evaporate between your pumping and your locked hands. Reduced to moans of pained pleasure. Marked by you and spoiled for any other man. Calmly. You can love for a fortnight without food or sleep. Just the dust in your nose. The women beneath you. Always young. Always different. Women chosen for you by the Turk in Islington. Especially for you. Used first by you and never the same again for any other man. Think of that. Calmly . . . anticipate . . . Beautifully. Yesssss . . .

The grey-haired man had turned.

Coward bobbed up beyond him. Almost in line.

Eliades squeezed off two shots. Shooting through Maitland at Coward. Both men fell together.

Lie still. Wait. Keep your aim locked off and count to one hundred.

A full seven minutes passed before Eliades decided to move.

I'll cross the canal bridge to the park. Stay back in the bushes until Moses returns. Then over the railings and into the truck without being seen. Simple.

21·23 hours

Coward pounded down the emergency stairs, mentally choreographing his possible actions, visualizing the layout of the forecourt. The street. The park boundary. The route of the canal. How the deer terraces sloped up to the rows of buildings and enclosures on the far bank. None of the details of the zoo came to him immediately. He had stared out at them so many times and for so long that their very familiarity made him blind to them.

Think, you clown. Think.

He skidded to a halt in the well of the stairs and looked around the deserted vestibule. The reception desk was unmanned and the internal fishpool chuckled to itself. The cork-tiled walls absorbed any echoes and the wall-clock was silently digital. Nobody stood on the outside steps and the forecourt was a puddled stretch of abandoned tarmac and flagstones. There was no real cover save for the parked cars on the southern side, and the decorative evergreens planted in the beds beside the low, flanking northern wall.

The street was empty for as far as he could see in either direction.

The gunman would have a clear shot if he chose.

Some choice, thought Coward. *Easy for him and none for me.*

He was too furious to talk himself out of what he had to do.

Thank Christ for adrenalin. Here goes nothing.

Coward threw himself out of the stairwell and took long strides to the glass doors, shoving through them and rolling down the marble steps. At the bottom he bounced to his feet, feinted, and zigzagged into the stunted firs. Nothing happened.

He could have gone into the zoo by any gate. How many are there? Three main ones? Two? How many side exits? I'm betting he went in this side. He must have a vehicle waiting somewhere.

Don't worry about it.

Coward threw himself over the wall. He loped across the street and jumped at the high park railings as though they had lost half their height. He caught at an ornamental spike and hauled himself up, swinging a leg. Gaining purchase on the crossbar with a heel. He went up and over in a clumsy, powerful vault, pushing and kicking forward into space.

Barbs tore at his face and hands. Something ripped his trousers from crotch to knee. He crashed down and through the mature hedge and tumbled on to flinty grass that bit at his back; most of the wind knocked out of him. He lay still. Only half-aware.

The deep shadows around him squirmed with microscopic life superimposed by the blood pounding behind his eyes.

Wait for night-vision, he counselled himself.

Long moments crawled by. A gibbon moaned from across the canal. A lion coughed at the night and the rain, smelling diesel instead of wildebeeste.

Coward moved crabwise towards the canal bridge. A dark slab against the loom of the water. Barbed wire and netting guarded the buttresses against climbers and the Victorian ironwork was out of reach. Coward slipped off his shoes and jammed them into his pockets. He tucked the ·38 down into his underpants and slipped into the dark water, swimming easily despite the biting cold. There was more cold heat in his blood than he knew what to do with. He crossed in the darker darkness below the bridge and flopped out on to the towpath on the opposite side. He had seen small boys sneak in this way. Under the wire and through the paddocks. Over the railings of the observation platform. He followed their time-honoured route and found himself flanked by dark buildings.

One of these roofs. Ideal.

He looked back across at his apartment building and

lined up his balcony with the structures on his side.

That one, he decided. *The Mammal House. Old Charlie Clore's money had built a platform for a sniper*. Coward bared his teeth in a hard, humourless grin. He fished the gun out of his trousers and padded through the shadows. He felt aware and taut and immortal. Even his hair-endings felt alive, bristling on his chest and scalp. He wanted Eliades very badly. The Cypriot's fate would not be decided by wig and gavel. He was Coward's for his very own.

A shadow stirred and a shape moved out of it, an amoebic black blob that became a crouching man with something that could have been a rifle swinging at his side. His head showed no features. No bone structure.

Masked, you bastard. You're my man.

Coward braced the wrist of his gunhand with his cupped palm and hissed the standard police warning:

'I am a policeman. I am armed. Stay where you are.' Knowing the man would not. Hoping he would not.

The shadow shied towards the greater darkness of a cage, rattling wire. An orange flash showed where he had been. The silenced shot whanged off into nowhere.

Coward fired a double-cluster to one side of the flash and knew he must have made a hit. Something clattered to the ground and something else slithered away, whining in a tightened throat.

Coward went forward on the balls of his feet, the gun out ahead of him as though it divined the way.

21·34 hours

Eliades heard the challenge and reacted.

He fired from the hip. Aiming at the voice. His brain flamed with fear. He knew the rifle had jammed itself. He tried to turn, to leap aside, to find cover. He almost made it. He hit wire just as a bullet ripped a hole in his upper right arm and shattered the bone. He was bounced away when the second slug punched into his hip, flattened against his pelvis and exited through his lower back. The rifle dropped away somewhere and he did not hear his own scream.

He followed his panic away from there on legs that seemed to be two odd lengths of tired rubber. And was he going blind? he wondered. His ski mask had slipped to one side, snagged by the wire, giving him only peripheral vision in his left eye.

He found the tunnel to the main gardens and panted down through it, emerging at the far end and sobbing past the Aquarium and the Reptile House. Liquid seemed to be running from too many places in his torso. Every breath forced a spurt of it through his black woollen shirt. It flooded down his legs and squelched in his shoes.

Forty quid a pair. They're ruined. Holy Madonna. I'm ruined.

There had to be a refuge. Somewhere to hide.

Eliades tottered past crane pens and the Zoo Shop. Beyond the gibbon enclosure was an expanse of grass and decorative ponds where flamingoes strutted and mallards stole bread from tourists on summer afternoons. Now it was just an open place with no cover.

The Elephant House could have been the slumbering outline of a stone pachyderm. Inside, a rhino snorted in his sleep and jiggled a tufted ear. Eliades did not hear him for the bubbling plasma in his mouth and nose. He had bitten through his tongue.

The North Gate. It's just past the Lion House and the Children's Zoo. Past the peacocks. I'll get over the stiles somehow. Past the wolves. Back into Regent's Park. Cover. Hiding. Rest and something to stop the blood. The world keeps going away.

Eliades crashed into a wall that would have been powder blue in the right light. He slid along it, caught at the rim. Held himself somehow upright. He ripped the blinding hood from his head. The North Gate was too far. He hadn't the strength.

Here. The Penguin Pool. Lower myself over and hide under the ramp that runs down into the pool. It's a chance. Take it.

Eliades got a leg over the sill and painfully levered himself off the floor, lying along the rim of the curving wall. He could just make out the water in the pool. Oily green dappled by rain.

Tired. Got to let go. Just roll off and down into the shadows.

Can't be far.

Eliades dropped the eight feet to the concrete ramp. His legs buckled on contact and he fell forward on to his smashed arm. The pain drove his senses away. With infinite slowness he collapsed like a melting bridge. His head slid over the lip of the pool and his face went below the surface with a quiet plop.

He drowned bare moments before he would have bled to death.

Coward padded past without a glance and did not see him die.

* * *

The ring road seemed to go on for ever as Moses kept his speed to thirty. He had been around the park twice without an opportunity to park or to double back. The reason was in front of him. A patrolling Panda, the two traffic cops inside chatting and laughing as they cruised the perimeter of the park.

Twenty minutes lost, thought Moses. *Me and Ellie should have brought radios. We would have been in touch instead of guessing what the fuck was going down. Motherhumping law. I should put both barrels up their flaming exhaust. All this piddling around at thirty. I'll have to pass them.*

Moses indicated right and eased out on to the crown of the road.

The Panda did the same.

What in rape's name were they doing? Moses braked and eased back, braking to a halt three car lengths back.

The Panda paused at an intersection and waited for the nonexistent approaching traffic to pass in the classic advanced-driving manner.

Like a pigging driving lesson. Turn, you bluebottle. Black pearls of sweat popped out on Moses' face and neck. He ripped off a sullen curse. The Panda made a leisurely right turn and went off down a slip road between naked trees and fat evergreen hedges. The driver was proffering his cigarettes and lighter as Moses moved off.

Moses accelerated and moved into a higher gear. He sped past the Crown-owned Nash terraces along the eastern edge of the park.

A full circuit would take all of ten minutes. Hot damn.

Moses made a U-turn and barrelled west, slowing where the Panda had turned, speeding up when he had passed. He was running with sweat now, and it collected in his crotch, prickling the waistband of his underwear. He wrinkled his nose at his own musk, knowing that the fastidious Eliades would complain on the long drive to Surrey. One day the whities would invent a deodorant that worked on Moses' strong body fluids.

Hell, some chicks like a man who smelled of strong meat.

Moses passed the main zoo entrance and coasted to a halt outside Coward's apartment block. Everything seemed normal and quiet. He craned to look up at the third floor. There was a neat double hole in the centre window. Moses felt his scrotum tighten.

Ellie had made the contract. But where was he?

Moses scanned the park railings, trying to see through the hedge. It was dark in there. Eliades could have missed the spot. Moses flashed the heads three times. He scooped up the Sterling and leaned it behind the seat where he could reach it easily. Then he leaned across and slid the passenger door open.

Nobody showed in the rearview mirror. Nobody walked anywhere. No traffic. Nothing.

Moses jerked his head towards the railings. Somebody was moving in there. Hands grasped the crossbar and a foot swung between the spearheads.

'Come on, man,' Moses urged. Eliades seemed to be having trouble.

Maybe he slipped on the roof. Twisted an ankle. Shit.

Moses slid along the seat and stepped down on to the pavement. He braced himself against the railings and reached up to guide Eliades' legs down on to his shoulders. One came down and bit into his bicep.

'Got you, man. Now the other one. That's it.' Thinking, *move ass.*

Moses was mildly surprised by how much Eliades seemed to weigh. Maybe he had heavy bones. It did not matter. What mattered was to get away from there fast. Moses grunted as Eliades dropped from his shoulders on to the paving behind him. The Cypriot must have eaten an elephant for dinner.

Moses turned to help Eliades into the truck. He was not there. Eliades rifle nudged the point of his chin and hot slate eyes glared into his, eyes he had seen briefly at the Bugalloo the night before. Now they were hard and flat under a mad frown.

This fucker gonna kill somebody.

'You ain't Ellie,' Moses said foolishly. He had time to blink before the rifle opened his cheek like ripe fruit. Then the pavement came up and mashed the opposite side of his face. After that he did not think much at all.

Coward leaned down and searched him. There was only money and the flick-knife. Coward picked Moses up by his belt and threw him into the panel truck, letting him land heavily. Then he handcuffed the negro by the wrist and ankle and rolled him into the back. When Moses woke up he was covered by the Sterling.

* * *

Her winds prevailed and rose to gale force.

The great eye circled and settled on a line between Aberdeen and Goteborg in Sweden. The great high-pressure front at her back fed her unstintingly. She grew secondary rings of power and she roared mightily, pushing the sea to the south.

The moon was exerting its influence as it rode above her. The sun, too, approaching conjunction with earth's satellite, pulled the tides upward, giving The Lady Kuklos more and higher seas to bend to her will.

10

Wednesday 3 October

21·56 hours

The saloon bar of the Magpie and Stump was deserted save for Dutton and Cave who had just eaten three courses of stodge in the dining-room. A log fire burned in the inglenook and the brass bygones nailed to the low beams shivered with reflected fire. A stuffed bear reared in a corner and mounted fish swam in cases. Cave swallowed half his whisky and water and belched long and softly. Rain shushed at the windows.

'That pie crust was made from cardboard and old shaving cream,' said Cave, holding back another bubble of wind.

Dutton suggested a game of cribbage.

'And that treacle pudding. Precast birdseed.'

Dutton washed his teeth with whisky. 'Has anyone ever told you what fun you are, Cave?'

'Not lately. Jesus, I can feel it setting.'

'You'll be suggesting we take a walk next,' said Dutton.

Cave's surprise could have been genuine.

'Who, me?'

'Yes, you.' Dutton jerked his glass in the direction of Poynter Hall. 'Up there. For a look around.'

'For what, particularly?'

'A deep freeze.'

Cave's 'Bollocks' was unconvincing. He forgot his digestion.

Dutton placed his empty glass on the table. 'That kid was stashed somewhere. Your round.'

Cave scratched a sideburn. 'You're getting at something, Inspector. Something more than another drink. You know what John Coward told me to do.'

Dutton pinged a nail against his glass.

'I heard. Buy a drink and think about it.'

'You mean *you* fancy trotting about up there with your Sexton Blake torch and Dick Tracy radio. You must be pissed.'

'Just enough.' Dutton's face was as smooth as a balloon. 'It beats chucking booze into our faces and snoring it off until morning. I've slept in the beds upstairs. You haven't. Anything's better than avoiding lumps in a mattress.'

Cave took the glasses to the bar and rapped a coin on the counter.

'Two large malts,' he told the barman who ducked around from the darts match in the public bar. The man was in such a rush Cave had to call him back to drop a shrunken ice cube into his glass. Cave returned to the table.

'Hardly worth the bother, was it? It's melted already. You should drink your booze like a Scot. Like me,' said Dutton, pouring water.

'I only do it to keep the staff on their toes. Christ, we invented pubs and we still run them like amateurs. No wonder Americans and Europeans laugh at us. Even the Irish have pros behind the bar.'

'Cheers.' Dutton drank with his teeth bared.

'You were serious,' said Cave.

'Malt drinkers always are.'

'No. About a fridge hunt.'

Dutton nodded with his eyes wide open. He blew smoke from a fresh Player. Somebody scored high in the other bar and was applauded. A glass shattered and somebody cursed. The silence came suddenly, broken by the loud, indistinct voice of a belligerent drunk.

Dutton sighed. 'Every time I go out for a quiet drink it happens. A drunk makes a scene. It's the copper's cross.'

'Shush.' Cave held up a hand.

'Don't hush me,' Dutton snapped.

'Listen. I know that voice.'

'Take it outside and sleep it off, Petrie,' said the barman. It had the sound of something he had said many times before. 'Go along now, lad.'

'Another one, Chas. C'mon. I'm celebratin', ain't I? They brown men got that bastard and hanged him. I knew he done it. I told you. I told all of you.'

'You talk too bloody much,' somebody said.

'Bloody rubbish most of it.'

'Have the bugger out, Chas. He's dis-bloody-gusting.'

'Yeah, Chas.'

'You don't put me out. None of you,' yelled Petrie.

'Don't forget he's lost his lad,' said Chas the barman. 'That earns a bit of charity. I don't want him muscled out. He'll go like a good'n, won't you, Petrie? They's coppers in the saloon. Don't want they to run you in, do you?'

'Coppers,' slurred Petrie. 'I'll show you coppers. I'll show 'em up for you.'

A door slammed open and closed and boots clacked along the interconnecting passage. Chas the barman ducked into the saloon bar, a paddle in his hand.

'Out,' ordered Cave. 'Back in the other bar.'

'On your head then.' Chas disappeared.

The saloon door crashed inward against its hinges and Petrie was there, weaving on unsteady legs. He was still unshaven and smeared with clay. He wore the clothes Cave had last seen him in. He fell in against the bar and a stool went over on its side. Petrie found the two policemen with his lidded eyes and he sneered elaborately.

'Buggering coppers,' he said. 'I've shot coppers. Shot 'em.' He pointed at Cave with a knotted fist. 'Seen you, copper. Haven't I seen you, eh?'

'You've seen me.' Cave made no move.

'Happens every time,' murmured Dutton.

'Leave him to me,' Cave said quietly.

'Pleasure.'

Petrie moved down the bar to where it curved back into the wall. He hung there drooling, the fist still pointed.

'Have a drink, copper. Have a big drink. We're celebrating, you and me. It's a fucking wake.' He laughed suddenly and swallowed something better spat out. 'They're both dead, see. Both of them. Laugh, eh? Laugh for you, copper. Big laugh for you. My boy and that fucking fat Ferris. You laughing are you, copper?'

Cave shook his head. 'No. What about you?'

Petrie threw his arms wide in a big sloppy gesture. 'I'm

bloody laughing.' He barely saved himself from toppling by grabbing at one of the beerpumps. Dutton half-rose out of his chair. Cave held him back.

'Let him talk.'

Petrie looked slyly around at an invisible audience.

'Hear that? Copper ain't laughing. Not laughing at all.' His slack yellow eyes swung back towards Cave. 'Should be laughing. They brown men hung the cunt. Right over there in they woods. Now my boy can rest. And me? What'll I do?' Petrie thought about himself, his chin tucked in against his filthy pullover. 'Yeah,' he said solemnly. 'What about me? D'you know, copper?'

Cave said: 'You tell me.'

'I'm celebrating. That's what. You want a celebration drink, copper? Drink with me?'

'All right.'

'Yeah?' Petrie grinned and giggled.

'I said so.'

Petrie's face contorted. 'You'll get some fucking drink. I'll give you drink.' He threw his head back, hawking in his throat. His head came forward and a gobbet of phlegm struck the beam above Cave's head. Some of it spattered his coat. 'There's your drink, copper.'

Cave did not move. His face was set. Almost pleasant.

Petrie glared owlishly.

There was no sound anywhere.

Then Petrie laughed. Loud and nasty barks that made the cords stand out in his neck. The laugh choked off and became a howl of loss that filled the room with an awful desolation.

Goosebumps grew on Dutton's arms. He swallowed all of his drink without tasting it.

When Petrie had laugh-howled enough he fumbled along the counter and went out through the door. His steps were slow, dragging things along the passage. A long moment later the outer door slammed and he was gone.

'Frigging Christ,' said Dutton.

'Yeah.' Cave agreed. 'Little brown men. You got it in one, John.

Dutton did not get it at once.

22·14 hours

The magpie on the painted sign swung with the wind and the unoiled metal hinges squealed. Rain made the magpie's feathers sleeker. Petrie liked the magpie. It held a full pint in its claws and had a knowing look. The magpie and Petrie were friends. When Petrie came for a drink it hung there outside the pub, waiting patiently in all weathers. When Petrie had a bellyful it watched him stagger home with big beady eyes and never a squawk of censure.

Petrie said good-night to the magpie and shivered. He could feel the shakes coming. He had to get home to the bottles of sweet cider he had hidden in the garden shed. When they were gone he would feel the click in his head and he would sleep like the dead. Almost as dead as Peter.

Petrie started walking. He ticked off the landmarks on his route automatically. There was the ring of white pudding stones around the pub forecourt. The slope down to the intersection where he must watch for traffic. Then the dark lane with its signpost to Salem woods where the brown men marched in line after nightfall. Then the leaning lamp-post and the long dark stretch of hedgerows where he must be careful not to trip in a rut or tumble into any of the flooded ditches. Then there would be the gravel path up to his cottage.

As he passed along the track beside Salem Wood his eyes hurt. He knew there was something out of place. Something different. He stopped and puzzled about it, shielding his eyes from the glare.

Two great fireflies hung in his way, guarding the path. Perfect orbs of light that lit him up and threw a long shadow away behind him into the darkness.

Unafraid, Petrie advanced between the lights and stumbled against the bonnet of a big black car. Petrie stroked the radiator and giggled to himself. He had solved the mystery. Drunk or sober he knew he was smart. He knew more than people thought he knew and he kept it all to himself. Even the marching brown men.

He liked them almost as much as he liked that old magpie.

'Petrie,' somebody said.

Petrie nodded. That was him all right. Feet scraped behind him and he pushed himself away from the car into the glaring headlights, blinding himself again.

'Hello, Petrie.' The voice was small and kind.

Petrie cuddled himself. Holding in the damned shakes. They spoiled everything. 'Going home,' he muttered. 'Home.'

'Of course. To your bottles of cider. Here's something better. Take it.'

An uncapped bottle was thrust into his hands and he smelled the spirit inside. He put the neck to his mouth and swallowed the whisky down. There were three mouthfuls, just enough to steady him. Not enough to make the click in his head. He let the bottle drop and wiped his loose mouth with the back of his wrist. It was all clear now. He knew who the voice belonged to.

'You're one of the brown men.' Petrie felt sly and knowing. 'I see you but you don't see me.' He was suddenly abrupt and erect. 'But I don't tell.'

'We know,' The small voice came from all around him. 'We knew about Ferris. We helped you. We gave you revenge.'

Petrie thought and nodded. He knew that.

'Now you have to do something for Peter. You on your own. There was another man who hurt Peter. Used him and killed him. An old and dirty man. He will escape, get away if you don't. Do you want that? Do you?'

Petrie shook his head. His hands hooked and extended, searching for a throat.

'He's in London, this foul old man. You must go there and kill him. Kill him for all of us.'

Again Petrie nodded. The brown men could not leave the wood. Here they could do anything. But not outside. He could go outside. Go anywhere. He thought of the foul old man touching Peter with yellow fingers. Hurting him. He squeezed his eyes closed in the blinding light and felt salt sting behind his lids.

'Where . . . tell me where?' he pleaded.

'St George's Hospital. On the third floor. Lying in bed pretending to be sick. You see how clever he is, this old man? If he is sick they will keep him in hospital where there is no justice. He will go free.'

'No,' Petrie promised the small voice. 'No.' He held his hands to his face and scrubbed away the tears that might mean weakness. There was a purr of an engine and the soft crunch of tyres. When Petrie lowered his hands he was alone.

He turned in a circle then began to run towards his home, the Land Rover and his shotgun.

22·15 hours

Coward waited for Moses to come back into awareness.

The home-movie of Maitland's stiff bearing melting into loose death played and replayed inside his head in full-colour and screaming stereophonic silence. Over and over. . . .

Coward wished he could bury his face in softness that smelled of lotions and natural girl. No face, no persona, just mounds and hollows and long legs he could wallow in until he felt quiet again. Not a package-deal of emotions and no's and coyness. No demands, no strategic headaches, no chocolates or flowers. Just the eternal mother-woman with no face. Gone at dawn with no face-powder on the pillow.

Coward shrugged himself straight. There was no time for that boy-man fantasy wishing. He had himself a black bantam to crack. How old was he, thirty? Younger? Good physique from working with weights, no fat. A trim one hundred and sixty pounds honed by steroids and jogging. Good cording in the neck and shoulders. Heavy wrists and dancer's legs. How much of him was ghetto blowhard? How much was built on the deeper, inner strength of the well-adjusted individual whose flag was his own?

The negro's lids fluttered. Nervous jerks of the limbs. The breathing changed rhythm, stepping up into small sips and long, shallow sighs. Both cheekbones were laid open and the closed left eye was as fat as a passion fruit.

The right eye batted sleepily, sorting in from out, light from shade, flesh from metal, Coward from the Sterling. A frown puckered the ridged nose and creamy white showed around the focused pupil. The pink tongue licked at the gap where a healthy tooth had lived.

'Shit, you fucked my smile.' The complaint was grounded in vanity. Delivered Caribbean soft. The mouth turned tough and petulant and the one good eye held Brixton cynicism, etched there by the mean streets and ghetto attitudes of South London.

The insolence died when Coward leaned into the light. Moses read his future there. Eliades had to be dead and he was going down the same deep pit. And he was not ready.

The more Coward just looked at Moses the more he *knew*. That man was *the* man. *Talk to the mother*. Die talking if you have to. But *talk*.

'Money buy anything?' he tried.

Nothing.

Moses nodded. 'Nothing, huh? How about talk? You want to hear anything I know? I know a lot of things. Lot of things.' *Try a smile. Maybe not*. 'Man, I *sweat* more facts than I do water. I'm known for it. Hey, when I dance I sweat. I could sweat a whole encyclopedia on the floor I'm so lively with facts.'

Silence. Just the grey eyes and the silver bore staring.

'If facts was lice, I'd be lousy with the mothers.' Moses ran with water. He wiped his face with his free hand and held out his wet palm. 'See? Come and collect some of this good stuff before it evaporates into thin air.'

No response.

'Don't read water, huh?'

Zero. The big fat O. Faster, Moses. That knuckle is whitening. Stop the flash from turning your ribs into a busted barrel.

'Names. I know names. That's it, you want names. I got 'em. Eliades. There's a name. Him.' *Sorry, Ellie. But hell, you flying higher than fucking Concorde. Me, I'm running just to stand still. I'll burn a candle if I stay breathing. Swear*. 'Cypriot guy. Shoots to contract, you know? He topped Mrs Pell. And uh, yeah, some City man. Name of Hudson. They were for the man in the Garden, you know?'

A nerve flicked Coward's lid.

Bingo and zap. That's the lost chord. Stay on target, Moses.

'You got him, huh? Eliades? Back there?' Moses nodded soberly. 'Yeah, I guess you did.' The eyes did a shy upward flick at Coward. 'You must be bad news. Ellie knew this was a bad contract. He was good, mister. A pro. Don't get me wrong, you got him and that's history. I just want you to know you wouldn't have if Kellerman hadn't nailed us to a time. Forty-eight hours. It was him got Ellie dead as much as you. He pushed us into making this mistake. You want Kellerman, I'll give him to you. Him for me, right?'

Was that a nod? Push for a yes.

'Two-way traffic, Mr Coward. You don't need me. Deal?'

'Depends,' said Coward.

'On what? Say it, you got it. Sheeit, I'm close to dead 'cause of that mother. It don't take no big brain to figure why I'm trussed here with my face all broken. Look at this face. There's something grating up here when I talk. You hit me, but that's down to Kellerman.' Moses shook his head violently, and spittle gleamed on his loose lips. 'Tonight, when we took the job, Ellie knew we were being written off. So what if he screwed up on that dish-washing lush? It happens. No *time,* see?'

'What about the dishwasher?'

'He was nothing. Somebody spotted him as a police snout. Ellie sent this new guy. Name of Riordon. From Dublin. Said he was bigshit in the IRA. He collected passports like trading stamps. He could shoot aspirin at twenty feet. But that don't make him a shooter. White tablets ain't a man. I told Ellie not to use him. Not that you tell Ellie anything. I said it anyway. He used him. Riordon tried a hit outside the club, man. Right outside the Bugalloo. Can you beat that? He missed, lost his gun, and raaaan for the boat-train. Man, I bet there was more in his pants than in his gut.' Moses grinned, winced and fingered his swollen gum. 'Nothing but chicken shit.'

'And Gerrard Street?' asked Coward.

The good eye showed white. 'I could lie. Make something up. But I won't. I don't know,' said Moses.

'I'd know if you did.' The eye of the Sterling could have been in a clamp. 'If Eliades knew . . . Kellerman . . .' Coward stumbled on the name. He sucked breath and tried again. 'If he knew Kellerman had him boxed, why did he take the contract?'

'We had to, Mr Coward. Kellerman figured Ellie screwed up on the dishwasher and owed him one. If the word went round, no more work. Eliades had to take it. They had Hammond up there. They cut on him with razor blades and he was about to swim the river in cement shoes. Ellie saved him from that. Said Hammond could finger you from eyesight, and that beats a photograph. I played dumb. Like I never got a real look at you when you threw me Riordon's gun. Sometimes it pays to look stupid instead of smart. That was one of those times. Hell, as it works out, I think Kellerman wanted us all together, all lumped together to make it easy for the clean-up team.' Moses laughed winced and smiled. 'Well, we moved too fast for that to work. We hit tonight instead of tomorrow. Would have worked too, if you hadn't . . . well, you know . . .'

'I know.'

Yeah? Well here's something you don't know, mother. 'If you hadn't happened, we'd have been half-way to Surrey for the second hit by now.'

You bit that, mother. That eyelid's flapping like semaphore. Moses leaned more comfortably on his free arm. 'Yeah, I'm stuck, Ellie's dead and old Hammond? Man, he'll be tucked up in his berth on that freighter to Rio. What you did to him in the Gents was mean. Funny mean, but mean all the same. That mother hates to be dirty. Old Hammond likes his linen clean.'

'That's enough.'

'Yessir,' said Moses.

'Tell me about Surrey.'

Moses looked sleepy. 'That's all you get for free, Mr Coward. You can't mash me much more. From here on you can only kill me. So, I think we continue this deal in a nice clean police station. With lights and lots of witnesses. Cups of tea and a constable taking things down on paper. I ain't very brave, but I know I got just one hand of cards left. You'll break me. In time. But you ain't got that kind of time left. I can hold out long enough to make what I know worth less than flyshit on a roll of sticky paper.'

Coward seemed to be thinking.

Moses went on. 'I'll give you it all. Written statements. Every last damned thing. And I'll get myself a nice official deportation order back to St Lucia. I wouldn't last a night in prison after I spill what I know. Queen's evidence, Mr Coward. Your bosses will yell and fuss and shit around, but they'll buy it. All the way.'

Coward's 'You're right,' was quiet. Ominous.

Moses missed it. 'Yeah,' he said, feeling better.

'I'll just have to kill you,' said Coward.

'*What*? You shitting me?' *This mother crazy.*

'No guns,' Coward could have been talking to himself. 'Beat you unconscious and float you down the canal.' He nodded, agreeing with himself. 'That's the only way.'

'You'll lose that way. You'll lose it all.'

Coward's arm blurred. Moses felt both legs go dead. The edge of Coward's hand struck both sides of his neck. There was no sensation. He was paralysed.

'This way,' said Coward. 'You'll know it's happening, and there won't be a damned thing you can do about it. How long can you hold your breath?'

22·38 hours

The black Bentley was back in the trees without lights.

Prebble walked up and down the path until he found the empty whisky bottle. It lay on a tussock beside the ditch. He gathered it up and took it back to the Bentley. It paid to watch details. He slipped off his galoshes and dropped them into a plastic bag, tied the end and tucked them under the seat. He fished the whisky bottle from his pocket and wiped it off with a wash leather. He dropped the bottle into another bag and put it back into his pocket. Then he sat and waited.

Minutes later, lights jogged into sight, gears clashed, and a muddy Land Rover bounced past. Petrie was at the wheel. He turned the Land Rover on to the main road in a slew of shale and roared away without pausing to check for oncoming traffic.

Prebble waited five minutes then drove back to the manor.

Petrie might kill himself on the motorway or get lucky, make it to St George's and kill Dutton's witness. Either way, it was a lottery he must lose. And either way, it made no real difference to Prebble. Any evidence the police might have would be lost in the coming confusion.

Confusion, he thought. *I like that. Such a deliciously innocuous word. Hardly sums up the holocaust I envisage.*

Prebble rolled the Bentley into his private garage to the rear of the stable yard and the electronic doors closed behind him. The same system cut in the overhead lights. Prebble pumped suds through a mixer tap and hosed the wheels and the mudsplashed body, sluicing off with cold water. The chauffeur would wax it tomorrow. Prebble rinsed off his galoshes and left them on the bench to dry.

Prebble let himself into the house and detoured through the kitchen where he fed the whisky bottle into the grinder, reducing it to powder. He went to his study, locked himself in and unlocked the telephone drawer. He dialled a local number and was answered with a simple 'Yes?'

Prebble said: 'O-six-hundred hours. Goodbye Piccadilly commences.'

The other end of the line was hushed.

'Repeat, please?' said Prebble.

'O-six-hundred hours. Goodbye Piccadilly commences. Roger, Leader.'

'Usual muster, twenty-three-hundred hours.'

'Understood.'

Prebble cleared down, locked up and went back to his guests in the withdrawing-room. Most of them seemed to have made for their beds. He patted Madeleine's hand in passing and did not notice her almost jerk it away. Her thoughts were in Nancy's bedroom.

'My sincere apologies, everybody. Something came up at the experimental station. How are your drinks?'

Calloway half-stretched from his chair, pale under his

tan.

Prebble smile-frowned at him.

'Taken care of,' he said. *Very much so.* He poured himself a generous brandy and beamed around the room. One last manoeuvre tonight and then . . . He moved Remy Martin over his tongue as *Tomorrow, tomorrow, tomorrow,* rang inside his head.

23·05 hours

Cave stepped out of his bedroom window, closed the sash behind him and inched along the sill of the pub fascia to the lower roof of the toilet block. He stepped down. The pegtiles creaked and held, slippery with moss and lichen. He crouched, gripped the gutter, swung over the lip, hung, then dropped to the ground. His toes made the barest scrape on the gravel. No lights showed, no dogs barked, nobody shouted alarm.

Cave walked around to his car, let off the handbrake and coasted down the slope of the carpark on to the road. When the car halted on the flat, he climbed out and pushed it another twenty feet. Then he turned the ignition and drove quietly towards Salem Wood.

'Not bad.' A match flared from the backseat and smoke billowed.

Cave reared in his seat. 'Jesus Q!'

Dutton grinned from the rearview mirror.

'I thought all that sudden yawning and scratching was a shill.'

Cave flathanded the rim of the wheel.

'Inspector, you're a . . .' He broke off, scalded by sweat. Then defensively. 'You were doing the same, dammit.'

'So I was. Must have caught the tireds from you.'

'I couldn't sleep.'

'Funny. Nor could I.'

'You catch that from me too?'

'Sure.' Dutton sounded comfortable. 'Watch you don't miss the turn.'

'What turn?'

'To Salem Cottage. That's where you're going. Park

the car and stroll across country to the manor? That's it, isn't it?'

Cave grunted irritably. 'Maybe. It wasn't clear.'

'Not like you Special boys, is it? I thought smart lads like you knew what you were about all the time.'

'Funny. That's funny.' Cave was not amused. He made the turn on sidelights, slow over the flooded ruts. He turned beneath the lych-gate and halted beside the cottage. The building was in darkness and the matted thatch dripped like wet hair.

'Right so far,' needled Dutton.

'So lay out the rest for me. If you please?'

'First I finish my cigarette. Can't go showing lights out there. Technically we're trespassing. Then into my gumboots and away we go. I have a flashlight and my plonker. Nine inches of sprung rod in a rubber sheath. Highly illegal and highly effective. It'll break a bone without bruising the surface of the most delicate skin. I confiscated it from a cabdriver who worked nights around the clubs. Specialized in drunks.'

Cave twisted over the driving seat.

'And what'll you do with it? Beat the deep-freeze until it confesses?'

One of Dutton's eyeteeth winked in the bad light. The red eye of his Player off to one side bobbed as he said:

'Come in handy for little brown men, I shouldn't wonder.'

'You picked that up too, eh?' said Cave.

'I get there, given time,' Dutton said comfortably.

Cave had no answer. He dropped the face of the glove compartment and slid aside the back panel. He pulled out two guns. The first was a ·22 Colt Woodsman with a custom stocked grip, chequered butt plates and a pyramid sight. He loaded it with steel jackets and tucked it into his shoulder clamshell.

The second was a gun Dutton had seen before. A Ruger ·33. Cave thumbed blunt-nosed magnum shells into the cylinder and passed it to Dutton without comment.

'You sure I won't give myself a nasty pedicure with that?'

'I know your range scores. Not bad for a CID inspector,' said Cave, no edge in his voice. 'You did a six-month tour in Belfast. Shot your way out of a roadblock with one of these. Got one of the sods too. Head and chest, wasn't it?'

'So they said.' Dutton sounded wistful. 'I don't like hardware.'

'That plonker of yours won't do much good at thirty feet.'

'I'll take my chances.'

'Nossir, you bloody won't, Sir. Here, twenty spare rounds should do. We ain't starting no war.'

Dutton said: 'Aren't we? Give me the Woodsman. I'll have to be close and sure to use it. It won't knock down a pudding unless it hits something vital.'

'Wrong, Inspector. I just hope I don't have to prove it to you. Ready for off?'

Dutton's cigarette glowed for a long, last drag then flew out of the opened back window.

'Yeah. Let's get our feet wet.'

23·20 hours

Platoon Sergeant Dennis crouched on the elevated platform built into the beech and watched his men advance through the broken ground in open order. The months of rigorous training were paying off in spades.

They covered the ground easily, carrying their weapons at high port, keeping point in the prescribed manner, using the sparse cover intelligently. They moved like wraiths, their dun uniforms merging with the general gloom, only their forward motion separating them from the terrain.

And this was the last training exercise.

In four hours' time they would be on their way to their targets. His squad would be the best. He had trained with the SAS in Germany, and he knew what his men would be up against if there were any opposition. He was not unduly concerned – if anything, the knowledge gave him an edge. Keened his senses.

Through his nightglasses he could see four other

platoons beating the slopes of the far valley rim. They would sweep down and meet his lads at the rendezvous in Salem Wood. His men could do it blindfolded. He hoped he had drilled them enough to follow the canal down to the lock and cross to the pumping station beyond as smoothly as they should.

He would know very soon.

The leader had struck medals for the occasion. Viewed as something of a joke at the moment, they would take on real significance after the successful assault. When they had brought down the bleeding-heart, left-wing pinkoes who held power. There was no 'if' in his mind. There was only a 'when'.

Hanging the Jewish pervert had hardened his men to the sight of death. A few of them had soldiered before in the regular forces, but not like this. He and the other sergeants had worked their men hard. Standard punishment had been a mile circuit in full pack at a dead run with a hundred fast press-ups at the end of it. At first, it had been resented. Then some of the lads had sought the punishment to set themselves against their fellows, a form of internal rivalry to prove their individual toughness.

The platoon sergeant believed the Nazis could have learned a lot from his lads. Toughness and smartness, that was the secret. He scraped his chin with his nails. He would shave before they pushed off. Shave and change his shirt.

He glanced idly towards Salem Wood. There was movement there. He raised his nightglasses and his lips thinned. The two coppers from the Magpie and Stump. He wished he had ground glass into their food when he had had the chance. Well, so be it. They would give his lads some sport when they crested the rise. A manhunt to limber them up.

He spoke into his radio, giving orders.

22·38 hours

The desk sergeant listened to his stomach growl as he manned the desk at Albany Street Police Station.

There was an hour or so to go before the drunks and dross were swept up and began to straggle in. The knife-cuts, the punk-rockers, the mugged old ladies who would carry their life savings in their purses when they walked their toy dogs. The odd junkie who talked to Martians, the odds-and-sods who slept rough in the park under wet newsprint. The self-confessed rape victims who might be on the game or wrongly accusing an ex-boyfriend, and the true victims of sexual assault, abused, confused and ashamed, most of them psychologically scarred for life. The sergeant had enough humanity beneath his callouses to treat the deserving cases kindly once he knew the score.

The desk sergeant watched the clock above the pretty WPC who typed reports with her long legs out ahead of her. Her tongue moved with her fingers as she stabbed at the keys. The sergeant rose above the contractions in his scrotum, blaming his desire on those bloody black stockings. Leave it to the young lads, they were better equipped. Had the stamina. Best for him to settle for his wife's more comfortable proportions and more reasonable demands of the flesh. He would be better off with a wad and a cup of tea in the canteen before the rush. He might get a game of cribbage in with the detective sergeant from CID for a penny a point. It would pay for the sandwich.

There was a scuffle at the door and a young black fell inside, one leg hooked up to his ankle. His face was a mess of blood and bruises. A tall white man with torn trousers pushed in behind and hauled the black up to the desk. He carried a . . .

The sergeant blinked as the Sterling banged down on the counter.

He tore his eyes away when the negro clutched his writing hand.

'Lock me up safe, man. This pig fucker gonna drown me. Gonna beat me shitless then slide me down in that canal. He gonna do it, man. I want protection. My fucking right, man.'

'Watch the language, laddy,' the sergeant said.

The standard caution for that time of night.

Coward identified himself with a flip of his wallet.

The sergeant sent for the detective sergeant and Moses was booked for unlawful possession of weapons. Coward hinted at a lot more charges and saw that the black was locked in the high-security cell. He was held under the aegis of 'Helping the Police with their Enquiries'.

Coward could not raise the Magpie and Stump on the telephone and nobody at the Incident Centre knew anything other than that Dutton and Cave had turned in for the night.

Coward knew otherwise but could do nothing about it for the moment. He made several other calls and left the station. Something in his face forestalled any questions. Moses was not the only one who saw death there.

* * *

Shipping fled from the North Sea where The Lady Kuklos held sway.

Those tankers that held station off Canvey Island battened hatches and threw out more warps. The storm cones were hoisted from the Faeroes to Portland. The seas mounted in the English Channel, held in check by the winds from the great eye in the North Sea. They banked higher and higher. And higher.

11

Wednesday 3 October

23·30 hours

The two policemen left the thick pinecover and crossed the raw stretch where tall elms had formed a stately barrier until flying insects poisoned them with fungus. Their rotted stumps were all that remained of their previous elegance, and young oaks had been planted in the gaps; thin saplings with few leaves and a century and a half to wait for their maturity. Another instance of Prebble building for the future.

Cave led Dutton down across the sucking flanks of the swollen river to the ornamental bridge. The slatted floor was awash and uprooted reeds had caught up in the rustic lattice, forming a slushy tangle underfoot. The stream had risen by more than a foot since the morning. Part of the bank had fallen away and a muddy wallow had formed on the sunken path.

The race pulled at their feet as they crossed to the shored gully that led off to the copse where Ferris had been found hanging. The elm uprights leaned inward from the crumbling walls and water ran from the plaited wattle.

'We'd better keep to the centre,' said Cave. 'The whole lot could come down any time.'

Dutton looked dispirited. One of his boots leaked and the whisky had died hard in his stomach.

'How far does this run?' he asked.

'About a hundred yards. Let's get on.'

'Whose idea was this anyway?'

'You're the senior officer.'

'Only on paper. I keep rolls of it in the loo.'

They sloshed on.

A fattened moon, one night away from waxing full, batted above the thick, erratic cloud. Playing peek-a-boo through the dull heave of low cumulus. Clarity then obscurity, detail then blackness. The two men climbed out on to the higher ground and waited for the maverick light to show them the valley.

Cave fished out his nightglasses and leaned against a silver birch. He scanned the immediate foreground and swept the skirts of Salem Wood. A hump of dullness moved and dropped. And another. He held on the spot and saw nothing. The light came and waned and came again. Still no movement. Then, just as the light fell again, a scurry and a fall from sight. The gleam of a rifle butt.

Cave made another, slower sweep. For a moment the rippled ground was alive with dim brown figures. Then they were gone as quickly as they appeared. Three, perhaps four squads, moving three-four-three in classic open order. A skirmishing line.

'Company,' he told Dutton. 'Here.'

He was handing Dutton the glasses when the birch rocked, chunking as lead drove into it in a controlled burst. Bark spat off in flat scales. The thwap and plod of disturbed air across the bridge of his nose and more holes in the tree.

The world slowed down as Cave moved.

He ducked in behind Dutton, scooping at his waist, heaving him up and away and down. Throwing himself into a dive on to his back, using the slope and their joint momentum to kick into a second roll.

Exertion and gravity took them from the ridge where concerted fire kicked clods and shale into the air. Scything off into the brush, driving into the copse with crisp little ticks.

They slid together and fetched up abruptly.

Cave heaved Dutton from off him, scrabbling around to face the upslope. Thinking, *dead ground to the left. Below us.* That was where the red darts had winked. Not from the squads flanking the woods. *They must have been waiting for us.* He waited for the firing to die.

Dutton's sheepskin had sprung its lower toggles and the skirt had ridden up under his arms. His belly heaved for breath. He rolled clumsily on to his side and worked the wet leather down around him. He somehow had the

Ruger in his hand at the same time. His hat had gone.

'Are you hit?' he asked hoarsely.

'No. You?'

'No. How come I don't feel lucky?'

Cave hawked moisture into his mouth.

'How should I know? They should have carved us three ways from Wednesday.'

'Deliberate, you think? Playing with us?'

A light knocking. Bark and twigs showered down around them. The bump of silenced automatic fire. Both men hugged the ground until it ceased.

Cave elbowed his way up the ridge. Cautious. Just below the brow a sapling fell in two and something slapped into the ground near his head. He allowed himself to slide back until he was beside Dutton.

'They've got us on two sides,' he said.

'And the third?' Dutton's voice came from the top half of his mouth.

'We're going to have to find out,' said Cave.

'Back down *there*. They catch us in the trench . . .' Dutton did not have to finish. He added, 'What about back behind us?'

'Open ground. Then a sharp dip. Down to an ornamental pond. No way round. Not now it's flooded.'

There was a flurry of single shots.

'And then what?' asked Dutton.

'What when?'

'When we go through that gully thing. There's open ground on the other side. Like a fucking fairground. Two rubber ducks.'

'You want to stay here?'

'No.'

'Then?'

Dutton shrugged in sudden bare moonlight. 'The next dark phase.'

'Right.'

The dark came almost immediately. Dutton turned on his own axis and sledged himself down the mudslick with an improvised butterfly stroke. Cave followed in much the same manner. They fell into the gully and helped each other upright.

'You know what I'd like?' panted Dutton, his face and hair thick with ochre mud. 'A demotion and a Noddy bike on traffic patrol.'

'See that your gun's clean,' ordered Cave.

'It's inside my shirt. Come on.' Dutton began to plod along the gully. He moved ten paces on one side, crossed over, walked ten more. It was a sensible pattern. Cave timed himself to do the same, out of phase with Dutton. That way they would not be an easy double target. They were about a hundred feet in when Dutton fell forward. Cave closed up on him, crouching against the bulging wattle.

'What?' he whispered.

'There's been a fall.'

'Damn. How bad?'

'About fifteen feet. The whole section's come down. We'll have to go over it. Don't touch the bloody sides. I'll go. Then you. Right?'

Cave nodded. Realized he could not be seen and said, 'Go ahead.'

He heard the ragged breathing, the creak of wattle. The sucking mud on Dutton's legs. Then a long silence. His ears ached from listening. The moon showed again and he used the light to watch their backtrail. It was empty. *Of course,* he reasoned. *Why bother exposing themselves? Easier to come up along the top and shoot down into the trench.*

There was a floundering and Dutton was back down beside him. He had lost a gumboot. The moon hid itself again.

Dutton was snatching his breath.

'Can't do it. Like walking through glue.'

'Okay, okay. Listen, it wouldn't have worked anyway.' Cave had worked out a gamble. 'They'll be all along this stretch by now. Probably boxed us in anyway. One thing to do. Stay right here.'

'What!'

'Keep it down. Think about it, Inspector. Let them backtrack. Let them find the fall. Let them come to us.'

Dutton sounded grim. 'You want to make that sound attractive?'

'Not trying to. You want to try climbing that shit again?'

'All right. I'll buy it. I don't have to like it.'

Cave grinned through filth, desperately humorous. 'You couldn't get through that slide. Neither can they. At least we don't have to watch our backs.'

'Great. Just the top and sides,' said Dutton. A smiling mud monster. He wished he had lost the leaking gumboot rather than the sound one. He said good-bye to his pension and retirement in his garden. It did not seem much to say anything to.

Cave's hand covered his mouth, silencing what he was about to say. The other hand pointing. A figure showed on the right bank. And another. Brief sightings of crouched men. Dutton nodded against the palm and it went away. He felt for the Ruger.

Cave could have been waiting for range targets to swivel at Bisley. There was no more doubt. He was doing what he was trained for. And that took all his concentration. He covered the slopes of the backtrail, leaving the top and rear to Dutton.

Dutton remembered the manual: reload after the first two clusters. Never leave yourself with an empty gun. *Who ever figured they'd need to remember it?*

A figure bobbed above him and ducked back again. Dutton gripped the wrist of his gunhand and braced an elbow against a raised knee.

And waited.

The wattle plunked and grew ragged spurs. Cave fired twice. The man behind the gun went down faster than he had raised up.

Two men came up on Dutton's side. He was thinking, *Good. They have to show themselves to get a shot in*, long after he had fired and dropped one of them for certain. There was some floundering in the bushes and a weight slapped down into mud. *Was that number two?*

Dutton was both agonized and exhilarated. *It was all so stupidly final.* He flopped down into the slurry as long bursts reached down into the gully from all sides. He felt a punch in the side that made him breathless. And calm.

Dutton fired two-handed at what might have been his

imagination. It cried out like a child and bounced down beyond the mudfall. He sucked in his breath as air got into his wound.

Cave had thumped off more shots and was reloading like a drill. Dutton watched him with dreamy intensity. There was a strange clarity to everything. The mud under his belly. The hair growing on his chin. The weight of his clothes on his back. The chips of water as shots struck into the ground near him. It was like that achingly wonderful moment before sleeping after a twenty-hour day. Just before one allowed sleep to come. When the pillow was crisp under your head and your body warmth hadn't permeated the bedding. That space in time filled by the ticking alarm at the bedside, the thump of blood in the temples. The last squeeze of the hot eyelids before sublime nothing came. The dead sleep that should be put off to savour the very need for it.

The pain was becoming a distant thing. Something outside the core of himself. *I'm retreating. Or is the rest of life ebbing from me?* Dutton wanted to go with the warmth but a chill was growing somewhere deep down. Roaring up to shake him, to bring him back to the caring, cold reality of the gully. That part of him that would not let go. Not take the easy way. Then the pain was a shrieking cleaver in his side, and breathing was a hard won and shuddering thing. Take in the air, hold it, let it go in a thin whistle that wouldn't jar the torn parts.

Reload, he told himself.

The shells were as long as cigars and as slippery as fish. The shell chamber was a dancing pinhead that would not stay still. One in. Then two. A third and a fourth.

Dutton craned to see the rim of the gully. It seemed closer and yet farther away. He carefully supported his gun-arm. His fingers had no strength. Cave was not firing. *I can't look away to see for certain. If he's gone, I hope it was fast for him. This lingering is for invalids.*

There was a spattering of falling mud gobbets. An upright near Dutton bowed inward and struck the opposite wall. A section of wattle slid down and over on to its face under a fall of earth and clay. A tree on the rim teetered and started down. There was a liquid tearing. A thick, viscous rending that shook the ground under Dutton.

The rim is closer. The whole thing's coming in.

'Cave. For Chrissake.' Dutton found his voice a croaking wail. Stuff was falling all around him. On to him. He pushed himself up on to his knees with the world swimming about. Men called and choked and the sounds were almost tactile. Dutton had his back against the wall and made his legs push him up over the shifting earth. He felt wattle under his sock and kept his feet on it, readjusting his balance with his arms and head. Keeping upright.

There was a man near him, covered by the slide, mud running into his opened mouth, drowning his eyes and his forage cap. Then he was gone. Dutton scrabbled upward, ever upward. He was slipping back. Then his heel was gripped, steadied and pushed. He was over the rim, rolling into brush, holding the Ruger like a talisman. Somebody was heaving up beside him. It could have been anybody. No, there was enough blue left to be the shoulder of a raincoat.

'Cave,' sighed Dutton and passed out.

The figure next to him emptied his mouth and stomach of cloying mud then crouched up, holding the Woodsman out, arcing it back and forth for targets. There were none. He stayed there until he was certain, then pulled Dutton up on to his shoulder and went through the copse in the direction of Poynter Manor.

12

Thursday 4 October

The Lady Kuklos held her position and her power increased.

24·06 hours

Cave could not say how much time had passed. A few seconds more than for ever. Dutton lay beside him in the copse, limp and silent. His heart still bumped along and Cave had covered the blue hole in Dutton's belly with his sweater and tied it around with most of his shirt. Cave ducked as combat boots padded past along the rim of the gully. Voices called and torches snapped on. Swearing and low instructions. Cave realised he had to think like Coward would think. Work through the problem and assess it from both sides. Make suppositions.

That gully had caved in like a mine shaft, bringing most of the brown men with it. They were buried back there. The rescue party must assume that he and Dutton were under the fall too. They had to.

Okay, assume they do.

The trail back to Salem Cottage would be patrolled by them. They would leave nothing to chance. There was no way out across the ornamental pond. That left one way. Down through the valley and across to the big house.

Then what? Take hostages? Think it through. Think beyond the immediate problem.

Prebble was playing soldiers. Had a private army. There were dossiers on such people. Gentleman farmers, right-wing reactionaries whose farm workers drilled and swallowed all that Column 88 garbage. The fear of the left-wing pressure groups. Union power. Immigrants whose skin was not as their own. The fear of difference. Fear for the purity of the race. Fear of the Russian and his infiltration. Fear of wealth taxes. Fear of the phoney equality Socialism brought by levelling down class, income, education and the traditional rights of the squire, the landowner, the man of property. Fear of change for change's sake. Fear of devaluation and not merely in the fiscal sense.

Devalued language, morals and manners.

Prebble would not see these changes as evolution, rather as revolution backed by red flags, muddle-headed liberalism, humanism and the great dead weight of the masses who followed the militants with enthusiastic apathy. Slicing more from a national cake that had once been owned by the few and their forebears for generations. Prebble must think it was time to take back the cake. To strike at the society he despised, to . . . *to what?'*

Cave did not know. He found too many complications in this simplistic view. He missed Coward who would rationalize the extreme views of the right, temper and sift them until he had isolated the core of looniness and made it laughable. Much as he would those equally nutty postures of the radical left.

But he was not here. Cave dropped it.

The way down into the valley seemed clear. Clearer than Cave's summation of Prebble's likely aims. He would find shelter. A doctor for Dutton. Find a telephone and get to Coward somehow.

Cave pulled Dutton's bulk on to his shoulder and began working his way through the copse. Thinking of nothing save keeping his feet and employing all the available cover. Making his lungs labour as quietly and as efficiently as possible. To keep going.

24·08 hours

Flashlights played over the fall of earth and men dug in the soft flanks searching for bodies. They had pulled one man out alive. Another was being worked on. The platoon leader watched it with a sour stomach. After a headcount he figured he had lost three shot dead and four more had to be buried in the mud with the two policemen. He would have to borrow men from the other squads. Men trained for similiar but different targets. He calculated them as casualties, working on the contingency plan he had in reserve.

His radio crackled, pinged and said: 'Report, Alpha-Five.'

'Alpha-Five, Leader,' he said. 'My status, seven lost. I say again, seven lost. The two subjects are believed lost too. I say, lost too. Over.'

There was static. Then, 'Understood, Alpha-Five. Make certain.'

'Affirmative, Leader. Out.'

A muddy private came up out of the gully shaking his head.

'A fucking daft way to start things off, Chas. I could use a pint of your ale now.'

Chas looked cold. 'Platoon Sergeant to you, Private. And don't ever use my Christian name again. Two demerits.'

'Dock my pay as much as you like, Chas. It won't bring Billy and Angus back. They're down there under that crud. You want to tell their mother, do you?'

'I'll forget you said that, Minschull. See what you can do, lad.'

The private saw Chas's face in brief moonlight. There was no room for argument. Nobody had forced him to join and there was no time for second thoughts now. He reslung his Armorlite and saluted.

'Yes, Platoon Sergeant.'

'Carry on.'

24·48 hours

Cave made it over the stile, stepping down into cloying mud.

The wind battered around him, almost a support for his back as he stumbled on across the ploughed field, bowed under Dutton's increasingly dead weight.

Something ahead was whining and clattering erratically. It irritated him. Set his teeth on edge. The wind was in his ears and eyes, blinding him with rain and deafening him to everything other than the clatter and whine.

He came abreast of the noise and recognized it for

what it was. The warning sign on the electrified fence. He no longer wished to curse it, it was friend, a beacon, a pointer. He was close to the drive to Poynter Manor. Just a few more yards and he would be walking on tarmac. He found the strength to lengthen his stride, to bear up under the inspector's weight.

The night turned upside-down and he was flailing in space.

He fell into the ha-ha without seeing it, losing Dutton in the rusty old nettles; falling up against the edge of the private road. He had to lie still. Just for a while. Close his eyes and enjoy the singing lightness above his cramped shoulders. It felt so good.

No, he had to go on. They were everywhere.

Cave found Dutton and hauled him up on to the road. He could not lift him although he tried with everything he had. His arms were cracked and his spine was jelly. His legs would not straighten, not even without Dutton's weight. Cave struck at his thighs with his fists and made them ache all the more. It did not help. He was used up. Nothing left.

He caught the sound of a motor changing up. Lights were turning on to the drive from the Manor. They would run him down. And Dutton. Cave drew the Woodsman and sank on to the road, aiming between the approaching beams, waiting for them to run him down, or stop and open the doors, to climb out to fire. Or take him alive. Whatever, he would take somebody with him.

The engine slowed and died down and the heads became dipped beams. The engine idled. The interior light came on as the driver's door gaped. Cave lined up on the single face there. A smooth oval with woman's hair. Huge eyes and a generous mouth he knew from another time when Coward had been married to them.

Then Nancy was beside him in the road. Calling his name. Helping him up.

'Not me, him.'

'You first, Frank. You first.' The deep voice taking charge as usual. Making decisions.

'You bolshie bitch. He's shot.'

'Stand up, Frank. I can't carry him alone.'

Cave told her not to be so smart-arse reasonable. When she slapped his face he saw things more reasonably himself.

24·06 hours

Gennaro's excellent pasta had not helped Kellerman's acid stomach. He could feel the gases building under his waistcoat.

He should have gone to bed with a toddy and a novel.

Instead, he was fretting in his darkened office with his two minders yawning in the vestibule. His eyes were sandy and the questions he asked himself grew a thousand ancillaries. All footling. All unnecessary. So many bluebottles buzzing around hung meat. Wave them away and they came back in thicker clouds. He should take a pill and sleep.

Kellerman mixed seltzer in water and drank it down when it was all but fizzed out, belching carefully. The body is a temple, he told himself. He should rest it before taking tomorrow's midday flight to Zurich. Let those he paid worry. He could stay in touch from Switzerland. Be informed about the outcome of the contracts and the flooding river. *If* it happened.

Eliades would take care of Coward and Prebble. The contractors would settle Eliades and the spade. And that gutless schmuck, Hammond.

With Prebble gone to the great social-climber in the sky, he, Kellerman, would finally control the consortium. None of the other guinea-pigs, all those toffee-nosed mucky-mucks from Old County, those bloody Belgravians with their cut-glass accents and elevated noses, could run a Monopoly game, let alone a consortium that would deal in billions.

Kellerman could and would. And when they knew what Prebble had done to them in the past, they'd get used to the idea. Money softened any blow, salved any conscience. He had never liked the other part of it anyway. Let the City bullion sink under the river mud and stay there. Let the whole banking fraternity of the City go hang. Let the government resite itself until the

Thames flood was over. Let them scurry around trying to evacuate London. Declaring Martial Law. Shooting looters. Chaos. Trying to make political currency out of that was crazy. Who needed it? Profit not politics.

Too much was being made of Calloway's predictions. Smart college boys. Two a penny. All the same. Brains and theories and no experience of life. Calloway's blisters came from the handle of a tennis racquet, not the handles of a street barrow for two shillings a week.

The telephone warbled.

Kellerman had it raised to his ear before his thoughts had disengaged properly. There were pips from a street telephone, a coin dropped and a voice said:

'Look out of the window, Kellerman.'

'You what?'

'The window. Look out of it. I'll hold.'

Kellerman pressed a button on his desk, his mouth dry. One of his minders looked around the door. Kellerman cupped the mouthpiece.

'Look out of the window.' He bobbed his head at the phone. 'Some nut on the line. What's in the street?'

The big minder spread the slats of the blind with two fingers.

'Some berk's parked his truck on the double-yellow line. Hey, that's Eliades' rig. What's that doing there?'

'You're sure?'

'Yeah, that's the bubble's wagon all right.'

Kellerman uncovered the mouthpiece. 'What's the gag?'

'Like Gerrard Street, Kellerman. No gag. You've got maybe two minutes to live.'

'Eliades?' said Kellerman, not placing the voice. 'That you?'

'He's past tense, little man. One minute and fifty seconds.'

Kellerman's pores opened like craters. He wanted to talk, to make a deal. Threaten. Nothing came to him.

'Listen, you . . .' he blustered.

'Goodbye, Kellerman. They won't find enough of you to fill a teacup.' The connection broke and the available tone buzzed. Kellerman dropped the phone as though it were hot.

'He says there's a bomb in the truck.'

'Who says?'

'I don't know. Him on the line.'

Scar tissue creased as the minder frowned.

'No. Oldest trick in the book that.'

'He said like Gerrard Street.'

'How'd he know about that?'

Kellerman's suit seemed to grow wrinkles and gas hurt his gut. His eyes and mouth were cramped and rimed with sweat.

'He said one minute and fifty . . . *Christ Alive*! The back way.'

'Yeah,' The minder was no longer slow. He made for the door with Kellerman clawing at his back. In the outer office Kellerman halted to tear at the drawers of his secretary's desk.

'The keys,' he screamed. 'We need the keys.' *Where did the silly bitch keep them?* The rear door was hardly ever used. Was barred and locked. *Christ, so was the desk.* 'Tony,' Kellerman yelled. 'Come back here and bust this bastard.'

The big man halted, stopped explaining the situation to the other minder, plodded back into the office. He threw the desk on its side and punched down at the upper, central drawer, mashing his knuckles. The wood splintered and gave. He ripped away the face and pulled out the rest of the box. Stamps, ribbons, notebooks and a cashbox spilled on to the floor.

'In the cashbox,' yelled Kellerman.

Tony smashed it with his foot. It buckled and held. He grabbed it up and ripped off the lid. The keys skittered off under a drinks cabinet.

'Hurry, you clumsy fuckup.'

Tony overturned the cabinet and it crashed against the door, slamming it closed. Kellerman scrabbled for the keys as Tony tried to pull the jammed cabinet from the door. His swollen fist gave him little purchase. He tore a nail and the top split across. The other minder hammered from the other side of the door, twisting the handle. The cabinet heaved away with a squeal of flaking paint and its doors slid open. Bottles and engraved glasses chinked out. The door burst inward as the second minder put his shoulder to it. He fell inside to embrace Tony who reared back against Kellerman. The three of them milled around in broken glass until Kellerman made a break. All three made for the stairs, ignoring the stately lift.

First floor. Ground floor. Basement.

They hit the rear door with Tony fumbling for the lights and Kellerman sorting the keys on the ring. He had no idea which key was which. A bare bulb clicked on.

'Here.' Tony snatched the keyring from Kellerman's hand, wrenching his ringfinger and smearing his cuff with blood.

Tony turned the Yale and locked it open. Then the combination Chubb. A bell clamoured.

'You've set off the alarm,' Kellerman raged.

Tony unlocked two bolts with the third key. The door opened and they were out in a cobbled yard in the rain. The walls were eight feet high.

'Help me over.' Kellerman flattened himself against the wet bricks.

Tony bent over, caught Kellerman's thin ankles and raised him above his head. Broken glass studded the top of the wall. Kellerman looked down at Tony, slapping the wall.

'Let me down. You'll have to throw me over. Mind the glass. Watch the suit.'

Tony let Kellerman down, gathered him and threw him up and over.

Kellerman felt glass rake at his waistcoat. A sensation of vertigo. Then he crashed down into a mews, rolling amongst garbage and dustbins. His head struck a pile of leaning paving stones and his hand slapped down into something disgusting. The cobbles beneath him ran with filth.

'Idiot,' he yelled. *Where am I?*

He found his feet. The mews ran off into the covered market. The opposite end was a cul-de-sac. Fruit crates and old cartons were piled everywhere. Much of the cardboard had been trampled to a slurry underfoot.

Lazy, degenerate bastards.

Kellerman jogged stiffly towards the market. *How much time had passed? One minute? More?* He quickened his pace, panting from the exertion. *More golf. More walking*. He must make more time for good exercise in the future. He reached the corner and looked back. There was no sign of Tony. Neither man had yet climbed the wall. *I can't wait. Think of number one.*

Kellerman pushed himself out of the mews, planning to make off down Henrietta Street. Cross Long Acre into Neal Street and the allnight garage. Get to the Rolls.

His feet left the ground and his shirt collar burst. There were knuckles in the back of his neck. He was slammed over a market stall. A hand gripped his windpipe, the thumb driving up under his jaw. Pinning his carotid artery with crushing pressure. He could not draw breath. Shout. Swallow. The yellow street lights blurred. Somebody was handling him like a doll. Like some *nebish*.

He felt outrage more than fear. Concern for his image. His suit.

Red darkness lapped his vision, making it hard to think. He was being hauled away, held by the throat and the seat of his trousers. Cobbles jogged past. Sodium turned the puddles orange. The pressure yammered in his head and made mush of his reasoning powers. He slid into a greyness of bursting lights, his cheeks burning, his eyes bulged and blinded.

There was nothing but being carried too easily.

An alarm bell rang close by. A metal door slid on runners. He was dropped on to a moulded metal floor. The door slammed and a motor caught. The floor bumped along beneath him and he curled up into himself, his thumb between his teeth. Sleep would give his brain the oxygen it was starved of.

He went under.

24·52 hours

He was kicked aware.

He should have been left. He needed his six straight

hours. Where was his orange juice and morning paper? He made to rub his eyes and found his arm would not come up. A stroke in the night? Kellerman worked on the theory that something was terribly wrong. He opened his eyes and proved it.

He was tied behind the wheel of the truck. Lashed upright in the driving seat. Cold metal bored at his throat, propping up his head. He peered down at himself and his stomach gas bubbled. The butt of a rifle was jammed between his bound ankles and the business end was aimed up into his jaw. His questing thumbs found the chill curve of the trigger inside its guard. One press in the wrong place and he would have . . . He jerked his thumbs away and dug them inside his contracted fists.

'Very wise, little man,' somebody said.

The voice on the telephone.

Kellerman eased his head to the left.

A man leaned against the opened offside door, one foot up on the sill. His calf showed through a rip in his trousers. The glow from his drawn cigarette showed a little of his face.

It was enough.

'Coward,' Kellerman croaked. He had a blinding headache.

The truck was parked on wasteland. One of those spots property speculators saved for infills. The backs of advertising hoardings ran all around the plot save for a gap that showed an oily stretch of river. There were cranes above the opposite bank, lights burning on their arms and cabs. Kellerman knew nobody came there. Knew it with dread certainty.

'You think you can get away with this?' Kellerman protested.

'I already have, little man.'

'You've gone off your head. Your superiors . . .'

'Look around you, Kellerman. Do you see any superiors?'

'You're . . . *Meshuggennar*. Crazy.'

'Probably. And that makes you in deep trouble. I can do whatever I damned well please. I plan to. Your plan went sour. The Cypriot is dead and Moses talked himself dry. You pushed them along too fast. They missed me and killed the wrong man. Commander Maitland. You know him, *knew* him, didn't you?'

'I know lots of people. Enough people to finish you, Coward. What should I know from this Maitland?'

Coward's move was almost casual. Kellerman's leg flared with agony. He nodded forward and the rifle bit into his bruised throat. He jerked his head back, gasping.

'All *right*. I know Maitland. Satisfied?'

'Better. What did you have on him?'

'Nothing. Not me. Prebble . . . maybe.'

'Maybe?' The soft question and the harsh pain.

'Ahhh . . . Prebble had something on him. Prebble.' Kellerman blinked tears away and tried to sound reasoning. 'Maitland was bent. Prebble had letters. Letters Maitland wrote to a young man. Years ago when he was at the university. Oxford, I think. Prebble bought them and got to Maitland through Peveril-Saunders. Prebble wanted his file pulled. That was the price. It's not a stroke I would have pulled. They were innocuous by today's standards. I mean, what's so terrible? Nowadays they do it out on the street and make the buses swerve. Who notices? I think nothing either way.'

Coward struck out and the leg ballooned with pain. Kellerman took a while to get his breathing straight.

'Where are these letters?'

'Please . . .'

'The letters, Kellerman.'

'In Prebble's safe. In his house. The study. Don't take it out on me. Just ask, I'll tell.'

'Any copies?'

'No. Straight.'

Coward pushed smoke into the night.

'Who put the contract out on him?'

'On who?'

'On Prebble. You?'

'Who says so?'

'Moses. Me.'

'No, that's crap.'

Coward's arm flicked and the fingers dug at the

kneecap. Kellerman's view of the night exploded. He rocked inside his bonds.

'All right. Yes, for Chrissake. I did. So *what*? Is this a court of law? Are you judge and jury? This is just you and me. Charge me and I'll do what I always do. The way I've always fucked you in the past. Buy the best legal brains there are. Deny all this. Be back on the street before your ears have stopped burning.'

'We'll see, little man.'

Kellerman almost spat at Coward. The pain gave him a strange courage.

'You should thank me for trying to have Prebble hit. He's crazier than you are. The financial part of the deal was terrific. That I could go with. But muddying it all up with this political shit? Out, mister. He had this plan to knock over the bullion vaults. The river is supposed to flood and he wanted to use that as a cover to take the gold out of the vaults. And that's not all. He had plans . . . make your cock play like a penny whistle. I don't know the details. I didn't get involved. But I can guess.'

'There was a map of the Thames in the Bugalloo safe. Marked with the flood areas. Bigger than the official estimates. You wouldn't know about that either, would you?'

Kellerman flinched, watching Coward's hand. His knee pulsed with heat, swelling visibly. He wanted to bite a knuckle.

'So I knew. I heard the deal and said no. I stuck to no.'

'Hammond said otherwise,' Coward lied.

'Hammond knew nothing. He was to organize some transport from here to the Continent. For the bullion. He screwed that up. Another reason I said no.'

'You must have thought twice before saying no, Kellerman. You blew up half of Gerrard Street to make certain your involvement stayed a secret.'

'You can't hang me with that.' Kellerman spoke too quickly, stumbling over the words, piling them up.

'Not in a court of law.'

'That's right.'

'Tell me about it anyway. Between you and me.'

'What's to tell? That dishwasher had to go. Eliades

recognized him as a copper's nark. Eliades had some Mick see him off. He botched it. The bomb made certain. I don't get involved. It's business.'

Coward leaned close enough for his breath to whisper against Kellerman's shivering cheek.

'So, good-bye Goldy Stern. And the little man keeps his hands clean. Just business.'

'You see,' said Kellerman, racing again. 'That proves it. I didn't even know his name. You see?'

Coward pushed himself away and watched the lights running with the river. His jaw clenched as though he bit off a yawn. He said:

'And now we come to Ferris. Do I have to freshen your memory?'

Kellerman pulled his leg as far from the door as the webbing would allow.

'Ferris? The mouse who worked for Prebble? He worked on this flood thing at Prebble's laboratory place. He's another bent one. Boys loving boys. You never saw it when I was at school. People made the best of things. Prebble had to dump him. He was an embarrassment. Those crazy toy soldiers of his found out somehow (who knows how?) that Ferris was a nancy. They beat him up a couple of times. Phoned him up in the middle of the night. Stuff like that. Ferris threatened to go to the police, cried all over Prebble's desk about it. Prebble had to let him go. He had enough of his own skeletons to hide.'

'Ferris confessed to assaulting and killing a boy-scout.'

Kellerman looked up from his knee.

'That little pouf? No way. He wouldn't pick flowers in case he hurt their stems, he was so tender-hearted. Him? No. Look elsewhere, Mister policeman. Do me a favour. I told you, skeletons.'

Coward's sudden, direct gaze made Kellerman feel naked. Hatred was too small a word to describe what showed there.

'Skeletons?' he said. Harsh and distinct.

'Yeah, skeletons. Prebble's fucking skeletons. Don't you get it?'

Coward made an impatient gesture.

Kellerman fled on.

'Prebble runs this column thing with a number. Column 88. Big deal *fascisti* fellows. Uniforms. Guns. Loudmouths. Bully boys who hate queers and talk dirty about yids, wogs, coons and pakkies. All that ethnic *schtick*. Those badmouths make the National Front seem like sweethearts from Sesame Street. You got it yet?'

'Keep going, little man.' Coward was dangerously close to exploding.

Kellerman took a huge breath.

'Listen, I'll go back to the beginning. I check out everybody I get involved with, right? I have a team of investigators who make your outfit sick. They're pros. One of them's a girl. Smart. She fell over this Sadler, a reporter who makes Prebble his life's work. She conned her way into his files and skimmed off the good stuff. She gave that to the fellows on the team and they went back to year one. When Prebble was ten he was expelled from school for maiming animals in the Senior Biology Lab. Blinded white mice and stuck drawing pins into goldfish. The family buried that and they moved around. The father was in the Civil Service, that made it easier to go abroad. The family came back to England when Prebble was fourteen. He went down on two young girls and the baby they were minding. Can you imagine? They sent him away for a long time over that. Cost the old man every penny he had. They kept their son in a special school until he was eighteen. Under supervision.' Kellerman shook his head and sweat flicked the windscreen. 'A year-old child, Jesus.'

'Kellerman,' Coward warned.

'All *right*. The last thing they came up with was recently. Two, maybe three years ago. In Turkey. I had to cable five grand out as a backhander to some official in charge of records. They have these, uh, special brothels for weirdies. Small boys trained to be used like women. Head jobs for Arabs, speciality numbers. Prebble got hold of one of these kids and rough-housed the kid into a hospital. The *mental* ward, Coward. The kid is still there. Crippled for life. Looks at flowers and cries when the colours are too bright. Prebble's an animal. How would he hold his head up if his soldier boys knew he was as bent as a square grapefruit? His feet wouldn't touch.' Kellerman sagged, blowing on the knee he could not touch. He dredged a grin from somewhere, a fleeting thing with ragged edges. 'I think he's crazy enough to take a flyer at grabbing power here. Like this was Germany forty years ago. And the irony is, if he'd been hit like I planned, I would have done everybody a favour. You saved the schmuck's life, you know that?'

Coward stopped being engrossed by the river and said, 'And my own, little man. Not much, but more than you can claim.'

Kellerman barked his laugh, his face contorted.

'Bitterness suits you, copper. Keep it up. Take me in. Book me. I'll take my chances against your pennyante lawyers anytime.'

'No,' Coward said shortly.

'No? Fine. So cut me loose and let me just sue you for all this.'

'No.'

'What d'you mean, no?' Kellerman was breathless from acid.

'This is it for you. Your final location. There's the river, and here's you. When it rises tomorrow, you can see it coming for you. You can watch it come across the rubble and junk and wash up around the truck. According to your map, there should be about nine feet here. Just about cover the top of your head. You can just sit there and wait to choke. If your bottle goes, you can use the rifle. Make the end quick. That, my little man, is truly poetic justice. That was the gun Eliades used on Maitland and missed me with. When the river goes down they'll find you. They'll check the rifle through ballistics. Match up the slugs. That ties you to Eliades posthumously.'

Kellerman said something foul in a stream, belching it out with force. He bit his mouth and sobbed deep in his throat.

Coward was untouched. 'One piece of advice, Kellerman,' he said, conversationally. 'Use the rifle before the webbing gets wet and tightens. Don't wait too long. And don't waste your breath yelling for help. There isn't any.'

He started to slide the door closed.

'*Wait!* Lunatic!'

'Good-bye, Kellerman.'

'Wait, I said.' A bloodspot had formed in Kellerman's left eye. 'I know where your wife is, Coward. You hear me? I know.'

The door froze midtrack. Slid open a little.

'Yeah, she's hired a stud to service her, Coward. He's got her on drugs. Hallucinants. Speed. The whole fucking chemists's shop. You like that? He fucks her for money.'

The door smashed open and Coward reached in, closing his hands around Kellerman's neck. Kellerman laughed wildly and spittle flecked the windscreen.

'*Liar!*'

'She's dying. You can't get her back. The big C. Cancer. The big crab's eating her insides. You've lost her. You've . . .' Kellerman gurgled as the thumbs dug deep. His mouth formed a lopsided rictus and his tongue popped out, coated and swollen. Then he was gagging into his lap. Coward had released him. *Too soon*. Terror brought Kellerman's voice back.

'I supply the drugs,' he croaked. 'Me. *Me*. Go ahead, Kill me.'

The door slid closed. Coward had gone.

'Come back and kill me, you cuckold. Kill me, kill . . .'

Kellerman choked on a sob of self pity. He was alone. Talking to himself. He stroked the rifle for comfort.

'Kill . . . me . . .'

Nobody heard.

* * *

The second call box had not been vandalized.

Coward ordered a car from Victoria and dialled the Magpie and Stump. When it did not answer he cleared down and called the Incident Centre. There had been no word from Cave or Dutton. Coward ordered the sergeant to send a mobile to the pub and break the door down if necessary. He would call back within the hour.

Coward rang off. His soaked clothes clung to him and

he stank of canal water. He shivered uncontrollably. He was tired and there was still too much to do. He caught sight of himself in the mirror above the telephone and shivered for another reason.

He did not like what he saw.

01·00 hours

Dr Buford shook his head at Cave and bit on his dead pipe. He flipped the end of the sheet over Dutton's face, a gesture more eloquent than words. Nancy lit two cigarettes and placed one in Cave's mouth where it burned with no help from him. She drew heavily on her own as the silence lengthened inside the Incident Centre; even the rain seemed hushed. The duty sergeant broke it when he informed Cave that all the telephone lines were dead and that the only power they had came from the portable generator.

'Frank?' said Buford, looking to Cave as senior man.

Cave bit back an expletive. It would not have helped. The whole affair had taken on nightmare proportions, made the night darker, diminishing his own capabilities to almost nothing. He could reach neither Coward nor Maitland, could lean on nobody around him. He found his voice and said:

'There's no choice, we go to London. We can't function here, we're too vulnerable. We'll leave the Panda and my car behind. We'll take Mrs Coward's Alfa and Dutton's Hillman.'

'What about him, the body?' said Buford.

'What more can they do to him now? We'll lock up and leave him here.' Cave's voice had less substance than the smoke he breathed.

Buford agreed without speaking.

'We can't leave the Panda,' said the duty sergeant.

'Then you drive the bloody thing if you want to end up like him.' Cave jerked ash at Dutton's shroud. 'There are a hundred armed men out there, and shooting coppers seems to be their main aim in life. Our only chance is unmarked cars.'

'I only meant . . .'

'I don't give a cold carrot for what you meant, Sergeant. Do what you please.'

'Frank,' warned Nancy.

Cave swallowed air and smoke and his temper.

'All right. Sergeant, you'll drive the doc, I'll drive Mrs Coward.'

'I'll drive you,' said Nancy.

Cave had no energy to argue.

'Let's get on with it,' he said. 'And if either car is stopped for any reason, the other car is to keep going, is that clear?'

It was.

01·45 hours

Petrie whispered to the brown men as he sat in the parked Land Rover. He had found a spot in the square across from the main gate of St George's Hospital, and had counted five policemen at various points in the building. There would be others, he knew. But he would fox them. He had emptied an old plumbing bag he used for his tools and his shotgun lay inside it with a box of cartridges, his skinning knife and his set of illegal wire snares. One jerk with those and game would throttle in seconds. Petrie grinned slyly – it took a poacher to catch a poacher. He hoped he would meet that copper who had pushed him around in front of his stupid wife, that stupid mooing cow with her rolls of fat and vapid eyes. Somebody would pay for that humiliation after Peter had been avenged. That came first.

Petrie left the Land Rover and walked towards the hospital, ducked through the gate when the keeper had his back turned and made for the casualty entrance where he took the stairs to the basement. He passed the boiler room and found a service lift used solely for transporting trolleys to the operating theatres. It only serviced the basement, third and fourth floors. A bold sign warned unauthorized staff against its use.

Petrie found the laundry room and shrugged into a fairly clean surgical gown and covered his face with a mask. Then he made a dummy figure of pillows on a trolley and covered it with a sheet, adding an oxygen mask and bottle, deciding it would pass anything but the closest inspection. He ran the shotgun beneath the sheet and filled one gown pocket with cartridges and the other with snares.

When he had explained what he was doing to the brown men he rolled the trolley into the elevator and pressed the button for the third floor. He was very calm as he rose up the shaft.

01·50 hours

'I must have dropped off,' said Cave, jerking up against his seatbelt as Nancy drove through Hammersmith.

'And you snored.'

'We have to find John.' Cave swivelled to see if the other car still followed.

'You have to. I don't.'

'Uhuh. What do I tell him when I see him?'

'Nothing that might give me the impression you were meddling, Frank.'

'You look tired, Nancy.'

'Look at yourself before you cast stones.'

'Look, I didn't mean . . .'

'You never did. Good old Frank, straight in with all four feet. Still, policemen don't need subtlety, do they?'

Cave felt better for his nap but was in no mood to fence.

'Take me to St George's Hospital. He could be there.'

Nancy turned the wheel a little too smartly and slewed on a corner. Cave's head thumped against the side window. He said 'Damn' and:

'What message shall I give him?'

'None, thank you.'

'He needs you, you hard bitch. What did he do to deserve a brass like you? He's never looked at another woman.'

'Deserve me, Frank? Easy. He was good in bed and looked good in a dinner jacket. The only trouble was, he was already married to the force, and I don't take second place to anybody.' Nancy shaved through an intersection on amber and ran into the square before the hospital, braking abruptly. 'This is as far as I go. Say good-bye and get out.'

'You're lying, Nancy. What went wrong for Chrissake?'

'St George's, Frank. Go and book yourself a bed.'

The naked suffering in Nancy's face made Cave look away. He stared at a muddy Land Rover and searched for something to say. He was at a loss for words. If only he felt close enough just to hold her against his chest, to stroke her hair. Anything. He looked at the Land Rover and knew he had seen it somewhere before, somewhere recently. He opened the door and released his seatbelt. A red light blinked alive on the dash.

'I'll tell John I saw you. And you looked . . . fine.' Cave swung a leg over the sill.

'No!' the denial was almost a cry.

Cave could not look at her. He was painfully embarrassed.

'Please, Frank. No.'

Cave wondered what that 'please' had cost her to say. He nodded vaguely and mumbled a farewell as he stood up and out of the car. Nancy slammed the door and took the Alfa away in a rush. He did not watch it go or look up as the Hillman swept in beside him. He was locked in on the Land Rover, his scalp alive with premonitions. Buford took his arm and said something which Cave cut through with:

'You know what Petrie looks like. You examined him.'

'Yes, why?'

'That's his vehicle, and that's the hospital where they're holding that vagrant Glass.'

Buford did not grasp the significance. There was no reason why he thought he should.

Cave walked around the Hillman and opened the driving door.

'Sergeant, go to the main gate and alert the third floor. Tell them an armed and dangerous man has possibly entered the hospital. Tell them me and Buford are coming up.' He added a general description of Petrie and hurried Buford through the gate yelling 'Police' at the gatekeeper. The sergeant took over the explanations and the gatekeeper lifted the phone to dial.

Cave started to run, dragging Buford with him.

* * *

The elevator had come to a stop on the third floor and Petrie stayed in the cage listening and hushing the brown men. They were laughing quietly all around him which should have made him angry but did not. They would not give him away, he knew that. The corridor was brightly lit and whitely silent, smelling antiseptic. Petrie eased the gate open and looked cautiously out.

Straight into the eyes of a seated, uniformed policeman.

'You don't want this floor, doc. This is the third and it's sealed. Must have pressed the wrong button. Where you going, four?'

Petrie nodded amid gales of silent laughter.

The policeman rose and stepped closer.

'I'll press it for you if you like. You'll be scrubbed up if you're on the way to surgical. I know a bit about it, used to porter at St Thomas's before I joined the force.'

Petrie nodded, feeling for a snare. Stepping back into the elevator.

The policeman's back was turning as he leaned around to press the right button. His back was fully towards Petrie. The wire went over his head and dropped on to the broad, blue shoulders. Petrie jerked it tight and watched the bright wire circle the thick neck and cut into the flesh until all that showed was the metal shackle. Petrie put a knee into the rearing back and pulled the snare tighter.

The policeman's arm smashed Petrie against the elevator wall with a metallic boom that echoed in the shaft, multiplying itself. The doors began to close as a wall telephone warbled in the corridor. Petrie pushed the thrashing man away from him and leapt for the gap, falling through on to the polished tile floor. As he rolled he realized he had left the gun behind. The laughter became mocking. They *had* betrayed him.

A door at the end of the corridor was pushing open and feet pounded up the stairs from the floor below.

Petrie sobbed to himself and ran at the opening door, smashing it closed with manic strength. He glimpsed a policeman through the round window before he ran on, finding another snare, looking for the room the old man must be in.

All the doors he tried were locked and he was suddenly at a dead end and the window showed him the street three storeys below. If only the laughing would let him *think*.

He whirled to face the men coming towards him.

Cave drew his Woodsman as he ran and Buford was close on his heels, his face pink from exertion. The door Petrie had jammed shut opened and another armed policeman was there, bulky in his flak jacket. Petrie could not believe it would end this way. He pawed the air before him and told them all to keep back. The wire snare whistled as he swung it.

'You lied,' he screamed. 'The brown men lied.'

Cave held out a placatory hand, holding his gun in the folds of his raincoat.

'It's all right, Petrie. Nobody will hurt you. Here's the doctor. You remember him, don't you? Petrie?'

'They lied. To *meeeee . . .*' Petrie held his vibrating head with both hands. The laughter was bass and coarse and roared around him louder and louder.

Cave took slow steps, speaking gently.

Petrie advanced to meet him, step by slower step. Then, gathering himself only inches from Cave's outstretched hands, he ran at the window and launched himself through it.

02·10 hours

The lights in the Control Room of the experimental station were dimmed, and Calloway sat next to Prebble, wishing for his Camels. Just to have held his Zippo would have been comforting.

He was seeing at first-hand what Coward was learning about Prebble from third-parties, and fear had formed a stone in his stomach. Calloway had seen men go off their heads during his tour with the army in Indo-China, but this experience was something else entirely. He had realized Prebble was strange and had made provision for it, as he made provision for most things, but he had not been prepared for what was happening now.

The hunt for the two policemen in Salem Wood came over the radio as it happened, and Calloway watched Prebble react to every shot and move of the firefight, his expression flitting between oddness and an assumed objectivity. By the time Sergeant Dennis reported the collapse of the trench and the loss of most of his squad, Prebble no longer seemed slack and overfed. He had swelled up like a great toad, his face mottled and his hands clenched, his eyes lost in swollen pouches. He had raised up out of his swivel and shook from head to foot as though buffeted by high winds. His breathing had become a contracted hissing as a muddy purple flush suffused his face.

To Calloway, it seemed as though two distinct people were trying to occupy the one body, and the weirdest manifestation was the way Prebble's voice remained cultured and controlled. If there had been a back window, Calloway would have cheerfully jumped through it; instead he sat still and made himself as small as possible, thinking of ways to bring Prebble back to normality.

Calloway shuffled papers and said, 'There goes the schedule.'

There was no sign Prebble had heard. His hands clutched at his chest as he slowly bowed forward.

'Yeah,' said Calloway. 'I guess I could rework the feasibility aspect of Alpha-5's role. Perhaps there's a possibility of having them act in a restrictive way, cut out their secondary target . . .' He talked on, wondering if what he was saying made any sense, hoping that something was getting through to Prebble. 'I'll punch out a revised programme for the computer. We already have a contingency revision in the bank. Let's see if I can patch something together . . .'

Prebble was looking down at him with a stranger's

eyes.

'Revisions . . . yes . . .'

Calloway swung to the tape deck, keeping his face averted.

'Let's see,' he said, selecting spools. 'Let's see . . .'

'The weather update,' Prebble hissed. 'Get the weather update.'

'Right. Wind rising force nine accelerating. Direction, north by west. Tides slacking at ebb, moonrise expected . . .'

Prebble's hand crushed Calloway's shoulder.

'Carry on. I'll just . . .'

A clipboard fell to the floor as Prebble turned and lumbered for the door. It swished open and closed and Calloway had the room to himself. 'Throw it up, honey,' he said shakily and reached for the telephone, dialling an outside line. He knew whatever he said would be recorded, but he doubted if anybody would check the tape before the operation commenced.

* * *

Prebble locked himself into the men's room where he coughed bile into a handbasin. His head was splitting and he could barely breathe. He must take more of his special medication. *How many capsules was that today*? he wondered, and did not know. Perhaps if he took two . . .

Prebble found his silver box and fumbled the capsules into his mouth, sucked water from the running tap, swallowing with difficulty, willing them to stay down.

Seven men lost for the sake of two unimportant policemen. There must be a scapegoat. No, I mustn't think that way.

Cold fire ran through Prebble's chest and his ears belled. He stayed bowed over the sink until the stomach cramps eased and ceased, replaced by the dull and nagging drumbeat of strained muscle. His legs had little strength in them.

Prebble threw water in his face and swilled aftertaste from his palate. There were thoughts in his head he did not like, thoughts that came unbidden from somewhere deep inside him. Vague doubts were forming too, and he knew he must control them before they controlled him. *Why weren't the capsules doing their job?*

Prebble's breath roared in his ears as his heart beat faster than it should. He raised his head and watched his reflection dab moisture from his jowls with a tear of paper towel.

I should have left Sergeant Dennis to his optics and watered beer. If only the noise and pain in my head would go away and take the dark, buried thoughts with them.

Prebble massaged his temples and stared into the mirror. His features were mottled in the fluorescent glare and he could not hold his own gaze. Something had come between him and his own image. Something that swam up out of the buried part of him, bringing all the forbidden thoughts he needed to suppress, blocking his view of himself. The something that made him do base and foolish things to the soft and yielding . . .

Prebble held his head and tried to see himself in the glass, his face struggling with itself. If only there were a deity he could call upon to help him. A Great One whose power might quell the something that fought him for supremacy. Prebble let out a hiss of breath and held his temples tighter.

No, he thought, *I must rely upon myself. I'm prepared by the red capsules, despite their awful side effects. However bad those are, I must prevail. Forget the loss of body hair and the effeminate swelling of the pectorals. Live with the painful corrective surgery in Switzerland. Accept the loss of physical desire, of sexual drive, the dulling of taste and appetite. And all because of the something that comes up from below myself, the something that floats in my awareness as a dark and confusing toad.*

The face in the mirror struggled with itself, fought over by two distinct personae, each struggling for control. On the one hand the aloof patrician, on the other, the cunning warted thing; both of them twitching the facial muscles, pulling at the mouth, both staring in turns from behind the eyes as the mind fought itself in the labyrinth inside Prebble's skull.

Prebble's face crawled with a thousand half-formed

expressions and the pressure inside his head formed purple veins on his temples.

I will not share.

Prebble smashed the mirror with his fist and it was over.

He straightened up and smiled his cool smile at the skinned knuckles and the torn skin around his bloodstone ring as the congestion drained from his face. He held his hand beneath the running cold tap as the blood ran pink over the white porcelain. He shuddered and his teeth unclenched.

The toad thing was retreating. Had gone.

Prebble's tongue darted playfully, slicking his lower lip with saliva. Even the taste of bile was now enjoyable. He had won his private battle, he would win the one waiting to be started outside. The hissing was something he now controlled. Prebble smiled into the mirror as an experiment and saw it succeed.

Somebody knocked, worked the doorhandle and asked if he was all right.

Prebble adjusted his tie and his battle blouse and admired his armband with its bright red H on a black roundel, a gold 88 over the central crossbar. He had designed it himself. Yes, he decided, he was presentable. He flipped the latch and allowed Calloway inside.

'What happened? I heard breaking glass.'

Prebble picked up his black gloves and worked one on to his good hand. 'The mirror,' he said. 'I slipped.' Thinking, *I shall have to carry the other glove, my hand is swelling*.

Calloway's face would not stay composed.

'You . . . you might have glass in there. You should get a tetanus . . .'

Prebble flicked a shard of glass from the rim of the handbasin.

'Shut up, Calloway. Have you worked out your probability factors, or whatever you choose to call them?'

'What? Yeah. It isn't good. We shall obviously have to cancel Alpha-5's target. Four men can't . . .'

'I could have told you that.' There was the right

amount of scorn in Prebble's voice. 'They were to have destroyed the pumping-station at Kempton Park. They can hardly do that with their explosives team dead. What does that inescapable fact do to our overall plan?'

Calloway chose a face and stuck to it.

'Well, accepting that, it does mean that the authorities would be able to restore the metropolitan water supply that much more quickly.'

'At least you haven't bored me with irrelevant technicalities. They would still have to repair the reservoirs. And we calculated, how long?'

'Two months or so. Subject of course to how quickly they can re-enter the area, bring in workers and supplies, restore the levels, purify the pipes . . .'

'Yes, yes. Cancel it and forget it. Alpha-4 can consider Kempton Park as a secondary target if time allows.'

'You could let me take it,' Calloway said quickly.

'I could what?'

'I know what has to be done. Five men could just about handle it. It would take longer and we should have less time to get clear. I've worked it out – we should have to swing north and west and come back into Surrey through Reading and Farnham. Alpha-4 could back us as you suggested. All they have to do is turn up and finish off if we fall behind schedule. That does mean that they'll have to follow our route out, and that means they're in jeopardy as we are, twice the number of men trying . . .'

'Yes, yes,' Prebble picked up his spare glove. 'I see that.' His pink eyes held Calloway steadily. 'And I thought you wanted to take the money and run. What suddenly makes you want to involve yourself in this way?'

Here goes the big lie, thought Calloway. 'Shows how little you know about people, Prebble. Politics apart, and mine kind of parallel yours, I don't plan to sit back biting my thumbs whilst you guys are out making my plan work. I want in.'

'*Your* plan? You're deluded. *Your* plan.'

'Yeah? My figures, my calculations, my predictions are what makes this operation viable. The big wave is on its way dead on time. Without my timing, your soldier boys would be picking fluff out of their navels in some cowshed, dreaming of some impractical way of establishing a new order. If your move doesn't coincide with that sea-surge, all this will be useless. I've guaranteed your timing is right.'

'And that makes you the great architect, does it?' asked Prebble with little warmth.

'Why not? It's true enough. You're the guy with the dough and the clout to get it done. But Uncle Dad here,' Calloway thumbed his chest, 'is the baby who made it all go.'

'That of course remains to be seen.'

Calloway moved his shoulders, shrugging athletically.

'You wouldn't move if you didn't know my calculations were right.'

'We must hope your expertise matches your self-regard,' said Prebble, moving out along the passage and back into the Control Room. He looked down over the ten squads formed up on the model beside their targets. Even Alpha-5 managed not to appear depleted.

'Well, do I go?' asked Calloway.

Prebble kept his ugly expression turned away.

'Yes, you go,' he said quietly.

02·30 hours

Platoon Sergeant Chas Dennis stood at attention as Prebble gave him his new orders. He could hardly believe it, they were going after all, Alpha-5 was going operational with the Yank in charge. That would take some swallowing, but it was better than being left behind. He could hardly wait to be dismissed, to get into action.

'There is just one other thing,' said Prebble.

'Yes, Leader.'

'Mr Calloway must be given every opportunity to place the charges. He is to be given every help your squad can afford him.'

'I swear, Leader.'

'Once you are certain that he has fulfilled his function . . .' Prebble's swollen hand made a vague gesture and the bloodstone winked red. 'He is to be lost in the action. He will not return with you.'

The sergeant's mouth thinned.

'You will make it your personal responsibility. It will go some way towards making amends for . . . well, I don't have to spell it out.'

'You don't, Leader. You can rely on me.'

'Yes,' said Prebble. 'Dismissed.'

Sergeant Dennis ran along the convoy of unmarked lorries and jumped into the driving cab of the fifth in line. Calloway was already there, an Armorlite across his knees.

'What was that all about?' he asked as Dennis started the engine.

'That?' Sergeant Dennis smiled. 'Just to make sure I took good care of you. Don't worry, Yank, you're safe as houses.'

'Take care of yourself. I'll be more than all right.'

'So long as you don't trip over your feet you'll be all right, you mean.' Sergeant Dennis let out the clutch as the convoy began to roll.

Calloway raised a foot against the dash and leaned the rifle across his knee, his face thoughtful. There had to be more to Dennis's antagonism than mere tension. He allowed the quarrel to die but knew he must watch his back. He opened the flap of his sidearm and checked that the Colt slid easily from the holster. Then, to forestall any further arguments, leaned back and feigned sleep. When trouble came he would be ready for it.

02·36 hours

Petrie's remains were sheathed in polythene, zipped into a canvas bag, strapped to a trolley and driven away to the mortuary. All that remained on the tarmac was a rusty puddle and a chalk outline of his body. There had been enough police witnesses to make the coroner's job easy. Another deduction was simpler: Petrie could only have learned Glass's location from Prebble.

Cave used the gatekeeper's phone to ask the New

Scotland Yard switchboard for Coward's extension and a taped Coward asked him to leave his message after the tone.

'This is Frank, John . . .' Cave got no farther. A second taped Coward cut in.

'Follow this carefully, Frank. This message timed at 01·32 hours. It will only play once, then automatically wipe itself. Maitland is dead. I think I was the target. Eliades was the gunman and he's dead or dying somewhere. I have his back-up man at Albany Street in solitary. We've held him on an arms charge to be going on with. He's your star witness if I don't make it. Don't go near him or think about him until you're sure you are in the clear. If they can come after me, they'll come after you. Don't think they won't. I've prepared the briefs for the DPP and the hearing for issuance is at eight o'clock this morning. The warrants are for Prebble and all his guinea pig friends. If I don't get there, you have to. And Frank, you have to serve them personally. You and nobody else, there's nobody else to trust. My not making it will make that apparent.'

There was a hissing pause on the tape, then:

'I've located Major-General Rawlings at the Flood Control Centre in Kingsway. I'm going through the tunnel to interview him. If he's in this conspiracy I'll have neutralized myself. If he's on the fence, the probability is he'll lock me up somewhere and watch how things go. If he's straight there's no problem. He might think me a bit strange and hold me until he checks me out, but that won't matter. Just remember the most important thing is to get those warrants issued by the DPP and see they are served. Don't waste time worrying your pointed head about my hide. Go get the bastards for me.'

The tape ended and hummed itself clean. Cave cleared down.

It seemed as though he and John had taken on the whole establishment and their relatives. The casualties were mounting and they were no closer to solving the whole mess. Petrie and his son, Constable Midgeley, Leon Ferris and Inspector Dutton. The poor copper garrotted on the third floor of the hospital. Goldy Stern. He did not count Eliades in his total. The Cypriot was a bonus on the road to evening the score. Cave knew he was no longer practising the objectivity of a good copper and did not give a good goddamn. He left the gatehouse and crossed the wind and rainswept courtyard to the hospital where he talked a doctor into giving him a stimulant to take him through the next twenty-four hours. There was no way he would leave John Coward to the wolves.

Then he took a cab home to Molly and a hot bath.

13

Thursday 4 October

02·40 hours

Another bloody flap.

Major-General Sir Jasper Rawlings moodily watched the clock blip to 2·41 a.m. He still wore his overcoat over his dinner jacket. The heating system of the underground Flood Control Centre had not yet been boosted to counteract the vigorous air-extraction.

You would think, wouldn't you he reasoned, that his masters would have devised a way of throwing ordure at a man when he was comfortably prepared? By elevenses perhaps, relaxed on his lawn in spring sunshine as China tea and Captains Number Ones settled into his erratic gastric flow. To attract his attention with a polite telephone call, and then to send a limousine for him after a decent interval. Allow a man to bid his wife a fond farewell, pick cat's hairs from his sober sleeve and stroll down the drive as a chauffeur saluted. Not them.

Had him waylaid at the Savile Club.

One moment he was enjoying a third crusted port with Charlie Maunders who moved knives and fruit about the dining table, choreographing some unlikely and hilarious withdrawal from occupied territory, the next: whoosh. Out into a police car and bucketing through a foul night on protesting tyres. All the blasted traffic lights at red and the siren seesawing away. Straight through the lot without a halt, crushed between two huge coppers with no conversation and sidearms. Streaking from Mayfair to Holborn in a record four minutes and twelve seconds. The springs still seemed to bounce beneath his haunches after how long? Two hours? At least that.

The flap had caught everybody by surprise.

There had been a skeleton staff of four when he had arrived. More had trickled in in ones and twos. Picked up, he supposed, by other racing police mobiles. It had been the same last month during the last period of high tides and northerly winds. Nothing done, nothing ready. *Civilians*, Rawlings thought dismissively.

He stared moodily at the dark rows of consoles waiting for their radar screens and solid-state innards to be fitted. When they were finally installed they would monitor London's smaller rivers for flood in the event of local outbursts of torrential rain. There had been one such overnight downpour in the north-east and many thousands were evacuated. Some roads had been under five feet of water. With the British Isles tilting to the south, inch by inch, the worsening weather and the rising tides, the problem of flood in the Thames Valley became more pressing year by year.

Well, do what you can with what you've got.

The giant illuminated map of the British Isles and the North Sea showed The Lady Kuklos holding her position. A blood red K inside a circle represented her centre and shifting white lines the high-pressure cold front at her back. To one side of the map was a long black panel where rows of digital figures represented planetary influences, windforce and direction, occlusion values, air temperatures, humidity factors, dew points and other data. Continually winking like a Tote board, they formed a technical portrait of the seas and estuaries of the eastern coastline and the bottleneck between Dover and Calais.

High tide at Dover was already higher than the expected 9·7 metres. A man who thought in Imperial measures, Rawlings automatically converted the metres to feet and inches. Two feet up on the expected seasonal norm. And the moon was only just sliding from her zenith, still drawing the tides with her. She would hold the levels high until she dipped below the horizon and released her influence to the rising sun. Another factor to be considered. It was clear something nasty was brewing. Tomorrow it would be worse, tomorrow the sun and moon would be in conjunction and then. . .

There was a sudden flurry of changing digits as fresh

data came in from the coastal stations and weather ships. They were clearly at variance with the lower figures produced by the computer model. Proof that meteorological prediction was anything but a precise science.

Rawlings slumped between his banks of telephones and watched developments. His real involvement would come should things become truly sticky. That moment had yet to come. If ever.

Rawlings knew his opening moves by heart.

He had first call on all army and naval helicopter squadrons on station in the Home Counties from Yeovilton to Plymouth. All army groups, Cavalry Units (transport), Pioneers and Sappers (bridges, pontoons and collapsible boats), Medical Corps (obvious) and NAAFI (covered by an umbrella government cheque being a private concern), to all the odds-and-sods the TA could usefully scrape together. The declaration of Martial Law would bring him all the bus fleets from London Transport, London County, Wye Valley and Green Line. The Metropolitan and St John's Ambulance Services. Anything with wheels. If it came to total evacuation of the capital, it would hardly be enough.

Two SAS units would drop on Horseguards and cover the evacuation of Whitehall. Other groups would . . . Rawlings stopped himself. It would be at least another hour or so before he knew for certain whether the flap was on or off. He suspected he would be able to stand down and get some sleep before tomorrow night which was more likely to be crunch time. Then, the sun and moon would be in conjunction and both would be exerting their highest influence on the sea. If that damned red K did not blow itself out before then.

If, if, if.

Rawlings wondered if the Civil Service Grade B girl who made the instant coffee had been located and brought in.

A yellow internal blinked at him. Rawlings flicked the voicebox diaphragm to open.

'Rawlings,' he said, not needing to hold a receiver.

'Braddock. Security.' Rawlings recalled a stolid man with large hands and feet.

'Yes, Braddock.'

'Sir, there's a man here from Special Branch. He wants to see you. He says . . .' Braddock worked suspicion down the telephone. 'It's urgent and private.'

'You told him I am . . . heavily engaged?'

'Yessir, however . . .'

'However *what?*' *These fellows would make a secret out of Christmas.*

'His name is Coward.'

'I am not enlightened.'

'He came through from Section A.'

'Did he now.'

Rawlings pondered. Section A was the underground link with the huge complex below Whitehall. It was possible to hike from Downing Street, through the bowels of the Ministry of Defence to the Churchill Bunker beneath Horseguards without once seeing the sky. One had to have high clearance to make the trip. And stamina.

'He also says he was sent by Commander Maitland. That's all he *will* say.' Braddock sounded unhappy.

Rawlings thought on in silence.

'Do I advance him, Sir? Or send him back?'

Advance him? Ye Gods, what language these people speak.

'Are you issued with a sidearm, Braddock?' Rawlings asked.

'Yessir.'

Rawlings could almost hear the heels click.

'Advance him then. Bring him along yourself. You have a relief there, do you?'

'Yessir.'

Rawlings switched to another extension and a girl answered.

'Coffee,' he ordered and switched again. 'I want to see the satellite pictures as soon as they've been analysed.' Again, he did not wait for a reply. The red K glared from a Tory blue sea and the northerlies prevailed at force-eight rising. The disparity between the factual figures and those from the model grew. If anything it would be touch and go.

Rawlings was swivelling with his head bowed when

Braddock brought Coward into his office. He looked up when the sliding door hissed closed and watched them come across the huge expanse of carpet. Rawlings was struck by several things at once. Coward's face was as grey as his eyes. He was also soaking wet. The fellow looked done in. He carried a plastic sack and Braddock gripped a holstered Smith & Wesson, his right hand on his own sidearm.

Rawlings identified himself and offered his hand. Coward's grip was firm and cold.

'He was armed, Sir,' said Braddock.

'So I see.' Rawlings patted a space on his desk. 'Put it here. Issue, is it? Indented for and all that?' he asked Braddock, his eyes on Coward.

'Yessir. Checked that first.'

'Well done. Off you go.'

Braddock reluctantly withdrew.

Rawlings toyed with a slide rule.

'Private and confidential, eh, Coward?'

'Yes.'

'And how is Commander Maitland?'

Coward dry-tongued his lower lip.

'He's dead.'

Rawlings stopped swivelling. He rode over his sense of loss. Cut himself off from shock. He forced himself to look again at Coward, seeing the exhaustion, the isolation of the man.

'Damn, how?'

'Shot. I was the target. He got in the way.'

'Lucky for you,' said Rawlings. Thinking, *what a bloody silly thing to say*. 'We went back a long way, he and I. We were close.' *Did that explain? Make amends?*

'I hope so. I hope you were bloody close.' Coward's voice crackled with force. 'I hope you shouldn't be on the list, either.'

'List?' said Rawlings. 'I think you'd best sit down and explain that.'

Coward swayed against the desk, his knuckles white beneath the dirt. Rawlings half-rose to help him. Coward spun the holster and laid his hand on the gunbutt, the index finger on the trigger. Rawlings sank back into his swivel, his eyes aware, his mouth closed.

'Here,' Coward tossed a crumpled envelope onto Rawlings's blotter. 'Read that, I have. It explains a lot. Then we'll talk.'

The letter went over three pages in Maitland's own hand. It was a resignation and much more. Rawlings skimmed through it then read it a second time more slowly, rapping the slide rule against his teeth. He laid the pages aside and said, 'Is this true?'

'Yes.' Coward retrieved the letter and lost it inside his coat.

'I know most of the people named there. Know some of them damned well. Who else has seen this . . . confession?'

'Nobody.'

'And who else will see it?'

'Nobody if I can help it.'

'That will take some doing, Coward. Can you verify any of it?'

'Some. Not enough to make it stick in time. That's why I'm taking a chance on you. A bloody big chance.'

Rawlings thought about that. 'Meaning I could be a bedfellow, eh? From your viewpoint that could be a possibility, I suppose.' He ran the slide rule through his fading red hair and pinched his nostrils with thumb and forefinger. 'You've picked a damned awkward time to come to me with this.' He released his nose to wave a hand at the activity through the glass wall.

'I may have come too late,' said Coward, watching the pinchmarks fade. 'All this could be a waste of time.'

An internal blinked.

'May I answer that?'

Coward shrugged.

Rawlings depressed a switch. 'Yes?' He listened and said: 'Do you take milk and sugar in your coffee?'

Coward blinked. 'No.'

'No. Both black.' Rawlings killed the connection. 'She'll bring it in directly. Try not to wave that thing at her.' He tapped the holster. 'Why have you come to me with this, by the way?'

'This.' Coward drew the map from his sack and

handed it across. 'Lay that out and tell me what it means to you.'

Rawlings used a telephone to hold one end down, rolling the map open across the desk and the holstered gun. Coward withdrew the gun, stepped away and held it down at his side. Rawlings affected not to notice. A girl came in with coffee in real cups and left again without a word. Rawlings grunted. He circled the Prebble Marine colophon with a retracted ballpoint and studied the water depths marked in red.

'Who,' he asked, 'supplied you with this?'

'Does it matter?'

'Damned right it does. This wasn't drawn up by some terrorist.'

'Wasn't it?'

'You know damned well what I mean, Coward. Did this come from Prebble Marine direct?'

'No. From Kellerman's club.'

'Who? Never mind. Glad I've seen it even if it is nonsense. Look here.' Rawlings pulled down a wallmap marked with the official waterspread along the Thames Valley. Although more extensive than those blue areas on the London Transport posters, the flooding was much less than shown on the map from the Bugalloo safe. 'You see, nonsense.'

'Unless the figures supplied to you were rigged.'

'Hardly,' said Rawlings, his manner didactic. 'That would require the connivance of every involved authority.' He ticked off his fingers. 'The Meteorological Office, Trinity House, The British Waterways Authority, The Ministry of Defence, The Hydrographic Department at Taunton, The Admiralty . . . the list's endless. No, groundless supposition. Groundless.'

'Somebody thinks it's kosher, Brigadier. The members of that consortium have got a hell of a lot riding on it.'

'Every year some lunatic makes for the nearest mountain to await the end of the world. As you see, we're still here.'

Coward moistened his tongue with coffee.

'That map wasn't prepared for fun. My information . . .'

Rawlings saw Coward was not going to continue. He said:

'Reservations, Coward?'

'Plenty.'

'You've pretty much put yourself in my hands.'

'Maybe.'

'A little more than maybe. He said you'd come bustling in here with some theory or other.'

Coward thought he had misheard. The tension in his jaw slackened.

Rawlings nodded.

'Yes, Maitland called me. He telephoned me at the Savile. Called me away from an excellent trout.' Rawlings's eyes lost focus. 'Wish now I hadn't been so short with him . . . in the light of . . .' He cleared his throat. 'I suppose there's no doubt, he is . . . ?'

'None,' Coward said brutally. 'And it's all for nothing if you don't come across with something concrete.' Thinking, *Maitland was ahead of the game again. Almost as though he knew he wouldn't be here. Could he have deliberately stood in front of the window? Dead end, stay out of it*. 'That map is some sort of key, Major-General. You must have some clue how those levels could be achieved.'

It was Rawlings's turn to bark.

'Apart from hiring twenty million Chinese to urinate along the length of the Thames simultaneously, I see no way. The Thames is two hundred and ten miles long. I couldn't police all of it, even if it was my function to do so.'

'So we sit here and wait to count bodies.'

'We do not. I just want you to realize how vast the problem is. The last thing I needed was for you to blunder in here with a map that compounds my overall problem. Did you expect me to welcome you with open arms?'

Coward shook his head wearily. 'No.'

'Then you aren't disappointed, are you?' Rawlings dropped into his chair and swivelled in a complete circle. 'Look, there are two tides a day in the Thames, and they are invariably slack, running sluggishly. At present, due to the rain, the river is running high at five knots. The reservoirs are full and we've drawn off all we can. There's only so much we can draw into the sewers, and even then the outfalls run into the river below the estuary. All the weirs are open and running to capacity. If we had a national water grid I guess we could pump it north to the midlands. We don't and we can't.' He made a tent of his fingers and pitched it on the map on his desk, staring moodily over the peak. After a moment he turned his head between the two maps as though a thought had struck him. He seemed to have forgotten Coward was there. Muttering.

'Yes, in that event, yes . . . my body count rises by two-thirds. I lose my bridges to the west. Another thirty or so electricity sub-stations are affectively knocked out. Gas towers, petrol stations, hmmm. The Hyde Park camps would no longer be viable. Nor Green Park. More pressure on Clissold Park and Finsbury. No, they're out. Nothing until the next high ground. Highgate in the north, Crystal Palace in the south. Telecommunications take a hammering. The Post Office Tower gets its feet wet, unless, hmmm . . .' Rawlings droned on in a monotone. Recalculating, reassessing. He could have been alone.

Coward selected a chair with a view of both doors and the room beyond the glass. The digital numerals blipped and changed and the red K glared. A girl shredded printouts and another collected punched IBM cards from programmers. Men spoke into telephones and analysed computations. Outside seemed a long way away. It would have been nice to unlace his shoes and strip off his socks. To lean against the upholstered chairback. To eat something. To close his eyes.

Coward stood and stamped his feet. Stretched his eyes wide. Dredged up recent angers to keep him going. Downed his lukewarm coffee in two gulps. The wall-clock lingered as time raced. His own wristwatch had been killed by the canal.

Rawlings ignored him, absorbed by the illuminated wallmap. The tides had eased at Dover and were reducing to their highest norm. The peaks on the Blackwater and across the Nore Sands remained constant. The winds prevailed.

A man separated himself from the general mêlée and wove through the desks and consoles with a folder of bromides. He caught Rawlings's attention and was waved on. The door swished aside and he entered to spread pictures on the desk. They were satellite photographs of the British Isles and the coasts of France and Spain, the tongue of Norway in the top right-hand corner. Cel overlays showed the outlines of the land masses below the cloud cover. Otherwise they were grainy sprawls of grubby cotton wool. To Coward that was all they were and the following verbal exchange meant even less. Rawlings seemed to draw comfort from it, however. He dismissed the man and pinned the pictures to a cork board. He was pinching his nose white as he said:

'We live again, I think.'

The wallclock tocked off another wasted minute. Coward felt he supported the whole of Holborn on his shoulders as he watched Rawlings's nose blush with blood, hoping he would not pinch it again. Rawlings dug at his scalp with the ballpen instead, saying:

'If we only had the Thames barrage complete, all this could go hang.'

Coward heard himself ask when it would be operational.

'Who knows? Three firms of international repute are involved in the construction. They won't even give the Greater London Council a final costing, let alone a finishing date. The barrage is arguably the biggest civil engineering project undertaken this century. The consortium started off with the greatest confidence, but that soon dissipated. There were the usual strikes. The English sickness. Apart from the labour problems, the river bed gave them a headache no proprietary medicine could salve. The chalk bed chewed up drills like sweets. They flew drills and bits in from South Africa and Japan amongst other places. The coffer dams they built to house the concrete piers during construction were hotter than any steel mill, the temperatures on the lower levels topped one hundred and twenty degrees. Even the toughest navvy passed out under those conditions. When they poured the concrete into one of the centre piers it cracked across. They still haven't sorted that one out. Do they blow it out, or try to strengthen it someway? Until that is resolved, neither the gates or the hydraulic systems can be fitted. And to date the cost is in the region of seven hundred million pounds. Daunting, isn't it?'

'So there's no barrage,' said Coward. 'All right, tough. The North Sea's still sitting out there, waiting to pile in on us. Look at the dates on that map. Tomorrow's the fifth. That's got to mean they know something you don't. Or maybe something you won't even think about.'

'Like what? Answer me that and I'll do something about it.'

'Use your authority, General. Which ever way I go I come back to Prebble and his private army. It all comes back to that. To him. All the people on that list are comfortably tucked-up at his estate in Surrey. He's there. His toy soldiers are there. They're armed as well as if not better than any of your SAS units. Given time I can get Prebble on a murder charge. That'll be too late. Don't ask me how I know, I just do.' Coward gripped the arms of Rawlings's chair, his face thrust close. 'We have to take him before tomorrow.'

'We, Coward?' said Rawlings.

'Yes, we. Round them all up. Sweat Prebble. I can break him.'

'You think so, do you? I don't happen to agree. You are deluded if you think I intend to act on this . . . fiction. You are overwrought. The death of your superior has obviously disturbed you. That's understandable. It might also explain this fixation of yours, this belief that somebody can control the sea. I'm sure that a proper investigation into Maitland's . . . demise, will prove the fact of the matter either way.'

'Don't play with me, Listen.'

'I have, patiently.'

'Hear what I'm saying,' Coward yelled, his breath stirring Rawlings's hair. He seemed to be seeing things through thick glass. The calm, florid face was too close to focus on. The oyster eyes merged into one great cyclopean stare. Both doors swished open and Rawlings's big hands clamped on Coward's wrists. Coward wrenched himself upright as Braddock's gun rammed into his kidney. A second gun cocked close to his face.

'Stand very still,' said Rawlings quietly.

'You're with them,' Coward said as Braddock took his holstered gun. The weight on his neck made him stagger. Cold metal circled his wrists as his hands were drawn back behind him, his feet kicked into a spread.

'Them, Coward? What them? Classic paranoia.' Rawlings looked past Coward at Braddock. 'There is a document in his inside pocket. Get it for me.'

Maitland's letter was taken and handed to Rawlings who weighed it in his hand. 'Better in my care, I think,' he said. He tapped the map. 'I'll have the river police alerted for any possible attempts at sabotage, although I fear the river is hardly navigable, being in spate. I'm having you placed in protective custody, Coward. For the best.'

Coward drew off a kick at the serene red face. It never landed. Braddock leaned on the handcuffs and Coward's legs were jerked out from under him. He fell with Braddock's substantial knee across his face.

'Take him away.' Rawlings swivelled into his desk, closing the episode from his mind.

The door swished open and closed and there were long anonymous grey corridors, an elevator that dropped several levels as the canal stink from Coward's clothes melded with Braddock's deodorant. More corridors into the secure section beneath the War House and signed clipboards and a body search. Through an electric cage into a box with a steel door, a hard bunk and a metal toilet cemented into the wall, a wired light globe in the high ceiling. Conditioned air that tasted used. Silence and claustrophobia.

Coward wadded his jacket into a pillow and laid himself on the bunk. There was nothing else to do.

03·45 hours

The roaring whine of the pump generators covered the

assault by Alpha-5. As Calloway laid charges along the outer pipes of the sewage beds the rest of the squad took the buildings with little effort.

Sergeant Dennis killed the first machine-minder with a snap shot to the chest, slamming the man back against the green generator cowling where he hung spread-eagled for a moment before falling on to his side.

The man beside him turned to face Dennis, his clip-board across his chest like a shield. He barely reacted before his face exploded in a spray of red gobbets and chips of bone.

The engineer died in his office as he spooned Typhoo Tea into a pot, brewing up for the entire shift. He was only five days away from his gold watch and pension and had been a widower for three months. He dreaded retirement without his wife. He never had time to think about that one way or another. His brain was dead before he fell among the mugs and digestive biscuits.

The fourth man tried to run from the building and lose himself in the sewage beds. He almost made a side door before he was brought down by a flurry of shots. The last two men died over a game of cribbage.

'This one would have lost anyway,' one of the guard said callously, turning over the cards. 'There's not a single point in his box.'

'Died in the hole,' said another.

'Cut that out. You. Put that money back. That's looting.' Sergeant Dennis was curt. 'Drag this offal away then get the main charges from the lorry. Move.'

'Yes, Sarge.'

Sergeant Dennis knew there should have been another man on shift. He went to the office and checked out the roster. It was all right, none of them had escaped. The missing man had reported sick and had not turned in.

Now for Calloway. Sergeant Dennis checked his watch. 3·56 a.m. There was less than ninety minutes left to complete the operation and to get the men back in the lorry. Even with a full squad they would have been cutting it fine. He strode towards the main door and was met by the two privates who manhandled a trolley of explosives inside. Calloway followed them in, weighed down by two heavy satchels.

'Have you finished outside?'

'The charges and pencils are sited. I'll set the timers later,' said Calloway, mopping his streaming face with a forearm. 'I'll mark a cross where the charges are to be laid in here and in the control room. Your guys can position them. That'll save time and leave me free to concentrate on the timers and fuses.'

'That leaves us without a lookout, Sarge.'

'You let me worry about that, lad.' Dennis saw the wisdom of Calloway's approach and grudgingly went along with it. At no time did he stray more than ten feet from the American who pretended not to notice.

04·45 hours

Cave sat on the end of his bed gripping the telephone in his left hand, his right in Maggie's. The sleepy voice at the other end oozed ruffled authority when it came on and said, 'Well, Maitland? This had best be damned important. I've only just flown in from Washington and I'm jetlagged to the hairline.'

'Mr Home Secretary,' started Cave, identifying himself. 'Commander Maitland is dead. Shot dead. I had to jump channels, there was no other way.'

'*Sergeant* Cave? Are you quite mad or drunk?'

'More desperate, Sir.'

'You are mad,' decided the Home Secretary. He turned and rapped something at his aide whose reply was shocked though muffled. 'You should have reported all this to your superior, Sergeant. Highly irregular,' added the Home Secretary. 'Give your number, name and rank to my secretary and expect to face a disciplinary board. I bid you good . . .'

Cave lashed at him, all caution gone.

'Listen, you silly, pompous bastard, will you? I'm the Sergeant Cave who handed you the negatives and prints of a certain dirty weekend in Brussels two years ago. I should have posted them to the *Sun*, they'd have made a lovely page three. All you have to do is listen and decide what you want to do about this fucking great conspiracy we've fallen over. You're not the only one who's tired. I haven't had a decent night's sleep in six weeks.'

'Language, Frank,' whispered Maggie.

'I haven't started yet,' snapped Cave, heady with benzedrine.

'Who're you talking to, Cave?'

'My wife. I sometimes get sense out of her. And she doesn't go on morality drives on one hand and grubby liasons on the other.'

'Say what you have to say, man. I remember you now.'

'What did he say, Frank?'

'He said he's listening, Maggie.'

'Well, Cave?' said the Home Secretary.

'Then tell him, Frank.'

Cave began talking and did not stop until the limousine came to take him to a personal interview in Whitehall. He rode there with an odd look on his face.

05·07 hours

'How much longer?' Sergeant Dennis asked Calloway, sweating now.

The American inserted a metal pencil into the oblong of plastic explosive and connected the timer before looking up. He lay on his side with both arms deep inside an inspection hatch in one of the generators, working by touch.

'Just this one in here, then those outside. Ten, maybe twelve minutes at the outside.' Calloway's arms ached abominably and he had the start of a pounding headache. The smell of oil was beginning to turn his stomach and he needed some air, not to mention relief for his bladder. Dennis's constant twitching concern was not helping.

'Why don't you get your men aboard the lorry? I'll finish up and meet you there.'

'I can't leave you here alone.'

'I could order you to go,' said Calloway.

Dennis's face became pinched and pale.

'Talking like this ain't getting it done, Sergeant. Goddamnit. Get your men loaded then come back for me if you must play mother hen.' Calloway turned back to his charges and missed the fury of indecision on the other man's face.

'I'll be back, Yank. Come on, you lot.' Dennis moved away, giving brisk orders. Calloway smiled into the cavity as he carefully replaced the hatch plate. He listened to the men leave the building then rose quickly to his feet and primed the last fuse in seconds. He used the remaining time he had to make up a special device he could hold in his hand and throw should the need arise. If he was correct about Dennis's intentions, the sergeant was in for a big surprise. He looped the satchels over his right shoulder and strolled outside to urinate luxuriously on the grass verge. The wind caught the parabola of water and threw it away in erratic streams.

When Sergeant Dennis caught up with him he was working on the pipelines.

'We're seven minutes behind schedule, Yank. You'll have to leave it.'

'No way, Limey. And I'm pretty tired of you calling me that. You know my name. Use it.'

'I said leave it.' Dennis ordered, shrugging his Armorlite from his shoulder.

'You want to go back and tell Prebble you chickened out for five small minutes? Jesus, if you want to go faster make yourself useful. Here.' Calloway scaled a small pack through the air and Dennis caught it one-handed.

'What's this? You shouldn't chuck this stuff about.'

'Bull. You can hit it with a hammer and play a blow-torch on it. It's just so much Plasticene until it's set off in the right way. The piece you're holding has a fuse in it and it still won't go off until I use one of these babies.' Calloway showed Dennis a timer. 'Now this one,' he said conversationally, 'is somewhat different to the others I've been using. This one can set off the charge you're holding without being connected to it.'

'Where do you want the bloody thing? I don't like holding it.' Dennis had lost all colour.

'Right where it is,' said Calloway. 'You even *look* like you want to use that rifle and I'll reduce you to ground chuck by simply pressing this knob with my thumb.'

'Stop arsing about, Calloway.'

'Sure, just as soon as you tell me what Prebble told you to do with me. I knew he was wrong in the brain when I met him, but tonight I realized just how crazy he is. A classic case of dementia praecox, I'd say. A schizophrenic to you. He was two distinct people when I caught him throwing up in the men's room just before we started. That's why I chose to come on this junket with you clowns. I don't have the stomach to be locked up with a nut like him. Ten to one he'll be out of his gourd completely when you guys get back to Poynter Manor. Me, I shan't be going with you. My money's in a Swiss bank and I have a plane ticket to foreign parts.'

'He told me to do nothing with you. You're the one who's crazy, Calloway.'

'That's a bad lie, Dennis. Now let's have it. Straight.'

'We're not even going back to Poynter Manor. We had orders . . .' Dennis shut up abruptly. He had said too much.

'More surprises, huh?'

Dennis shook his head, his mouth clamped closed.

'Won't talk, eh?'

There was no response. Dennis dropped the charge and brought up his Armorlite in a sharp jerk.

Calloway let himself fall backward, pressing his thumb in against his palm. There was a blue-white flash and Dennis was bowled away as his rifle pumped shots into the ground and scaled paint from the pipes. His head and legless torso struck the grass and skidded to a halt.

Calloway did not bother to look at him. He brushed himself off and jogged across to the lorry, checked that the rear doors were firmly locked and then took the wheel. He made good time to London Airport, stripping off the uniform as he went. Underneath he wore the clothes he had flown in with just four days before. He abandoned the lorry in the long-term carport, caught the ferry terminal car to Terminal 1 and boarded the Dublin flight with minutes to spare.

Major-General Rawlings had pinched his nose crimson.

He had split his time evenly between The Lady Kuklos and Maitland's resignation. He had read the letter so many times he felt he knew it by heart and the implications it contained deserved serious consideration. When he blinked, the glaring, circled K blazed in his mind like the afterburn of a flashbulb.

Now that the moon had set and the tides seemed to be behaving themselves he gave himself entirely to the consideration of his actions over Coward. Rawlings thought he *might* have been somewhat precipitate but failed to see what else he should have done under the circumstances. The Special Branch man had obviously been labouring under enormous strain and might well have been close to breakdown. Or was he just a tired copper doing what he thought best for Queen and Country?

Rawlings did not know. He had certainly baulked at the idea of involving the higher civil authorities at that time of the morning. Anyway, was there a Minister for Floods? Of course not. There had been a Minister for Drought and Snow in the previous administration, but these posts seemed only to be created in the teeth of the fact and never as a sensible precautionary measure. A Scot himself, Rawlings thought the English a tardy, muddling race whose genius for improvisation flourished only because they abhorred proper Germanic preparation as though it were somehow unEnglish and smacked of foreignness. They also excused their lack of forethought in economic terms.

Rawlings fingered his tender nose and frowned at the red Whitehall telephone. He supposed he must wake somebody up. Probably get himself lumbered with some snotty Under-under Secretary with a bored manner and carefully trimmed nails, snowy cuffs and several University degrees in Creative Buck-Passing.

Rawlings lifted the receiver and punched the contact button. As a considered afterthought he plugged in the black box tape to record the outcome of the call. He wanted some record of the conversation with the Home

Office.

And the merry-go-round started.

06·00 hours

To the residents of Stanwell the first explosions came so close together that they sounded like a massive sonic boom.

Early risers felt the ground move beneath their feet, saw their curtains dance as the pressure wave flexed then blew window panes in. Soot fell from chimneys. Dogs howled and ran in circles and cattle on Staines Moor stampeded. Water birds on the surrounding flooded gravel pits took to the air and circled in frightened banks.

A ragged gap had appeared in the northern flank of Staines Reservoir, which widened as tons of water pushed the weakened wall outward, punching through brick and earth in a brown torrent.

The central dividing causeway had also been breached, and the higher level of Staines 2 rushed in upon the waters of Staines 1. Ten thousand million gallons began to run towards the Longford River and the southern perimeter of Heathrow Airport. British Airport Authority switchboards were jammed with calls of protest and enquiry. Many thought Concorde had flown too low and crashed in the area.

Before the local telephones went out, hysterics reported wreckage in Slough and Windsor, and others reported strange lights in the sky.

The dark waters swept through Stanwell, swilled into basements and flooded houses up to first-floor level. People began to drown before they were hardly awake. Some of the older cottages collapsed on to their occupants, crushing many in their sleep. Close to the electricity sub-station the current lasted long enough to shock to death those who waded to safety. The hydrostatic pressure in the sewer tunnels blew manhole covers high into the air and raw sewage mixed with the river water. The death toll rose into the low hundreds during the first thirty minutes.

06·08 hours

A Panda despatched from Staines Police Station crossed the

Crooked Billet Roundabout and raced along the A3044 between the west wall of the King George VI Reservoir and the eastern wall of the Staines Reservoirs.

The road heaved and the Panda slewed to a halt, battered by blast. A great lick of muddy orange flame rose from the south-east corner of the King George VI, blackening as it rose into the overcast. A stately column of earth and brick followed; almost a lazy, dynamic afterthought. The flash lit the entire stretch of road. A wall of water came from the northern breach, a great ragged V funnelled by the high and sloping walls. The two policemen abandoned their Panda bare moments before the first dark wave struck the vehicle and carried it back towards the roundabout like a buoyant toy. They climbed the wire fence and ran for the high ground through milling, frightened sheep.

Neither man saw the dead watchman and his alsatian being claimed by the waters that almost took their legs out from beneath them. They hung on to the upper fencing and watched the level of the reservoir lower. Nine thousand million gallons began to decant into the River Colne, swelling it to a torrent as it rolled through Staines, hurrying to void into the Thames, accelerating and unstoppable.

06·11 hours

The southern wall of Datchet Reservoir blew out.

A huge wedge that widened as the deluge gouged at its sides and hammered down across Datchet Common. The B36 was cut along with the Windsor–Staines railspur and Sunnymeads Station was inundated.

Spreading south and east over the already waterlogged ground the surge struck into the Thames at Ham Fields and swept through low-lying Wraysbury into Runnymede, where it smashed through the waterside bungalows, battering to death those it did not carry away and drown. An electrical fire set off a cylinder in a Calor Gas store and the explosion reduced the building to charred cinders. The unignited gas flowed over the surface of the river like a veil, waiting for the next naked flame.

As the Thames rose above its banks it drowned four miles of the B3021, Magna Carta Island and the Kennedy Memorial. Boats were ripped from their moorings and raced down the river at twelve knots, turning themselves to matchwood at Bell Weir.

Cats, dogs, sheep and horses were caught by the flood and their carcasses were carried eastward by the river, adding to the pollution.

06·22 hours

An explosion fractured the wall of Wraysbury Reservoir and water spurted from the faults, gouging at the topsoil and grass, gradually and steadily cutting itself a wider channel. It would take another forty-seven minutes to blow out entirely.

At Heathrow, groundstaff reported inches of fouled, fast-running water on the perimeter road, and that the entrance tunnel was flooding. Passengers aboard a stalled airport bus were forced to swim to safety. A party of old people were trapped on the upper deck and sang as they waited to be rescued.

Egham Roundabout and the main village street went under two feet of turbulent water, and blocked traffic tailed back on all roads for several miles.

The Colne rose above its banks and flooded across Clarence Street into Staines Market Square where it boiled around the Town Hall, sweeping the stalls into the river. The war memorial was toppled as the waters ripped through the riverside gardens, drowning two winos who slept on the benches. The road surface began to break up and a fractured water main added to the turmoil.

06·25 hours

Several more explosions were heard.

The Littleton side of the Queen Mary Reservoir was breached and a great torrent spilled into Shepperton Film Studios where it destroyed the sets of a multi-million-dollar science-fiction epic. The flood spread west and east in a great wedge and poured into the swollen race of the River Ash. The suddenly formed body of water milled and swilled about, then, after some initial reluctance, began to surge with the riverbed towards its natural outfall at Walton.

Heathrow Flight Control diverted all incoming flights to other airports and grounded all outgoing flights. The BAA began the evacuation of both staff and passengers as the runways went under a deep blanket of water.

The huddle of small reservoirs at Molesey went up in concert.
Chertsey, Sunbury and Walton began to flood as rain and heavy wind made the mounting chaos worse. Local emergency teams could not muster, let alone reach their fire appliances or ladders. More and more telephones went out and electricity pylons close to the river shorted out. Cars and lorries were swept from the roads and lost with their drivers in the swollen river. Miles of low-lying roads were made impassable and communities on the relatively high ground found themselves marooned on newly formed islands.

The houseboats moored on Laleham Reach rode up on the sudden high water, and those that did not capsize and sink slipped their moorings and sailed off into Chertsey Weir where they jammed themselves into the sluice-gates or disappeared beneath the race.

Slowing now to a steady ten knots, the swollen Thames rushed eastward towards Richmond and London.

There were already three thousand dead and the toll mounted rapidly as the waters advanced into the built-up areas.

06·28 hours

Water had found itself in Heathrow Underground Terminal and had flooded the track, shorting out the power. London Transport closed off the Piccadilly Line at Hatton Cross, and British Rail suspended all services on that part of Southern Region.

Both the Birch Green and the Kempton Park Pumping Stations were destroyed by a series of explosions, ensuring that the capital's western water supply was severed.

There was no bore on the Thames.

The level rose gradually and steadily and faster. The river topped Bell Weir and fled on into Staines where it rode over Church Island and the Lammas, and rushed beneath the road bridge to join the turbulent outfall of the River Colne. Uprooted trees and smashed boats, garden furniture, gates, fence-slats and corpses formed into rafts of debris on the creaming surface. The A32 flooded and the waters spread out into the marinas and flooded quarries on the Surrey bank. The Thorpe Water Park became part of the Thames and the riverside houses went under water along with the many residential caravan parks. The people there had no chance of escape – there was nowhere to go.

Where the Thames widened on the long curve into Laleham, the flow tumbled less and less and ran with greater power, a rushing brown snake that gradually spread from its banks as it travelled east.

06·31 hours

Nancy came to Coward through the dreaming darkness, swimming easily, her smile malicious. Even so, he knew he must reach her and warn her of a danger he could not identify. He only knew it was there and he had somehow failed her.

He had neither voice nor limbs and hung suspended as she moved around him with easy flicks of her long and silver fingers. He had to make her listen, make her come to him and away from the greater outer darkness. He felt suffocated. Something dark was rising at her, reaching with great snapping pincers . . .

Coward came awake with a shout that died in his throat.

There were orders and steps racketing in the passage and the outer door opened. Keys sought the lock of the cell door. Coward lay still with his eyes closed, thinking he might get lucky if both guards came into the cell together and one leaned forward to rouse him. Stiff fingers to the throat and a knee to the stomach or groin, push him aside and take the second man any way he could. The steel door opened, a match snarled alight and smoke streamed into his face. Coward smelled the sharp fragrance of a small cigar.

'Tricks, John? That one's so old the manual's printed in Latin.'

Cave sat down as Coward swung his legs to the floor. Braddock held a pile of clothes in the doorway, his face a closed book as he did his best to seem invisible.

'Are you coming in, or are we going out?' Coward asked as the bad dream faded.

'Out,' Cave jerked a thumb at Braddock who held out the clothes for Coward to take. Coward recognized his blue safari suit, his white sea-island cotton shirt, his black leather casuals and black tie with grey chalkstripes. 'Get yourself out of those rags. The man's waiting. This time, we got all the way to the top.'

'How?'

'By mentioning a certain weekend in Brussels.'

'Oh,' said Coward, stripping off.

'Shower's along the passage, Sir,' said Braddock, shoulders back and thumbs rigid down his seams.

* * *

The Home Secretary came around his desk and shook Coward's hand.

'You know the Commissioner of the Metropolitan Police, of course,' he said.

As well as I know the roof gardens of Buckingham Palace, thought Coward who had only once been in the same room with the man.

'These others are colonels whose names you need not know. And you've had one unfortunate interview with the Major-General.'

Rawlings and Coward exchanged glances and nods. Cave had lost himself among the antiques and the gilded sidechairs, and the colonels lounged as only military men can. The Thames map was unrolled on the desk and Maitland's letter lay on a sidetable where only the Home Secretary could reach it when seated in his upholstered swivel. A svelt aide in pinstripes took notes in shorthand.

Coward was waved into a chair facing the Home Secretary who sat himself and said:

'This is a civil operation that will be run from this office. The army will be aiding the civil police in every way they can. There can be no question of imposing military law at any time, that must be firmly understood.' He then went into a concise update of events as he understood them, impressing Coward with his ability to strain extraneous verbiage so that the bones of the matter were exposed by the precise use of simple language. It was agreed by mute consent that the figures and depths on the map were wildly exaggerated and that the current contingency plan for the evacuation of London was adequate. The Home Secretary shook his head when Coward started to speak, saying abruptly, 'I want an immediate assault on Poynter Manor. Mr Coward will head it and direct operations. How many SAS units can he have?'

Rawlings said, 'Two.'

'That's barely fifty men.' The Home Secretary allowed a brow to rise over a widened eye.

'Sir, we have barely eight hundred men in or around the capital as it is, and most of them are clerks. No more can be spared. The security of the Prime Minister and Whitehall itself must take some precedence . . .'

'Yes, yes, Rawlings, I know all about that. You well know I've delayed any further cutbacks on military spending. Let's just take our inadequacies as said, shall we?'

'Sir,' Rawlings said stiffly, chastened by his recent private interview with the Home Secretary.

'What about police?'

'We have some four hundred with firearms training,' the Police Commissioner said. 'A good half have qualified as marksmen.'

'A mixed force, then. Sergeant Cave here estimates there are about a hundred of these lunatics. This has to be handled quickly and quietly. I should like it to be steamrollered so that it does not escalate into a prolonged firefight.'

A colonel said, 'So long as we don't mean to withdraw personnel from Northern Ireland. None of us would recommend that.'

'Fine, I shouldn't accept it as a serious solution anyway.' The Home Secretary turned to Coward. 'You've got a sticky job. What do you know about these northern groups of Column 88 I see mentioned in this file on Prebble?'

Coward was startled.

'Nothing, Sir. The file was withdrawn from circulation.'

'God in Heaven. Am I the only one in this room with a clear picture of what's going on?'

Nobody answered.

The Home Secretary leaned on his snowy blotter.

'It seems there are four groups in the north of about the same size. They've been monitored of course, that's standard form, but up until now there's been no indication they had anything planned except to rally once in a while and hold clandestine meetings. And what's more important, there's no indication that these groups are a party to this action of Prebble's. I doubt if they even know about it.' He broke off and gnawed a thumb knuckle. 'This can't be the proposed action of a single, isolated cell, can it? What on earth do these people think they can achieve? A hundred men? It's ludicrous, isn't it, Rawlings?'

'Quite.' Rawlings allowed himself a dry cold smile.

'Well, you'll have to pull all these northern fellows in anyway, David,' The Home Secretary told the Police Commissioner. 'And be bloody nippy about it. I don't want them playing silly buggers as well.'

'I'll alert the relevant Chief Constables, right away, Home Secretary.'

'After some judicious vetting, David. I see a few names here who have to be pulled in themselves, rather than directing operations against their fellow conspirators.'

Rawlings pinched his nose to hide a second, wider smile. He was delighted to see the Police Commissioner discomfited. The Home Secretary looked at his aide who looked at his notes. The colonels looked away and only Coward held his direct gaze.

'I don't think Prebble wants to achieve anything, Sir. Just cause chaos any way he can.'

'I see. Could he be taken easily? Alive, that is?'

Coward thought and said: 'No.'

'Then don't bother to try. And that's an order I'll promptly forget I gave. Trials are expensive affairs, and this fellow's psychological profile leads me to believe he wouldn't be fit to plead in the event he was taken alive. Of course, if you *can* take him with no fuss and tuck him away with the rest of the Napoleons, all well and good. Then he can't be turned into a martyr for the cause. You, incidentally, are now a Commander, and Cave is an

Inspector. Congratulations. Now, the sooner you get on with this the better I shall like it. When can the SAS units get airborne?'

Rawlings said: 'Immediately. A Wessex can pick Coward up in fifteen minutes, Home Secretary. Just give the word.'

'I give it. Anything else before we give ourselves over to the evacuation plan?'

Coward stood and said, 'There is for me.'

'Well?'

'Commander Maitland, Sir. Does he have to be . . .' Coward sought the right words.

'Commander Maitland died doing his duty. He will be buried with full honour and his widow's pension rights will not be affected. He was a friend of mine, a close friend, but don't confuse this with charity, Coward. Nor any of you. I want that fully understood. It is just good politics. We need heroes more than we need bent coppers. Nobody smells good after a conspiracy of this magnitude, and this administration must survive whatever comes. Does that answer your question?'

'Yessir, and I thank you.'

'For what?' asked the Home Secretary briskly.

The telephone light flickered and the aide lifted the receiver to his face. Coward and Cave shook hands all around and made for the door. The aide was whispering urgently into the Home Secretary's ear. His face tightened and paled. He held up a rigid palm.

'Wait, gentlemen,' he said. Then into the telephone: 'And why wasn't I informed of this before? Confusion is a word I won't tolerate. No, immediately.' He slammed the telephone down. His face had a bruised look. 'They've bombed the reservoirs to the west of London, and Heathrow Airport is non-operational.' He raised the telephone again and waited for the Prime Minister to come on the line.

Rawlings pinched his nose and Cave forgot to reach for his cigars.

'Does that give us our higher levels in London, General?' Coward asked bitterly. There was no reply.

'Yes, Prime Minister . . .' said the Home Secretary.

'I've just heard myself . . .'

* * *

The local radio stations picked up snippets of the Flood from their traffic helicopter patrols and began broadcasting what they could sift from the garbled reports. Londoners came awake to the news of the flooding in the upper Thames and shrugged it off as they usually did – it was all happening out of town and had nothing to do with them. Such floods had never reached their doorsteps. They shaved, ate breakfast and read their newspapers; it was the usual start to a wet Thursday.

At the river bend between Thames Ditton and Surbiton the racing water lapped out over Hampton Court Park and turned much of it into a boiling brown lake before rushing towards Kingston upon Thames.

As the day quickened the spreading devastation could be clearly seen from the air. The flow of the Hogsmill River was baulked and it rose over its banks across Norbiton Common. People drove away from their homes with no clear idea where they were going, channelled by overworked traffic police who were too thin on the ground and had little guidance from control.

And the weather worsened as the gale-force winds struck inland.

07·38 hours

Madeleine Prebble put the breakfast tray she had prepared for Nancy on the bedside table and looked around at the signs of hasty departure – the half-opened drawers, the spill of powder on the dressing-table, the single curled stocking on the floor – and she sighed deeply. The scrawled note propped against the lamp read:

Dear Maddy,
The night was too long. Remember me kindly,
Nancy

Madeleine crumpled the note and dropped it into her robe pocket, grateful she had houseguests and therefore no time to dwell on morbid thoughts. Her guests would have to be entertained inside the house since the weather made shooting or riding impossible. She took the tray back to her room and sipped both orange juice and black coffee as she dressed.

When she was happy with her appearance she knocked on the door connecting her bedroom with her husband's and slipped through. When she had pulled the drapes she saw that his bed had not been slept in.

Madeleine was not unduly concerned. Her husband often spent all night at his experimental station and seemed to require little sleep for days on end. He would probably appear at some time during the morning, if not for breakfast itself at eight o'clock.

Madeleine went down to the kitchen wing to give her cook her orders for the day. Luncheon could be a lengthy affair, she decided, and would break the day in two nicely. The well-fed could more easily be left to their own devices.

The kitchen radio was on and tuned to a news report.

There had been some terrorist activity during the early hours of the morning and the reporter promised more details during the day. Madeleine tuned to Capital Radio for music. Giles hated the cheerful, popular stuff and called it banal pap, which was why she allowed a radio in the kitchen. The staff appreciated it and she enjoyed the cheerful simplicity of it herself. She wrote out a menu and to the driving lyricism of Paul McCartney and Wings calculated amounts to be drawn from the deep freezers. Then, taking her keys to the storeroom, she searched for veal and capon.

A methodical woman, she had six bin freezers labelled with their contents and amounts, and she went to the ones she needed without hesitation. As she checked through the bins he became both confused and slightly cross. Somebody had been moving the frozen food around and had muddled her whole system. To double check, she opened all the freezers and found that the sixth bin was empty. It should have contained ice-creams and gateaux, but they had been spread throughout the other five machines and tumbled in anyhow. Furiously, she checked back to the last time she had drawn anything and found it had been five days before. All the subsequent meals had been prepared from fresh food.

Madeleine's eye was caught by a shining item at the bottom of the sixth freezer and she leaned in to pick up the tiny metal badge, a gold fleur-de-lis from a scout cub cap.

She was staring at it when the first Wessex blatted in overhead.

14

Thursday 4 October

08·09 hours

Madeleine whirled about as her cook screamed and dropped pans.

There were soldiers and policemen in flak jackets in the kitchen, their faces blackened, their guns pointed. She instinctively moved to slam the door closed but a combat boot was in the gap and the door burst wide. An SAS man jumped past her as another covered her with a Sterling. The rear door slammed open and more men streamed in behind her. An officer checked her name off on a clipboard and she answered all his bewildering questions in a hushed monotone.

The tall policeman with slate eyes came in and confronted her.

'Which is your husband's room, Mrs Prebble?'

'Up the main stairs to the right. But he isn't there.'

'Have we missed him?' asked an SAS man with a radio that gave out a steady stream of codes and coordinates.

'Where is he?' asked Coward.

Madeleine said she thought he was at the experimental station.

'No, we've been there. Search this house from cellar to attic. Bring everybody into the banqueting hall.'

'I'll bet the butler did it,' grinned a soldier passing through.

'Move,' snapped an NCO.

'Sah!'

'Will you please tell me what this is all about?' asked Madeleine, her nerve returning little by little.

'Just answer my questions. Name your houseguests for me.'

'I've got that all here,' said the officer with the clipboard. 'Seems we've bagged them in one go.'

'Except one.' Coward's mouth clamped on itself and it

took all of Madeleine's courage to look him in the face. 'I ask you again, where is your husband?'

'I have no idea and I do not take kindly to hectoring. Kindly tell me what this is all about.'

'I am here to arrest your husband on a charge of treason. I might well be cautioning you as well.'

'What do you mean? I don't . . .' Madeleine could not accept what she had heard, felt the ground roll under her feet. She swayed and her hand opened as she raised it to her brow. Coward caught her as her knees jellied and she dropped something small and metallic to the flags. He stooped and gathered it up as she sagged against him. Madeleine heard Coward ask her where she had got the badge through a woolly and airless tunnel.

'Over there,' she somehow said. 'In freezer six.'

Then she was lowered into a chair and made to sip water from a breakfast cup. *How does one act treasonably? What could Giles have done to warrant this massive and intolerable intrusion? Surely there had to be some mistake.* But she knew there was no mistake and wanted to understand without *knowing*. To comprehend without being touched by what Giles and his business partners had done. She took great draughts of air and felt the room steady itself.

Coward was inspecting the freezer without touching it and she watched him from the edges of her eyes, ready to look aside if he glanced her way. He seemed to have found something that both angered and gratified him, hardening his face even more and pinching his eyes almost closed. Despite her fearful anxiety, Madeleine found herself wondering how much tenderness there would be in those long hands. How he would use his mouth in an embrace. Whether he would be hard and capable or warmly responsive. Shocked by her own sensual curiosity she turned her mind back to Giles and his alleged treason. She also knew that the tiny badge had a significance that she could not bring herself to consider directly.

Hating her lack of fibre, Madeleine blanked off her mind and tried to think of nothing, to see nothing, to feel less. She could not. She heard Coward order the storeroom sealed and allowed herself to be guided towards the banqueting hall where her houseguests waited in uneasy silence, most of them in bathrobes and slippers.

She had time to notice Calloway's absence before the harder questions started.

* * *

The Thames boiled over Teddington Weir and through the hastily opened lockgates towards Strawberry Hill, Eel Pie Island, Richmond upon Thames and Twickenham.

Special railway buses could not reach the stations to carry commuters to the nearest working rail-links. Road traffic was in chaos and there were hopelessly snarled tailbacks on all those major roads that had not been blocked off in time. A juggernaut carrying imflammable chemicals had jack-knifed on Twickenham Bridge and ruptured its tank. Noxious liquid had spilled over the surrounding vehicles and been ignited by contact with an overheated exhaust pipe. The bridge became a wall of flame, punctuated by explosions as the flames reached the other petrol tanks. Blazing chemicals spilled into the river and the Thames burned for a quarter of a mile. A row of houseboats moored nearby caught alight and burned down to their waterlines. A family of four were crisped as they tried to take their inflatable through the flames to the opposite shore.

The crew of a single fire appliance stood helplessly by and watched it happen, unable to reach the spot through the traffic jam.

08·50 hours

Coward sprawled in a footman's chair in the withdrawing-room of Poynter Manor and sipped a glass of black lemon tea as he wolfed down digestive biscuits. He shook his head at Cave.

'None of them know nothing about nothing not never. They have enough lungpower to want their solicitors and baldly talk of suing for wrongful arrest, but they act dumb about Prebble's private army. I've lost count of the times I've been threatened with the Police Commissioner. He must have a lot of friends down here in Surrey. The same old lyric set to music. Like wind you can't break.'

'Drug the sods,' said the SAS officer from the fireplace where he lounged.

'No comment,' said Cave, looking up from the military map he studied. 'Mind you, John . . .'

'Don't give our friend the wrong impression, Frank.' Coward snapped a biscuit and dunked it. 'Waste of time anyway. I believe them. This whole affair is Prebble's own. He's got them all tied into this consortium of his, but guns and bombs ain't their bag.'

'Except for a hundred boyfriends with Armorlites, you mean,' said the SAS officer. 'Where did he recruit them, I wonder? Are there really that many psuedofascists in this green and pleasant land?'

'Under every stone. Flip one, find one. There are hundreds of weirdos who need to herd together and be something clandestine, the nuttier the better. From the Church of Sexual Revelations to the Society of Sodomites. Fringe groups are rapidly taking over from strikes as the English Sickness.'

Cave crayoned a ring around an area of Essex to the north-east of London. 'There,' he said. 'Has to be.'

Coward rose and studied the map with the SAS officer.

Cave said: 'That's the next largest complex of reservoirs. And there,' he scrawled another circle, 'is Debden where they print the Bank of England notes as well as other foreign currencies. If Prebble got hold of the plates and paper he could make a real mess of the economy.'

'And use Harwich as an escape route?' Coward asked himself.

'Or private airfields. There are two up there. And Stanstead Airport. They could have chartered a plane and be travelling as a group,' offered Cave. 'Maybe I should have that checked out with the charter companies.'

'Do,' said Coward. 'Although I wonder if they will leave the country. Why cause all this chaos if it isn't a bid for power?'

'A pretty lunatic scheme, I'd say,' said the SAS officer.

'What do you think this stunt was all about?' Cave said hotly, ringing the western reservoirs. 'If not barmy?'

'I see your point, Inspector.'

'We can't cover all these points, we'd spread our forces too thinly.' Coward chewed a ballpoint. 'What do you say? You're the military expert.'

The SAS officer pulled at his lower lip and let it pop back against his teeth. 'I suggest a central muster point where we are close to any further possible targets, and have patrols out spotting. If only we knew how they were travelling.'

There was a rap at the door and a corporal of Signals entered.

'Sir,' he said, offering the officer a note.

'Give it to Commander Coward.'

'Sir.'

Coward took and read the note and smiled for the first time in weeks. He handed the slip of paper to the officer with a jaunty salute.

'A break at last, Frank. An army mobile aiding the evacuation of London Airport came upon three men trapped inside a truck in the long-term carpark. Shots were exchanged and resulted in the death of two of the men. They were found to be wearing uniforms and were armed with Armorlites. Frank, we've got a live one.'

Cave's grin transformed his lined face.

'How do I respond, Sir?' asked the Signals corporal.

'Tell them we want him,' said Coward.

'Soonest,' said Cave.

* * *

The rising water swung around Marble Hill and tumbled into the narrows below Richmond Hill where great swirling undertows formed as the water piled up upon itself. There were wind-whipped whitecaps and the seething surface smashed up around the bridge pilings to pound over the parapet of Richmond Bridge.

09·20 hours

Private Michael Minschull had done his best to look arrogant in defeat but he had lost too much too soon.

Watching your mates die messily and noisily was a lot different to the sport of hanging a fat old homo, and the hard Scottish SAS sergeant who had him at the point of a Sterling had spent a lot of time telling him how he would carve Minschull's slats if the officer would just turn his back long enough.

Minschull kept his hands clasped over his head and maintained his balance in the speeding Wessex by spreading his feet wide and pressing his spine against the metal wall. Every bump of turbulence cost him a strained neck, each banking turn a rap to the head. The Scottish sergeant had taken his armband and blown his nose on it before grinding it under his heel. Then his belt and bootlaces were taken along with his ammunition pouch. The body search had left him bruised and shaken. For Michael Minschull the gilt had definitely peeled from the gingerbread.

What had happened to Platoon Sergeant Dennis was a bloody mystery.

And that Yank, Calloway.

And how in the name of blazes did they all get themselves dumped at Heathrow like that? Somebody must have driven the truck there and then gone walkabout. *Christ, nine of our squad dead, two missing and me captured. So much for Alpha-bloody-5. I don't even know if we got our target. All we did was knock off the two coppers from the Magpie and Stump. How much time would I get for that if they nail it on me? About eight years, counting on remission? Yeah.* Minschull smiled and held up his cropped blonde head. He could do that standing on his head.

Then he was hit in the pit of his stomach and was gasping saliva between his knees.

'Lost my balance,' said the Scottish sergeant.

'Very well. Carry on,' said the officer.

'Thank you, *Sah!*' The sergeant's Sterling forced Minschull's head up. 'Stand up for yourself, laddy. This is how *we* play soldiers.'

Minschull's eyes began to stream and mucus clogged his nose. He sniffled and pressed himself back against the airframe, praying he would not be bumped forward. Dreams of medals and six adoring girls on each arm faded as if they had never been.

The Wessex sideslipped and lost height and Minschull vomited down his front. Even the gingerbread had crumbled.

* * *

The river rose over the Richmond Lock and rushed down either side of the Isleworth Ait to rejoin at the lower reaches of Syon Park as a rushing brown chevron. The waters spread out over the Old Deer Park on the western bank, running at about eight knots towards the Royal Botanical Gardens at Kew.

10·06 hours

They made Minschull stand in the rain until Coward was ready for him so that he was soaked to the skin and thoroughly chilled when he was doubled into the withdrawing-room. Minschull had only seen Poynter Manor from the outside and despite his nasal congestion he was curious enough to take in the gilded frames and the rich furniture.

'Eyes front.'

'Give him a chair,' Coward ordered from behind an Empire table. 'Cigarette?'

Minschull's 'Don't use 'em,' was sullen and glottal. He dripped on to the Persian carpet.

'Don't use 'em, *Sah*!' the Scottish sergeant bellowed into his ear.

Minschull flinched and said nothing.

'You do have to call me sir.' Coward was mild.

'You hear *that*? You nasty, scrofulous little *tick*!' yelled the Scottish sergeant. Then to Coward: 'Give him to me, Sir. I'll show you the colour of his lights. I'll haul out his slats and number them for you.'

Coward's 'No,' was quiet. 'Leave us please, Sergeant.'

'Sah!' The Scottish sergeant slammed to attention and marched from the room. A tocking pendulum clock made the silence and peace that much more sudden.

Minschull was surly. 'I know what you're doing. Seen it done in the films.'

'Sir,' reminded Coward.

Minschull told Coward to do something obscene with his mother's old fur coat.

Coward feigned regret. 'Very well.' He rose and walked into the passage. Cave came into the room almost immediately and kicked the chair away. Minschull fell, barking his elbow and numbing his chin. Cave pushed him on to his face with a foot and Minschull tried to crawl away, to use his feet in self-defence.

'Stay down.' Cave emptied Minschull's lungs with a stamp. 'Stand up.'

Minschull was hauled to his feet and harangued for a full three minutes as he caught at his breath and made both eyes work together. Then Cave was replaced by the Scottish sergeant whose graphic descriptions of the pain he was about to inflict were coarse and blunt.

When Coward and the SAS officer re-entered the room fifteen minutes later, Minschull was as compliant as a child. He was given back his chair. The questions started simple.

'How many trucks does Prebble's force have?'

'Ten Ford panel trucks.'

'Number of men?'

'Not counting me and the rest of Alpha-5, ninety.'

'Where is your next target?'

'Dunno.'

Coward and the officer started to leave the room.

'Wait. I don't know. We just had a map reference.' Minschull gave it and the SAS Officer checked a map of Essex. It was an old holiday camp on the River Crouch.

'That can't be your target.'

'It's the muster point. I don't know about the target except it's a building where they print money.'

There was an exchange of glances. Coward asked: 'Why don't you know?'

Minschull shrugged and flinched.

'The Leader said it was best if we only knew what we had to know. In case . . .'

'In case any of you were captured and interrogated?'

'What do *you* think? I suppose so, yeah.'

'I see. And what was your group supposed to do at the

target you seem to know so little about?'

'Make an assault.'

'Destroy the building?'

'No.'

'Come on, Minschull.'

Minschull shifted in the chair, leaving damp patches on the tapestry.

'We were ordered to go in quick and quiet. Look, all I know is that Alpha-5 was to act as a perimeter guard. That's all. Then, when the other groups had regrouped, we were to join up and leave.'

'Leave for where?'

'Nobody said, did they? I left that to the sergeant. He was in charge of Alpha-5.'

'That's taking a great deal on trust, Minschull.'

'That's how it works. Too many questions and I was out. It was the same for all of us.'

'All right, how were you all to leave? In the trucks?'

'No. They were being left behind.'

'Then how?'

'Ask Sergeant Dennis, he knows. If you can find the sod. He swanned off though, didn't he? Left us three in the bloody truck, locked in.'

'Not very loyal of him.'

'Maybe he had a reason. I dunno.'

'Do you believe he did?'

'I dunno, no.'

'You don't seem to know much.'

'Then ask them that does bloody know.' Minschull's buttocks left the chair as he yelled. He sagged as the burst of spirit evaporated as quickly as it had flared. 'Looks like I carry the can for the lot.'

'You chose to join this group of nasties.'

'Yeah, well, I didn't think it'd turn out like this, did I?'

'Weaklings like you never do,' sneered Coward.

'*We've* given *you lot* the big runaround. You want answers, ask the Leader, if you can find him.'

'We will,' promised Coward as the SAS officer whispered something.

'I doubt it,' said Minschull.

'Why?'

'He's the only chance this rotten country's got against all you bastards who gave it to all them bloody immigrants. Never asked us what we thought about it. In my grandfather's day you only saw the bastards in Tarzan movies or in Sanders of the River. Now they're walking down every high street. It's sick.'

'This building,' said Coward. 'It wouldn't take ninety men to assault it, even if they are all as wet behind the ears as you.'

'Who's wet?' bridled Minschull.

'Would you like to ask the sergeant that? I'm sure he'd enjoy a further chat.'

'No,' mumbled Minschull.

'Sorry, didn't catch that.'

'Please, Sir. No.'

'Better. Now, were there other targets?'

'Transmitter, I think. I'm only guessing. Some of the lads were talking about pylons and such.'

'Reservoirs?'

Minschull shook his head dumbly. He did not know.

'Sergeant,' called Coward.

Minschull threw himself from the chair into a foetal position, his face contorted and his mouth wide with terror. He grovelled before the ornate table. 'I don't know,' he wailed. 'Please, I don't.'

Cave and the sergeant were in the room, ready to gather him up.

'Lose him somewhere,' said Coward, pressing a thumb and forefinger to the bridge of his nose. The sergeant dragged Minschull from the room and Cave perched on the edge of the desk.

'Well?' he said.

'It must be Debden. My guess is they're holing up at this holiday camp during the daylight hours and making their next move tonight. If that storm comes in from the North Sea on schedule, they'll have chosen exactly the right moment.'

'Do we go in after them?'

'Not if I can get clearance from the Home Office to do otherwise.'

The SAS officer looked concerned.

'My dear Commander,' he said. 'That seems to be playing with fire. We could surely locate them when they're least expecting it – if we go in now. They must be bivouacked and resting. We could take them off guard.'

Coward looked jaundiced.

'There might be other groups, have you considered that? If Prebble is working in concert with other extremists, they could all be coming together tonight at Debden. How does he plan to evacuate if he doesn't plan to use his trucks?'

'Ah,' said the SAS officer, his nose tilted back. Considering.

'You're the military adviser, you come up with a plan of campaign.' Coward yawned and scratched his neck, shivering with fatigue.

'What do we do?' asked Cave.

'Let the military work on it and get some shuteye.'

Cave looked stricken.

'But I've taken a wakey-wakey pill.'

'Shame,' Coward said insincerely.

'Even so,' said the SAS officer. 'I strongly recommend we nip this whole affair in the bud now. I cannot see any other sensible option. I'm certain that Major-General Rawlings will agree with me, as will the colonels.'

Coward became white-faced and savage. He opened a manila and spilled photographs on the table, portraits of Peter Petrie in life and death. He came close to rubbing the SAS officer's nose in amongst them.

'Listen, you,' he said in a voice nobody recognized. 'That kid is the essence of what this is all about. Prebble did that, and that in microcosm is what he'd do to the rest of humanity if he could. Take something good and honest and turn it into twisted rotting meat. I want him for that. I'll have him for that. Protest all you want, Captain – you and all the rest. I want that animal dead to rights. And, you know, I will.'

'Good God,' said the officer, pale under his outdoor windburn. Shocked on several counts.

Cave's restraining hand was thrown away as Coward stalked through the tall, elegant door and slammed it closed behind him.

'He'll do it too,' said Cave, massaging his fingers. 'This is not a personal vendetta, Inspector.'

'No?' asked Cave, wondering. He held the officer's wrist as the man reached for an outside line. 'This is still a civil operation, Captain. Leave your shoulder pips where they are. If the Home Secretary doesn't buy his plan you'll get your chance to shine.' He left the withdrawing-room with the officer staring at his back and found Coward rummaging through the safe in Prebble's study.

'You want to tell me about it?' he asked as Coward riffled papers, separating several letters in Maitland's juvenile hand.

'No,' said Coward, setting a match to them.

11·80 hours

The high water slowed as it ran against the prevailing wind.

Kew Palace grounds were under water and Grove Park was flooding. Dukes Meadow and Barnes were being evacuated in piecemeal fashion as the advancing waters reached out for Hammersmith, gathering on the river's bend before striking around at Putney and Fulham. The Underground system was hastily closed and commuters travelling on delayed trains were sent back to the suburbs. Those who tried to cross the river were sent back and rerouted. The western suburbs of central London were effectively cut off from the south and east.

Radio bulletins warned people to stay at home if it were at all possible, and the catch-phrase, 'Is your journey really necessary', was dredged up from the Second World War. One flippant disc jockey was disciplined for playing a whole section of Handel's Water Music *and threatened with dismissal.*

After consultation with the Prime Minister, the Home Secretary gave Coward the green light to act as he saw fit.

There were only eight hours and seven minutes before the full moon reached its zenith and was in conjunction with the sun. From that point, a sea surge from the east was possible.

12·00 hours

Prebble was now certain that Alpha-5 had been lost.

He had monitored all the BBC radio broadcasts and knew that the authorities were playing down the reservoir bombings. No private aircraft were being allowed to overfly the area either, otherwise the media could not have been stopped from filling the airwaves with news and conjecture. He thought there must be something on *The World at One* on Radio Four but he would have to wait another hour and he ought to get some sleep. He had not slept now for thirty-six hours and would probably need to remain alert for another twenty-four. Now was the only time he could afford to nap.

If he could only be sure Alpha-5 had not fallen into government hands.

Prebble knew his hands shook and that there was a palsied nodding in his head and neck. The men must not see that at any price. He took a green and red capsule and washed it down with brandy from his flask. Then another. Sometimes when he stayed alert for too long, the dark thing came for him. The last time had been the worst for a long time, since he had met the boy in green on the road and coasted to a halt beside him and . . .

Prebble shuddered and leaned a hand on the chalet wall until he could control his limbs and his facial muscles, wondering if the capsules worked as well as they once did. His vision was sharpened and his hearing became acute. He could hear men in the farthest holiday chalet snapping cards on to a table. The snap and hiss of a beer can opening. Could see minute highlights in the raindrops on the cracked window. The weave of his uniform jumped at him like deep furrows in a freshly turned field. His polished buttons flared like brass suns.

Prebble groped for the portable cot and lowered himself into it. His limbs were made of helium and he could hear the blood pumping along his arteries and pinking in his veins. His heart drove like a great muscular engine and made his lungs labour too hard. He fell back on to the opened bedroll with his hangar-door eyelids closing. Although he could not see them, his irises were black pinpricks in small blue marbles.

He fell into a dark spiral and lost himself trying to think of cleverness.

15·05 hours

The upper reaches of the river were draining slowly towards London and the previously flooded areas below Windsor began to rise above the waters, discoloured, fouled and littered with polluted debris. The forward flow had swung through Hammersmith, was spreading into Wandsworth and Chelsea and forcing itself beneath Vauxhall Bridge. Moving ever more slowly, ever more certainly into Westminster as the waters went in search of the sea and The Lady Kuklos.

15·50 hours

Wrapped against the driving rain in his black Crombie and a hand-knitted scarf, the Home Secretary stood on the terrace outside the Members' Restaurant of the House of Commons and stared gloomily at the rising river. It was sluicing past the stone embankment well above the seasonal high water marker, and was the oily brown of discarded coffee. Even the fast police launches could not live on it.

The Home Secretary wished he had been able to give Major-General Rawlings more than a roasting for his crass tardiness. The trouble was he could see why a career soldier avoided political issues. The previous two governments had reduced the army, the forces in general, to mere ciphers with outdated equipment and no prospects for the able younger ones to gain promotion, to do anything worthwhile with the services. That was changing, but slowly. When he considered that the Iranians had more and better arms supplied by the British than the British themselves, he was chilled and somewhat ashamed.

There would be hell to pay if the Thames did decide to swamp London. His own career would end as abruptly as a switched-off bulb. Less than a thousand soldiers to defend the capital. Ridiculous. He smelled ordure in the air, aimed directly at his head. He would brazen it out as best he could and take the axe bravely when it came. Eighteen years in the House had taught him how to die gracefully if that time should come.

Well, he thought, *I'm damned if I'll recommend we suspend the House until it's damned well necessary. Even if it does mean we are all evacuated by helicopter. The Prime Minister will agree, I'm sure. No anti-establishment terrorist, including Guy Fawkes, has achieved that, and won't if I've got anything to do with it. Still, discretion being the better part of valour, wouldn't hurt to ask the Speaker to push things along. There's only a second reading of an amendment to the Right of Tenure Act to include houseboats on residential moorings. That, under the circumstances, should be passed as read. They can have the blasted river.*

Soaked and cold, he hurried inside to have the appropriate note passed to the chair.

16·20 hours

The members of Prebble's consortium arrived at London's Heliport and were driven in unmarked cars to West End Central Police Station where they were formally charged with conspiracy to commit treason and various other serious allied charges contrary to the Queen's Peace and the Defence of the Realm Act. They were then ferried independently to various prisons to the north of the capital where they were all held in solitary confinement in high-security wings.

Madeleine Prebble was not amongst them. Coward had insisted she remain at liberty so long as she agreed to stay within the house and grounds of Poynter Manor, to hold herself available for further questioning and to voluntarily surrender her passport.

16·30 hours

A high-flying Nimrod photographed a holiday camp on the River Crouch and printed the results through to Major-General Rawlings's staff who had them analysed.

There was no question that several heavily-laden vehicles had recently driven over the verges and were under cover in the dining-room block. An enlargement processed through a NASA computer-enhancer clearly showed a face at the window of one of the chalets. Infra-red prints registered radiated heat from a large body of men which caused a colour change in the roof tiles.

18·00 hours

Cave entered the master bedroom to wake Coward with a cup of tea and the news that Prebble's column was preparing to move from the holiday camp. A Wessex equipped with air-to-ground radar was spotting upwind to smother its engine noise, prepared to follow the column in any direction. Commercial flights had been directed away from the area to avoid collision since she flew without lights. Holding the Wessex on station in the gale-force winds tested her pilot to his maximum.

Coward sat up in Prebble's bed and sipped his tea. He had slept soundly without a hint of a bad dream. Darkness had fallen and there were forty-one minutes to moonrise. Wind from The Lady Kuklos smashed the rain in trickling dance on the windows and rattled the sashes in their frames.

'Commander Goldilocks in the big bear's bed,' said Cave.

'What does that make you, Inspector?' asked Coward.

Cave laughed. 'Haven't got used to it yet. Maggie's made up with it. I thought she was going to burst into tears.'

'That's the best sleep I've had in who knows how long. What have you been doing, Frank?'

'Solid police work. I've been through Prebble's study with a fine comb. I've sent all his codebooks and ciphers off to the Yard, along with his diary and his business papers. There was another safe behind the panelling. If he does stand trial it'll be an open and shut case. He logged everything, a barrister's dream. The hair samples and the blood smear from the freezer matches Peter Petrie's, so that's tied up too. There's only one problem I can see.'

'Oh?'

'You'll have to wrap this up in the next four hours or do it without me. That's when the benzedrine will wear off and the medics won't allow me another. So get on the stick, eh?'

'Frank, you're a nag.' Coward threw back the covers and made for the en-suite bathroom to shave.

Cave sat on the bed and watched him through the opened door.

'Oh yes,' he said. 'We found some capsules in a secret drawer of the desk. The analyst says they're used to treat schizoid patients. Only these would work on an elephant. No British psychiatrist would prescribe them, and the guess is they are privately manufactured in Switzerland.'

'So?' said Coward, lathering with Prebble's expensive shaving cream.

'So, the analyst says that doses of those massive proportions would depress one half of the split personality to such a degree that that persona would wither and probably die.'

'Which one?'

'That's the nub of the matter, nobody knows. All he would say was that it would be the dominant personality that survived. So, if that *has* happened, which one will we be arresting? And could it be legally argued that the "dead" persona commited the crime and not the surviving "half"? It's going to be a nasty puzzle in court, a battle royal of expert witnesses.'

'I don't give a damn,' said Coward, nicking himself.

'Somebody's going to have to.'

Coward's 'No they won't' was too quiet to be heard.

* * *

Deep and fast-moving cloud cover hid the moon as it rose. Nothing could be seen with the naked eye so it was left to radar and the weather satellites to record the phenomena in their special and various ways.

The tidal streams were baulked and then held by the moon's increasing pull, springing to their highest peaks. The waters to the north of Scotland were stopped from voiding naturally into the Atlantic – were drawn back into the North Sea where The Lady Kuklos ruled.

Her breath raged and the seas banked beneath her, held in thrall by her retarding winds. Very slowly she made them run to the south, down the eastern coast of the British Isles towards the bottleneck of the Dover Straits where the high tides piled up against her forward winds, rolling higher and heavier – forced to wait for the surge she sent against them. Already high from the moon's rising influence, they peaked and swilled and waited.

When the two walls of water conjoined, they must assault the land through the estuaries. There was nowhere else to go.

15

Full Moon

20·35 hours

The spotting Navy Wessex reported that Prebble's column was splitting into single units.

Alpha-3 turned north at Latchingdon and drove north through Maldon before swinging east along the B1026 towards Colchester. There were only three possible targets – the reservoir at Abberton and the television masts at Mistley and Manningtree.

Coward despatched a helicopter with orders to stop Alpha-3 on the open ground beyond the Abberton Reservoir.

Suddenly blinded by the searchlights of the swooping Wessex, the driver of Alpha-3 tried to turn away across the open fields. The front wheels jumped a low wall and dropped into the ditch beyond. The vehicle somersaulted twice and disintegrated in a flash of lilac flame. Caught by the blast, the Wessex was blown sideways and beam on to the wind, forcing the pilot to make a high banking turn before the gyros brought it back on to an even keel. When it returned to the site of the crash there was nothing but a smoking crater, a twisted chassis bar and a burning tyre.

The Wessex swung west and awaited further orders.

* * *

The Lady Kuklos was now a dark and awesome tyrant who sent many little sisters out ahead of her to worry the mounting sea with their cold and constant winds. Her skirts were shredded by lightning and her cape trailed torrential rain as she built the sea into a rolling wall and blew it south.

The flanks of the black wall barrelled into the coastal defences and rode over them as though they were nothing. They gnawed at the foreshores and threw craft they did not swallow far inland. The surface of the sea rose and swept south with no show of whitecaps or theatrical squalls. A monumental surge whose power was greater than stone or metal or brick.

The great wash rolled in upon the swelling southern waters and climbed against them, seeking a way through to the narrow straits beyond. Crest after crest crashed south in huge and tumbling falls, building a shifting, tortured mountain of water that could fall neither north or south. To escape The Lady Kuklos and the plunging moon, the great sea ran both east and west. The larger western wave surged in upon the esturies of the Blackwater, the Crouch and the Thames. The tallest crest was seventy feet above the sea.

21·00 hours

Alpha-6 and Alpha-7 sped along the A127 Southend Road towards the entrance of the M11 as the remaining six vehicles turned north through Brentwood. None of them was aware they were being monitored. A Signals officer had located the wavelength and frequency of their radio signals and was set to jam them should he be ordered to.

Coward was happy to wait.

21·30 hours

Major-General Rawlings was firmly convinced that the situation was critical. He advised the Home Secretary and strongly recommended the four-hour warning be given and suggested immediate evacuation.

The House had risen early and key Cabinet members were gathered at 10 Downing Street, ready to be flown to a highly secret alternative seat of government. Built during the fifties and designed to withstand nuclear attack, it had been extended over the years and was equipped to be self-sufficient for several months.

All television and radio stations gave updates on the situation and BBC2 broadcast a specially prepared programme on how to guard one's home and family from the flood menace.

The Royal Family flew to Sandringham and the Horse

Guards removed their horses to safety.

Insurance brokers no longer quoted for flood damage and security firms were telephoned by eager new customers and concerned existing ones. Boat-owners who advertised their craft for sale in the *Exchange & Mart* could have sold them sight unseen ten times over. The far-sighted filled their baths and handbasins with water and made certain they had candles, torches and matches. Camping enthusiasts broke out their portable stoves and gas bottles. The stupid and the ambivalent did nothing.

21·40 hours

Coward watched the SAS officer plot the Alpha units.

Alpha-6 and Alpha-7 had turned on to the M11 and were racing north as the other vehicles crossed to the A113 at Stapleford Tawney and split into three groups. Two of them turned towards the airport, two followed the parallel secondary road, and the third group took the road to the north-east.

'It looks to me,' said Coward, 'as though they are meaning to converge on the motorway. What the hell are they up to?'

'Two units on the motorway, and the other four making for elevated crossing points. I wonder . . .?'

'What?' Coward wanted a cigarette or some paper to tear. Something to do with his hands. He clasped them behind his head and forced his shoulder blades together, got up to pace and found it was not enough. He had to be doing something.

'I suppose they wouldn't be planning to cut the motorway?'

Coward stopped pacing.

'To make certain pursuit is impossible?' he said. 'It makes some kind of sense. Let's get airborne. Handle it from the air.'

'We can,' said the SAS officer.

'We will then,' Coward decided. He pushed Cave's shoulder. 'Come on, Frank.'

Cave slid from the chair and rolled on to his back, dead

to the world and snoring peacefully.

Coward grinned.

'He'll not forgive himself for missing this. Give me a hand, we'll carry him aboard. If he does wake up, he'll have a ringside seat.'

For a moment the SAS officer saw his dignity in jeopardy. Then he called the Scottish sergeant.

'Sah!'

'Take this man to the Wessex and board the men.'

'Sah!' His face impassive, the sergeant carried Cave outside.

'Tell me something,' Coward asked the SAS officer as they followed. 'Do you ever question your own decisions?'

'Constantly, Commander. If one doesn't tighten the old scrotum once in a while, one can't be much good.'

'I must be a constipated genius then.'

They made a ducking run across the grass and boarded the Wessex which took off with a fluttering roar.

Coward slumped against the vibrating wall and wondered if he had made the best use of the facilities he had been given. He had cleared the printing and security staff from Debden and replaced them with armed volunteers. Dummy plates and paper had replaced the genuine article and he had set up a loose perimeter around the building and grounds with orders to allow Prebble's column through before tightening the circle.

An SAS unit from 22 Group patrolled the string of reservoirs that followed the course of the River Lea. Their Wessex was to make a rocket attack on any vehicle that approached any of the five installations.

But was it enough?

Coward realized it was far too late to make changes now. Let the deck fall how it must and hope he had all the aces and court cards, he decided, thinking of Nancy.

When this was all over he would find her and bring her home where they would fight the filthy illness together. Others had done it, why shouldn't they? She must come, she had to.

The helicopter was shuddering in the headwind, fighting to keep a constant speed and altitude.

Coward went forward, walking like a drunk on the pitching deck, picking his way through men and equipment. As he squeezed on to the flight deck he was greeted with the news that one of the Alpha units had blown the elevated section of the B170 flyover and blocked both lanes of the M11. The spotting Wessex had also lost two of the other units. They had simply stopped blipping on the scope.

Coward swore and the pilot gave him the look a pro gives the amateur. Without a word he managed to convey his belief that the spotting crew had done better than anybody could reasonably expect when flying in a gale. Coward let the pilot see he understood when he said:

'Our luck was too good to hold. Pull all units out from the reservoirs and converge on Debden.'

'Commander,' said the Communications officer. 'They've blown the feeder ramp from the A1168. That whole section of the M11 is now isolated.'

Gripped by sudden nausea, Coward wondered why.

'One thing,' said the SAS officer. 'It won't help the evacuation of London any.'

For a brief moment the massing clouds parted and shafts of moonlight picked out the swollen snake of the Thames far below. Here and there, the odd roof or stand of trees made dark patches on the flooded waterscape. Sobered into silence, the men on the flightdeck stared down until the cloud rolled in and surrounded them with blind rushing night.

Behind them, Cave dreamed of Maggie in black chiffon.

* * *

The great wave stretched from the Naze to the North Foreland, a distance of some twenty-eight miles.

With The Lady Kuklos screaming through its tumbling peaks, the northern flank smashed over Clacton Pier and rushed along Jaywick Sands into the mouth of the Colne.

That part of the wave following the Wallet channel advanced faster into the Blackwater where it surfed across the mudflats to inundate Osea and Northey Islands before striking up into Maldon.

A mile-wide surge rolled down the Whitaker Channel and into the Crouch as its flanks shredded themselves into foaming disorder on the flat siltlands of Dengie Marshes and Foulness Island where fierce bores raced through the creeks and tributaries to throw the Roach into a seething turmoil and back it towards Rochford.

The southern flank crashed over the sea defences of Sheerness and gouged at The Swale oyster beds before assaulting Chatham, Whitstable and the Kentish coast; tearing up marine cables and smashing the sewer outfalls.

The massive central wave made erratic progress where it crossed the Gunfleet, Buxey and Foulness Sands. The crest began to tumble and turn into tormented white water full of mud, sand and shale, lagging behind the green mammoths that coursed through the deeper waters of the Middle, Barrow and Black Deeps, surging into the Swin, the Warp and the Cant, and on into the mouth of the Thames itself.

With the triple-headed forward wave making twelve knots between Shoeburyness and the Isle of Grain, the massive following sea rolled after, ready to make a series of secondary assaults.

Southend Pier took a wave along its entire length and was picked clean of its superstructure, literally exploded into matchwood before it was carried away up into the town itself. The metal pilings were ripped out, twisted like soft solder or punched flat. Hundreds of tons of Victorian ironwork were carried west by the swollen waters.

A broken sea swept across Hadleigh Bay into Benfleet Creek and poured into the streets of the town.

The Robert Montgomery*, a Liberty Ship that was swamped and sunk during the Second World War, still held its cargo of fragmentation bombs as it lay in two halves off Sheerness. The wave completed its destruction and seeded the river bed with the still lethal ammunition.*

Canvey Island took the wave broadside on.

A great wall of water broke over the coastline, smashed into the packed rows of bungalows and destroyed them in their hundreds before rolling on towards the tanker jetties at Shellhaven and the oil refinery beyond. A great hammerblow of water struck a moored Japanese tanker and threw it ashore with a broken back. The prow swung into the storage tanks and cut through them like a huge dull knife. Oil and petroleum spilled into the flood and was carried upriver. Liquid gas holders were breached and a toxic cloud streamed towards London on the gale-force winds.

And losing none of its power, the central wave rolled into the bend of the Lower Hope towards Tilbury and Gravesend.

22·30 hours

'I've found the two missing Alpha mobiles,' said the spotting Wessex. 'They are at Stapleford Tawney Airport. Alongside the perimeter fence. I say again . . .'

'Roger,' replied Coward's pilot, 'stand by.' He turned to Coward. 'Action, Commander?'

'Nothing – just to keep watch. Now the other two Alphas are at Debden, we can sweep up. How soon will we be there?'

'Four minutes to ETA.'

'Thanks,' said Coward. 'We'll be just . . .'

'Good God!' said the spotting Wessex.

'Advise on the expletive,' said Coward's pilot.

'Sorry, Command. But the buggers have just blown up. Lit up the whole field. Fantastic.'

'Don't ask me,' Coward told all the questioning faces around him. 'Just get us down there yesterday.'

* * *

Running strongly, the wave swept over Tilbury generating station and reduced its two chimneys to rubble before powering past to gnaw at the buttressed docks along Bill Meroy Creek. Its southern flank bored in amongst the jetties and piers of Northfleet as the following sea threw itself at Gravesend and surged up the hill with incredible force.

The men in the Custom House saw the Royal Terrace Pier tear itself apart and disappear into the mountainous race. Water surged into the northern entrance of the Dartford Tunnel and flooded it. The storm signals hoisted near the Tilbury tide gauge were swept away.

The wave was only twenty miles from London Bridge and the death toll was over twenty thousand.

22·35 hours

Prebble saw the brief double flash from the north-east because he watched for it. Dead on time. He visualized the trucks vaporizing as his men made for and boarded the big Sea King helicopter. Any ground staff would be heading for the explosion, should any be about in this wonderfully foul weather. No trucks, no evidence.

Although he had hired the helicopter through one of his foreign paper companies, he wanted it to appear to have been hijacked. There would be nothing left to lead the disrupted authorities to him when he had finished. Prebble had planned to the last detail.

He leaned through his car window and watched his men slide from the elevated motorway down a pneumatic chute, landing on the open ground beside the Debden printing works. He had got the idea from the emergency deboarding procedures of the commercial airlines. Simple and effective.

Prebble lowered his nightglasses and giggled, his face bloated and running with sweat. Sipping air between each burst of hilarity. *Cleverness*, he thought.

His men should take less than half an hour to locate and bring out the plates and paper, come back across the fields and be winched aboard the huge Sea King. Then away across country using the contour beam he had bought on the American black market, right under any radar and away to the Continent.

As soon as the helicopter was airborne he would detonate the remaining Alpha mobiles and return to Surrey in his Bentley as calmly as he pleased. When the other northern groups realized what he had achieved with his tiny force, they would have to join him for a final push against the disorganized government.

They would *have* to.

Within a fortnight he would be flooding the country with counterfeit money that nobody would be able to distinguish from the real thing. Once that happened . . .

Prebble sipped and giggled and activated his portable radio.

'Alpha-11, Alpha-11, this is Alpha-1. I say Alpha-1. Do you read?'

'Alpha-11 acknowledge we copy, Alpha-1.' said the radio.

'Alpha-11. Proceed to rendezvous. Proceed.'

'Roger, Alpha-1. Alpha-11 out.'

'Alpha-1 out.' Prebble dropped the radio on to the seat beside him and sat back to watch the fun.

* * *

'A new call sign,' said Coward's pilot. 'Alpha-11.'

'That's what we've been waiting for. That's the last link,' snapped Coward, faint with relief. 'Right, tell that Signals officer to jam their broadcasts. They must be committed now.'

'Debden Command,' said the radio. 'Men approaching from the east. On foot.'

'Take them,' yelled Coward. 'We're coming in.' He slapped the pilot on the shoulder and the Wessex dropped like a steel safe. The SAS officer went back to get his men to stand by.

The wave had stormed through Halfway Reach where it rode over the Kentish embankments and swept through Dagenham Docks. It had met with the slackening western floodwater and burrowed beneath the less dense fresh water, casting it from its salty back so that rolling streamers of it swilled over the banks on either side. Fierce undertows developed, clawing the debris down into the deeps, only to release it to the following sea where it rose up to form a great bobbing crust.

At the King George V Docks it battered the cranes and swept tons of heavy equipment away. At Woolwich it overturned and sank the car-ferry, and threw explosions of spray over the pontoons of the unfinished barrage.

People who had gathered on Shooters Hill for safety heard the surge pass as a continuous mindless roar.

22·50 hours

Prebble heard the Sea King before he saw it through his nightglasses.

It approached the motorway with its tail in the wind, edging in until it hovered over the downlanes between the parked Alpha units. Then, swinging carefully to face south, it dropped squarely on to its marker, its rotors feathering. The winch was swung out and ran a cabled pallet to the shadowed open ground below the elevated section. Men reached to secure it.

Prebble pressed the cigar lighter in the dash and selected a havana one-handed. When he drew breath through the cigar there were bubbles of saliva at the corners of his shivering mouth. His hair clung to his streaming scalp and his eyes were bare scratches of light.

He would watch the helicopter away and then leave.

Prebble was reaching for the ignition when the first lights crackled on. A flare bleached the detail from his nightglasses and caused him to jerk his head against the door rim. His cigar lost itself between his legs.

Prebble threw open the door and levered himself from the car to sweep burning ash from his crotch and the carseat, trying to find focus through his glasses.

His men were caught flatfooted in crisp white light as a bullhorn distorted commands to surrender.

This could not be happening. How?

There was the light chop of Armorlites and the chatter of Sterlings.

Men were dropping and running, trying for the darkness.

One man was hurled into a concrete wall as the surface exploded around him, another died with his legs cut away. Grenades cracked and hung balls of smoke in the air, diffusing his view of the action. Prebble sagged against his car unable to look away, riveted by the sight of men and dreams dying together. A few sprinted for the motorway, more lay strewn about on the black grass.

The helicopter, he thought. *Make for the helicopter.*

The Sea King rocked from side to side as it tried to achieve lift in the howling crosswind. A man was at the bay door trying to free the winch cable, to abandon it with his friends below. He squinted upward as a dark shape drifted in above the Sea King, glaring lights picking him out.

Prebble recognized the outline of a military Wessex and knew it had to be over. He let himself fall into the Bentley and closed the door. He did not care that he had left his nightglasses and havana on the grass verge.

Prebble breathed through his mouth. There was little oxygen in the night air and it tasted wrong. His head was split down the middle and banded by steel coils. He drooled over his lap, searching frantically for his silver box and the last three capsules.

He must feel better, and quickly.

He got the first one down dry, but the second made him gag. In his haste he crunched at it, biting through the webbing inside his cheek. The taste of blood was lost in the cloying bitterness of the drug on his tongue. He swallowed what he could and got the third one into his mouth, panting as the familiar punch to the heart took his breath away.

There was a darkness inside his mind that overwhelmed him as he felt himself lose stature, his personality crushed smaller and smaller like a ball of soft tissue.

He moaned aloud and held his chest.

The flares were bursting inside his head but the darkness only intensified its grip on him.

Somebody must have talked, must have given him away.

Kellerman? Calloway? No, Kellerman didn't know enough and Calloway was lost along with the rest of Alpha-5.

Who else? Madeleine?

Madeleine, he thought, and the dark overwhelming presence agreed with him, *made* him see it was her; took the initiative as it forced him lower inside himself, losing him inside dark pressures that were too strong for him, making him become part of that *other*.

It was Madeleine. The whore. She must have planned and waited and planned some more. Why did not matter. The knowing mattered. *You should have known,*

Madeleine, known I'd know sooner or later.

Now it's too late for you. I'm coming home.

It was Prebble who found first gear, but it was something else that drove away.

*   *   *

Coward's pilot brought the Wessex in fast and low along the motorway until the Alpha units and the Sea King were in sight. Then he gained altitude, throttled back and swung down over the other helicopter, denying it airspace.

The flarelit ground below the elevated section was littered with dun bodies and Coward could see a small group of Prebble's Alphas surrendering to advancing SAS men and armed police.

Coward looked for a tall and thick-limbed figure and did not find it.

Damnation.

A sudden engine surge cannoned Coward backwards as the nose of the Wessex tilted and elevated at forty-five degrees. He hauled himself upright and forward in time to see the Sea King rise beneath the Wessex, its huge rotors screaming only inches from their own forward canopy as it edged upward, sideslipping ponderously.

Coward knew the Wessex should have been sliced into Meccano if his pilot had held position above the other craft. Not knowing the proper military language, Coward said: 'Kill it.'

'Commander?' said the pilot, manoeuvring.

'Shoot it down,' ordered Coward. He could see the face of the Sea King pilot in the reflected dazzle of the Wessex searchlights; could have shot a pip off the man's nose at the distance.

'Too close, Commander,' said the Wessex pilot, making a climbing turn, rising up and away from the other machine as it banked to the east, directly above the soldiers and Alphas below. A shot then would have dropped the Sea King directly on to them.

Christ, good-bye, everybody, thought Coward.

'He must have been counting on that,' said the pilot,

reading Coward's mind.

The Wessex came around and followed the Sea King into the headwind, picked it up in the searchlights and pinned it against the boiling sky. Gradually, it was pulling away as the Wessex pilot waited for open countryside before he opened fire.

There was a glimmer of lights off to the left and the Sea King veered and dropped closer to the whipping ground. It had seen the spotting Wessex as it came from the north to join the hunt.

The gap widened. Five hundred yards, six . . .

'Stand by.' The pilot armed his controls and watched his sightscope bring the Sea King to its centre.

Then the Sea King faltered, swung, and flashed along its length. Great streamers of electric fire arced along the shredding rotors and made hard white rosettes in the air. Sputtering tracers of blue fled to the ground.

The Wessex ruddered right, crossing above the stricken helicopter as it dropped after the trails of spitting glare.

'What happened, for Chrissake?' asked Coward, craning to see the impact, but they were past and banking around again.

'He flew into overhead power cables,' said the pilot. 'The one thing we all fear most. I lost some friends in Ireland just that way.' He was badly affected.

The Wessex made a pass over the crashsite before landing. There was little to see through the smoke and flame.

23·59 hours

The sea-surge was already at Greenwich.

Major-General Rawlings decided he would wait until the clock blinked to 24·00 hours before he gave the order to evacuate the Flood Control Centre. There would still be time enough to leave the capital and install his staff at the secondary command post centre before the wave struck Holborn. His staff had calculated that the high levels of water already in the Thames before the surge came in were enough to make the disaster more cataclysmic than could ever have been imagined.

And today was only the beginning, he knew.

There would be higher tides over the following three days. What was happening now was a mere foretaste of what was to come. He monitored the updates on the casualty figures and the spread of destruction and already thousands had perished, the loss of property was incalculable. There had been a vast explosion of natural gas at Canvey Island, completely destroying what had been standing after the great wave had passed. Debris had fallen as far away as Basildon and Gravesend. When the waters did finally retreat, he knew that plague and pestilence would be sure to follow. Then the panic and the looting. He wondered if UN troops would have to be called in in the final event. The thought shook him to the core. He opened the general switch on his telephone and said: 'Evacuate, ladies and gentlemen. You know the drill.'

Wondering if listening to Coward would have made any difference, he slowly stacked his papers and charts on to a trolley and had them wheeled away.

Too little, too late, he thought. *Much too little, much too late.*

He walked to the elevator like the old man he felt himself to be.

* * *

Coward checked the faces of the fourteen surviving Alphas and shook his head. They were a sorry-looking lot and Prebble was not amongst them. He handed them over to the SAS officer and ordered him to sweep the area thoroughly. Nobody must slip through the net. The Scottish sergeant slapped him a perfect salute as he walked away through the screaming wind.

Coward found his pilot smoking at the controls of the Wessex as though regulations were made for others. He was listening to his radio, monitoring the commercial and official broadcasts. The BBC World Service was off the air and he could only receive Radio 4 at strength 2. Most of what was coming through sounded like prerecorded tape. There was little real information about the conditions in the capital. Coward listened with him for a while; it seemed that the Signals Section of the army had patched in with the police bands to keep communications going. There was very little to be heard on long-wave, even the French and Dutch stations were coming in low-power.

'We're not the only ones taking a pasting,' said the pilot, shouting above the wind noise, offering his cigarettes.

Coward refused. 'Feel up to some more flying?'

'Depends where. Circuits and bumps are all right. Anything longer means we need to refuel. I can't raise the local airfield, Southend's out, and Stanstead seems to have stood down. Nobody expects to have to fly in a force ten to twelve north-westerly, Commander.'

'How do you feel about it? Will this thing fly in these conditions?'

'Only if I have to. Normally we're grounded automatically.'

'This isn't normal, is it?' said Coward, wondering about trying to go by road. Surrey suddenly seemed a long way off.

'Well, we can but try. There's no way this bloody wind is going to drop. She'll drink a lot of juice though. Where're we going?'

'Along the Thames to Surrey. Poynter Manor.'

'That'd mean crosswinds until we turn our arse into it, then we'll have a following wind all the way. We'll need a full tank for that. You expect any stragglers to make for there, do you?'

'Just one,' said Coward. 'Keep trying for fuel.'

'Will do.'

16

Friday 5 October

The wave threw itself upon Greenwich, flooded the pedestrian tunnel, mauled the commercial buildings on the north bank and battered the elegant frontage of the Royal Naval College. Fouled water poured into the Painted Hall and created a nightmare for future restorers. The following sea rolled on into the National Maritime Museum then fell upon the Cutty Sark. *Torn bodily from its dry dock, the famous old clipper was carried into Limehouse Reach where it swung beam on to the surge and sank.* Gypsy Moth II, *the yacht in which Sir Francis Chichester made his round-the-world voyage, was snatched from its display mooring and sailed up into the Pool of London.*

Baulked by the higher ground on the southern bank, the surge barrelled into Whitechapel and Tower Hamlets where it trapped many hundreds in their highrise flats without power, water or lighting. As many of the older sewer systems collapsed under the huge water-pressure, whole streets fell into deep trenches and hundreds of thousands of rats swam through the foul waters, savage with fear.

As the surge rose in Limehouse Cut, water poured into the River Lea and the Regent's Canal and a great shoulder advanced into North London whilst the Lea, unable to make its outfall, rose above its banks and caused local flooding deep into Essex.

Smashing through the wharves and piers of the Lower Pool, the wave ran on towards London Bridge and the Tower of London.

01·56 hours

A train yammered in Kellerman's head and brought him out of his stupor.

He had soiled himself and stank of his own stomach disorder. His hair fell in two lank horns over his forehead, his eyes were slow and overbright and his mouth gaped loosely. He had long given up fighting his bonds or calling for help, for his wrists were raw and there was no saliva in his mouth. Swallowing was something he had forgotten how to do. He had no idea how long he had been in the truck – it could have been for ever or a mere eternity and he no longer minded.

Kellerman heard the train come closer.

It was not inside his head after all, but came from his left, from the east. He cocked his head to listen and realized it was running up the river. The oblong of Thames he could see between the hoardings was pitted with rain and ran slack, hardly moving at all as it lapped against the stone parapet. Every once in a while, a lazy wavelet slopped over the sill and ran down into the rubble and weeds. Kellerman stroked his friend the rifle and rested the point of his chin on the bore. Holding his head erect was beginning to take too much of his strength.

His slow eyes scanned the sky to the east. If there was a train there must be a track with lights and signals. Kellerman's dulled mind accepted hallucinations very readily.

There had been sculls on the river. Girls under parasols trailed their hands from punts as they were poled past by men in boaters. A monkey had danced on the waves without once dropping a banana or wetting his paws. Eliades had shot neat holes in floating tins with an ornate pistol Mae West had given him as a keepsake. Kellerman's long-dead wife came to beg his forgiveness for being so cold in bed. And now there was the train he could not see as its coming vibrated the side window, thundering in, closer and closer.

The oblong of Thames began to undulate as it rose over the parapet and began to cascade towards him. Water spurted through the latticed supports along the base of the hoardings as they rocked backwards and forwards, creaking on their struts and uprights.

Kellerman's nose itched with vexation. He had liked the other things he saw, but these were different and awful and made him want to be someone somewhere else. He was remembering things he had blanked away, things that would make him hateful and hating. Hated things that would bring the fear and the loathing and the knowing.

Kellerman's head ached as he was brought back to reality.

Some roaring thing glistened black far above the hoardings and the sound racketed off the sky, through his frame, inside his head.

The wave had come for him as Coward said it would.

God rot you in hell, Coward.

Kellerman thrashed inside his bonds, scaling off dermis, soaking the tough straps with sudden blood. His pathetic attempt to scream lost itself in the outside roaring.

The hoarding bellied towards the truck and came apart in ragged sections, water spurting through the breaks. The first waters slapped in against the truck and rocked it on its springs. The second wave lifted the truck and ground it in a half-circle. Water ran in through the door seals and swilled up through the floor plates, running cold over Kellerman's shoes.

Then there was the great water rolling wider than the river, angry white spume along its scouring flanks. As it came bellowing across the waste ground to swallow the truck, Kellerman found the trigger and pulled it hard.

The flash lit up the windows a bare moment before they were battered inward.

The truck was swept up and carried into the side of the nearest building where it was hammered into unrecognizable junk.

His death brought the toll to twenty-nine thousand and seventeen.

* * *

At Tower Bridge, the peak of the great wave broke over the bascules supporting the roadbridge, twenty-eight feet above the river. Spray cascaded over the four towers and the lifting machinery was badly damaged.

Confused water broke over the cruiser HMS Belfast *where she lay moored on the southern bank. Her enormous natural buoyancy held her up and she heaved against her warps as they tried to restrain her. Finally they gave, and with a great rolling shrug she moved up river with her guns aimed at London Bridge Station.*

The wave struck hard against the ancient and massive stones of the Tower of London, and for the first time this century there was water in Traitor's Gate. A Beefeater with foresight and a sense of history installed himself and the ravens in the uppermost rooms of the White Tower with enough rations to last him several weeks. He was to need them.

After breaking over London Bridge, the wave rolled on.

At St Katherine docks it sank millions of pounds' worth of class boats in the marina. On the north side of the river the following sea spread out beyond the Guildhall and inundated both Liverpool Street and Broad Street stations as it turned the streets of The City into fast-running open sewers.

On the south bank the water began to run downhill through Waterloo and on towards the Elephant & Castle.

The great wave ran on to the next bend and the Houses of Parliament.

02·00 hours

Nancy had slept most of the day and woke to confused noise in the corridors as her bedside telephone shrilled at her.

An excited Spanish voice told her the hotel was being evacuated and would she please go directly to the lobby where a coach waited to take her to safety. As she replaced the receiver she picked out the warning sirens above see-sawing police cars.

She dressed in her warmest trouser suit, wrapped a scarf around her head and took the service elevator to the rear mews.

The noise in the streets was appalling as car horns sounded throughout the city. Drivers over-revved their engines as they edged through the jams. Most of the streetlighting was out and none of the traffic lights worked. The only light came from the streaming cars and the whole world seemed to be on the move.

Nancy wove through the traffic and skirted Sloane

Square where an armed and mounted police sergeant commanded the centre reservation as his constables kept the cars moving. He had already shot and wounded two looters with a pantechnicon full of Marks & Spencers garments, and they lay under blankets waiting for the ambulance that might not come. Broken-down cars were pushed aside and cars with single occupants were ordered to take passengers.

The police were too distracted to notice the lone woman who slipped through their warning barriers.

Despite her pain, Nancy felt an excitement she had not known before as she made her way past the dark and deserted Chelsea Hospital. The city seemed to wail like a huge stone animal and she wondered if it had been like this during the Blitz. She supposed not, for there was an hysteria abroad that bordered on panic, and nothing of the like was recorded in any history she had read. She leaned against a run of ornate railings to catch her breath.

She turned her face to the sky and allowed the rain to spatter her dry cheeks with chill drops, enjoying the moisture on her skin. It felt so *clean*.

Before that moment she had no clear idea where she was going or what she meant to do when she got there. Now she knew, and when the pain had subsided she made for the river, making her good-byes as she went.

The Embankment had been closed off and was guarded by blinking amber lights on low stands, winking solemnly at the darkened buildings and deserted streets like visiting Martians whose arrival had been ignored. Nancy almost felt sorry for them, but she, like every other Londoner, was in too much of a hurry to stop and chat. She patted the nearest yellow plastic head and passed on.

She walked out into the centre of Chelsea Bridge and looked towards Battersea Park on the far bank. South London was still lit and some of the sodium spilled on to the river's swollen surface.

Nancy had never seen the river so high or so slack. Almost the only movement was from rain breaking its surface and the odd scurrying eddy from the cold and driving wind.

The wind brought something else.

A distant roaring from the east. Nancy crossed the road to lean on the opposite parapet and gaze past Grosvenor Bridge to the bend before Vauxhall. There was little to see. Most of the northern bank was a confused black fret where fleeing headlights blipped through far intersections. The wind whipped her face and she almost lost her headscarf. Then the surge came.

First there came a long and humpbacked swell that lapped above the embankment wall and sent skittering spills of lather over the parapets to wash the road with hissing streamers, scattering the lonely Martians before drowning them.

A second and larger swell broke against the bridge and sent dull hammer-blows through the entire structure. Spray whipped Nancy's face as the road heaved beneath her. She staggered and hung on to the ornate wall with all her strength, her scarf gone and her hair billowing behind her. She opened her mouth wide and tasted brine on her tongue.

The river rose into great shoulders that shook spume into the wind before crashing in against the bridge. Great white fountains burst up all around Nancy and she almost lost her footing as water plucked at her lower torso. Somehow she stayed upright as the black hill of water rounded Vauxhall and bowled towards her, roaring forward faster than a man could run.

She was laughing wildly when it smashed in and took her with it.

02·12 hours

Madeleine Prebble switched on her bedside light for the third time since midnight and piled pillows behind her back. Sleep eluded her and she was plagued by the growing recognition of her lack of awareness, her blinkered view of the life around her.

There must have been a thousand clues she had failed to pick up, a thousand more she had studiously ignored; all of them pointing to an oddness in her husband. The frequent trips abroad when he came home introspective and silent and locked his door against her. His almost pathological aversion to children. To small boys in particular, and the tight paleness of his face when he had to be in the same room with one. The almost cunning manner he had of observing the child from the very edges of his eyes, the saurian heat that lurked there. The way he clenched both hands around his cigar as though to hide shaking and sweating palms. He had once gripped a glass so hard he had shattered it and cut his hand badly. That was the day one of the local cub scouts had come to the door for Bob-a-Job week and surprised Giles in his study.

Madeleine realized the boy had been Peter Petrie.

She remembered the metal badge in her emptied deep-freeze, and solids of shock blocked her throat.

A rare smoker and a rarer drinker, she needed both now. She slipped on a dressing-gown with a fluted skirt and white nylon trim, toed on her slippers and went downstairs, fearful of the shadows between the ancient beams, yet more fearful of making light, as though to do so would make a beacon for Giles.

In the withdrawing-room she lit the apple logs with the electric bellows and curled up with a bottle of Napoleon VSOP and a box of handmade cigarettes from the House of Dunhill. At least they tasted like tobacco, unlike the modern machine-made things with filter-tips, high-porosity paper and gaudy packaging. She lit up and blew a ring into the fireplace where it warped in the updraught and was swept up the wailing chimney.

Lost souls, she thought, goosebumping.

Shivering, she caught sight of herself in the gilded mirror above the fireplace. She looked soft and lost and ten years younger than her thirty-four years. So much time seemed to have gone by without her noticing how set and dull she must have become. What a boring creature she must seem to somebody like Nancy who ate every God-given day as though it were a huge creamy sundae she must consume because it might be her first and last.

Madeleine poured another stiff brandy – the first had evaporated somehow and she had no memory of drinking it – tilting the bottle further than she ever had before. It was truth time and she might need a cushion.

Might? Christ, imperative. I even need alcohol to soften the edges of this private stocktaking. How pathetic. How me.

Madeleine threw her cigarette into the crackling flames and took another. As she did, her eye was caught by the files on the long Empire table the policeman with the slate eyes had been using. There must be material there about Giles, facts that might help her understand better. Help her understand *period.*

Madeleine emptied her glass, uncurled from the chair and approached the table. She did not have to search for what she needed, the pictures of Peter Petrie were scattered all over the table. Life and death, black and white. Raw unretouched colour. She steeled herself to pick up one of the body in death, naked on a pathology trolley, one suffused red eye starting from the calm, dead face. She was staring at it when she heard the door open behind her. Clutching the print to her breast, she turned to face the shadowy figure who stood there silently watching her, an alsatian on a tight chain at his side. It was the police doghandler.

'It's only you,' said Madeleine gratefully. 'Only you.'

'Keep to your room, please, Mrs Prebble. Those were Commander Coward's strict orders. Best to do as he says.'

Madeleine shivered.

'It's cold. Would you like a drink?' She would have done anything to keep the man in the room with her.

'No thank you. Are you going to bed?'

'Some water for the dog?'

'I'll see you to your room.'

There was no room for conversation or compromise in the man's tone.

'Very well, but I need to go to the kitchen first. I want the radio to take up to my room,' said Madeleine, dropping the colour print and gathering up the brandy and the glass.

The dog watched her come with flattened ears.

02·24 hours

It had taken Prebble three hours to reach Rickmansworth along the M25 and his patience was already exhausted when he found the A412 intersection closed off, both lanes carrying traffic away from the upper flood areas.

His fuel gauge read close to empty, he had to fill his tank.

He took the ramp to the service station and found the queue for petrol tailed back three hundred yards. He swung along the outside of the double line of vehicles and put his foot down, swinging on to the forecourt from the wrong side and scraping the front fender from a family saloon. He halted with smoking tyres and levered himself from the driver's seat, drawing his sidearm.

'Hey, *you*!' a pink-faced man yelled, pointing down at his saloon then back along the queue. 'Look what you've done to my bloody motor. I'm calling the law.'

Prebble ignored him. He thrust his Colt against the temple of the pump-attendant who was triggering fuel into a Vauxhall.

'Leave that. Service mine.'

'I'm talking to you, Fatty.' The pink-faced man clawed at Prebble's sleeve, swearing.

Prebble shrugged him away and shot him through the mouth, throwing him and his exploded skull back over the bonnet of his car. His wife screamed through a bloody windscreen.

The attendant sprayed petrol over the floor and his foot, unable to move or comprehend as Prebble tried to move him towards the Bentley. He simply went down on his knees. Prebble wrested the pump from his hand and knocked him away with the barrel of the Colt. The screaming woman had locked her door so that the noise was less. Prebble was grateful – he did not want to waste another bullet.

He filled his tank and drove west to pick up the A412 to High Wycombe, knowing he would have to swing south-west to Reading.

Nothing would stop him from getting home.

I'm coming, Madeleine.

* * *

Water poured into the Underground system at Charing Cross, Embankment and Waterloo stations as the long, following sea rolled the river up the hill to the Strand and along Northumberland Avenue into Trafalgar Square and The Mall. The Landseer lions on the base of Nelson's Column were up to their paws in water. A swift current ran through Admiralty Arch to join with the greater waters that had rolled around the Houses of Parliament and now swept across St James's Park. Parliament Square was a boiling lake and Churchill's bronze statue stared over the waters with lowering disdain.

Hasty sandbagging had done little to save Westminster Abbey or any of the other historic buildings from water or wind damage. High winds howled over the spreading waters.

The gale ripped the upper branches from a plane tree in Hyde Park, hurled them through the window of a second-storey apartment where they threw the brocade curtains across the bars of a lit gas fire. Fanned by the wind, the fire caught hold and swept through the building. The resulting gas explosion ripped off the roof, scattering blazing debris on to the surrounding properties. Within half an hour Porchester Terrace was alight from end to end. With nobody to put it out, the fire rapidly spread to the adjoining streets.

In the higher areas of North London the sewers filled and backed up. Black untreated sewage ran from the manholes and pure drinking water was unavailable.

The city began to stink and the rats came up everywhere.

* * *

Madeleine leaned back against her closed bedroom door and listened to the alsatian's claws scratch on the oak treads as the dog handler took it below. The main door slammed and she had the house to herself. She shivered and held the transistor radio, listening to it crackle instead of playing Capital Radio as it should. She felt more isolated than she ever had and the house noises she had lived with for years were now strange and worrying.

Her room was as alien as a shop window display, the carpet too white, the bed too goldly rococo; too frivolous for her depressed mood. The wind-driven rain knuckled the windows and the floor beams creaked. She ran to the bed and burrowed into it, plumping the pillows up all around her. She poured a measure of brandy and tossed it off, feeling nothing until it bit the back of her throat. She put the bottle on to the sidetable and fiddled with the transistor, feeling she must make some noise of her own.

The radio broke into a short musical figure and a solemn voice said: 'This is the BBC Emergency Service. Stay tuned to this frequency for information about all flood areas. We shall be broadcasting on the hour and every hour. Flood relief centres are being set up and the homeless should make their way to the one closest to their immediate vicinity. A list of locations will follow. Those of you who have radios are asked to pass all relevant information on to those who do not. Those of you who are trapped inside your own homes should stay where you are until help comes, or until the water level falls . . .'

A burst of static lost the voice in crackling fat. Madeleine worried her lower lip with her teeth and shook the transistor, unnerved by a hard knock of fear. The room seemed to have shrunk about her and she was glad she had kept her slippers on.

'. . . Certain parts of Central London have been designated as "no-go" areas. The police and the army patrol these areas, they are armed and have orders to shoot looters on sight. I repeat, on sight. These "no-go" areas include The Mall and St James's, Whitehall and its environs, Piccadilly and Leicester Square, Tottenham Court Road and Shaftesbury Avenue . . .'

As the solemn recitation continued, Madeleine's head bowed over her breast and she sobbed quietly, holding the radio to her for comfort.

Then the overhead lights dimmed, brightened and went out.

Madeleine screamed without uttering a sound.

03·00 hours

The Wessex could have landed anywhere.

All Coward could see in the headlights were the men huddled around the bowser as they handpumped fuel to the helicopter; the rest of Stapleford Tawney was lost in rain-whipped darkness. Now and then the pilot would duck inside to check the gauges, grunt and leave again. His last estimation for how long the refuelling would take had run out fifteen minutes before. Coward had given up asking anything. He checked the load in his revolver and tried to work out how long it would take Prebble to travel overland. It was something to do.

The Wessex shook in the wind, threatening to turn on its side.

Coward would not think ahead to the takeoff, telling himself that was the pilot's department. He chewed a nail and waited.

03·08 hours

Prebble stumbled along the grass verge of the unlit road.

He had killed his Bentley at the service-station by filling his tank with two-star petrol. It had pinked along for a couple of miles and then stopped. The rare passing cars had sped past without stopping and Prebble was soaked and savage. He had fallen many times and was streaked with clinging black mud. To keep himself going he thought of complicated new ways to prolong agony whilst not causing death too quickly.

Then he saw the dog.

Almost purring, he went towards it, his hands trembling with anticipation.

03·12 hours

Charlie Glass had been one of the last evacuated from St George's Hospital. A police car had taken him to Highgate where one of many rest centres had been set up, and Charlie was issued with a blanket, bread and a mug of soup. A WVS woman gave him tobacco and matches. The place overflowed with bedraggled people and their snivelling children. No great lover of the human race, Charlie took great satisfaction from seeing so many so miserable at one time.

He had seen the river rise over the embankment and surge through the streets of Hammersmith from his hospital room. A free grandstand seat. A policeman in waders had carried Charlie through the flooding lobby and out to the waiting Panda.

Charlie grinned his toothless grin.

They were taking the knocks now. *They* were having it bad as he had all these lonely, downtrodden years, and serve them right. Now they would know from first-hand what it was like living on their wits and going hungry. Getting through a cold night without a bottle or a smoke. Now Charlie was the professional in a world filled with amateurs. For the first time in his life, Charlie had the edge.

He stowed his tobacco inside his shirt and went looking for anything that might be useful on the road. He stole several ounces of tobacco and ten boxes of matches. There were some tins behind a trestle table and he tucked as many as he could into his overcoat pocket. He took toilet paper from the lavatory and several disposable razors from the bathroom. What he couldn't use he would trade.

When the rain eased, he decided, he would make a break for it.

He rolled himself into his blanket and went to sleep, still grinning at the greatest black joke of all time.

03·14 hours

Gluckman had slept through the sirens and was woken by silence.

The screens of his machines no longer showed him price indexes from around the world and his ticker-tape no longer chattered. He worked the lightswitch fruitlessly and called for malt and Peg. When she did not respond he wheeled himself through into the outer office where he found her staring out at the night, her back to him. He called her more sharply as he wheeled himself to join her at the window, feeling slight alarm.

Tears had streaked Peg's thick make-up and her lips shivered around her porcelain teeth as she took his hand in hers without turning her head. Gluckman craned to see what had upset her.

Monmouth Street seemed to have risen towards him and he felt he was closer to the ground than he should be. The Thorn Building had lost the lower half of its glass fascia below a turbulent rush of brown water. The upper part of a car moved past with the flow and nosed into a floating body, nudging it gently aside. A swimming dog beat across the intersection with Long Acre, paddling wearily for the roof of an abandoned articulated lorry that blocked the entry into Charing Cross Road.

The usual sodium glare was absent and Gluckman could see the scudding night sky as clearly as though he were in the depths of the country and not in the centre of London. No lights showed anywhere save for the glow of a fire off towards the upper West End. A crackle of shots came to him on the wind and he knew the police must be firing on looters.

The two old people held hands for mutual comfort as they viewed the deluge, neither of them trusting themselves to share more for fear of showing emotion. Peg's cat moved against Gluckman's leg and purred around a male rat it had caught and killed in the lavatory.

Gluckman stroked the glossy responsive fur and felt colder than he had in his life before.

* * *

Light jumped through Madeleine's fingers.

She flinched and burrowed deeper into the bedclothes, still trying for the scream that would not come. She lay rigid and unmoving before realizing that light was what she wanted, what she needed.

She unlaced her fingers and stared around her bedroom, taking in the décor and the furniture as if seeing it for the first time, seeing the hand-blocked wall-covering, the elegant Chinese lamps Nancy had given her as a wedding present, the thickness of the fitted rug, the whiteness of the paintwork.

Her style, her taste. Her ghetto bedroom.

All lit by the blessed return of power. Of course. She suddenly realized that Giles had installed powerful generators during the last power workers' strike. As always, Giles planned ahead. As always . . .

Madeleine's head jerked towards the unlocked bedroom door. When Giles came, as she somehow knew he would, he would come through there.

She vaulted from the bed, throwing the covers away from her, and turned the big brass key in the lock with a satisfying click, withdrew it and thrust it deep into the pocket of her robe. The door was four inches thick, prime Honduras mahogany, he could not get through that before she had roused the police patrolling outside.

Comforted, she went back to her bed, poured another brandy and selected a third cigarette, tapping it against the red and gold box.

She had not remembered the interconnecting door with her husband's bedroom, perhaps because it was so rarely used.

Madeleine lit her Dunhill and listened to the rain.

03·52 hours

The AA patrolman watched the cars whip across the intersection, content to sit in his van with the heater and the wipers going. The traffic was like a crazy bank-holiday as thousands fled towards Basingstoke. He had heard that public buildings were being opened as relief centres, and that boarding houses were doing land-office business. When they were all full the authorities would have to open the camping sites. Going under canvas in these weather conditions held no appeal for him and he was glad he had moved out of London the previous year. With hindsight he knew it had been a smart move.

He yawned and poured tea from a thermos, blowing on the scalding liquid before sipping it.

He saw the man stumble from the hedgerow and weave along the sideroad towards him, moving like a drunk or a traffic accident victim. He made an odd series of noises too, half-grunts and bubbling coughs, as though he had a bad chest injury.

The AA patrolman poured his tea back into the flask, screwed on the cap and climbed from his van, leaving the door open so that the interior stayed lit.

The man came slowly into the spill of light, big in the gusting darkness, staring from a face smeared with blood and filth. His clothes were stained as badly and his hair was spiky and stiff with the stuff. He could have been rolled through an abbatoir.

'Here, old man. Let me help you,' offered the patrolman.

The man struck at him with something that slapped stripes of crimson on his raincoat. It was bigger than a cat or a rabbit and a dead tongue lolled from the carcass's mouth.

It was a gutted dog.

The patrolman backed into the side of his van as Prebble swung the carcass at his head, reaching for his throat with his free hand. Lifted from his feet, the patrolman died as his neck was broken with a savage twist.

He and the ruined dog were left in the ditch when Prebble drove away.

04·00 hours

The Wessex went upward, nose into the wind, turning on its axis.

The pilot killed the forward lights as he fought for height and a course parallel to the beam wind. There was no skyline, no light, nothing to give Coward any feeling for up, down or sideways. All there was was the trapping harness and the bucketing canopy streaming with water, tinted green and crimson by the instrument lights. The radar scope swept itself and threw a circling beam across the pilot's visor as he talked to his black box in a language with technical conjunctions Coward had no way of understanding. He sat in his bucket seat and tried to think of nothing as the rotors blatted and the gyros tried to keep to a mathematical horizon. There seemed to be no ceiling to the weather and the dials recorded extremes of windspeed.

'Say again,' said Coward as the pilot spoke to him over his headset.

'I said, the old clichés come true sometimes. This is real wing and a prayer weather.'

'There are no bloody wings.'

'Be glad of it,' said the pilot, his features obscured by his tinted visor. 'Twenty minutes to the river, *if* we don't dig ourselves an underground hangar.'

Coward muttered, 'Tally ho,' and shrank in his seat.

Eight feet behind him, Frank Cave lay on his back under two army blankets and snored gently. He and Maggie swam in Mediterranean waters with dolphins and seahorses, and he had turned down several film stars and heiresses in favour of his wife, which pleased her.

He did not know she had left their Camden Town flat and had caught the last Underground train to her sister's house in Cockfosters where she brewed tea and sat wondering if he were safe and well.

The television was dead for lack of power and the radio simply repeated the same recorded broadcast. She had turned it off to save the batteries, and had decided she would go further north at daylight, keeping her sister's car to the backroads.

She had enough vision to see that staying close to the capital would be a grave mistake.

04·32 hours

Sadler carefully removed the last of six roof tiles and fed clear polythene into the gap to form a makeshift window.

He had left Fleet Street just before midnight and driven to South Kensington where the jammed traffic forced him to abandon his Vanden Plas on the pavement.

Walking as fast as he could, he was forced to make detour after detour to avoid road-blocks and roving gangs of youths who sensed they could vandalize and mug to their heart's content with no interference from anybody. At the Queen's Elm a black and a white gang clashed, brawling all over the intersection. Sadler back-tracked through sidestreets and reached his mother's street around two o'clock in the morning, feeling his way down the familiar unlit street like a newly blinded man.

The gutters were already filled with rushing water when he opened the front door.

His mother had installed herself on the first floor and was knitting something in veridian by candlelight, saving her precious primus fuel for another time. She would not leave, this was her home and had been for fifty-three years. The German bombers had been unable to shift her to the shelters, and what was a bit of water in the streets to a Londoner of her years? It would eventually go down, she would scrub through and carry on as before.

She had always kept a larder of tinned things since wartime rationing had ended, replacing the items each year. She had bottled gas and paraffin, a first-aid kit with splints and bandages, needles and pins, tinned butter and meats, soups and bottled vegetables; an entire outer of toilet paper and litre bottles of disinfectant and bleach. She even kept a gallon of distilled water in case the mains were bombed.

Mrs Sadler had been caught out in 1940 and now, at eighty-four, she was too canny to allow that to happen again. She scolded and knitted as the waters rose around the house, and had Sadler stuff an old mop down the toilet so that the sewers would not rise up through it. She had read the leaflet the Council had issued to all ratepayers, and had taken note of the precautions described there.

By four o'clock the water had swilled up to the top riser of the staircase, and furniture on the ground floor bumped and scraped against the ceiling.

Sadler moved everything up into the loft and was helping his arthritic mother up the ladder when the water rose over his shoes.

Now they sat in darkness waiting for the dawn.

04·22 hours

The Wessex dropped lower as it approached the river.

The sky ahead had taken on a lowering brownness, and the western horizon was punctuated by scattered patches of diffused scarlet. Dark drifts of rising smoke ran before the wind and the undersides of the rushing clouds were sculpted by licks of fierce crimson.

With a shock, Coward realized that London was burning.

The Wessex made a slow, banking turn over Poplar, settled into the tailwind, and the swollen Thames was suddenly below, silvered by the moon and reddened by the many fires; an ugly sprawl of white-capped water spreading far to the north and farther to the south.

Coward recognized nothing until the Wessex passed over Tower Bridge and saw waves breaking all around the curtain walls of the Tower of London. Many of the bridges were intact and served to show where the river usually ran, now they were isolated, cut off from the banks by several hundred yards of water.

There were fires in Westminster, and Belgravia blazed from Eaton Place to Lowndes Square. Bonfires twinkled along the banks of the Serpentine.

A great lake spread from Battersea Park to Earl's Court, and the river's bend between Clapham and Parson's Green was now a wide and rushing torrent.

The Wessex flew on.

04·52 hours

The props were still feathering when Coward jumped on to the lawn below Poynter Manor to return the dog handler's salute.

'All quiet?' he asked.

'Yes, Commander. Haven't heard a peep out of anybody. Except Mrs Prebble.'

Coward looked off towards the house and saw the lights through a chink in the bedroom curtains.

'She's still awake, I think. I asked her to keep to her room, Sir. She was wandering about the house earlier on. She's got a bottle.'

'Don't blame her.' Coward shifted his holster so that his gun was a twelfth of a second from cock and fire. 'Keep on your toes. How are the others deployed?'

'Four men at the experimental station. Forensic have a team inside. Two dog teams are covering the stable block and the back of the house, and the army have a patrol in the wood.'

'Fine. I don't want anybody inside the house. Clear?'

'Right, Sir.'

'Carry on.'

Coward turned up his collar and walked off up the waterlogged lawn, hunched against the wind and rain. He let himself through the main door, locked and barred it behind him, and stood listening in the shadowed hall.

When he had prowled through the lower rooms, the kitchen annexe and the banqueting hall, he went upstairs to stand outside Madeleine's bedroom. The transistor was repeating the broadcast he had heard over the helicopter radio, muffled by the heavy locked door.

He went along to the adjoining bedroom and let himself inside. It was empty. He closed the door and the curtains and turned on a sidelight. The room was much as he had left it the previous day, except that the bed had been made and the covers turned down. Coward shrugged off his wet jacket, hung it in the dressing-room and crossed to the connecting door. The radio still played and there was no other sound. His neck prickling, Coward eased the door handle down and cracked the door, peering inside.

Madeleine lay naked upon the bed, much as though she had been thrown there. Her gown and nightdress lay on the floor and the transistor was on the pillow beside her sleeping face. Her breath stirred her hair, still damp from a recent shower, and there were beads of moisture on her cheek. Damp prints led from her dressing-room.

Coward eased inside, walked around the bed and lifted the brandy bottle. There was a bare inch of liquid in the bottom. She had drunk herself insensible. An empty glass had fallen from her hand and dropped to the floor, staining the bedsheets and filling the room with raw fumes.

To Coward she was a poor, frightened bitch with a good body and little else going for her. He felt no desire as he regarded her naked sprawl – he had a horror of drunken women. She was just one of a million people who would have to come to terms with life. She would have to make her own adjustments and deserved no special sympathy. Christ, he had to make adjustments himself.

The sight of the transformed river was still with him, and the past five days had cost him far too much both emotionally and physically. He instinctively knew he would never get Nancy back and could see no way of continuing with Special Branch. He had murdered Kellerman as surely as Prebble had mutilated and killed the Petrie boy. All that was different was the motive and that would not stand up to moral scrutiny. There had been a time when he could have defended his actions with one breath and condemned Prebble's mindless cruelty with a second – would have made a strong moral case for the death of the small, ugly racketeer. Now he could not and never would again.

Tomorrow could take care of tomorrow.

Coward set the glass beside the bottle and covered Madeleine with the rumpled sheet. Then he went back into Prebble's room, turned off the light and lay on the bed, his revolver in his lap.

06·01 hours

Prebble drove the AA patrol van deep into the trees of Salem Wood and covered it with brushwood.

The journey had been long and there were memory gaps that worried him in a vague, peripheral way. There was something he should consider, should remember, should take with him up to the manor to confront the whore with. Trying to remember her name, he set off through the trees.

He sniffed at the night as the wind whipped at the skirt of his battle blouse, smelled his own stinking strength through the clothes that hampered his movements and kept him from the raw, rainswept night. As he wove through the trees he tore them off, leaving a trail on the carpet of pine needles. The noises he made deep inside his chest were not human.

He cleared the wood and padded through the wet grass of the lower lawn where he found the dark shape of the Wessex. Prebble hated its mechanical smells and knew it was dangerous. When he heard snoring from inside he knew it was asleep and could not harm him. Hissing quietly, he skirted it and moved up the rising lawn, cooled by the streaming rain.

A heel crackled on gravel and Prebble ran in against the side of the manor, crouching to peer and listen. He made out the shape of a guard with a four-legged shape behind him. The smell of the alsatian tempted Prebble, but he resisted it, turning away and loping to the entrance to his study. Why there was a guard did not concern him. He sprung the catch hidden in the stonework and slid inside.

When he had selected a knife from the kitchen he made for the stairs. He had remembered the whore's name.

He found the bedroom door and carefully turned the handle – there could be no noise to spoil the surprise. It was locked. He wanted to tear the frame from the hinges, but he thought of cleverness and he moved along to his own room to use the interconnecting door. He entered and crossed the darkened room, feeling around the furniture, his bare feet silent on the carpet. He felt for the architrave and found it, running a hand over the mahogany doorface to the handle.

As his hand gripped the cold metal the light snapped on behind him.

Prebble froze, hissing.

He caught the stranger's smell and knew he should have picked it up as he entered the room, had overlooked the scent in his hurry to reach the whore. The cock of a revolver was very loud. Prebble heard controlled breathing from the bed, *his* bed. He located the source as precisely as he could, ready to turn when the somebody spoke. That would be the best time.

Nobody said anything.

Prebble could not wait, he swung around and threw himself after the kitchen knife. Powder exploded close to his face and he was punched hard in the chest and side. Half-blinded, he felt the knife drive home close to bone and lodge itself in the wooden bedhead. Using the knife as a lever, he sought the man's neck and face with his free, reaching hand. The gun ploughed a furrow in his calf as he found a throat and brought his teeth in against it.

* * *

Coward heard the alsatian's low, warning growl.

He swung from the bed and opened the door to listen. After a while there was a soft padding along the lower passage and the clatter of a knife drawer in the kitchen. A cold part of Coward was glad the man was coming armed as he heard hissing from the bottom of the stairs. He closed the bedroom door and felt his way back to the bed. A thin wedge of light showed from beneath the interconnecting door and he hoped Madeleine stayed sleeping.

Coward's throat had dried and a nerve fluttered in his jaw.

He wanted to be finished with this mausoleum of a house. It overshadowed the present and made itself more important than the people it housed, and made him feel shrunken and claustrophobic and less of a man. He needed sun, air and sleep to help him rebuild.

The opening door caught him unaware and the odd, hissing breath was in the room with him before he realized. Thick ankles blocked the light from under the door and Coward switched on the light.

The room jumped at him, and the figure trying the handle was gross and naked and streaked with mud and dried blood, the buttocks and thighs crisscrossed by bleeding scratches where they had been flailed by undergrowth. The half-turned head was a bloated parody of the man he had known as Prebble. This was a thing that looked like a man.

Coward mastered the shock and cocked his gun.

There was a whirl of motion and the naked thing was upon him, moving too fast for its bulk. Coward fired and fired again. The big body jumped from the double impact as it bored down upon him and the knife swung in to take him through the upper arm and pin him to the bedhead. Coward pulled the trigger a third time, a moment before the big belly trapped his gunhand and a knee came up into his crotch.

Nausea took the room away from him momentarily, and he came back as his throat was clamped and stinking breath bloomed in his nostrils.

Coward drove the edge of his hand against the gaping jaw, and again at the nape of the neck. Blood burst from Prebble's ear as he nuzzled in strongly, searching for the big vein in Coward's neck.

Coward struck at Prebble's eyes and nose and felt cartilage give, felt himself weaken from the pressure on his throat. He seemed to be hitting rubberized steel. The roaring in his ears rose to a crescendo as lights spangled his failing vision and a rising scream came from beyond the bed. He could no longer feel the gun or the compressed mattress beneath him. He gave himself up to the screaming spangles and ran from the pain of being.

* * *

Prebble too heard the scream and he smelled the smell of the whore.

She stood in the doorway unclothed, her mouth full of noise, showing herself to him without decent darkness to obscure her body. He must teach her chastity through pain. Prebble hauled himself from the bed and found his feet through a mounting dizziness. He had lost too much blood through the blue holes in his chest and side but he knew he could finish the lesson. He needed the knife for that, and he reached it from the bedhead with a single pull.

The man on the bed fell sideways, his head loose on his neck. Prebble would finish him later. He turned back for the whore but she had gone away through the opened door. Prebble padded after her, vaguely registering the bay of dogs from outside.

* * *

Madeleine fumbled the key from her gown pocket, unlocked her bedroom door and ran. The gunshots had brought her from sleep and she had made her way into Giles's room before recognizing what she did.

There on the bed, obscenely straddling Coward, was somebody who might have been Giles. Gouts of blood pumped from the naked back as the gory head sought to tear at the limp throat. It had turned at her cry, hissing blood from its smashed nose as it freed the knife.

Madeleine lost her footing as her ankle turned under her and threw her down the stairs. Her head struck against the stone flags as she sprawled in the lower passage. When she pulled herself upright she found her twisted foot would not bear her weight. She fell in against the banister rails and used them to haul herself towards the sanctuary of her kitchen. Half-way there she realized her mistake. The annexe was blind. The only exit was through the freezer room and the police had sealed it. Turning, she hobbled back the way she had come and found Giles there, casting about for her in the shadows.

Keeping to the wall she edged up and past him, pushing herself as fast as she dared. He caught the movement and swung the knife at her in a hard arc. The blade sang against the stone wall and skittered off into the shadows.

Hissing and spitting, Giles went down on all fours and scrabbled about in search of it as Madeleine made her halting way through the banqueting hall and into the gunroom. She slammed the door and sought the lock.

There was no key on the inside.

Madeleine sprawled against the guncases and found they were all locked, just panes of glass between her and the rows of twelve-bores. Close to hysteria, she picked up a chair and smashed it against the nearest cabinet. Glass showered in her hair and across the floor. She threw the chair from her and lifted out a Browning.

She was trying to open the ammunition drawer when Giles filled the doorway.

Madeleine swung the Browning at the filthy and naked man, using it to fend him off. He came on as though she held nothing, his bulged yellow eyes clamped on her as he crunched through glass, closing in to finish the lesson.

When the double-bore buried itself into his stomach he forearmed it aside and it crashed off somewhere, breaking more glass.

Backing away, Madeleine found herself wedged in the corner of the room and she allowed her legs to buckle, sinking to the floor with her arms raised to save her face from the first slashing cuts she knew must come. At least she was going to die as herself and not in some negative state. She had that consolation.

With the last of her courage she spat up at the mad face.

There was a cracking flash and part of Giles's stomach spattered Madeleine and the wall with sticky gobbets of running warmth.

Giles halted as a great terminal shiver went through him. He grasped the knife in both hands and raised it high over Madeleine's head, bunching his shoulders, ready to make a last plunging cut.

His left hand was thrown away from the handle as the fingers shattered. A gaping hole appeared between his pectorals.

Giles showed the sour belief of a child who finds immortality is reserved for greater beings. His face slackening, he turned to see who had dared to do this to him and he saw Coward sighting at him a moment before his eyes rolled and died. His great legs turned to fat and he fell to the flags with a meaty slap.

The hissing slowly died away.

Coward stepped over to the body and aimed his revolver at the head, squeezing off a last deliberate shot.

The hammer clicked on an empty chamber.

Coward held the pose for a moment then dropped the gun to the floor and looked across at Madeleine as though she were just another shadow in the room.

When he had looked enough, he turned and walked away.

* * *

Epilogue

The Lady Kuklos lived on for three more days and blew herself out on the morning of the fourth.

For three consecutive days great seas followed the moon into London, each wave higher than the last.

The levels of water rose and spread out to the suburbs where they formed stagnant salt lakes that stayed for many weeks before draining slowly back into the sea.

Then the looters came and the shooting started. Cholera swept the surrounding areas of the drowned city, and the spring brought bubonic plague, malaria and blackwater fever. Tuberculosis swept the camps where tobacco trading and the barter system replaced money. Wild dog packs roamed the western marshes and rabies returned to Britain. Only the rats flourished and multiplied.

Of the three-quarters of a million people who died, less than half had drowned; disease and violence had taken their toll.

Not until the following summer did the waters retreat from the city centre, by which time it was too late.

London had died.

PETER WAY

Super-Celeste

The year is 1982. Behind the cool façade of international aviation, a deadly contest is taking place. Euro-Aviat, headed by Henri Levitte, the grand old man of French aviation, is battling with the American giant, North-West Aerospace, for the big Australian order which will guarantee its future. But can the Super-Celeste, Euro-Aviat's superb new jet fighter, win the vital order? Or must both sides resort to trickery and threats in the deadly battle for survival which is the reality of modern aviation?

For Henri Levitte there are family problems too, for he has created a family which hates him. His adopted son – who was to fly the Super-Celeste – is shot dead. His daughter commits suicide. And his remaining son vows a terrible revenge . . .

Sunrise

'Plot boils with crude energy' – *The Guardian*

The Secret – a safety network beneath London's streets, an escape route for the nation's leaders and the location of its devastating retaliatory weapons.

The Operation – 'Sunrise' is the code name for the most closely guarded plans of all – survival in the aftermath of World War III.

The Mission – journalist David Marriott's determination to penetrate the Operation at his discovery of a horrific plot which could alter the West's sunrise for ever.

STEPHEN KNIGHT

Requiem at Rogano

London in 1902 is shocked and terrorised by an extraordinary series of murders, the work of the so-called Deptford Strangler. Although retired, former Scotland Yard inspector Reginald Brough is drawn into the inquiry by his nephew Nicholas. For Nicholas, unbelievably and terrifyingly, is beginning to believe that he himself is the Deptford Strangler. But the true solution of the mystery is even stranger and the extraordinary chase leads the two across Europe to Italy and a conclusion beyond their wildest imaginings.

Requiem at Rogano is a thrilling and suspenseful novel of rare originality and fascination, and marks the arrival of a major new fiction talent.

'I have not had such a good weekend-with-a-thriller for years . . . The ingenious twists go on until the penultimate page. The writing is crisp and highly intelligent . . . The author's ingenuity is breathtaking, and he keeps the pace up throughout the book' – *Financial Times*

'A stupendous winner. First time originality' – *Yorkshire Post*

GRAHAM LANCASTER

The Nuclear Letters

Plutonium, that deadly radioactive material, had been disappearing all over the world. Someone was amassing enough to obliterate whole populations. And someone was sending letters, marked with a strange code. Cold threats of chaos if certain demands weren't met.

Neil Janner had everything: a successful dental practice, a fantastic car, a warm woman. He was torn from this secure life to work for the CIA. Inexperienced and vulnerable, it seemed that he alone could crack the code and smash the deadly plot . . .

GORDON PAPE AND TONY ASPLER

Chain Reaction

In a political reaction of devastating force, one man's death could lead to global confrontation.

Ever since the 'free Quebec' movement started, and particularly since de Gaulle made his encouraging 'Vive Quebec' speech, Canada has been a political flashpoint. Now, assassination tears her apart; moderates and radicals battle in the streets for control. On America's doorstep lies a land weakened and open to invasion – but America will not tolerate an enemy so close. One by one the major powers are drawn into the conflict – a chain reaction that threatens total confrontation and war.

CECILIA BARTHOLOMEW

Outrun the Dark

Billyjean is twenty-one and just released from thirteen years in a mental asylum. Inside, she's still a frightened eight-year-old, clutching a bloody spanner and staring down at the dead body of her little brother sprawled in a pool of blood on the garage floor. Her memory of that moment has gone. Did she kill him – or is she too an innocent victim of evil?

The plot moves into a terrifying spiral of fear, spinning to a heart-stopping climax – *Publishers' Weekly*

'Compelling, vivid and terrifying' – Arthur Herzog

'A spine-tingling page-turner' – Mary Higgins-Clark, author of *Where Are The Children?*

'A chilling melodrama filled with psychological tension' – *New York Times Book Review*

PATRICK ANDERSON

The President's Mistress

Ben Norton is determined to uncover the truth about the murder of his former girlfriend, Donna Hendricks. With the aid of a brilliant, if eccentric, Washington reporter he begins to penetrate the tangle of deception surrounding the affair. But each time he gets a lead there is someone around to put him off the scent. Powerful White House officials, corrupt senators, his own one-time friends in the Washington social set, as well as the dirty tricks department, all conspire in a massive cover-up operation – with bribery, blackmail and sudden death. Why? Because Donna Hendricks was the President's mistress, and Norton's enquiries seem to be leading straight to the Oval Office itself.

The Senator

Charles Pierce epitomises the American Dream – young, handsome, rich. But when he becomes the Senator, something goes wrong, his world crumbles against the backdrop of the J. F. Kennedy assassination, the Vietnam war, the hippy era, and the increase in drug addiction and racial tension. His loyalties are split by his personal experiences and his role as the Senator. He has to choose between his true conscience and bettering his career.

JOHN D. MACDONALD

Dead Low Tide

Suicide . . . or Murder?
Her name was Mary Eleanor – the boss's wife. She was one of those dark-haired Alabama girls and had on a sort of blue denim play suit. She slouched in the chair and crossed her brown legs. 'Will you find out something for me?' she said. 'Will you find out what's wrong with John?'

Andy McClintock had no wish to start spying on his employer, and said so firmly. Nevertheless he became involved, and still further involved. The clincher was the body on the sand with a harpoon barb through the throat.

'Delightfully lively' – Maurice Richardson, *Observer*

A Key to the Suite

When a giant hotel is booked for a business convention its luxury suites soon start to hum with plots and savage manoeuvrings. Floyd Hubbard, cool top corporation executive, arrives at the hotel with one thing on his mind – to make recommendations that would get rid of the ageing sales chief, Jesse Mulaney. But his move is anticipated, and in the heady convention atmosphere of bars, girls and loaded drinks he falls for one of the oldest tricks. Cory, the strange and elusive girl he is set up to meet, proves difficult to resist, and the urgency of his mission fades as he becomes just another footloose businessman. Then the convention turns into a nightmare.

HAROLD KING

Closing Ceremonies

'Equals *The Day of the Jackal* – subtle, complex and exciting' – *Publishers' Weekly*

Hidden deep in a deserted mineshaft in the remote mountains of Paraguay lies the most bizarre memorial to evil. In an incredible duplication of Hitler's Reich Chancellery, guarded by exiled Nazi war leaders, is the shrine to an urn containing the ashes of a dark deity – Adolf Hitler. Four armed men, on the trail of a Nazi war criminal, blast their way in. But only one escapes, taking with him the sacred urn. He was the Hunter, driven by an all-consuming thirst for revenge against the men who guarded the urn and who had killed his beloved brother. Yet he was also the Hunted – by both Israeli Intelligence and by a cold and ruthless killing machine, a man known as Der Kettenhund, the Chain Dog – the perfect creation of the ideals of the Third Reich. It was a manhunt that spanned the continents and that ultimately threatened the life of a world leader . . .

'Makes *The Boys From Brazil* look like child's play . . . A real page-turner' – Robert L. Duncan

BOB RANDALL

The Fan

A dazzlingly suspenseful shocker of love, hate and fear, *The Fan* unfolds its horrifying story by letting the reader in on the private correspondence of a famous movie star. Little did glamorous Sally Ross imagine that amongst the pile of letters dealt with by her tough secretary Belle there were many from one who signed himself Douglas Breen, the Fan. Nor did Belle realize that behind the calm, polite phrases of the Fan's letters lurked the crazed mind of a psychopath – a deadly killer for whom overwhelming love could turn overnight into violence and terrifying hate.